A second b[...]
blazing white and hot

Edwards scrambled to his feet, standing on the front of the Manta. The machine pistol snapped down into his fist, ready to go into action, but the strange glowing disc wasn't moving. He put on his shadow suit's faceplate and hoped for the visor to screen and filter out the blinding light, as well as analyze the object in the sky.

The range was ten miles, and it was advancing quickly.

He activated his Commtact microphone. "Guys, wherever you are..."

Nothing. No response, not even static. He turned his gaze back to the sky. For all the polarization of the lenses, he couldn't make out a detail of the blazing comet looming ever closer. But in the space of fifteen seconds, it had closed to nine miles. He couldn't get details about the shape of the object, only its range, and there was no guarantee that was right.

Edwards turned to open the cockpit, but the command signal to remotely open the canopy was also jammed.

He was in a complete blackout.

Other titles in this series:

James Axler
Outlanders®

ANGEL OF DOOM

A GOLD EAGLE BOOK FROM
WORLDWIDE®

TORONTO • NEW YORK • LONDON
AMSTERDAM • PARIS • SYDNEY • HAMBURG
STOCKHOLM • ATHENS • TOKYO • MILAN
MADRID • WARSAW • BUDAPEST • AUCKLAND

Recycling programs
for this product may
not exist in your area.

First edition August 2015

ISBN-13: 978-0-373-63887-1

Angel of Doom

Copyright © 2015 by Worldwide Library

Special thanks to Douglas P. Wojtowicz for his contribution to this work.

Printed in U.S.A.

A dreadful ferryman looks after the river crossing,
Charon, appalling filthy he is, with a bush of unkempt
white beard upon his chin, with eyes like jets of fire.
—Virgil, *Aeneid*

The Road to Outlands—
From Secret Government Files to the Future

Almost two hundred years after the global holocaust, Kane, a former Magistrate of Cobaltville, often thought the world had been lucky to survive at all after a nuclear device detonated in the Russian embassy in Washington, DC. The aftermath—forever known as skydark—reshaped continents and turned civilization into ashes.

Nearly depopulated, America became the Deathlands—poisoned by radiation, home to chaos and mutated life forms. Feudal rule reappeared in the form of baronies, while remote outposts clung to a brutish existence.

What eventually helped shape this wasteland were the redoubts, the secret prehocaust military installations with stores of weapons, and the home of gateways, the locational matter-transfer facilities. Some of the redoubts hid clues that had once fed wild theories of government cover-ups and alien visitations.

Rearmed from redoubt stockpiles, the barons consolidated their power and reclaimed technology for the villes. Their power, supported by some invisible authority, extended beyond their fortified walls to what was now called the Outlands. It was here that the rootstock of humanity survived, living with hellzones and chemical storms, hounded by Magistrates.

In the villes, rigid laws were enforced—to atone for the sins of the past and prepare the way for a better future. That was the barons' public credo and their right-to-rule.

Kane, along with friend and fellow Magistrate Grant, had upheld that claim until a fateful Outlands expedition. A displaced piece of technology...a question to a keeper of the archives...a vague clue about alien masters—and their world shifted radically. Suddenly, Brigid Baptiste, the archivist, faced summary execution, and Grant a quick termination. For Kane there was forgiveness if he pledged his unquestioning allegiance to Baron Cobalt and his unknown masters and abandoned his friends.

But that allegiance would make him support a mysterious and alien power and deny loyalty and friends. Then what else was there?

Kane had been brought up solely to serve the ville. Brigid's only link with her family was her mother's red-gold hair, green eyes and supple form. Grant's clues to his lineage were his ebony skin and powerful physique. But Domi, she of the white hair, was an Outlander pressed into sexual servitude in Cobaltville. She at least knew her roots and was a reminder to the exiles that the outcasts belonged in the human family.

Parents, friends, community—the very rootedness of humanity was denied. With no continuity, there was no forward momentum to the future. And that was the crux—when Kane began to wonder if there was a future.

For Kane, it wouldn't do. So the only way was out—way, way out.

After their escape, they found shelter at the forgotten Cerberus redoubt headed by Lakesh, a scientist, Cobaltville's head archivist, and secret opponent of the barons.

With their past turned into a lie, their future threatened, only one thing was left to give meaning to the outcasts. The hunger for freedom, the will to resist the hostile influences. And perhaps, by opposing, end them.

Chapter 1

They had marched from the sea, landing on the western coast of Italy after a long journey, and when they arrived, they were a full expedition. Three of the fifteen-foot-tall Gear Skeletons, the walking combination of body armor and tank, had been the heavy muscle of the Olympian expedition to Italy. Forged from secondary orichalcum, which combined both lightness of frame with incredible durability, the fearsome war machines were armed with shoulder-mounted light machine guns. But the Gear Skeletons were also versatile, their strength obviating the need for bulldozers or other heavy machinery.

Captain Myrto Smaragda and nineteen of her brethren, brave Olympian men and women, were the bulk of the expedition escorting the powerful war machines. They were experienced soldiers who wore Praetorian armor, a blend of leather and polymer to pay homage to the armor of ancient Greek warriors, all the way down to the odd officer's side arm: a three-foot falcata such as Smaragda's own keen sword. The human troops were no more primitively armed than their walking robotic companions. Each soldier was equipped with a helmet with advanced night-vision optics and built-in comms that would keep the warriors in touch with each other. The radio with the power to reach back home to New Olympus rode on the broad back of one of the three Spartans. The device was capable of broadcasting hundreds of miles, thanks to the ancient Annunaki technology, especially the charged energy modules that were built into the millennium-old skeletal robots.

The Gear Skeletons had been designed for use by a smaller race. Former archivist Brigid Baptiste of the Cerberus Redoubt had explained that they were made to accommodate trans-adapts: half-size humanoids of great cleverness, density and durability. As such, there was nearly no leg room for a full-size human. Fortunately the horrors of war had meant there were plenty of capable amputee volunteers to ride in the chests of these great war machines. Amputees were the only norms who could pilot the machines from their truncated cockpits.

Despite their impressive weaponry, Smaragda and her unit were not here as conquerors; they were here as explorers. Even so, they came equipped to defend themselves from whatever horrors lurked on the Mediterranean Sea or in the Etruscan countryside. For years Smaragda and her fellow warriors had battled against the mutated hordes unleashed from the Crack, an abyssal canyon wherein the genetic weapons of long-lost eras were rekindled and turned into a means of ensuring the domination of the young Greeks.

"Remember this. We believed in the ideals of freedom, even as Hera covered our eyes with the scales of her deception," Diana had told them. "Zoo gave his life so that we could be free of the facade of a false war and to ensure our freedom and self-determination. We can do no less to protect the liberty and freedom of those who will be our neighbors and, hopefully, allies or friends."

The caution toward gentleness was accompanied by another admonition. "I also will not throw away twenty-three lives and three ancient, alien artifacts to prove how nice we are. If someone tries to kill you, you kill them right back! We're not loading cupcakes and cotton balls into your machine guns."

So here the group was, the Spartans ambling with their long brass limbs taking enormous but slow strides so that they didn't force the New Olympian soldiers to march too hard or heavy. Smaragda knew the giant machines had the ability to cross a hundred miles in the space of an hour, their nimble, precise legs allowing them traction and sure footing on even the roughest of terrain. Even so, the pilots weren't impatient, allowing their machines to move at such a sedate pace. The Charged Energy Modules that activated and motivated their limbs were remarkable pieces of technology thanks to the Annunaki, the same aliens who had at once created the warrior robot suits and the ones who had kicked off the massive, crippling war that had left New Olympus slow to recover.

Even so, there was little assurance that the CEMs, despite capturing and recovering them from the crashed scout ship that inserted itself into the war, were an inexhaustible supply of power. Just because they had not run one down completely didn't mean they could not be drained. No one knew how to recharge them, despite the combined efforts of New Olympian and Cerberus scientists.

Unnecessary wear and tear on the crystalline jewels of concentrated energy was to be frowned upon, as well as pain and injury to the pilots. The properties of secondary orichalcum made it rustproof and immutable from hammering or cutting by conventional tools. It also did well to absorb even the hardest of falls and other impacts, lessening the effects upon the pilots. But even with those amazing attributes, the amputee warriors nestled in their chests were still vulnerable. They had not been called Gear Skeletons for nothing, requiring conventional vehicle panels to enclose the users to shield them from the elements and oncoming attacks.

Even with their cushioned pilot chairs, however, movement at high speed and the prodigious leaps the war suits were capable of did leave their pilots with pulled and torn ligaments as well as minor fractures in their spinal columns, even whiplash.

More vulnerable to attack, the body-armor clad Praetorians at least didn't have to worry about their own physical abilities ripping them or shattering them when they fought to the limits of their bodies.

Smaragda flicked the visor of her helmet to scan mode, sweeping along the sides of the road, searching for unusual heat sources on infrared. The last thing they needed was an ambush. There was not supposed to be an enemy force in this part of the country, despite the rumors that had drawn them here.

Something dark had been awakened in recent days. Towns and villages in the interior had stopped communicating, stopped trading, disappearing as if they had never existed. One man returned from a visit to such a village, his hair turned white, speaking of "they who walked as ghosts" and of winged angels, both horrible and wonderful.

The Italians had turned to their neighbors, seeking help, and New Olympus's new rulers sensed that such occurrences bore the stink of urgency. A full army would be too much, but with the stories of the horrible angels, the trio of mobile armor suits was, hopefully, going to be sufficient. There was a line between coming in too hard or too soft. Smaragda felt better with the Skeletons lumbering at her side.

All being well, with them present, they would be prepared for the very worst. Three giants with shoulder-mounted machine guns and enormous axes and swords would dissuade any opponent, even if they were winged angels of gigantic proportion themselves.

Smaragda scanned the sides of the road leading to the town that had spooked the Etruscan traders so badly, looking for signs of what could have terrified the lone survivor. She gripped her M-16 rifle tightly, but she kept her finger wrapped around the handle, firmly under the trigger guard so as not to accidentally set off the weapon. She was in no mood to waste ammunition or to cause undue injury. Carrying your gun with your finger on the trigger was a sure way to do both.

Over the heavy, ponderous thuds of the Spartans' gigantic claws, Smaragda picked up something that she couldn't quite make out. She immediately held up her fist.

The trained Olympians came to a halt.

Deafening silence descended upon the Greek column and she realized what felt so odd.

There were birds on the branches of the trees along the road, but they made no sound. They were still, no nervous tics she'd seen other birds display as they, even in rest, continuously turned their heads, making certain nothing was creeping up on them. The visible birds, however, was not what had truly disturbed her.

There were trees, heavy and dense with foliage, but the impunity of nests of hidden birds was not accompanied by the riot of tweets and chirps that warned any intruder of how outnumbered they would be if they dared enter the thicket. The countryside was silent.

Smaragda stepped off the road, closing on one of the closest trees. Her men watched as she slung the rifle, then drew the falcata. With a twist, she rapped the spine against a low-hanging branch where a songbird perched.

The creature turned its attention toward her, blinked with eyes slow and gummy, but did not launch. Even the turn of its head was casual, unconcerned, not the flicker movement of a normal bird. Smaragda gave the branch another tap with the spine of her sword. The songbird took a clumsy sideways step further along the branch, then unfurled its wings.

Just before she could tap the branch a third time the songbird took off, wings flapping powerfully, moving with the natural strength and speed of the creature, the limbs beating with the urgency necessary to keep the tiny thing aloft. It wasn't as if the songbird was in some sort of debilitating trance. It flew straight and true.

It just didn't seem to care. The normally skittish creature would have taken off on Smaragda's approach, let alone not stay in place for two raps on its perch.

"Not good," she said.

Niklo spoke up. "This place has bad mojo."

Niklo had ten years on Smaragda and it showed in his gruff, grizzled looks. He'd been through plenty of battles, before Hera and Z005 arrived in Greece, mixing it up with bandits and other coldhearted thugs who made their living preying off the defenseless and helpless in postapocalyptic, shattered Greece. When the hydra drones rose up, Niklo had been one of the first who knew what to do back when the best weapons were swords and muskets. Before Hera had opened the Olympus Redoubt and its stockpiles of late-twentieth-century armaments, it was a matter of toughness.

Smaragda and Niklo had been thrown together in the madness of the hydra wars, quickly gaining each other's trust as they'd stood the line against swarms of mutant clones bred in the ancient vats of the Crack.

Niklo's unease at the strangeness of this dead countryside echoed hers and, with those five words, cemented Smaragda's instincts. Despite the fact that Smaragda had gotten an officer's commission and Niklo remained master sergeant, there was no jealousy or animosity between them. Smaragda's role entailed much more red tape, something Niklo could pawn off onto her. In the meantime, officer corps didn't regularly get issued a Squad Automatic Weapon, either, and the brawny, grizzled Niklo loved using the light machine gun to plow their way out of an ambush with a long belt of ammo.

"Tan, get on the radio. We're experiencing something weird. Everyone, if your weapons aren't hot already, safeties off," Smaragda ordered.

"You heard the lady!" Niklo bellowed. "Heads on swivels, standard perimeter protocols!"

"Movement!" came a cry from their scout up the road.

Smaragda turned and jogged toward the man. Niklo cut her off.

"You talk to home base," he told her.

Smaragda wrinkled her nose, not wanting to expose any of her men to danger while she was busy on the blower back to Olympus. Even so, she was the one in charge and she was the one whose opinion and authority mattered. This was a chain-of-command decision.

"If things look bad, you hold down the trigger until you melt the barrel laying down cover fire for our retreat," Smaragda ordered him. "And you make damn sure you come back, or I'm swimming across the Styx and dragging you back to life."

Niklo smirked, his lined face a road map of seventy years lived in the space of forty, dark eyes twinkling. "Myr, I'm counting on you getting me back from Hades."

The Olympians, turned into a well-oiled military machine of professional warriors, remained in their defensive positions, alert and ready for trouble. No one was in the line of fire of the other and each had a designated vector to scan and search. Everyone knelt, making themselves smaller targets and bringing their knee and thigh armor up to their chests to bolster the protection of their vital organs against incoming fire.

Thanos—"Tan" to his platoon mates and friends, who seemed to be everyone—looked concerned as he was on the radio. "Not getting a signal. Something is jamming us."

"How can that be?" the pilot of the Spartan asked. "This radio is designed to transmit across hundreds of miles. It's predark technology, solid-state and can cut through any interference like a knife through mud."

Tan shook his head. "Listen to this."

Smaragda took the receiver. The only sound on the other end was…unnatural.

A knocked-out radio should only receive static, white noise, the pop and crackle of random frequencies and the hiss of electromagnetic radiation pouring off the sun onto the surface of the Earth.

A jammed radio should not be singing in unholy but beautiful tones. She couldn't bear to listen to the blasphemous signal for more than a few seconds before handing the radio back to Tan. He didn't seem to be in a hurry to put it back to his ear, either.

She tried the helmet comm. "Niklo, come back."

As soon as she stopped transmitting, there was that song; a high, melodic tone, singing verses in a long-forgotten tongue. But even without understanding the words, Smaragda knew it spoke to something that did not belong on Earth. It was a *prayer*. What was worse, she *knew* something was listening and somewhere, beyond the veil of her senses, it was struggling to respond.

"Karlo, Rosa, go grab Niklo and Herc and bring them back. We're heading back to the boat. If you see anyone or anything that's not Niklo or Herc, open fire," Smaragda said.

So much for a mission of peace and mercy. Smaragda

didn't like the idea of sending off her soldiers to retrieve their teammates under orders to kill any strangers. However the singing and the odd behavior of the wildlife around them added up to this road being nothing less than a murder trap.

And she'd led her platoon right into it.

Karlo and Rosa jogged up the road to where Herc, the scout, had called back about movement. Niklo had only been out of radio contact for a minute, but it felt like a lifetime. The only heartening thing was that there had been no sound of gunfire. After all, if Niklo didn't cut loose with the SAW, that meant there was no enemy force rising to engulf them. The Olympian sergeant would have made any ambush pay for their surprise, and the light machine gun would have been heard for miles.

The silence around them, the damned silence smothering the platoon, ate at her. Smaragda upped the magnification on her helmet optics, scanning the road ahead. It had been midday when they'd stopped, clouds moving in. The day had been growing steadily grayer and dimmer, but now the light was fading even faster, when the sun should be highest in the sky.

Her blood seemed to thicken in her veins as even the high-tech optics in her Praetorian helmet, the same advanced night-vision and telescopic lenses that Kane and Grant had as part of their Magistrate armor suits, showed nothing.

"Captain?" A voice spoke up.

"Movement?" Smaragda asked.

"No. Just...smoke," Tan said.

Smaragda flipped up the visor on her helmet. There, invisible to the infrared scanners, was a roiling, spreading cloud that billowed out onto the road. She glanced through on infrared again. No one seemed to be inside the cloud, utilizing it as cover or concealment. Who knew if the smoke had some properties that could be filtering out even the body heat of her fellow Praetorians?

"Should we open fire?" another soldier asked, nerves jangling in his voice.

"On what?" Smaragda asked. "We might just end up cutting Niklo and the others apart."

"But they're not on the infrared," Tan noted.

"Retreat," Smaragda ordered.

"Smoke's closing in on the road behind us," announced the Spartan at the back of their formation. "I'm going to…"

"Stay put!" Smaragda commanded. "Don't enter the smoke."

Every instinct told her to open fire into the infection of black ink spilling onto the road on either end, bracketing them in.

Smaragda wouldn't risk the lives of her men in a friendly fire incident.

"GS 26, knock us a road through the trees, now!" Smaragda ordered.

The suit in the center of the formation reacted quickly, plunging into the woods. Large, brassy arms wielding unimaginable strength pushed against trunks, shoving trees out of the ground, roots snapping. Branches shattered against the suit's broad shoulders and Smaragda waved her men into the gap being created by the bulldozer-like robot. She stayed at the back of the group, watching as the walls of inky, foreboding smoke began to close in on where they used to be. It was as if the clouds were only following the road, forming perfect columns, not spreading out into the forest and upon the path that Skeleton 26 pushed through. Smaragda continued stepping backward, minding the exposed roots and splinters left in the robot's wake.

She kept the muzzle of her rifle aimed at the wall

of darkness and turned sideways, skipping back after her men.

"Niklo, I'll be back," she whispered. "If you're alive."

Silently she repeated that thought. Leaving soldiers under her command behind, in a lurch, was as bad a defeat as seeing them fall in bloody heaps.

"Everyone comes home." Smaragda repeated the motto of the Praetorians. "Sooner or later, we'll be back for you."

A scream split the air. She whirled and looked down the trough cut through the woods. Of the three Spartans in the unit, she could only see one, the other two having disappeared behind a wall of darkness that intercepted them. Of the fifteen soldiers she'd pushed into retreat in the wake of the Spartans, she saw only six, and they were in full retreat.

The mighty robot's shoulder guns opened up onto the shadowy smoke as it lunged for the brass giant. The flash and flicker of muzzle-blasts did little to dent or illuminate the choking, inky fog that seemed to grow tentacles with which to entrap the robot.

Smaragda shouldered her rifle, but realized that opening fire into the fog would mean that she could be blindly gunning down fellow soldiers taken captive by the cloud. She wanted to yell for a cease-fire from the robot but, watching the giant fight for its life, she noted that tracer rounds struck the smoke, then bounced off the cloud.

GS 26 lashed out with its battle-ax, the edges heated to steamy white by elements inside the gigantic weapon. The ax seemed to fare better, lopping off solid hunks of the darkness, but only if they were slender tendrils. Anything thicker than a human torso caught the ax, forcing the Spartan to struggle and wrench the blade free.

Tendrils whipped out, snatching up another of her men.

Smaragda lunged, drawing her falcata and slashing at the tentacle of living night. Blade met alien smoke and it was as if she tried to chop a tree branch. The solidness of the tendril of cloud rattled her arm, tendons popping as she put enough force into the swing for a follow-through.

The soldier in the fog's grasp turned ashen, eyes wide with horror. He breathed out, wisps of frosting moisture escaping from his lips.

"Run!" he rasped. "Get away! Live to…"

Another whip of darkness wrapped around the Praetorian's head and, within moments, he was wrenched off of his feet and into the smoke as if he was never there.

Lashing smoke fingered out toward her, but she swatted the pseudopods aside, scrambling into retreat.

The Gear Skeleton still fighting the fog disappeared; one hand reached up, clawing at the air in the hope of grasping some anchor, but the robotic claw stilled and was sucked into the darkness.

Smaragda turned and raced off a side trail between the trees. Whatever the smoke was, it seemed to have trouble flowing through and around the trunks of the forest. She swerved and wove, bounding over fallen logs and branches. She regretted lifting the visor so that she could see the midnight horror that expanded onto the road as leaves and fronds slapped and slashed at her face and eyes. She struck a tree trunk at full speed while half blinded by a leaf raking her naked eyeball.

The impact jarred her, but she seized the trunk, using it to maintain her footing.

She glanced back and saw that there were three tentacles winnowing their way around trunks, stretched out at far back as she could see through the trees. Smaragda raised her M-16 and opened fire. Rifle rounds shattered the eerie silence that had fallen in the wake of the last Spartan's disappearance, but they did nothing to dispel the living darkness stretching and seething after her.

Smaragda turned and ran again, having paused only

to slide down her eye shield, leaving the advanced optics out of the way.

Smaragda ran for as long and as hard as she could.

Within an hour she was at the coast, on her knees, her chest burning, shoulders aching, trying to vomit but having nothing to spit up.

Twenty-two people were now gone.

She was the lone survivor.

She pulled off her helmet and, for a moment, thought something else had come after her. A sheet of white spilled down over her eyes and she screamed in shock.

Then she realized why she was so stunned.

Before the smoke her hair had been as dark as a raven's feathers.

Now the tresses that she could see were as pale and wispy as silken icicles.

Trembling, Smaragda looked around for the boat that had brought the expedition.

"Live to tell what happened," she said in a terrified murmur.

"Live to tell what…happened…" she repeated.

Tears drenched Smaragda's cheeks as she struggled to her feet.

Chapter 2

Domi crouched deeply as she faced off with the man in black. Perfectly balanced in her hand was the handle of one of her favorite knives, its flats gleaming under the harsh lights. She was a small woman, hardly five feet in her bare feet, and Domi was almost constantly barefoot. Her body looked thin and frail, her complexion was white as bone and her hair was wispy, silvery and trimmed short so as to provide little more than peach fuzz for an opponent to grab on to. Most startling about Domi was her eyes, ruby-red gems that denoted the cause of her pale flesh and translucent hair.

The girl was an albino. And yet she was facing off against a man a foot taller and easily a hundred pounds heavier than she was, her muscles tense, ready for battle. In the centuries before skydark, the cataclysmic nuclear Armageddon that drove humankind to the brink of extinction, albinos had been considered frail. Indeed, as a child, she had been, but surviving in the deadly world outside of the villes, in the harsh wilderness between tiny islands of civilization, had hardened her.

She was thin of limb, yes. But her muscles were corded tight and had strength and swiftness within them, making her akin to a panther. Her "claws" were her knife and her "bite" was a deadly little .45-caliber Detonics Combat Master, which she didn't have access to now.

The big man in front of her was powerful, armored,

and even inside that armor, had a lightness on his feet, bouncing on the ground in a taunting dance, making it apparent that he expected her to charge him. He was dangling himself as bait, waiting for her to commit to an attack before he turned it around.

Domi was a survivor, though. Before she'd begun to learn how to read under the tutelage of Lakesh and Brigid Baptiste, her school had been expanses of desert or gnarled, predator-stalked forests. Her teachers had been the cruel and the powerful, seeking to use her as meat or pleasure or, in some grisly cases, both. And the feral albino girl had been a quick student, passing every test thrown at her.

This was not the first time she'd faced the armored brute in front of her. His head was encased in a glossy but tough helmet, shielding his face and preventing her from seeing if he was blinking or shifting his glance. Without a view of his tells, Domi was partially blinded, at her usual disadvantage. With nothing to betray her enemy's thoughts, and even his body language distorted by the bouncing dance he shuffled, all of her usual cues as to where or when to strike or even to defend were gone.

The brute lunged. He had his own blade, twice the length of Domi's, almost a short sword that looked normal-size in his massive fist. The movement startled the wild girl, but even when reflexively responding to the sudden rush, Domi's body reacted with speed and agility. The edge of the knife whistled through the air and she could feel the brush of wind off its cold, unyielding dagger on her bare upper arm, the lethal edge missing her by fractions of an inch.

Domi's swift sidestep planted her left foot down hard for support, bracing her so that she could kick up with her other leg, the knee striking the big knife-man in the side. She'd aimed instinctively away from the bulletproof polycarbonate shells that shielded his abdominal muscles and into the ballistic cloth side panel. The impact was more than sufficient to elicit a grunt from behind the opaque black visor of her foe's helmet.

Domi brought her knife around, finding a brawny shoulder and stabbing into it. Even as she plunged the blade down, she wrapped her other arm around his, snaring it tightly to give her leverage on him and to make her harder to reach with his free hand. The armored brute lurched erect and Domi's feet left the ground. Now she was riding a bucking beast, and just to make certain he couldn't shake her free, she wound her muscular legs around his forearm and wrist.

Suddenly the brute not only had to deal with the bulk of his armor and the throbbing pain of her stab, but also the unbalancing, unsettling weight of the feral girl.

"Dammit!" Edwards shouted as he toppled off balance, bringing them both down to the exercise mat.

Domi stabbed again at the ballistic cloth between the polycarbonate plates that would have provided protection against slashing, stabbing steel. Fortunately for the former Magistrate, Domi's knife was a blunt-edged aluminum copy, meant for training. Even though its edges were soft, rounded, unable to cut anything softer than mud, when you stabbed someone with the tip, it still was hard, unyielding metal slamming into soft flesh.

And it hurt, much to Edwards's dismay.

"I thought these things weren't supposed to injure you," Edwards grunted as Domi slithered off his arm.

"Not normally," Domi replied, her verbiage clipped as she was still brimming with adrenaline from the training session. "But 'm not normal."

"You can say that again, runt." Edwards looked her over. He was used to her dropping pronouns and adjectives while stressed or energized for combat, so was not worried about her suffering some sort of episode or being too out of breath. Indeed, the comment about her not being normal showed she still retained her wits, sense of humor and a significant skill at wordplay.

"Still, I'm damned glad I was wearing armor," Edwards added, giving her a poke in the shoulder with his fist. "Just too bad you found the kinks in it, little cheater."

"Was the point," Domi answered, rubbing her knuckle-brushed upper arm. She smirked at his accusation of cheating. "Pardon pun."

Edwards grinned, pulling off his helmet. His hair was a close-shaved scruff around his melon-size head, showing off his bullet-bitten ear. Though the Magistrate armor was designed to be environmentally adaptive, beads of sweat still formed thanks to the exertion and condensation of Edwards's breath inside the helmet.

When they'd met at first, and were being assigned to either run or be a part of the Cerberus Away Teams, Edwards had bristled at the concept of working "beneath" such a young, tiny female.

That was dozens of sparring matches ago, across the past several months. Since then the brawny former Magistrate had come to respect Domi. There were times when she sounded barely more educated than a toddler, and she always looked like a frail wisp of a creature, but there was strength and intelligence in there.

It wasn't the kind of phenomenal intellect as displayed by others such as Brigid Baptiste or Mohandas Lakesh Singh, who boasted unique scientific and mathematical acumen. It was more the wisdom and agility of mind showed by fellow former Magistrates Kane and Grant. It was knowledge that didn't involve splitting atoms, but observation of her surroundings, instincts that helped her react and respond to danger at speeds beyond even the most trained soldiers that Edwards knew of.

Being under her command, even if it was a mere three people in the whole Cerberus Away Team, was no threat to his abilities, his prodigious strength and paramilitary Magistrate training. His teammate, the beautiful and bright freezie Sela Sinclair, was another sharp mind and strong woman Edwards had learned to respect.

The Magistrates had been a strictly masculine community, a group of men who were of similar size, similar strength, each picked and groomed from even before birth to become part of the hybrid barons' elite enforcers. They had been forged as rough, macho and gung ho, their individuality limited by the stripping of their first names. Edwards had been born Edwards, as his father before him and that father before him. His mother had been a donor, a handpicked maiden chosen to bear a healthy child, to mix with the genes of a soldier and warrior to produce an ideal fighting man.

Edwards had been given very little of a normal youth. It was spent physically training, learning the laws and procedures of the Magistrates, not being a boy. For him, as well as Domi, the luxuries of childhood were absent, little chance of play or exploring and nurturing a sense of awe and wonder.

Now, in the wake of the barons' evolution and shedding of their hybrid-human forms, Edwards was a lawman who found a new vocation as a warrior in the defense of Cerberus Redoubt, and an avocation as an adventurer, a hero to swoop in to the rescue and restore order.

Through this selfless assistance of others, Edwards felt awakened. Reborn even. In helping others, in traveling the world for the purposes of growing knowledge, for the effort of building a world, he was young again. He was alive whereas before he'd merely survived and existed. It was a lesson, a transformation, that Domi had also undergone.

Domi herself was a child of the wilderness. Later, in the

Tartarus Pits, the hellish subterranean area in the shadow of the Administrative Monolith in the center of Cobaltville, she'd had to scrabble as a petty thief and was pressed into servitude as a prostitute. It was only her acceptance as an ally, the affection of Grant as a surrogate father and protector, the gentle love of Lakesh, that had turned her from a feral savage into an avid student. She'd gone from a slum criminal totally out for herself to someone who understood that love and affection were not necessarily displayed by sexual desire, as with Grant, and that intimacy could come with gentility, not cruelty, as with Lakesh.

Given such an environment that nurtured goodness, growth and intelligence, Edwards found himself only mockingly grumbling about "babysitting trips with nerds to ruins" and actually showing excitement about learning about the history of the strange planet they lived upon.

"Hey, you two!"

It was Sela Sinclair, who herself had not become involved in the ever-escalating sparring matches of Domi and Edwards. Sinclair's preference for combat was not the close-quarters of knives and fists but rather the application of leverage and focused energy, usually in the form of the collapsible baton she had become intimate with in her pre-skydark life as an Air Force officer. It didn't mean she didn't lack for bare-handed skill, but when things came to a hands-on approach her preference was for the strength-amplifying qualities of an ASP telescoping fighting stick, the same way that Domi preferred a sharp knife. And even then, the ASP was only for situations where she didn't necessarily require the killing of an opponent.

Sinclair folded her arms, leaning on one leg, hip tilted jauntily.

"Something come up?" Domi asked.

"The CAT teams are being called in for a briefing," Sinclair said. "Something about a call from New Olympus."

Domi perked up at the sound of that. Edwards and Sinclair had joined her in that prior mission, arriving later with armor kits meant for Sandcats and Humvees that would be adapted to the Olympian Spartans. They had also been present when Hera Olympiad had gone berserk with power, standing their ground against her madness and the ever-growing energies and mass of her corrupted command node.

Hera, a Cobaltville scientist who had been sent to retrieve Annunaki artifacts from Greece while the Overlord Marduk was still Baron Cobalt, had acquired a smart-metal control nodule when one of Marduk's Nephilim drone troopers was captured. Using the knowledge she had gained from her exploration of the Crack, she'd manipulated the smart-metal pod to provide herself a new form of clothing. Because the pod was now reacting with an intelligent mind, it followed her commands rather than simply existed as a suit of body-conforming armor.

Of course, Marduk had known of her interference with the Annunaki electronics. He'd tried to take control of her and, barring that, his psychic assault had driven her insane.

Hera had bonded that module with another piece of Annunaki technology, a Threshold, and an electrical drone weapon on top of that. CAT Beta—Domi, Sinclair and Edwards—had been at the forefront of the battle against the out-of-control Hera as she'd continued to add mass and energy to her suit's frame, assisted by Brigid Baptiste.

Despite the defeat of the superhuman Hera, the damage to New Olympus had been significant. There were sorties from Cerberus to the Grecian nation, teams mostly there to excavate and open up collapsed and damaged tunnels in the deep underground military base that had been the Olympian redoubt. The digging and rebuilding were necessary, as Hera's destruction had cut off access to redoubt supplies of ammunition, food and medicine stored for the hundreds of years since before skydark.

Rebuilding had been going well, but for New Olympus to actually send out a call for help meant something big had popped up.

"Shower and change. You've got fifteen minutes," Sinclair told them.

The two Beta Team members headed to the gymnasium locker room where Domi helped Edwards out of his bulky Magistrate armor, cutting the usual de-prep time by half, allowing Edwards to do more than just let the showerhead spit on him for a second. That both teammates were naked was not a distraction to either.

Domi had her devotion to Lakesh, and Edwards was uninterested in settling down and of no mind to steal the scientist's woman. Indeed, Edwards was a man of personal discipline, and while he believed that men and women could be lovers and work together, he personally did not want to complicate his relationship with the tiny Domi. Edwards also had a preference for taller, fuller-figured women, and to the massive former Magistrate, Domi's appearance was more of a prepubescent boy's than an object of sexual desire. Hell, knowing her for this long, becoming nearly a brother to her on the CAT team, she was not an object. She was Domi. Friend. Living being. Person. Not an object of lust.

From what Edwards had read or seen in vids from before the destruction of mankind, he could appreciate that at least one thing had advanced forward since the age of "civilization." Humanity needed to grow up, to not just focus on their baser instincts and rut like animals. Reproduction was important, but there were other much more vital matters that needed attendance.

By the time Edwards finished his shower and dressed, he and Domi arrived at the briefing with minutes to spare.

In fact, they had both entered sooner than Kane and Grant, and were there to see Brigid Baptiste, the third member of the group that had been entitled CAT Alpha. Brigid was not happy to see Kane and Grant ambling in so slowly after their counterparts had showed such promptness, and she let her distaste for the situation show in her scowl.

"I told you we shouldn't have stopped for coffee," Grant said, catching the disgust in Brigid's glare. He slid into his chair at the meeting table, setting the travel mug down in front of him. Kane shrugged at his friend's statement of being "busted."

"It's not like we're the B-team," Kane noted, giving a wink to Domi, who wrinkled her nose at the mock insult. If there was a rivalry between the CAT teams, no one on either of the two squads had been made aware of it. They were comrades and allies. The only rank came from the fact that Sinclair was awakened after Kane, Brigid and Grant became a team, and Edwards had only recently found himself a free agent in the wake of the collapse of the baronies. Kane's joke was taken in stride, not in malice, and Brigid rolled her eyes.

"As you know, ever since our first contact with New Olympus, we've been sending over manpower and assistance to help them with their rebuilding," Brigid began. "They've reciprocated by helping to design Kane's exoskeleton during...recent troubles."

"I didn't get to blow-dry and curl my hair for this recap?" Edwards asked, rubbing his closely shaved pate.

Brigid chuckled. "Sorry, but you know I try to be as completest as possible."

Edwards shrugged. "Not a problem. I just needed something to...distract me."

Domi nodded in recognition. Edwards was referring to Ullikummis's attack and conquest of the Cerberus Redoubt. Not only was Edwards present for that, but also he'd been infected with one of the stony Annunaki's seeds, making him a puppet, a pawn of the exiled godling. Memories of that time, the loss of life and the madness of their enslavement, were still recent and raw.

"Right now, they're starting to expand their area of influence over there, peacefully." Brigid quickly added the *peacefully*. "They'd sent out an excursion into what used to be the Etruscan countryside."

"Italy?" Sela Sinclair asked.

Brigid nodded.

Sinclair smirked. "I always wanted to take a vacation in the countryside with the vineyards."

Brigid gave the Air Force veteran a one percent salute, akin to the gesture that Kane and Grant gave each other. She continued speaking. "Out of twenty soldiers and three Spartans sent into the Italian countryside, there was only one person who returned. The commander of the ground platoon. She was in shock to the point that her hair turned white. She claimed they had encountered an amorphous, seemingly sentient darkness that was immune to gunfire and had swallowed people. Even their robotic support team was unable to break the bonds."

"Bulletproof fog that eats soldiers," Grant murmured. "Do you have any historical correlation and background for that, Brigid?"

"Nothing so far," she replied. "The only possible link to an inky, all-enveloping blackness is the relation of one of the old gods of Italy—Charun."

"That sounds like the 'mythological guy who has a boat on the river of the dead' Charon?" Kane asked. Brigid acknowledged that Kane got the pronunciation and identity correct. "Any relation?"

"Charun, it is believed, was a renamed chooser of the slain in Etruscan mythology. He was a winged god of death," Brigid explained. "An invulnerable fog or a wave might be in reference to the river Styx's alleged properties of making anyone dipped in it invulnerable, like Achilles."

"You've been hitting the research hard enough," Kane mentioned. "Sometimes, it's best to put speculation aside and put feet on the ground."

"And hope that we're not stumbling into a trap," Sinclair added. "You want us to come with you?"

"In general, we rarely send both teams into the field together, but in this instance, it would be beneficial to have you along. My ankle still isn't at a hundred percent, so my running and jumping will be impaired, and DeFore still wishes to make certain Kane hadn't received anything permanent in regard to the crack he received on his head. I'm under the presumption that the reason the expedition encountered such a powerful surge was due to the size of the intrusion," Brigid said.

"So if we show up with three to six people, we can slip under their radar, so to speak," Edwards concluded. "I can figure out why you want Beta with you." He glanced toward Domi as if to provide clarity.

"Indeed. We'll also be heading to Olympus in two groups. One via traditional mat-trans, and Edwards and Grant in the Mantas," Brigid added. "We'll see if our jerry-rigged weapons systems for them might prove sufficient to deal with a superhuman threat."

"If we have a target that we can use the Mantas against," Grant added. "Who knows if the thing generating that weird black mass will be out in the open."

"We'll cross that bridge when we come to it," Kane said. "The first thing we need to do is get to New Olympus."

"And since we're taking the Mantas, we'll catch up to you in a few hours," Edwards pointed out. "Don't drink all the hospitality before we get there."

Kane chuckled. "It's not the hospitality you should worry about."

Edwards didn't say it out loud, but looking at the concerned features of Brigid Baptiste in the wake of the briefing, he knew that something out there was going to be a terrible challenge.

Then again, that was the reason for the existence of the Cerberus Away Teams, he added grimly and silently.

Chapter 3

The arrival of the strangers was nigh, as the radio signal came through from across the gulf of land and ocean that separated New Olympus from the Bitterroot Mountains. Diana Pantopoulos was at once relieved at the response, and guilty for having drawn the Cerberus warriors back into their continent.

Diana had inherited the role of "queen" of New Olympus, an unenviable task alongside Aristotle Marschene stepping into the "boots" of Z00s, in the wake of that last visit. As of now, Greece was actually working on a charter and constitution allowing a representative government, but also allowing Diana and Ari to act as "ranking managers."

The two were still commanders of the Gear Skeleton forces, having risen in rank with the loss of Z00s—the Magistrate formerly known as Thurmond—and Hera Olympiad—Helena Garthwaite, the scientist sent by Baron Cobalt to uncover ancient technology that the baron recalled on a genetic level. Those two, and another Magistrate, had been sent on an expedition to find the tools of Marduk, Cobalt's original Annunaki form, and in the process, they had built Greece into a fortress-like society with remarkable Spartan Gear Skeletons as the backbone of their mechanized military force.

It was an empire built upon clay feet. Through the use of clone production facilities, Helena Garthwaite had initiated a program of terror to unify the Greek countryside.

It was the effort of Kane, Grant and Brigid that ended that deception, the years of death and violence, but in such a spasm of destruction that it had left New Olympus heavily damaged and many of its heroes fallen on the battlefield. Diana didn't want to think if they had not showed up. The true evil behind the whole society, Marduk, the former Baron Cobalt, arrived to claim his storehouse in the Tartarus Crack.

Though teams had come and gone, assisting in the reconstruction of New Olympus in the wake of that war, this would be the first time the men and women of the Cerberus teams would be returning as a group.

Diana smiled at the thought of her friend, the small, feisty Domi among them.

"Incoming mat-trans event at the old Oracle Temple," came the announcement from her wheelchair's built-in comm panel. Diana pressed Send.

"Alert received. Reporting to command center," she answered.

"Shall we get your suit ready?"

"No. Let the new Artem15 meet them," Diana said.

And with that, the wheelchair-bound administrator of New Olympus felt a pang of regret at her promotion. She'd loved being the armored suit named for the goddess of the hunt, Artemis. But as Aristotle had been promoted to Z00s, a new "queen" was necessary for the rankings. Now, she was H34a, as Zeus and Hera were the king and queen of Mount Olympus. Whereas the previous Hera was petty and manipulative, Diana tried to be a little nobler, a little more righteous. She'd learned from the mistakes of the past.

Or had she? Wasn't she just buying into the same level of hero worship? Hadn't she and Ari just taken the place of a manipulator and a man who, up until his final battle, had been happy to deceive others for the sake of his own power?

Rolling herself into the command center, she noted that Aristotle was there, along with the rest of this shift's personnel. They were watching the progress of Artem15 and two other suits as they bounded across country, taking enormous strides that ate up terrain at great velocity. Diana held a wistful moment for the days when she'd needed to bolt across countrysides on emergency missions. Artem15's long legs allowed her to easily top 100 miles an hour, and those speeds were necessary in defense of the people under New Olympus's protection, townsfolk who'd easily be outnumbered and slaughtered in the assaults made by deadly hordes of Hydrae.

That kind of rapid response gave Diana a little wear and tear as she sat in the control couch of the mighty Gear Skeleton, but the hero suits and the Spartans were often ridden hard, beyond acceptable limits. Now, they were only on their way as a means of ferrying the Cerberus visitors from the parallax point atop the remains of the temple of the Oracle to New Olympus itself. There was still a lot of digging to be done to get to the mat-trans buried during the old Hera Olympiad's rampage.

Those damaged tunnels and elevators themselves were made all the more inaccessible by the fact that there was little way for the fifteen-foot armored titans to fit into the redoubt and dig. Smaller conventional exoskeletons, one of which Kane had utilized during his "infection" by Ullikummis, had provided some ease. But they were not based on a frame constructed of alien technology alloys, nor were their charged energy modules able to operate at maximum capacity due to the conventional human-designed metals not being up to Annunaki-level snuff.

"Queen on the deck!" announced First Officer Orestes, standing to attention, clicking his booted heels together in a sharp salute.

"As you were," Diana said, waving off the show of respect. She'd earned her place as an officer, but she didn't feel that she warranted all of this attention or adulation. Even so, Ari gave her a wink from across the room where he was watching the main screens that displayed drone camera views of the countryside.

"ETA to their arrival?" Diana asked.

"They're a half mile out, sir," Comms Officer Kindalos said, looking back over her shoulder. As always, Diana felt a little self-conscious. Whereas Helena Garthwaite/ Hera Olympiad was beautiful to the point of perfection, the former Artem15 pilot had more wrong with her than merely amputated legs below mid-thigh. The same battle that had taken her lower limbs had left scars spiderwebbed across her forehead and right cheek. Diana's pride forced her to wear her hair flipped over, her blond locks masking her deformity with a curtain of tresses.

Unfortunately, since her ascension, she'd been forced into a more face-to-face role. Hiding her features, no matter how insecure she was about them, would not do when it came to projecting her authority. Ari had tried to tell her that she did not appear bad-looking, even with the crisscross of healed flesh patterned on her face. Diana didn't believe him. Even though he was in love with her, she still didn't trust his opinion.

Ari rolled around to her, gave her a clap on the shoulder. "Honey."

Diana smiled, resting her hand atop his.

"You ever get tired of all these snap-to's?" she asked her king and lover.

Ari shrugged. "Occasionally. But it reminds me not to mess around with my power."

"What power? We're stuck with all the decisions but none of the fun," Diana told him.

Ari looked to the trio of running and jumping robots. "That was fun, wasn't it?"

Diana gave him a pop on the biceps, but laughed. "I'm too young to be nostalgic and shit."

"Just keep smiling. You look prettier," Ari told her.

"Liar," Diana called him, but she still leaned over and kissed him on the cheek.

The two returned their attention to the screens. Mounted on tiny motorized planes, the pursuit cameras enabled the New Olympians the ability to keep their eyes, remotely, on things without endangering the cameraman. The unmanned drone concept was still in its earliest developments when, in 2001, the world had been blown to hell by a global nuclear cull, all caused by a renegade dimension traveler by the name of Colonel Thrush. But, thankfully, in the postwar era, more than a couple survivors had come to Greece from Israel, which had been extremely active in such technological development.

The tiny airplane zipped ahead of the trio of welcoming robots toward the ramped natural obelisk upon which the Oracle Temple had been built. There were four people visible atop the clean-cut "table" at the peak of what had been a spire of granite. The structures atop, walls formed from a henge of natural-appearing stones and a long-gone roof, wood and thatch rotted away by the passage of history and impact of storms a millennium ago. It bore more recent damage; burns from ASP blasters striped the massive, lithic columns, evidence of a more recent battle between the heroes who had arrived back then and Marduk's ASP-armed Nephilim. At the base of the ramp was a golden puddle, a mirror made of the molten remains of Hera Olympiad and Z00s, and the metals surrounding their bodies as Z00s had made the final sacrifice to end her unholy rampage.

The puddle itself was a reminder of wounds, the deaths of four other Gear Skeleton pilots slain at the talons and blasters Hera had absorbed into her extended, reprogrammed body. It also commemorated Thurmond's end, especially in the face of his admission of his wrongs and his ultimate betrayal of Hera's foul protection scheme. It was now an honored tomb, a memorial to true freedom, and the birth of equality under law for all of New Olympus.

As the drone swooped closer, they saw four people in the midst of the henge that formerly held the temple roof and walls together. Three women, one man and the sight of small, slender, spider-limbed Domi, her bone-white complexion a stark contrast to the deep ebony of her shadow suit, made Diana's heart skip a beat. A kindred spirit had returned. She imagined this was what it felt like to have a visit from a sister after a long time, Diana being an only child.

The other woman was undoubtedly Brigid Baptiste; Diana quickly recognizing her on the screen thanks to her flame-gold tresses, vibrant and noticeable. The tall woman knelt, punching the recall code into the small pyramid-shaped interphaser, sending it back to Cerberus Redoubt. The small device exploited the intersection of naturally occurring energy paths or "parallax points" as referred to by the designer of the interphaser, Mohandas Lakesh Singh. It was a priceless piece of technology, so recalling it to the redoubt would keep it from ending up in the wrong hands.

This was not Cerberus's indictment of New Olympus as "the wrong hands," but as there was no way to penetrate into the mat-trans chamber for New Olympus's redoubt, it would be useless to Diana and her people, and leaving it out in the elements would make it too vulnerable.

The third woman was also familiar to Diana—a slender woman with a dusky complexion, her short hair arranged in braids. She stood at attention, maintaining the demeanor of even the highly trained New Olympian troopers, keeping the frame of her Copperhead submachine gun clasped, muzzle down to her belly and finger off the trigger. It was just a brief inkling of Sela Sinclair's Air Force officer's skill and mental alertness. Though it was unlikely she'd accidentally tug on the trigger of the compact, bullet-spitting weapon, a true professional never took chances. If the firearm discharged without Sela's will, the gunfire would only harm the ground at her feet. At the same time, her eyes scanned their surroundings.

"This is Grant to New Olympus command and control." Another familiar voice piped up. "We are approaching your airspace in two Manta craft."

"Edwards here, in Manta Beta" followed the other aircraft's radio.

"Welcome to New Olympus airspace. Antiaircraft measures are being tuned down for your safe passage," Kindalos announced loud enough for the rest of the command center to hear. Quietly, in a lower tone, she switched channels on her headset and contacted the air defenses. While it was unlikely that mere .50-caliber machine guns could bring down two transonic Manta craft, it was better to not have even that slight risk.

"Sir? Majesties? We just got word that there were two aircraft coming in, and from the west, of course, right?" radar station officer Niko Mikoles asked. "I've got *three* contacts on radar. All from the west."

Diana and Ari immediately tuned in on their observation screen.

"Kindalos! Let them know," Diana commanded, sharp and urgent.

Kindalos's fingers flew to the frequency switch, linking back to the fast-flying Mantas. "Cerberus flight. Be advised. Unidentified flying object flying in parallel," the comm officer said quickly.

Before there was a chance for Grant or Edwards to reply, a loud screech blazed over the speakers.

Kindalos, wearing her headset, was literally slammed from her seat by the sonic burst exploding so close to her ear. At the same moment Mikoles's radar screen blazed brightly, energy seeming to pour into the readout. After another instant the screen cracked down the center, wisps of ozone rising from the shattered glass.

"Medic to C-and-C!" Orestes yelled into the intercom.

Diana and Ari turned to the armrest comm-links on their chairs, but discovered that whatever odd pulse that had literally floored Kindalos and caused screens to die in a spectacular manner had rendered their radios equally useless.

Aristotle didn't delay an instant, dropping himself from the seat of his chair to the floor beside Kindalos. Though king, the training and instincts of a soldier were hard to bury and the former Are5 showed that he was as skilled in the ways of emergency medical treatment as he had been in waging war. He laid Kindalos so that there was no strain or stress on her neck, in the event of reflex-inducing whiplash. The headphones were swiftly discarded.

The young woman's left ear was drenched in blood. Ari tore a kerchief from his breast pocket, applying it gently to the side of her head to keep away infection and stop the slow trickle pouring from her burst eardrum.

"Come on, kid, don't do this," Ari murmured. Other officers joined Ari in looking over the injured Kindalos. In the meantime Diana and Orestes checked on Mikoles for injuries.

"I'm fine," the young man told his superiors. "We need a fire ext—"

As if to answer his incomplete suggestion, a guard pulled the trigger on a CO_2 canister, blasting through the radar screen to whatever produced the stink of ozone beneath the broken glass.

Diana spared a small part of her mind to show pride in the military precision and loyalty presented in responding to the injury and the damages done to their electronics. While there would always be those who thought of soldiers as nothing more than mindless thugs and fodder, *real* troops would band together and move quickly with calmness, practiced problem-solving and true care for their fallen comrades.

However, with the pulse that had knocked out both radar and the radio communications, they were out of touch with Grant and Edwards in their Mantas.

Right now, all they were able to do was to get their own comms back up and running. Even as she thought this, there were already guards racing on foot to convey alerts to the rest of the Olympian redoubt.

So much fixed, and now another attack had driven them back to blindness and primitive messages.

At least we got the fire extinguisher on the radar screen, Diana thought to herself. Otherwise, we would have been sending smoke signals.

THE SUDDEN BURST of feedback that struck Grant brought a mixture of good news and bad news to the brawny pilot. First was good news, in that the Commtact's new frequency filter had managed to minimize the brain-rattling discomfort of…whatever that electronic howl was. One of the weaknesses of the implants and their plates was that it was quite possible to blow out the hearing of someone listening with either too loud a response or via electromagnetic interference. Fortunately, Lakesh and the other whitecoats back at Cerberus had been diligent in improving the Commtact network and the electronics within.

Unfortunately there was more bad news. The navigational instruments based off radar, which was pretty much everything in the Manta cockpit, were rendered as useless as his Commtact. There was little to tell if the systems themselves had suffered catastrophic damage or if they were merely jammed, dazed by the sudden wave of energy.

At the very least Grant and Edwards had been able to hear the majority of the warning coming from New Olympus. Grant would have felt a lot more confident had not the Heads Up Display on the pilot's helmet been equally invalidated by the interference pulse. Still, there was a dome of glass, and Grant was an expert pilot, so at least he wouldn't find himself crashing. Just to make certain, he pulled on his shadow suit hood. One thing the faceplate allowed for, in addition to being a self-contained environment, was advanced optics and sensors.

Grant glanced back and could see, in the distance, the outline of Edwards's ship. They couldn't talk by radio, but maybe they could communicate with hand gestures, especially with the telescopic zoom available in the eyepieces.

He throttled down only a fraction, steering to parallel Edwards, when he caught a flicker of darkness from the corner of his eye.

So much for being able to use sign language with Edwards before the UFO arrived.

Grant turned his head, swinging the Manta into an S-turn that would allow him to survey a maximum of sky around him. The cockpit glass of the high-velocity ship allowed him a fairly good panorama of the Mediterranean airspace. Edwards was visible, as well. He was keeping his distance and was focused on something Grant couldn't see at this moment.

"Deaf and mute, and half blind," the big, former Magistrate grumbled to himself. "I might as well be a sitting duck…"

With that thought, however, Grant noticed Edwards suddenly accelerate his Manta, as if to engage ramming speed against his fellow pilot. There was only a brief instant of confusion until he realized that whatever had drawn Grant's attention as the UFO was now flying on his tail, sticking to his blind spot.

That turned out to be a much better form of nonverbal communication that instantly clicked in Grant's mind. Within a moment he throttled up to near escape-velocity speed, tearing away from his pursuit utilizing the scram jet engines built into the moon-base-built wonder craft. He only maintained escape velocity for a few seconds, but that was more than sufficient to have created a few miles of space between the Manta and his pursuit.

With a deft spin, Grant was able to see the UFO as it raced to catch up. He could see a pair of powerful wings, but what hung beneath them was no mere bird, not even a pteranodon.

He employed his optic enhancements and zoomed in, focusing on a man.

No, to call it a man would have been a misnomer. With electronic readouts on the transparent shadow suit's faceplate, Grant could see that the entity had a wingspan of thirty feet, its skin tone blued like that of a pallid corpse. Around its bare, brawny arms, he saw what at first appeared to be coiled serpents, but recognition immediately kicked in. He bore some version of the serpentine ASP blasters worn by the Nephilim drones who served beneath Enlil and the other Annunaki overlords. They glinted like metal in the sun, but those weapons seemed puny in comparison to the winged humanoid's handheld device. It was a gigantic hammer, gripped in sinewy, powerful hands.

Grant looked at the face of his foe, one twisted in grim rage, tusks protruding and curving out over his mustached upper lip, a black beard of writhing worms crawling up the sides of his face before they lengthened into serpents like a male version of the Greek monster Medusa. His nose plunged down over his peeled-back lips like the hook of a vulture's beak and its eyes were shadows beneath bulging, clifflike brow ridges.

Grant's shock at the hurtling creature knocked him from taking a mental inventory of the beast's appearance, and he flipped the circuits to activate the weapons recently added to the Manta. As he did, there was a whine of protest from the systems, informing him that whatever had negated radio communications had likewise disabled the weaponry controls.

"Isn't that just great?" Grant growled, throttling up the engines and hurtling toward the flying humanoid. Though he was certain the hammer was far more than just a brutish weapon meant for crushing skulls, he was gambling on a Mach 2 impact stunning the flying opponent. The creature was not thematically different from the gigantic Kongamato from Africa, and he always wondered how one of those muscular horrors would have dealt with being run over by a supersonic Manta.

The tusked mouth turned into a semblance of a smile through the telescopic magnification on Grant's faceplate and immediately he started to regret playing chicken with a flying demon.

He didn't have long to doubt his course, though, as a moment later the Manta jolted violently. Even strapped into the pilot's couch, Grant's head and arms flailed wildly in the cockpit. Alarms and lights jerked to life around the cabin, the violence of impact making the horizon cartwheel in the cracked windshield of the supersonic craft.

Stunned, Grant tried to will his hands back to the joystick nestled between his knees. Unfortunately centrifugal force and a stabbing pain in his back and shoulder kept them dangling at the ends of his ropy arms. All the while, his optics displayed a countdown of the Manta's altitude as it spiraled toward the Mediterranean Sea below. At this speed, striking incompressible water, it would be like hurling a melon against a stone wall, except the meaty fruit disgorged would be Grant's internal organs.

Chapter 4

Edwards was aghast at the sight of the winged monstrosity flying to meet Grant's Manta at ramming speed. At the same time he grimaced at the inconvenience of having his weaponry disabled by whatever had knocked out the radios. As it was, the flying monster itself was spiraling out of control, seemingly as stunned as the Manta, its pilot locked in a fatal corkscrew heading toward the waiting sea beneath them. However, even as the hammer-wielding flier toppled head over heels through the empty air, Edwards's Commtact came back online.

"Grant!" It was a chorus of alarmed cries in familiar voices.

Edwards looked between the stunned monstrosity and his fellow Cerberus warrior plummeting toward the ground. With a pit of disgust in his belly, he realized that the newly armed Mantas had very little that could be used to save another aircraft from crashing. The upgrades were meant to swat threats from the sky, to ensure that they crashed.

And if Edwards could not rescue Grant, he'd sure as hell avenge his friend. His thumb flicked up the safety switch on his joystick and he pressed down on the trigger. In a moment a pair of .50-caliber machine guns roared to life beneath the keel of his Manta, streams of lead locking on the falling humanoid. As tracers described the path of fire from Edwards's guns, the winged creature jolted to alertness. One bullet smashed through the beast-man's wing, but no pain registered on his target.

Instead the huge hammer was raised in both hands. It lowered its head and the hammer's bonce began to glow brightly, turning into a blazing sun at the end of its two-meter-long shaft. Edwards watched as the air in front of the hammer and the falling devil sparked to life. Instinctively the former Magistrate realized what those individual flares were as he eased off the trigger. The hammer was incinerating the massive bullets in flight, shielding the stunned opponent.

"So, if you want to play it that way," Edwards murmured, "let's try something that won't burn up."

Edwards kicked in what passed for afterburners on the Manta, and the crush of acceleration pushed him deeper into the pilot's couch, the transonic aircraft blistering along at escape velocity. This low, he wouldn't be able to keep up the pace very long, but it was merely a short burst of speed that roared him past their winged opponent. Unlike Grant, he wasn't going to ram his enemy, but rather, let the sonic boom in his wake beat at the odd, hammer-wielding being.

And since the interference had stopped and the Manta's cockpit was now receiving camera images, he was able to spot the effects of the thunderclap of his passage on the creature. It had lost its hammer and, once more, it was working into a spiral. Unfortunately this spiral was slow and winding, lazy and controlled.

Even so, there was no way that Edwards was going to allow it anywhere near its fallen hammer, wherever it would have landed. He swung his Manta around, all the while hoping that somewhere Grant had regained control of his craft.

The winged creature spotted the incoming scram jet and righted itself, putting on its own burst of blinding speed. Within moments it was out of sight, a spray of .50-caliber lead chasing it over the horizon.

"Guys? How's Grant?" Edwards asked, still distracted by whatever it was they'd encountered.

IT COULD HAVE been adrenaline surging through Grant's limbs that gave him the strength to pull his hands back down to the joystick, or it could have been the more automated systems on the Manta kicking into gear, providing just enough of an iota of balance and slowing for him to regain control of himself in the death spiral. Or it could just have been the mental image of him exploding like overripe fruit against the surface of the Mediterranean Sea that found Grant with his fingers wrapped tightly around the controls once more.

Whichever it was, he hit full reverse on the thrusters, jets blasting out bellows of air to slow his twirling descent, even as his other arm seized fast to the stick, bringing the control surfaces back to level.

With that all going on in the space of a few moments, the inertia of Grant's insides caused a sour ball of bile to roll up into his throat, acidic taste making him grimace in disgust as the Manta's crash course with oblivion came to an abrupt halt. It wasn't like crashing into a wall of stone or an ocean from nearly a mile high, but it certainly was an upsetting experience. He couldn't see through the gloves of his shadow suit, but he could feel how whitened his knuckles were as he clutched the throttle and collective.

Despite the environmental protections provided by the full-body shadow suit, Grant was drenched in sweat, his heart hammering to the point where he wondered if it would burst through his ribs. Adjusting the thrusters in VTOL mode, he steered a course toward the Oracle. He wanted to set down because he could feel a stream of cold air hissing through the cracked windscreen, hear the flap of torn seals and bouncing metal holding the cockpit's canopy in place.

In the distance Grant heard a sonic boom and wondered if it was the explosion of Edwards's ship or the detonation of some other weapon. It might have been the distraction of keeping the Manta on course for its emergency landing, but it took a moment to sink in that Edwards and his ship had gone supersonic.

Whatever Grant had collided with had proved to be more than capable of standing up to the incredible withering power of the jerry-rigged .50-caliber machine guns and missiles on their ships. And since Edwards saw with his own eyes what "ramming speed" accomplished, the big, bald brute went with a balance of raw power and ability. The blast of air parting and then clapping back together at Mach speed was the trick he'd opted for.

"Grant, you all right?" Kane asked over the Commtact, his voice showing far more emotion and concern than the stoic Cerberus warrior had displayed in a long time.

"Yeah. I've got my Manta limping to a landing near you," Grant responded. "Any clue as to how much damage I'm suffering? Systems are still on the fritz here and there in the wake of that feedback blast."

"You can see it for yourself once you land," Kane replied, his voice growing harder.

Grant curled his lip. It was likely that it was more than just a scratch. He kept the pace even and steady, knowing that imperfections in the hull would make a renewed effort at supersonic transit a very messy method of suicide. The shadow suit provided a modicum of small-arms protection and had kept him from shattering limbs on short falls or minor crashes, but should the cockpit split open and the restraint belts on the pilot's couch fail, no amount of non-Newtonian fabric would keep him from being crushed as he hit the ground after thousands of feet of free fall.

"Guys?" Edwards spoke over the comm-link. "How's Grant?"

"Limping along. What happened to the winged bastard who ran me over?" Grant asked back.

"He took off running after I knocked the hammer from his hands," Edwards replied. "Do we have contact with New Olympus yet?"

"You got a hammer from him?" Brigid interjected.

"Big bad hammer. It just missed opening Grant's Manta like a can of rations," Edwards explained.

"That's a fair assessment," Grant added. "He was an ugly cuss, with blue-gray skin and snakes for hair…"

"Charun," Brigid stated.

"So much for a skeletal boatman," Grant murmured. "What, we have the cross between Thor and some ugly angel?"

"No, Charun was a god of the dead. Edwards, you going to keep watch over where the hammer landed?" Brigid inquired.

"Damn straight. Once I knocked the thing out of his hands, we got our comms back," Edwards explained. "So keeping the hammer away from him is, in my humble opinion, a great plan."

"Good," Brigid said. "Then we can see if we're dealing with Annunaki technology or—"

"Charun had some metallic snakes wrapped around his arms that immediately reminded me of Enlil's ASP blasters," Grant said, cutting her off. "But these were bigger, thicker. Presumably more powerful. And being wound around his arms, he likely still has them."

"Confirm on that," Edwards advised. "We'll need people on the ground to get to the hammer before Charun returns."

Grant's mood was not good as he grew closer to the spire where his compatriots had landed with the interphaser. So much for having the advantage of air superiority, he mused.

He grit his teeth. Of course they had air superiority. Edwards's Manta still was in perfect condition, and as long as the strange, hammer-like device was out of the hands of their enemy, their weapons systems would operate and they could communicate with each other. And from the way that Edwards seemed dead set on protecting the airspace over the fallen weapon, it occurred to the CAT Beta ex-Magistrate that the hammer was special.

Maybe the winged humanoid had access to powerful arm blasters, but there were bigger and more impressive tricks in his lost tool bag.

Grant frowned, swinging the wounded Manta closer to the ground, making the decision to land near the puddle of molten secondary orichalcum. There was more flat ground and he didn't want to damage the wings or harm his friends with too clumsy of a landing. The henge stones would likely add to the damage of his wounded aircraft, making repairs even more difficult.

Soon he was in range so that he didn't even need the telescopic zoom on his helmet to inform him that three Gear Skeletons, one adorned as a "hero" suit, two others as Spartans, had arrived at the base of the ramp leading to the top of the oracular spire.

The giant exoskeletons spread out, forming a perimeter in which Grant could set the Manta down. Even as they did so, they extended their arms upward to cushion the descent of the craft in case it had suffered more damage and couldn't extend its landing gear.

Grant kept up his vigilance upon landing. The last thing he needed was to get sloppy, no matter what kind of help he had available to him. Even so, when he felt the powerful robotic hands latch on to the hull of his Manta, Grant was relieved.

Unfortunately the big man realized that such relief was only temporary. This was only his first encounter with a winged monstrosity powerful enough to engage an armed Manta. Another godlike being, different in some ways from their usual Annunaki opponents, but still formidable, still extremely dangerous.

He hoped that Charun was alone, but even as he did so, he realized that things were never that easy.

EDWARDS DIDN'T HAVE to search too hard for where the hammer went down. It had produced so much energy in its shield against the twin machine guns on his Manta that it left a smoke trail and its landing produced a highly visible scar on the countryside. So far, his systems were continuing uninterrupted, but that didn't mean the winged enemy wasn't trying to slip back into Greek airspace after being driven off.

However, he didn't want to waste any more of the Manta's endurance than necessary, so he swung the aircraft low over the crater. As he did so, sensors in the Manta's cockpit measured the width and depth of the dent the hammer had made in the ground. It was only two feet in depth, and little more than two and a half feet wide, but it was a crater carved into solid rock.

Edwards was no expert at mathematics, but he'd seen large bombs go off before and placed the power of the hammer's impact equal to about twenty-five kilograms of plas-ex. That was merely from falling from a great height, not being thrown.

Now he could see why even a glancing blow had almost crushed Grant's Manta.

Edwards landed the ship and used the shadow suit on his forearm as a keyboard and monitor to gather the crater's information and transmit it to the others. If anything, Brigid Baptiste would want to see the physical environmental effects of the artifact. It might be only pure trivia, but it could also give the brilliant archivist some form of scale from which to determine just what they were up against.

Edwards got out of the cockpit and jogged closer to the hammer, letting the optics in his shadow suit faceplate continue to record information about the hammer. As he closed with it, he could see that the handle was fully two meters in length, and it was not made from any material he recognized. It was dull, not resembling the polished brass of secondary orichalcum or any other natural alloy the Cerberus explorers had encountered.

No, that was wrong, Edwards thought. There was a woodlike grain to the handle, but the shadow suit's analytical optics were not registering it as anything carved from a tree that he'd ever seen. He frowned. He'd seen something made of wood but not wooden before, and he wished he'd had a hint of Brigid Baptiste's photographic memory at times such as this.

"Brigid," Edwards called.

"Thank you for the camera footage of the artifact," she answered. "What are you going to ask about?"

"The handle. It looks like some kind of material I've seen before, but I can't place it. I'm hoping…"

"The Cedar Doors we encountered underground in Iraq," Brigid responded. "In mythology, they were the gates to an entire Cedar Forest, whose fruit, when eaten, would provide immortality. Unfortunately said eternal existence came in the form of zombie-like reanimation and was not full of cedar trees as we understood them."

Edwards took a deep breath of relief. "That's what was bugging me. So, this is fake cedar? Or a petrified tree material?"

"It is possible," Brigid answered. "But I would prefer a closer look."

Edwards grunted. "I'll babysit this thing until we can get a recovery team here."

"Do not attempt to move it yourself," Brigid admonished. "Who knows—"

"Yeah, I wasn't going to get zapped by any security systems built into a hammer that can punch a hole in rock like fifty-five pounds' worth of TNT," Edwards murmured. "And while I don't know the kind of heat that could incinerate two ounces of armor-piercing shell, let alone a whole volley…" Edwards trailed off, hoping for her to give him a bone of information.

"Even that calculation is beyond my current knowledge," Brigid interjected. "But the melting point of lead is 328 degrees Celsius."

"That'd be nice if I were shooting a handgun, but the Fifties fire tungsten-cored bullets."

"Three thousand, four hundred and twenty-two degrees Celsius," Brigid offered. "Oh, my."

"Ten times hotter than you thought?" Edwards asked.

"Ten point four-three-three rounded to the nearest hundredth, but, yes," Brigid said.

Edwards could hear the smile in her voice as he demonstrated at least a semblance of mathematical skill, so that the big brawler showed that he wasn't a complete drain on the brains of the assembled Cerberus Away Teams. "This is very disconcerting."

Edwards nodded, even though he knew the head-bob wouldn't translate over the Commtact. But if he gave voice to his personal fears, he would lose more than a little of his appearance as a tough guy. Even so, he couldn't disagree with Brigid's own outwardly calm evaluation. The hammer's powers were formidable, easily as dangerous as the glove that Maccan utilized in his attack on Cerberus, maybe even worse, since it was a larger item.

Edwards's curiosity led him nearer to the deadly hammer, examining the crater even more closely. For all the force of its impact, it stood flatly on its head and had not penetrated the bottom of the bowl. This set the hairs on his neck on edge, because that was not how it should have been naturally. He recorded this, and transmitted it to Brigid.

"Edwards, do not approach any closer," she warned.

"It fired off something like a braking rocket, didn't it?" Edwards asked.

"Yes," she told him. "Which means that the artifact, indeed, has some manner of autonomy."

Edwards took a couple of strides backward, but even as he did so, he recalled the shape of the head. It was not the normal shape for a sledgehammer, nor was it a stylized T shape with Celtic carvings enmeshed on the sides, as the holy symbol for Thor that Edwards had seen before. This was a more crystalline structure, semitransparent, flat-sided but held in place by webbing forged from molten metal. It was a hexagonal prism, with a pair of hexagonal pyramids forming the caps on each end, as if it were a gigantic piece of quartz.

Except this quartz was bloodred and glowed from within as if possessed by a hellish flame at its core. The whole thing had an eerie electricity that made Edwards's skin crawl, even behind the protection of his shadow suit. As he was fully environmentally enclosed within the high-tech garment, his instincts were on maximum alert simply due to the crackle of energy he felt in the air.

Brigid Baptiste, as usual, had been correct in her assessment. He'd gotten too close to an entity that could protect itself with the same facility it had protected its wielder from the heaviest "small arms" that had ever been developed. Edwards flexed his forearm and the Sin Eater automatically launched into the palm of his hand, ready to spit lead. He didn't think it would be any more effective than the heavy machine guns he'd fired earlier, but Edwards was not going to go into death without a fight.

The throb of dread in the air lessened the further he backed from the alien weapon.

"Okay. If I don't mess with you, you won't mess with me," Edwards murmured. As he spoke he could feel a tickle in his forehead, right from the spot where the inhuman Ullikummis had inserted the seed of his flesh into his brain. With that action, the ancient stone godling had gained total control of Edwards, turning him from a protector of Cerberus into an oppressive, dangerous marionette. The feeling was still raw inside his skin and spirit.

Whatever the source of the odd reminiscent feeling, it made him angry, reminding him of his violation by another alien mind as well as his failure as a protector of freedom. As much as he fought, he'd still ceded his will to something else, no matter how powerful. That even Brigid had likewise been changed and abused by the same godling didn't help, as she'd found a way to fight Ullikummis's control. Edwards hadn't.

It still didn't matter that the would-be conqueror was no less than the son of Enlil, nor engineered to even greater abilities than a standard Annunaki overlord. Edwards had fallen, and he still hadn't felt as if he'd washed that stain from his spirit.

And right now, he felt as if the alien artifact in front of him saw that stain, smelled the stink of failure upon him, and saw an opportunity.

Edwards grit his teeth and settled in, standing guard.

The anger spurred by the shame he felt made him wish someone would try to steal the hammer.

He wouldn't even have minded going into battle against the winged monstrosity when it returned for its property.

Chapter 5

Perched on the nose of the parked Manta, his Sin Eater retracted into its forearm holster, Edwards knew he'd be waiting a while for someone to show up for Charun's fallen hammer. Even at this distance, thirty yards from where it'd cratered the rocky hillock, its emanations whispered promises of ancient evil up and down his spine.

He checked his wrist chron, a display built into the forearm of the sleek, body-conforming shadow suit, actually. Brigid had contacted him again, alerting him that they would be on his position in about two hours. The big Magistrate passed the first hour and a quarter thinking about the brief, brutal aerial chase and battle he'd undergone. At supersonic speeds, even a few seconds of movement translated into miles of ground to cover, especially since there were a couple of ranges of mountains between him and New Olympus.

Even with the mighty strides and leaps of the Gear Skeletons, it was unlikely that there would be an arrival within the next thirty minutes.

Edwards started to inform himself not to take aerial combat so far away from friends who could come to his aid, but his common sense kicked in. The whole purpose of air support was to *distance* aerial combatants from troops on the ground. Getting the horrific Charun as far from his compatriots was the best thing to do. He couldn't have anticipated the presence of a powerful artifact in need of recovery.

For a moment he saw that he had two shadows on the ground, looking past the wrist chron. Edwards squinted, then looked back up into the sky. Up there, somehow, had appeared a second brilliant sun, blazing white and hot. He scrambled to his feet, standing on the front of the Manta. The machine pistol snapped down into his fist, ready to go into action, but the strange, glowing disc was not moving. He put on his shadow suit's faceplate and hoped for the visor to screen and filter out the blinding light as well as analyze the object in the sky.

The range was ten miles and it was advancing quickly.

He activated his Commtact microphone. "Guys, wherever you are…"

Nothing. No response, not even static. He turned his gaze back to the sky. For all the polarization of the lenses, necessary for use on walks outside the Manitus Moon Base, he could not make out a detail in regard to the blazing comet looming ever and ever closer to him. But in the space of fifteen seconds it had closed to nine miles. He couldn't get details about the shape of the object, only its range, and there was no guarantee that it was right.

Edwards turned to open the cockpit, but the command signal to remotely open the canopy was jammed. He was in a complete blackout. He ground his teeth behind the faceplate and looked back at the hammer. "You *wouldn't* be alone, would you?"

The hammer didn't speak, but it didn't have to. There was a new malice hanging in the air; a smug sense of superiority that proved annoying in humans but was infuriating when it came from a supposedly inanimate object.

Edwards tried to open the manual hatch, a backup in case of the failure of the remote access. The only problem with that was that now the hatch was shut; immobilized by a force so strong that even using his foot-long fighting knife he couldn't budge it open. He bent the blade by sixty degrees and gave up for fear of losing an important survival tool or causing himself injury should the blade shatter. In frustration, he gave the cockpit a hammering blow in an effort to somehow override the Manta's security systems.

"Come on, open," he growled.

The Mantas, however, were machines meant to withstand the stresses of supersonic flight and re-entry flights from the moon. As strong as Edwards was, he was nothing compared to the force of air pressure striking the atmosphere at multiples of the speed of sound. And with the Manta sealed tight by the interference put out by Charun or one of his partners, it was far too late to grab a few grens from his war bag.

All he had were his Sin Eater and his Copperhead. It was formidable firepower when dealing with bandits or mindless mutants, but the mind behind the ever-approaching torch was encased in a body that had survived a crash with a Manta. Though his gun's bullets moved at the same speed as a Manta in full acceleration, neither of them possessed the raw mass of the orbital transport. He might as well be throwing kernels of rice at the opposition.

Edwards grimaced in his impotence. He could stay and provide a brief, valiant, but ultimately doomed resistance, or at least try to do something useful. Thinking ahead, he knew he had to opt for the latter choice.

Edwards sighed, looking at the hammer in disgust, then ran, bounding off the Manta. Sticking around would be suicide, or worse, get him captured and used against the others. Running away was not going to be his course of action, though.

Edwards raced to find a good spot wherein he could hide his bulk. At least the shadow suit's fiber optics were still in working condition, picking up the surrounding dirt and scrub brush to disguise him among them. It wasn't invisibility, but it was still great camouflage. The suit's fibers were also radar-absorbent, so that meant he might not be picked up by any form of detection.

The environmental seals in place with his faceplate also prevented his scent from escaping the skintight garment. With all of these precautions, however, Edwards was still worried. This wasn't his first go-around with entities of superhuman weaponry or ability. One of the previous had strung him around like a marionette, turning him from an individual fighting for the future of the planet to a foot soldier trying to conquer it.

There was a bowel-chilling sense of dread as the blazing sun died down. Two winged figures hung in the air at least a hundred feet above the hammer. Edwards almost flinched as the faceplate optics zoomed in on them, almost as if they could hear the electronics focusing. He held his breath in an effort to further lower his profile. With his body mass draped over the Copperhead and Sin Eater, there were no metal objects to reflect radar pulses or show up magnetically, he hoped.

His thoughts were racing, so if either of these two were telepaths, they would hear him as if he were screaming at the top of his lungs. His fists clenched and he fought to control himself, to deaden his frantic mind. All the while, he hoped that the faceplate was still recording the image of these two entities.

Though they were winged, neither set of appendages on either appeared to move, not Charun and his leathery, demonic adornment, or the other's feathered limbs. The other was far from being Charun's equal in ugliness. Instead of a scaled, lipless crack with curved tusks sweeping up from his jaw, her mouth was lush with lips like flower petals or succulent as orange wedges and the color of wine. Instead of a scraggly black mane, thinning and pierced with yellowed horns, her brow was smooth, with auburn tresses cascading in looping curls that spiraled down past her shoulders.

Charun's skin was blue-gray, holding the pallor of a near-mummified corpse, despite the vital and bulging muscles beneath that ashen, crinkled hide. Hers was deep and richly tanned, vibrant and glowing from within; a decidedly Mediterranean bronze gained by long hours taking in the sun. She, like he, was topless, her full, pendulous breasts jostling as they were framed by an X of leather straps that seemed to connect her to either the eerily motionless wings or the quiver across her shoulder.

Both of them were the same height, nearing eight feet from toe-tip to the top of their heads.

In one hand she held a great, hornlike torch that had faded to merely the brightness of ordinary flame now. In the other she held a bow. But even with his greatest magnification on the shadow suit optics, he could not see the string on the ancient-seeming weapon. Instead, where the bowstring would have been notched, on each arm of the bow there was a bejeweled block of golden metal that shimmered with the same brassy sheen of a Gear Skeleton. There was a hand-molded grip in the center, with a stubby projection making it seem like some form of pistol around which a bow had been built.

Edwards couldn't help but think that this device might be more than gaudy, ornamental, ancient weaponry and more a piece of alien technology. The resemblance of segments to secondary orichalcum, the same Annunaki alloy in the Olympian war suits, was all the evidence he needed to make the assumption.

Speaking of the devil, the woman extended her arm with the torch. With a flash of brilliant flame, the ground suddenly came alive with several pillars of sprouting light. Edwards's stomach twisted as either his eyes adjusted to the brilliance or the shapes of the pillars solidified into human forms. There were two Gear Skeletons, and from Brigid's briefing, Edwards could recognize the Spartans as having the same ID numbers as those reported missing.

There were about twelve soldiers with the two battle robots, and the Cerberus Away Team member let out a low hiss of his retained breath, inhaling to replace the stale air. The armored warriors were clad in the familiar mix of modern Magistrate polycarbonate and classical Greek leather armor.

The faceplates were open on their helmets, though, and through the empty space, Edwards made out the white-eyed, slack-jawed expressions of the Olympian soldiers. They moved with normal agility and walked apace, but there was literally nothing but pinholes in the middle of their eyes.

Edwards's molars ground together until they locked in place. Not good. Not at all, he thought.

The fluid nature of their movements indicated that the blank-eyed soldiers were in perfect health and ability, but the unblinking, slack nature of their features warned of something darker, deadlier, at work than hammers capable of smashing Mantas from the sky or torches that burned with the brightness of a sun. These were thralls, lost completely to the control of an outside entity.

And yet, for the soulless, zombified expressions, they were spread out, searching carefully for any sign of Edwards, their guns at arms. The two Gear Skeletons walked over and seized the Manta, picking it up as if it were a toy, further testimony to the kind of raw power of ancient Annunaki robotics. The mecha began walking to the west, carrying the aircraft in their powerful arms.

"The pilot might not have gone far." The woman spoke, lowering closer.

Again, the motionless nature of those wings, despite their classic angelic or demonic shape, dug into Edwards's nerves. It only took him a few moments to realize that the appendages wouldn't be natural, but artificial constructs designed to match a human's view of a winged deity. He'd been around with Cerberus long enough to know when technology was the explanation of something occurring in mythology, be it the hammer of a god or something as simple as flight.

The wings were silent and motionless on the backs of Charun and his beautiful partner, which took away one possibility that they were some manner of jet pack or rocket belt. Indeed, the eerie quiet pretty much narrowed things down to some manner of antigravity system. As to why their flying devices were so similar to wings… well, even the Manta had wings. It just made flight and maneuvering easier. He couldn't see flaps or ailerons, but given their biological appearance, they could have been supple, enabling them to steer.

This also explained the lack of pain or reaction to injury when Edwards had put a .50-caliber round through Charun's wing. He saw the scorched hole, flesh split and tattered at the edges of the "wound." His optics couldn't detect any mechanics sandwiched between layers of leathery skin, but nor could he see blood vessels or other signs that the wing was alive.

As if on silent, telepathic cue, Charun looked down at his injury, the limb bending around so he could look at it more closely. That tusked maw turned up at the corners in a smile.

The woman looked across and met his smile with her own. Almost playfully, Charun brought the bullet hole up to eye level and peered at his partner through the aperture, which elicited a laugh from the angelic female.

It looked like a true friendship between the two entities, reminiscent of what he had seen between Kane and Brigid, the ability to communicate entire ideas in just a few gestures, because the audio pickups on his suit's hood were not conveying anything more than breathing between the two. The only words she had spoken seemed to be toward the slave stock searching the Manta's landing area.

That spoke to either telepathy between the flying pair or an intimate friendship that often did not require a single word. Edwards, at this point, was desperately hoping it wasn't telepathy. Such doomie powers would make all of the camouflage and hiding a moot, useless point. Thankfully, it didn't seem as if the zombified Olympian troops had any more special senses as he lay, still as a rock, his suit's camouflage system making him look like inert stone and soil piled as a short berm.

A soldier walked to within inches of Edwards's motionless form, even looked right down at him, then continued on. The big brute of a man made a convincing pile of rocks, but that did not give him the freedom to breathe a sigh of relief. Instead he kept frozen, muscles tense to the point of aching. His breathing ran shallow and he only allowed himself to blink when his eyes were dried and burning.

It seemed like hours before the soldiers moved on and Charun and his "bride" rose further into the sky. She waved her torch, almost dismissively, and suddenly streaks of the same light that deposited the Olympian zombies on the ground flashed up, sucked into the tongue. Charun alighted on the ground just long enough to lift the massive hammer.

Edwards didn't move his head, didn't do more than sweep his eyes to the periphery of his vision at either angle. He waited, remaining still despite the growing ache and fatigue in his shoulders and neck.

He didn't know how long it was, but finally the heavy tread of Gear Skeleton feet resounded again. Edwards almost didn't want to relax.

"Edwards!" a voice shouted. When he turned his head toward the sound of that call, he could feel tendons popping at the base of his skull, making it feel as if hot, wet gore splashed down on his neck. He winced and gasped.

"Here," he croaked.

A slender but muscular figure raced to his side. It was Kane.

He helped Edwards to his feet.

Looking around, he could see one of the suits, complete with a quiver of javelins and brassy, steel-wool curls flowing down over her shoulders. That had to have been the new Artem15.

"We've been trying to contact you for an hour," Kane said.

Edwards pulled off his shadow suit hood. Beads of sweat splashed and evaporated in the cool air of the Greek afternoon.

Kane tilted his head and looked at the Commtact plate on his friend's jaw. He snapped it off its mounting and looked closer at it. "Your Commtact looks like it burned out. What happened to the Manta?"

"Charun and his girlfriend showed up," Edwards explained. "With two of the missing mobile suits. The suits picked up the Manta."

"Girlfriend?" Kane asked, fishing into a belt pouch for a replacement plate. Once he did, he handed it to Edwards, who donned the new communicator.

Almost instantly he heard Brigid Baptiste's voice. "Give me a description of this girlfriend," she ordered.

Edwards launched into his recorded memory, then tapped the interface on his suit's forearm. "I'm also sending you the vid my suit captured."

"That is Vanth, and her torch is of equal power to Charun's hammer," Brigid explained. "And, yes, they are partners. Psychopomps."

"Psychos? Yeah, I can see that," Edwards grumbled. "Psychopomp...that's not the same as crazy, right?"

"The term 'psychopomp' is Greek. Literally translated, it is 'guide of the soul,'" Brigid told them both. "Choosers of the slain. Angels or sub-deities who take people to the afterlife."

"That explains the zombie-like appearance of the Olympian soldiers searching for me," Edwards added.

"The theft of their spirit is a concerning development," Brigid mused over the Commtact. "As do Charun's recovery of his hammer and the disappearance of our second and currently only flight-capable Manta."

Kane frowned. "You said this torch could spit out the bodies and then pick them up again. Don't yell at me for being wrong, but that sounds an awful lot like the Threshold or Lakesh's interphaser."

"If that," Edwards mused. "It could be like one of those traps in the old vids. The ones with the four guys fighting the ghosts?"

"Turning the humans and the mecha into energy, then storing it in that format?" Brigid inquired. "And, yes, Kane, I can see the similarities in your assessment, as well."

Edwards frowned. "Great."

"What's wrong?" Kane asked.

"I'm getting used to this crazy shit," Edwards grumbled.

Kane clapped his friend on the shoulder. "Come on. There's room for you on Artem15's other arm."

Edwards nodded and the two men were picked up, gingerly, with a gentle touch belying the robot skeleton's massive might. Once they were settled into the crooks of the giant's elbows, it turned and began to run; long, looping strides that crossed first fifteen, then twenty, then finally thirty feet in a single bound.

The wind in Edwards's face was cool and refreshing, a

release from the paralyzed caution and stony patience he'd had to endure while waiting for the arrival of his allies.

He still couldn't shake the feeling that he'd let everyone down. No matter how much information Brigid and Kane got from his report and his vid.

Chapter 6

Smaragda sat at the conference table, her shoulders slumped, shocks of her white bangs hanging low over her baggy eyes. She stared at the top of the table, but she was so deadened, so numbed by the trauma of losing her platoon, she didn't even register the grain of the faux wooden veneer topping the furniture in front of her. All she could do was fight the need to close her eyes, to dispel the horrors of her platoon's swallowing, to keep the echoes of their screams from ringing in her ears.

She was clad in a nearly shapeless sweatshirt that covered her arms, hiding the recent work she'd carved into it with a razor. The flesh of her forearms was heavily checkered now and was raw from the disinfectant she'd poured over the dozens of new cuts to prevent sepsis. Smaragda hadn't cut herself since she was a mere teenager, the focus and élan of being with the New Olympian military stealing not just privacy for the act, but also drowning out the need for controlling her pain.

Now her forearms stank of hydrogen peroxide, dampened somewhat by the loose bandages and the rumpled sleeves of her top. She didn't know if her acknowledgment of the odors was just a strong memory or if she truly was literally reeking of it. Either way, it was too late now as the lights came on in the conference room, people filing in through different doors. Smaragda's eyes rose slightly and she watched her queen roll herself along on her wheelchair.

Their eyes met as they were at the same level, and Smaragda instinctively looked back down, wishing that she could wither away, shrinking into the ground and out of the presence of Queen Diana.

She pressed her forearms harder against the tabletop and the pressure on her skin allowed slowly healing snips and cuts to pop open. It wasn't the same kind of rush as she got from pressing a razor blade against it, but the pain still clouded her perceptions, taking her out of the moment, out of her self-loathing for…surviving.

Conversations murmured around the corners of her consciousness and it was something that helped her to muffle the distant memories of her dying friends. If only she'd stood her ground…at least she wouldn't have felt so useless. No, she would have had the beautiful darkness of oblivion, her body and soul swallowed completely by the Stygian cloud, her suffering ended by its ravenous greed.

"So we have a new development," Diana announced, her voice cutting sharply through both the conference room and into Smaragda's numbed mind. "Our people are still alive."

Smaragda looked up, staring at her queen, her hands clenching into tight fists so that even her closely trimmed nails threatened to spear through her palms. "What?"

"They are alive and under some form of mind control, or have had their bodies commandeered by the Etruscan menaces," Diana clarified for her. "We have video of both the intruders and our missing people, thanks to Edwards over there."

Smaragda glanced in the direction Diana pointed and saw a brawny, brooding figure, he having cast his eyes downward.

"Just trying to get as much as I could. I sure as hell was useless in terms of fighting those two," Edwards grumbled.

Smaragda turned and glanced toward the screen, the lights dimming.

"Myrto, see if you can recognize anything off of the initial parts of the video," Diana ordered. The queen's voice held more than a little concern, something the disgraced soldier couldn't understand. If anything, she should have been executed for such a disgusting failure.

Why worry about me? Smaragda mused silently. Why even have me here at this table?

But even as she did so, a small monitor was slid to her section of the table and she looked at the flying entities.

"Did you see anything like that?" Brigid Baptiste asked.

Smaragda shook her head. "The only thing any of us saw was a literal flood of dark, churning smoke. However, we were in the woods, and I couldn't see through the canopy of trees."

Brigid nodded. "Perhaps that is why there was that form of manifestation."

Smaragda looked down at the screen, watching as her friends suddenly appeared, deposited on the ground by streams of light emanating from the torch held by the flying female figure, Vanth.

She could recognize them by the subtle differences, the little bits of customization on each of her fellow soldiers' armor, even before the camera focused on the faces inside their open-visored helmets. She looked at one set of eyes and her heart sank. Every instinct was to grab the tiny monitor and hurl it aside, but she didn't even possess the will to lift her arms, to even touch the image of lost brothers.

Edwards leaned across the table, his long arm snatching up the tablet and turning it away from her.

"She doesn't need to see that shit," the big man gruffly announced. "Pardon my language."

"It's excused," Diana stated. "I'm sorry, Myrto."

The failed soldier just shook her head, tried to say, "It's okay," but could only manage a mumbled, garbled semblance of human speech.

"Are you sure you're all right to continue this debriefing?" Edwards spoke across the table.

A hand rested upon her shoulder and she looked up to see that it was Brigid Baptiste. Her touch was delicate and her expression was one of concern. "Let me talk with her alone, everyone."

Smaragda shook her head. "I can be useful…"

"We know that," Brigid answered her. "I just want to talk to you. One-on-one."

Smaragda looked into the emerald, shining eyes of the tall woman, seeing a warmth that made her dislike herself even more, not wanting to deserve any of that for all that she'd failed to do. And yet the offered hand was irresistible and she rose, guided to a doorway.

EVEN IF BRIGID BAPTISTE were not possessed of a photographic memory, enabling her to recognize the signs of severe emotional trauma, she would have noticed the turmoil that wrapped up the frost-haired Smaragda. Taking her into the hallway, away from the presence of others, she managed to give the young woman some privacy. The corner of the corridor was well lit, but no one was using it.

"I'm sorry for dragging down the debriefing…" Smaragda began.

"You aren't," Brigid told her. She braced Smaragda's face in both of her hands, locking eyes together. "Just look into my eyes and concentrate on my voice."

"Why? What are you doing?" Smaragda asked.

"First, I'm going to get your complete testimony without causing you more conscious mental harm," Brigid explained. "I'm hypnotizing you now, lulling your senses, making you feel more and more comfortable. As the notes of my voice strum gently in your ears, I am commanding your visual attention. With sight and hearing focused, calmed, you will become more attuned toward the cues that interfere with your detailed memory, as well as separate yourself from your emotional barriers."

Smaragda's dark, red-veined eyes slowly unfocused with Brigid's continued description of the hypnosis process, calming her, fixating her until Brigid was able to draw her hands away from the girl's cheeks.

Smaragda stood stock-still and the Cerberus archivist began asking her questions and receiving honest answers. The trick to hypnosis was simply a case of distraction of the conscious mind, taking away filters of behavior and emotion that would otherwise interfere with clarity of communication.

The shell-shocked soldier was much more forthcoming in her responses, and didn't seem as if she wanted to fold herself away under the table. And since this was Brigid Baptiste, not a single syllable, not a single impression, would be forgotten or lost in the translation. Her brilliant mind absorbed every fact and description uttered by Smaragda, as well as opinions and impressions on things she could only speculate about.

The whole hypnotic session took only fifteen minutes for the direct questioning and Brigid was partially of a mind to continue, digging into Smaragda's self-loathing and attempt to take care of it, like a surgeon having discovered a tumor in the midst of an operation. However, Brigid realized that if she attempted to dig too deeply, she could cause as much harm as she'd attempt to undo. No, meatball surgery on the traumatized young woman was not going to be on the menu today.

Smaragda's healing would have to come from a more conventional source, but even as Brigid closed out the hypnotic session, she complimented the woman on her observational skills and her ability to bring vital intelligence to New Olympus. Positive reinforcement on the subconscious level could be a minor salve, but it wouldn't upset the Greek woman's thoughts such as an attempt to bury her feelings of self-loathing and survivor's guilt. Putting that down deeper in Smaragda's mind would be exactly the opposite of removing a tumor; it would be pushing a packet of septic and diseased flesh into a vulnerable set of organs, waiting for one moment to split and infect the rest of her, poisoning everything else she did.

No, Brigid couldn't sublimate the raw feelings on Smaragda's part. She could only attempt to leave an impression that she actually had done some good.

With a snap, Smaragda blinked her bloodshot eyes.

There was a moment where the soldier seemed unsteady on her feet, but Brigid assisted her with a firm hand on her shoulder.

"What happened? It feels like I fell asleep," she said.

Brigid nodded. "In a way you did. I hypnotized you."

Smaragda's brow wrinkled as she looked up at the tall Cerberus woman. "Hypnotized. You didn't do something like make me cluck like a chicken if someone says 'dinner' or something, right?"

"Nothing like that," Brigid answered.

Smaragda managed a brief flicker of a smile before she cast her gaze to the floor. "At least I was good for something."

Brigid put her arm around the soldier's shoulders. "Come on, let's get back to the meeting."

This time she sat Smaragda right next to Edwards. The big man seemed confused for a moment.

"She's too hard on herself, just like you," Brigid murmured. "Maybe keep an eye on her and take your mind off of your ill-perceived failures."

The CAT member nodded. "All right. I can take a hint," he added with a mock growl.

"How'd you screw up?" Brigid heard Smaragda ask as she returned to the head of the table. At this point, Kane and Grant put away the cards they were toying with as they'd waited for her to return. She chuckled at the two of them sitting back up and looking interested, as if they were schoolboys afraid of being busted by their teacher.

"I thought you would be getting more information from Diana and Ari," Brigid said.

"We did. But after we got all of that, and showed more of the vid, we had time left over," Kane told her.

"What did you get?" Grant asked her.

"I got deeper information on the situation," Brigid said. "And it contrasts with the interview in only a few minor errors and differences."

"I told the truth," Smaragda interjected.

Brigid nodded. "You did. But human memory is, for most people, a fickle thing. The human mind alters perceptions upon reflection, adding details that might not have been there in the original case, and ignoring others that seemed irrelevant at the time. A study in the late twentieth century proved that eyewitness testimony was only accurate in one instance out of ten where there were other forms of corroboration such as audio and video recording."

"Really?" Kane asked.

Brigid nodded. "In my instance, that kind of filter for memory is missing, most likely a genetic anomaly."

"Like a doomie." Edwards spoke up.

Domi shook her head. "Brigid's too smart for that. Doomies can't handle the future. They get crazy. Brigid looks straight back."

Brigid managed a weak smile. She didn't want to correct her friend and oft-times student Domi. She could see the future, but only via educated calculations based upon prior data, a cause-and-effect form of premonition. She didn't engage in it too often, only for the purposes of planning for battle and avoiding dangers. And even then, her calculations were not one hundred percent.

"Did Myrto see anything?" Diana asked.

"She described the fog she mentioned in detail," Brigid stated. "And as our initial evaluation of potential myths, there was a Stygian aspect to the cloud. And yet there was something equally familiar to us. During a recent expedition to Africa, we encountered a similar unnatural darkness. To every one of our senses, it was something that was a truly physical entity. Not even a flashlight or high-tech optics could cut through it."

"What was it really?" Aristotle asked.

"It was a psychic projection. One that was so strong, it even numbed tactile senses," Brigid stated. "So, what Myrto saw could have been something similar. A form of smoke screen."

"Why not just use an actual smoke screen? Wouldn't that take a lot of energy?" Aristotle persisted.

"Because they were facing soldiers. There had to be a focus for them to counter. Something akin to my hypnosis of Myrto," Brigid explained. "The black, invulnerable fog was something that could draw the fire of the Olympian troops without endangering them in the process."

"You mean that my men were opening fire on a cloud that wasn't there, and it wasn't even concealing the ones attacking us?" Smaragda asked.

Brigid felt some relief as the soldier regained some of the fire in her belly.

"It may have, in some instances. But being a black fog to your conscious mind, it allowed you to shoot into it and not even register any impacts. You could even have been steered to shooting between your friends. Or have known, subconsciously, where your brethren were. It is no good to take people as zombie prisoners when their own compatriots open fire and cut them down," Brigid told her. "In that way, you protected your brethren, deliberately shooting not to hit them."

Smaragda rested her forehead on her palm. "Wouldn't it be a mercy just to kill them than let them be zombies?"

"We shall see. There may be a means of recovering them from this current state," Brigid offered. "And if there is…"

"Then shooting them would be condemning them to death for no reason," Smaragda concluded. "Damn."

Brigid nodded. "There is hope."

"How did you tell that?" Smaragda asked.

"I asked for every detail, and more than once you, in your hypnotic state, told me that you shifted your aim so as not to hit your friends. Even when you were alone," Brigid said.

Smaragda's voice rose in frantic intensity. "But the cloud was bulletproof. It even was capable of smothering a Gear Skeleton!"

"So it appeared. But that wasn't the case," Brigid replied. "But your unconscious mind could tell that the pilots of those suits were floundering, hesitant to strike into the fog. When their guns went off, they were shooting at empty air. When the fog reached at them, it was actually the captured soldiers and townspeople from the Etruscan countryside."

"Those were…townspeople." Smaragda looked down at her hands. "Did we…?"

"Again, the purpose of expanding your zombie army was not to lose them as cannon fodder," Brigid said.

"How are we going to deal with them, then?" Grant asked. "It's not as if we've got a means of blocking out enemy thoughts."

"Maybe we do." Edwards spoke up.

Everyone looked to him and, as one, the group understood what he was saying. Edwards *saw* the zombified Olympian troops, and saw Charun and Vanth. As did the recording equipment on his hood.

"Either the sealed helmet or the optics provided everything you needed to immunize yourself against the mind-muddling effects," Brigid said.

Smaragda nodded, catching up. "Our helmets aren't environmentally sealed and the 'fog' was invisible in our multioptic visors."

Brigid nodded.

"What about anyone inside?" she asked.

"Only the two we sent in initially. And then the two we sent for Niklo and Herc. And they were gone on the IR," Smaragda said.

"Were you still listening to the prayer on your radio?" Brigid asked.

Everyone turned toward her.

"Prayer?" Diana asked. "What prayer?"

"Myrto heard a voice inside a radio note while her helmet radio was jammed," Brigid advised. "You didn't remember the anomaly on your radio consciously."

"To be honest, all I remember is that comms were all jammed up," Smaragda replied.

"Just like with us," Grant pointed out. "Except we didn't hear anything other than static."

"But that is because we set the Commtacts to filter out bursts of transmission or white noise, and modulate the volume down low," Kane offered.

"I had my microphone off and I set the Commtact to passive, only activating on…a recognized call from another on the same Commtact network," Edwards added.

"So it was not even some form of atmospheric hallucinogen. It was a post-hypnotic suggestion carried on the radio interference," Brigid noted. "One that allowed you to remember the alien prayer, but not enough that you could translate it."

"Even so, we won't take chances for our infiltration," Kane said. "Shadow suit hoods on at all times. Myrto, we brought a suit for you, as well."

"Me?" the woman asked.

"You were there. Your friends are in peril. You can guide us to the spot where they were taken, and their familiarity with you will provide us with a coordinated group once we free them," Brigid told her.

"'Once,'" Smaragda repeated. "You think they can be saved?"

"It's what we do," Kane informed the soldier. "Especially when someone has their life literally pulled from them like this. I can't imagine a worse punishment than losing your own will."

Grant looked to Brigid. "So, half-hour hypnosis. I know you got the entirety of the chant that Myrto heard on the radio."

"And I've been attempting a translation as we speak. That was why I had overlooked the possibility of the transmission being a carrier signal for the origins of the fog and its effects upon the Olympian soldiers," Brigid returned.

"Multitasking in your mind," Kane mentioned. "I'll never get over how you pull that off."

Brigid frowned. "Especially while being cautious about my efforts at translation. There seem to be phonetic cues that manipulate thoughts in each word. I have to separate the whole of the context to the point where only one word is transcribed, and out of order."

Grant winced. "I'm already getting a headache trying to figure that all out."

"So when do we leave?" Sela asked.

"In the morning," Brigid said. "I'll need time to work

on the translation. It is a frustrating blend of Babylonian and Etruscan, which is annoying as it's a prototypical language to Latin...and there are only ten thousand textual examples of the tongue that I can work from in this mix."

"Only ten thousand," Diana murmured.

"And most of which I have not read," Brigid confessed. Even though she couldn't have been expected to know everything, she hated feeling underprepared for this mission, especially in regard to linguistic translation.

"Get some sleep at least," Kane ordered. "And I mean you, too, Myrto. We're going to pay a visit to Vanth and Charun. Without the benefit of armored support."

Aristotle frowned. "I'm sorry, my friends, but that sounds too dangerous."

"To you, it sounds dangerous," Grant interrupted. "To us, it's another day at the office."

Chapter 7

Brigid Baptiste made her way to the quarters she was sharing with Sela Sinclair and Domi. The Mount Olympus barracks were full, so the accommodation of an individual room for each of the Cerberus envoys was an unlikely thing. The other two Cerberus Away Team women had agreed to share their quarters while Kane was stuck with the gigantic Grant and Edwards as his "dorm" partners.

"Still not walking good?" Domi asked.

Brigid had wrapped her sprained ankle underneath the leg and boot of her shadow suit. It had been all right for the start of the day, but as the time stretched later, the ache grew and grew.

"It's just slowing me down a little," Brigid returned.

The little albino slowed her pace to match Brigid's, then let the taller woman drape an arm over her shoulders. Brigid appreciated Domi's tightly muscled arm supporting the small of her back. Sinclair dropped back and lent her shoulder for the other side.

"Honestly," Brigid said. "I'm not a cripple."

"We're a team," Sinclair told her. "We watch out for each other."

Brigid smiled. "Thank you."

"Besides, you interrupted workout," Domi added.

Brigid looked to the ruby-eyed girl, a frown turning the corners of her mouth down. "Are you saying carting me around is a workout?"

"It's not like toting Grant around, but…" Sinclair piped in.

"And it's a big butt." Domi giggled.

Brigid wrinkled her nose.

"Just kidding, girlfriend," Sinclair said.

"I know you are," Brigid replied with more than a little indignity. "But you two jokers wouldn't be having as much fun if I took it in stride."

With that, Brigid lifted both feet off the ground with a grin and Sinclair and Domi let out gleeful yelps as they were suddenly off balance. Before anyone fell, though, she put her feet back down, wincing as that action only aggravated things more, which only added to Brigid's laughter, this time at herself for being so silly that she ended up hurting even worse.

The three of them reached their quarters and Domi and Sinclair helped Brigid onto her cot. It had been a long day of preparations and briefings, so getting some rest would be good for all of them. Tomorrow would be a huge day and there was no telling what Charun and Vanth were truly up to.

Brigid was glad for the sheer comfort of the shadow suits. Their body-conforming nature and environmental adaptations made them quite easy to sleep in without need of a cover, so she merely stretched out on her cot's mattress. There was a stretch and a tentative pivot of her foot on the other end of her sore ankle. She hadn't caused serious harm to it with her horseplay, so once that was done, she closed her eyes.

Even as she did so, she was only resting some of her brilliant brain. The other part was still working, separating and attempting to translate the individual syllables of the ancient song. Brigid imagined herself sitting in an empty room, the object of her translation separated onto different note cards that she could arrange appropriately.

There were great segments of this blasphemous-feeling chant that had grammatical syntax that made German seem blunt and straightforward. Merely moving words and syllables seemed to alter the chant dramatically. All the while, she kept herself on guard against any hidden message that could manifest itself as an "information virus" that would threaten her.

In her barren, mentally constructed study, she held one of the cards, and thought back to Zaragoza. There, too, had been a hellish song, which had stolen lives, literally. This had been done mathematically, and as soon as she thought of that, she mentally summoned a chalkboard with Ereshkigal's song upon it.

That had been an easier translation simply due to the fact that it had been spoken in a living language, not one dead, without the option of a still-extant speaker providing a verbal context. Brigid had thought about speaking the song that Smaragda had heard and allowing the Commtact and its built-in translation matrix to take care of any understanding.

This one was different, though. Ereshkigal sang her call of suicide in Spanish.

This language was a dead and gone variant of Italian, much more primitive, and seeded with words originating on lips not too different than those of the Annunaki overlords who had been the origin of far too many threats to the world.

Brigid turned to the shadowy tune of Ereshkigal, then back to the song of Vanth and Charun. The ancient goddess who tormented Zaragoza ferried her tune of reanimation on temple bells, urging life to the townspeople who had taken her song to heart and killed themselves. The shambling walkers were of a different flavor than the Olympian troops who carried a lifeless, dead-eyed pallor. Those were actual revenants, horrors that should have been buried or returned to the cycle of death and life being eaten by scavengers.

This instance was the theft of some form of energy, rendering them as operatives for the two winged horrors. Brigid didn't want to speculate on the potential of a human soul as that kind of power source, but as she ticked down through the possibilities, eliminating all the possibles, no matter how improbable, she found herself coming to the conclusion that it was the theft of just such a higher mental function that was at fault. And why preserve the bodies?

Charun and Vanth both showed the capability to over-whelm even the armed Mantas, as well as other phenom-enal feats. The very act of using her torch as a kind of threshold/interphaser proved to be more than sufficient as a weapon, to the point where she'd been capable of trans-porting a dozen humans and two giant humanoid robots.

Brigid looked closer at the monitor, studying how the Gear Skeletons were not summoned back to the torch; they were too busy carrying the Manta overland, back toward the west. This momentarily confused her, when she realized that the Manta wasn't connected to a living being, much like the piloted oversize battle suits. The am-putee pilots were literally plugged into the powerful ro-bots by means of a cybernetic access point on their spine. As much as the Olympian soldiers were able to be trans-ported along with their weapons and armor, there must have been some form of "life prerequisite."

Or, simply, it could have been that there was an actual limit to how much the torch could pick up and deposit. Occam's razor. Vanth had come to retrieve Charun's ham-mer, and possibly take the human pilot who'd disarmed her partner. That was why there was a limit of how many soldiers and Gear Skeletons were transported in.

"So you do have limits," Brigid mused, quickly adding up the combined weight of the deposited Olympian troops, the two skeletons and the Manta. "And on closer examination, she decided that she couldn't ferry the weight of the Manta. However, rather than destroy the ship, she's using it as bait for the pilot and his companions…namely us."

Brigid rubbed her chin as she watched the two beings. They weren't moving their lips and neither of them had spoken aloud to be heard on the audio pickups in the shadow suit hoods. And yet they did seem to have a shorthand; gestures and facial expressions that told each other as much as any conversation could. Brigid had seen similar relationships, between Kane and Grant, primarily, and it was slowly growing among the members of CAT Beta.

It was also an element of her friendship with Kane. These two had been together, seemingly forever. And yet, if they had been around for so long, what would have been the impetus for their suddenly expanding their influence?

Of course, there had been the war with the Hydrae and Danton that kept New Olympus from hearing about the winged "soul thieves." With that kind of distraction, there could have been endless wars going on on the Italian peninsula, and the besieged Olympians wouldn't have heard a clue. Only recent expansion of trade and exploration allowed them the luxury of exploring further than their doorstep.

Brigid went back and played the testimony she received from Diana and Aristotle. In her memory construct, she put down a small room, the conference table where the Olympian regents spoke with her.

She knelt to look into the room, to play back the scene…and something gave her pause. She looked around at the note cards strewn across her work area. Even as she was multitasking mentally, there was an anomaly, an oddity that was itching in her mind.

Brigid cleared the distractions, returning her white room to its clean state. It was a symbolic means of cleansing her mind of everything competing for her attention, and it usually worked.

Not now.

The mental note cards, for all their existence at the whim of her will, had not disappeared.

"Dammit," Brigid murmured. "There is much more psycho in these psychopomps than I anticipated. Even Smaragda's testimony has a dangerous weight to them."

The note cards began to swirl around, building into a twisting dust devil. Though this was all occurring in Brigid's mind's eye, she *felt* the pressure of the winds building. She pursed her lips tightly and immediately summoned a brick wall between herself and the rising storm.

"You're in my mind, whoever you are," Brigid announced. "And you walk here at your peril, intruder!"

The note cards rattled against the wall she'd constructed out of her will and she then heard a hiss she wasn't quite certain of. Within moments, however, she saw sharp corners slicing through the wall, trying to dig deeper, to penetrate the barrier of her mental defenses.

Brigid slammed another wall against the other, buying herself a moment more. In the same instance she armored up, summoning a variant of Kane's and Grant's old Magistrate armor, a carapace that in the real world was composed of black polycarbonate materials and Kevlar, rendering her two partners immune to all small arms. This one, however, was cast in the same shade of emerald as her eyes, a small amount of narcissistic affectation on her part.

Within a few moments the second wall was sliced to ribbons by the active, dangerous song of Vanth and Charun.

Brigid held her ground, summoning her own version of a Sin Eater.

This one, however, was not a mere gun. This was a

focus of her personal will, a twin-barreled beast that bracketed her right hand like the claws of a crab.

The notes stopped swirling, the tornado of force that made them up fading and settling into a shape. It was a winged woman, tall and beautiful, with flowing hair.

It was Vanth, and she did not have her torch. But she did possess her bow.

"Pitiful human." Vanth spoke. "You have let me in, and that is your doom."

Brigid smirked. "I've had worse between my ears, lady."

In a flicker of motion Vanth raised her bow and opened fire with it, arrows spitting out as if she was firing a machine gun. Had Brigid not steeled herself behind the armor of her will, it would have proved impressive, but even as she stood her ground, she felt the pricks of dozens of impacts. The archivist swept the ends of the arrows, snapping shafts off her armor. A moment of concentration and the winged huntress's arrowheads popped from her shell, clattering to the ground.

"You resist," Vanth mused.

"Because I know what you are. I know what these attacks are. And having looked behind your curtain..."

Brigid swept up her double-barreled Sin Eater, spitting out molten yellow spears of flame that lashed toward Vanth. The goddess let out a wail of surprise, folding her wings around herself as Brigid's mental counterattack splashed against her feathered shields.

Brigid could feel the blazing heat of her own onslaught and watched as feathers fluttered away, burning and flickering out of existence on the battleground of her mind.

Brigid opened fire again, slashing another searing swath of destruction. Vanth spread her wings and flew at the last moment before the Cerberus warrior's beams struck. Vanth shot up like a rocket, accelerating away from Brigid.

"No. This is not how we play this game," Brigid growled. She gave a moment of concentration and then in the next instant she was parallel to Vanth, who hurtled through the white void.

Vanth's face flashed from grinning victory to shock and surprise. "What?"

"I've spent a lot of time alone in my mind. I know everything inside it. It is large enough to encompass a universe, but there is nowhere that any intruding program, no mathematical trick of thought, can escape my focus," Brigid told the envoy of the goddess. "You are inside my brain and I am *everywhere*!"

With that, Brigid cut loose once more. This time Vanth was unable to bring her wings up to shield herself, nor could she swerve. The twin-barreled burst of energy slammed into Vanth's near-naked chest, the heat of the Earth's own blood searing and charring flesh. Instead of the stench of human flesh, however, it was odd, twisted, alien. It did not matter, for Brigid's take on the Sin Eater held a bottomless supply of the blazing energy of her will. She held down the trigger, blocking out the huntress's screams of pain and the snap-pop of roasting flesh and fatty tissues.

A charred wing swept around, slamming into Brigid hard enough to break her concentration, ending the fountain of lavalike fury that she'd unleashed. The blow sent the archivist into a whirl and she took every ounce of willpower to stop her dizzying spin.

"I am a song that has swallowed hearts and minds across two universes," Vanth's avatar said as Brigid "landed," lying prone from the dizzying impact. "Girl, you have no concept of how in over your head you truly are."

Brigid looked up. "I'm in my own head. Not in over it."

Vanth fluttered down closer to the prone Brigid Baptiste. It had replaced its bow with a spear. "I will peel you out of your defenses, and then I will add you to…"

Brigid narrowed her eyes and Vanth paused as she felt changes around her.

"…add you to the…power…"

Figures began to appear around the winged huntress as she floated over Brigid. First dozens, then scores, then by the hundreds until the two of them were surrounded by a sphere composed of women who looked exactly like Brigid Baptiste, complete in her armor of will.

"The power of what?" Brigid demanded.

"Who…what?" Vanth asked, turning, looking up and down. "Thousands of you. How?"

"You're the one who is in over your head. And under mine," Brigid returned. She rose from the "ground," floating up to the avatar of Vanth unleashed in her mind.

"You want my intellect, for what?" Brigid asked.

"The torch," Vanth answered. "To open the portal for the bodies to pass through."

"To go home?" Brigid continued, getting closer to her. The goddess was now sufficiently cowed. Vanth's sharp senses picked up that every one of the other Brigids held a Sin Eater similar to the one that had hit her so hard, caused her so much pain.

Vanth's attention locked onto Brigid. "Your world will become my race's new home, human."

Brigid nodded. Her lips curled with anger at this entity inside her mind, being proud and cheerful over such a blasphemous ideal.

"And when we come, it will be as a plague," Vanth warned. "An endless horde…"

Brigid floated backward from the armed huntress. "It

sounds fascinating, but I'll keep my brain here…and your plague on the other side of our dimension."

With that, Brigid willed herself into all of the copies she'd placed around the intruder in her mind. To Vanth, it looked as if she'd dissipated like a windblown fog. In actuality, Brigid now looked at the mathematical virus input into her mind from thousands of points of view… over the sights of her will weapon.

"Goodbye," the millions of Brigids told the Vanth avatar, and she pulled the trigger. The universe of Brigid's mind's eye turned to the color of raw, blazing lava, the roar and heat manifesting into actual sweat on her brow where she rested on the cot.

"Brigid?"

It was Domi's voice, from the real world. Brigid could feel the slender but rough fingers of the girl pressing on her shadow-suited shoulder, hear the notes of concern in her little friend's voice. Her million guns opened up, working to crush the Vanth avatar, and even as they attacked her, she watched and felt as slashes of sickly light carved through her duplicates.

That hurt. The torch's searing light felt as painful, as horrible, as her own counterattack seemed when she damaged Vanth.

"Brigid!" This time there was panic in Domi's voice. "Wake up!"

"One moment," Brigid called out.

The Vanth entity continued to crumple under myriad relentless counterattacks from Brigid's will. The intruding… virus. The intruding virus wasn't letting go, firing back with everything she could summon. In addition to the torch's flame, arrows flew, darting out, and Brigid felt her chest tighten, stung by those phantom shafts. Inside the Magistrate armor of her will, she was soaking wet, trying hard to breathe while the spike of agony stuck in her breastbone.

"Go away. Die now!" Brigid growled. She realized that she was in such a mental struggle she'd reverted to how Domi would speak in this situation.

Domi, help.

And with that summons, a simulacra of the feral albino girl appeared, clad merely in her black suit, bare-handed and barefoot, but drawing twin daggers from sheaths on her hips. Like a snowy owl, she swooped down upon Vanth, those black talons of hers carving deep into the burned and battered goddess. The creature sang out a wail of pain as diseased blue pus erupted from each of Vanth's wounds. The once soft and supple-looking torso of the woman was in places blackened, charred, and where the shell of its skin split, the milky blue gunk seeped, blackening like oil when it lit against the surrounding flames.

Somewhere in a part of Brigid's mind, she realized that the tint of Vanth's blood resembled the sickly pallor of Charun. Perhaps a sign of ancient injuries incurred in the deep past.

In the meantime Brigid summoned up Kane and Grant, as well as Sinclair and Edwards. If Vanth wanted to take her over, then Brigid would take strength from her friendship, the very reason she was fighting so hard to prevent the winged huntress's takeover of her mind. For should the alien goddess take Brigid over, turn her against the others, then there would be very little to stand between the two winged invaders and the rest of the world. They'd already showed their deadly adeptness at taking over the Gear Skeletons and Olympian soldiers. They were giving her a struggle to the point where she was suffering psychic and physical exhaustion.

And with her five friends leaping into action, hammering at the Vanth virus, Brigid had a breather. Her chest no longer felt as if it were pinioned by an arrow when she breathed. The sweat was cooling from her brow. Her strength grew.

No more cockiness. She left up her friends and dove in herself.

For it was through teamwork that Brigid was at her ultimate strength. Too many incidents had reinforced that it was the combined talents, skills and attributes of the Cerberus explorers that provided the best results. Together, they had dared the gods themselves, and this fragmentary essence was now crumbling, pieces shattering off of her charred form, bursting into puffs of ash, thanks to that knowledge.

Her summons of friendly thoughts gave her all she needed.

And as soon as the virus attack had begun, it was over.

Brigid knelt, her friends fading back to where they'd come from, the images dissipating as quickly as the charred embers of Vanth's intrusion. Merely getting back to her feet took as much will as it had taken to battle the virus. Her legs felt like rubber and when she was fully stood, she gulped down deep lungfuls of air, trying to recharge and replenish what little remained in her reserves.

She spent more of her mental energy, taking inventory of herself, scanning for signs or remnants of the Vanth entity that had invaded her mind via the song. All that was left were the actual words and notes of the transmission that tormented Smaragda so. Finally, during the battle, her translation of the enemy message had been completed. It was assembled on a board, giving the archivist all she required for understanding the ancient rhyme.

It also felt hollow, again like the song of Ereshkigal when she'd read it in English from the Spanish. Whatever information virus, whatever hypnotic energy, was in those words was gone, stripped away. Its remnants were also expunged from her mind.

She hoped.

"Brigid!"

With that she opened her eyes and was back in "the world." Both Sela Sinclair and Domi were standing over her on the cot. Domi had a towel in her hand and was blotting away sweat on her brow.

"I'm fine," she muttered, mouth dry and gummy.

"You didn't sound it," Domi returned. "You were drenched with sweat and muttering in your sleep."

"You didn't listen closely, did you?" Brigid asked. She didn't know if her partners could actually handle the song if she'd spoken it aloud while in the throes of battle with Vanth's avatar.

"You were sputtering gibberish," Sinclair offered, "and given what you are translating, we pulled on the hoods and killed the audio feed. Once you stopped moving your lips, we slipped them off. But you were still laying there and sweating up a storm."

"You were right to do that," Brigid said. "It was the song of Vanth. I was fighting its effects inside me."

Domi helped Brigid to sit.

As sore as she'd been in her "white room," Brigid felt a similar dull ache from where Vanth's arrows had struck her in the chest. She touched her wrist, taking her own pulse and doing a mental inventory on her body.

"Let's see if there's a doctor on duty," Sinclair suggested.

Before Brigid could say anything, the rest of the Cerberus Away Team members came in.

It was all she could do to lay back, the burning beneath her breastbone a reminder of the brutal battle she'd just fought.

Chapter 8

"You nearly died in *your* adventure with Enlil and got right back to work!" Brigid snarled at Kane.

"The doctors want to have you wait on your cardiac enzyme results," Kane responded. "Just to make certain you aren't flirting with a heart attack."

"And we let you…" Brigid murmured.

"Don't get excited, Baptiste," Kane ordered. "The last thing we need is for you to rush into action. That's why you wanted us to bring CAT Beta along with us, right?"

Brigid's lip curled in a sneer.

"Besides, according to Domi and Sela, you had your fair share of adventure before the rest of us, fighting that thing in your mind," Kane added.

She folded her arms, body language for cutting herself off from him or what he'd say.

Kane knew that when she got into one of these stubborn moods, it would take a shifting of continents to get through to her. No matter how much he repeated that *she* was the origin of the idea of relying on CAT Beta to make up for weaknesses and injuries among the CAT Alpha team, she was in a snit.

"Baptiste?" Kane asked, trying to draw her out of her grump.

"Go on the mission, Kane. Just go. I brought this onto myself by trying to translate that chant," Brigid grumbled.

Grant leaned his head into the hospital room. "I'd say she learns fast, but that's pretty obvious."

"Once she was the student, now she's the master of grump," Kane said back.

"You think this is funny?" Brigid challenged. "Not only am I sidelined, but I'm sidelined because of my damned curiosity!"

"So because you're mad at yourself, you threw a metal pan at my head?" Kane asked.

"Like I could hit you with such a non-aerodynamic object." Brigid grunted. "You could duck that in your sleep."

"Well, thank you for the vote of confidence," Kane answered as Grant handed him the now-dented bedpan.

"How's the ankle?" Grant asked.

"I aggravated it in horseplay with Domi and Sela," Brigid said.

"You *have* been a busy girl." Grant chuckled.

"Not another laugh. Not. One. More," Brigid threatened.

Grant showed her the palms of both of his hands in a sign of surrender. "Not another."

Brigid sighed and lowered her gaze at herself, reclined in the hospital bed. "How come neither of you get hurt badly enough to miss out on all the fun?"

"We'll transmit as much information back to you as we can, if we find relics," Kane offered.

"Go on. Just make sure you know how to program the interphaser," Brigid insisted.

"We know," Kane returned.

"Don't make me hobble out of this bed and come to your sorry rescue!" Brigid added.

Kane backed into the hallway, handing off the dented bedpan to a nurse. "You and your partners have my deepest sympathies."

The nurse peered around the corner. "Don't worry. She's not the first soldier we've had to deal with."

"She's a beast of a patient…" Grant warned.

"We've dealt with Queen Diana when she was still Artem15," the nurse returned. "She was the definition of the beast."

"I hear you talking about me!" Brigid spoke over the Commtacts for Kane and Grant, causing both men to wince.

"Aw, crud," Grant rumbled.

"We'll never get rid of her," Kane added.

"Damned straight," Brigid concluded.

"Behave, Baptiste. Just because you hypnotized the CAT teams and Myrto to guard against the song of Vanth doesn't mean you can be lazy. Heal up and join us," Kane told her before turning off his Commtact.

A moment later he felt Grant slap him in the back of the head.

"What was that…?" Kane began. Then he shook his head. "Brigid wants the last word."

"Getting so you won't need these things anymore, partner," Grant concluded with a laugh.

THE CERBERUS EXPLORERS and Myrto Smaragda were back at the Oracle, just as the interphaser beamed in from their redoubt. Kane knelt and entered the coordinates onto the small keypad built into the side of the pyramidal device. The interphaser was a means of expanding the reach of the CAT teams beyond the limitations of the mat-trans network in various redoubts. There were weaknesses in utilizing the local matter transmission chambers as the damage to the Olympian redoubt proved.

Their Greek allies literally could not receive or send visitors via the mat-trans, though thankfully the Cerberus Redoubt was able to rescue people trapped behind collapsed tunnels within the Hera Olympiad-ravaged headquarters. Rescue teams, including Kane and the rest of CAT Alpha, as well as CAT Beta, retrieved the injured and the imprisoned and brought them back via the parallax point atop the Oracle peninsula.

Hundreds of lives that could otherwise have been lost were given a second chance. Efforts to retrieve further supplies trapped within the depths went via the same circuit, but not like the hectic, constant matter jumping of those first few days of search and recovery. It was also the only means of getting maintenance teams down to work on the deep underground nuclear reactors, sent in for week-length shifts along with appropriate supplies.

The last thing that Kane and the Cerberus staff wanted was a nuclear meltdown in the Mediterranean, causing loss of life throughout New Olympus and its environs. They had too many friends and there were also too many potential allies out there for them to risk a failure of those reactors.

"We're still going to have to walk a ways," Sinclair mentioned. "According to Lakesh, there had been a parallax point on the Italian peninsula until three months or so ago."

Kane frowned at the idea they had been literally so busy over the past months that the disappearance of a major parallax crossroads was something listed as far down on the priorities of the Cerberus explorers. Only the mention of a danger in the Etruscan countryside sparked the memory of that mystery in Lakesh's mind. "Three months."

"The point is turned off?" Smaragda asked. "How is that possible?"

Kane tapped in the coordinates to the interphaser. "Vanth and Charun have to be behind that development."

Smaragda's eyes narrowed. "So, they haven't been

awake for long. The stories that we received go back at least six months. What were they doing the first two or three?"

"Waking up. They've been asleep for a while," Grant said. "Brigid said that the worship of Charun and Vanth ended around three thousand years ago. They only woke up recently."

"Gathering people to power the device that has hijacked the parallax point," Sela added. "Because there's no way that you can do something like cut off access to a wormhole without an assload of power."

Kane frowned. "Gathering up the energy to shut down the parallax point using brains. Human and otherwise, given your account of the birds."

"Zombified humans is one thing. But the songbirds were downright creepy," Smaragda responded.

"Brigid did say that Vanth wanted her brain and soul to add to opening a door," Domi added. "The points are already doors for us. Maybe they want to change where the door opens."

"To unleash the hordes as a plague," Grant repeated from Brigid's debriefing.

"If I didn't know any better, I'd think that when she hypnotized us, she planted seeds of answers for the questions we're asking right now," Sinclair mused, her arms folded.

Edwards chuckled. "Like none of us have learned anything from our adventures?"

"Yeah. We picked Edwards for the Cerberus teams for more than just the muscles he's wearing on his arms," Grant added. "There's some working muscle between his ears."

"All of our ears, yes," Sinclair answered. "But we're thinking about parallax points as doorways that can be hijacked. And the whole 'dragon roads' thing as a circuit board that can be rewired."

Kane stood, looking down at the interphaser. "What's wrong with that? I mean, it's not as if Lakesh hasn't explained that in simple terms for us foot soldiers enough times. Nor Brigid."

The air around the group began to hum, laser beams spraying out in a pattern around them. The interphaser created a matrix of energy surrounding them, plasma vortices taking on the appearance of mist and fog, lit and glowing under the ray beams shimmering from the pyramidal device's top. The five people were transformed from solid matter into cohesive streams of atoms that could be slurped through the wormhole. All of this energy was poured out at Cerberus Redoubt, from the long-running nuclear reactors that were the only power source at their beck and call that could open such a wormhole.

The interphaser simply found those crossroads of magnetic lines crisscrossing the surface of the world, and in finding the nexus, beamed those massive energies through the thinning of reality, literally opening a door between universes, folding the space on the other end. To an observer, the effect was sprays of misty Technicolor energy flying outward in sheets, and then five humans clad in skintight black leather materializing, rather than the interphaser reconstructing the bodies of the travelers in their journey across hundreds and hundreds of miles and across two dimensions.

The process was painless, if disorienting for first-timers or those entering an improperly programmed mat-trans. Kane was familiar with "jump dreams" and more than once these very same disconnects from reality actually gave him glimpses into other lives, other incarnations.

The interphaser, however, had cleared up much of that interference that resulted in a nauseating landing or that wave of delirium making the jumpers sensitive to odd psychic vibrations. In a way, it felt less like a dangerous leap into the unknown than it had before, where every redoubt was still an unknown, potentially inhabited by coldhearts or other menaces.

The world phased back into view around the Cerberus adventurers and Smaragda, becoming more and more visible through the "bubble" of laser-lit smoke around them. Within moments they were at a small clearing in a forest, one adorned with stones arranged in a form of henge.

The warriors immediately scanned the surrounding tree line, though part of Kane missed the presence of Brigid to explain to them what this circlet of standing rocks signified. It was already evident to Kane and Grant that the stones meant that ancient peoples knew of the presence of a parallax point in this location. Those with sensitivity to extrasensory phenomena knew to associate these places with a means of contacting the gods.

There was scarcely an interphaser landing point that hadn't showed some form of marker that it had once been a spot of worship. While there was no real confirmation that the Annunaki threshold jewels operated on the same parallax point principle, this would have been a likely landing point for the overlords themselves as they'd visited the Earth.

Kane remembered that he had his shadow suit hood recording vid, and Brigid *was* looking over the scene here. Their landing point was not far; only about seventy-five miles from where the major nexus had been before it became a black hole on Lakesh's observations.

Domi was crouched, her hood down. Though the girl was not averse to technology, there were some things that only her feral instincts could pick up on. Smells and behaviors of local wildlife were as much in the cues she could pick up on instantly as Kane's own point man's instinct.

Her ruby-red eyes locked in one direction. "Heavy steps."

"Beta, disperse. Myrto, go with them. We'll stay, observe and initiate contact if possible," Kane ordered.

There was no disagreement among the three CAT Beta members and their Olympian companion as they gathered their effects and disappeared into the tree line.

"At least we've got backup out there this time," Grant murmured, shouldering his war bag. "I'm not picking up anything on the Commtact."

"Me, either," Kane returned. "That means something else might be up."

"Charun and Vanth might have figured that if they couldn't brainwash Edwards, or get Brigid with their little virus, we might be immune to their subtle ways," Grant offered.

Kane nodded in agreement. "So they sent Gear Skeletons."

"Capture or kill?" Grant proposed. "That's what we have to figure out."

Kane and his friend went to the tree line, looking for a good hiding spot. "We've got the same dilemma here, partner."

Grant's lips pursed in thought. "We've brought the materials needed to incapacitate the Olympian troops without much harm, but the Spartan pilots...we would have to donate armor to them."

Kane chuckled. "A cloud in every silver lining. Don't ever change, buddy."

The large Magistrate had a shotgun out. Loaded with less-lethal loads, mainly neoprene slugs that would punch with enough force to stun and bruise, but against the Sandcat panels enveloping the Spartan pilots it might as well have been a handful of marshmallows to be hurled at the giants. There was one saving grace, though, but they didn't know if it would work.

Under the pump on Grant's and Kane's less-lethals were Taser units. Each of these little electric guns fired twin prongs via compressed air at a target. On humans, the barbs would stick in clothing or stab shallowly in skin, and the fine wires attached to the tines would ferry forward a powerful pulse of voltage, capable of freezing a person's muscles and nervous system, effectively paralyzing them.

The theory, as devised by Sela Sinclair and Brigid Baptiste, was that maybe, if the electrical current somehow connected to the Spartan war bots, their pilots would be affected. The pilots commanded the powerful robotic suits through a cybernetic node installed at the base of their spines, so that the mighty Gear Skeletons could actually conduct the electrical shock of the Tasers.

"If it's one or two, we'll be fine. If it's all three, we're going to have to get creative while one of us reloads," Grant noted.

"Or if we miss," Kane offered.

Grant narrowed his eyes.

"This is a new system for us," Kane added. "So we won't be as good and accurate with it as we are with our usual arms."

"If I can hit targets with a bow and arrow, I might be able to compensate with Taser tongs," Grant grumbled.

"Hush, I can hear the stomps of a Spartan closing," Kane returned.

Kane knew he didn't have to say anything. Grant might have been famous for his gruff, grumbling nature, but when it came time for serious work, there were few people quieter than he.

The two men slithered deeper into the cover of the

tree line, eyes open, ears peeled for the approach of the robot or robots.

There was also the potential that the Spartans weren't alone. Who knew how long the two mysterious godlings had been ready for an arrival by the Cerberus contingent? There had been hours between the time Edwards was picked up, the debriefing, and then finally the very hectic night in the wake of Brigid's battle against the deadly song of Vanth.

So far, things seemed in the clear. Neither Kane's cunning nor Domi's feral instincts had been tripped by the presence of soldiers camouflaged among the forest surrounding the little clearing. The only signs of an enemy presence were the leaden footsteps of the robot approaching. Enemy ambush was not close enough to be on the agenda, but then, these two Etruscan entities had lived as contemporaries of the Annunaki overlords. Maybe they were other Igigi, or they were an entirely different species, but whatever the case, they didn't survive the intrigues of the dawn of humanity by being easy to predict.

Then again, wits and cunning often did wonders for Kane and his allies in dealing with deadly overlords. One of the problems of being a being with access to armies and nearly magical technology was a tendency to overlook the scrabbling little apes and their resourcefulness with nothing more than twigs and pebbles.

Too often, in Kane's observation, these "gods" forgot that they were mortal, flesh and blood as the rest of the planet. Enlil and his surviving brethren had learned that lesson at the cost of more than a couple of their fellow Annunaki. Brigid mentioned that there were similarities between the hypnotic song of Ereshkigal and that of Vanth. Vanth's version, however, had a much more mathematical base, she'd told him, which made it into an aggressive, human-brain-based piece of malware.

If these bastards can nearly give Baptiste a heart attack, then they definitely are in full Annunaki range of powers, Kane thought. He remembered his own psychic duel with Enlil in India, one that had almost crushed him mentally and physically. Kane never claimed to be any great shakes mentally, and that he survived the telepathic conflict instigated by Enlil seemed merely stubborn resolve and dumb luck rather than anything else. Vanth's attack against Brigid still weighed on Kane's nerves.

There was nothing more that he would like to do than wring Vanth's neck, should she show. Kane and Brigid were *anam-charas*, and harm to one was literally harm to both.

Bide your time.

Going off in a knee-jerk reaction was not the key to victory here. He wasn't even certain that either Charun or Vanth would be showing. As such, he remained patient, his less-lethal shotgun ready for action. The Sin Eater, folded away along his forearm, would be for someone or something worse. Brigid had stated for the entire Cerberus group that they would do their best to rescue and recover their lost soldiers.

The monstrous steps slowed. The walker was on the far side of the clearing, fifteen yards away, and obscured by the tree line. One thing, though, had become apparent. What they had mistaken for the ponderous bulk of a walking Spartan war bot wasn't a thing forged of alien alloys and cobbled Sandcat armor.

Fingers, the size of sausages, swept aside the crown of a tree, branches shattering under incredible pressure. The splintering limbs weren't violently thrashed, merely shrugged aside with a casual brush of an arm as long as Kane himself was tall. The creature that the arm attached to was a thing of horror, its face just as twisted and inhuman as Charun's own.

This was not an automaton, and it was far too large to be an Annunaki or one of their servant Nephilim. This was a gargantuan creature, not unlike another horror that Kane had encountered. It had been in the Appalachian Rift, and his name was Balor of the Baleful Eye, an entity of horror and suffering created by another scion of Enlil, the brutal yet eternally handsome Bres. This thing was not a Fomori, but he could already "hear" Brigid's explanation of how the Celtic Fomorian demons and the Greek Cyclops were likely different cultural observations of the same creatures. And these giants were the creations of horrible technologies that made flesh and bone flow like molasses.

Because of the power it instilled in them, and because of the continuous agonies it ravaged them with, the one-eyed giants were fearless in the face of danger and death. Kane watched as splinters of smashed branch speared into thick, elephantine hide, taking only trickles of blood, eliciting a smirk on the titan's face. Anything that sparked its way from the endless existence of dull ache was a moment of pleasure, a relief from the sameness of eternity. According to Bres, when they'd last battled, the constant state of their bodies was breaking and tearing their deformed figures, and instantly healing. Only the worst of agonies could penetrate such a fog of constant ache.

It had made the Bres's Fomori formidable, utterly fearless in battle, even enjoying receiving injuries. Added to that was the riot of cellular activity that made them heal almost instantly.

Less-lethal shotguns were not going to be the order of this battle. Not with eighteen feet of rippling brawn and the splinter injuries on its arm closing, the trapped wood being scabbed over to become part of its uneven, alien dermis.

The big, ugly eye swept the tree line as the creature inhaled deeply.

"Smell you," it rumbled.

The fat, knob-knuckled fingers wrapped around the trunk of the tree it'd mangled and twisted, wrenching the field maple from the ground. Clumps of dirt fell away from the gnarled roots, the three-foot-diameter log easily grasped by the cyclopean horror.

"Smell you. Kill you," the thing grunted.

Kane rose and rushed away from his position as the massive trunk slashed through the air, propelled by mighty muscles.

Chapter 9

Five or so years ago, when he'd been a Magistrate in Cobaltville, there were lengthy lists of things Grant never thought he would run into, encounter, let alone be threatened by. Sure, he'd heard stories of genetic mutants unleashed upon the countryside in great hordes just to enforce a feudal lifestyle among the survivors of the apocalypse back in 2001. But those things had been hunted down, thanks to the reunification program that had trained and armed Grant and Kane, equipping them with polycarbonate armor and high-tech weaponry from full-auto side arms to Deathbird assault helicopters. After a while, the muties were exterminated, something that Grant regretted missing out on.

Since then, however, he'd faced biological and technological wonders without end. Pan-terrestrial aliens such as the Archons, the hybrid barons who commanded Grant and Kane, the Nagah, the Fomori, the Annunaki themselves. Grant even recalled the time his tesseract "time shadow" faced off against a living Minotaur in a brutal battle thousands of years prior. Grant even regularly visited New Edo and Thunder Isle, where time-trawled dinosaurs lived and thrived.

None of them quite matched the scope of eighteen feet of rippling muscle, topped by a grotesque head with a huge, watery green eye. At eighteen feet, it towered over even the largest of predatory dinos that he'd encountered, the Acrocanthosaurus. Fortunately the cyclops stood bi-pedal-erect, so its entire body was in a column of flesh, bone and muscle, unlike the forty-foot-long Acro, which squared its bulk on two massive hind legs, balanced out by a muscular tail.

Even so, nearly twenty feet of humanoid was impressive, especially since it was no mere inflated person. This was a creature with broad feet and fat legs, its girth slowly tapering, but not by much, to shoulders that were "only" seven feet across, and arms that, while seemingly spindly, were still thicker than Grant's by a factor of three.

The moment Grant saw the brute rip up a thirteen-foot tree by the roots with no more effort than he would have pulled out an annoying weed, his mind raced. The cyclops had announced its intentions in a manner that would have made Domi seem loquacious and then fast-balled the maple like a javelin. The three-foot-thick trunk smashed against other trunks with the crash of thunder, and only the grunts of Kane's efforts over the din informed Grant that his friend was all right.

"Yo! One-eye!" he bellowed, stepping into the open. "Pick on someone your own size!"

The giant had been reaching for another tree trunk when it paused, looking aghast at the dark-skinned human who rose to greet it, shotgun clutched in fists that would have been massive to any other entity.

The cyclops reared back and whipped its head forward in a challenging roar. But as soon as the creature opened its mouth, Grant shouldered his shotgun in one smooth movement and fired.

While there wasn't much hope that a neoprene baton would do much to penetrate its hide, getting whacked in the epiglottis by a rubber slug that could break normal human ribs *did* send the giant into a stunned coughing fit.

That single shot purchased several seconds for Kane to get his feet back beneath him, and time enough to come up with a coordinated plan.

"Fall back into the heavy woods—he'll have a hard time moving quickly in there," Kane ordered.

Grant turned and broke through the tree line. As soon as he was out of sight, he immediately cut to the left, running perpendicular to his prior course. That change of direction was a lifesaver as the enraged giant plowed through trees, bellowing like a wounded bull. Yard-thick trunks exploded under the pressure of the cyclops's passage.

Grant, thanks to his time on Thunder Isle, was intimately aware of the square-cube law. The giant was three times the height of a human being, but the nature of such growth was that its volume and mass grew much faster than its surface area. As a "normal-size" human, the beast would have easily been about 300 pounds. Due to that mass increase, the thing was now more than a ton in weight—2,700 pounds by his mental calculations.

Since the creature's musculature and bone structure had been altered by Annunaki technologies—nanomachines rebuilding the entity to properly support all of the added material—there was little doubt the cyclops had few physical impairments in regard to its enormous weight. By the thickness of those massive legs, there was little question that just taking a single footstep would shatter its own bones. It was mutated to be that large.

Such incredible power inherent in its limbs was enough to give Grant pause.

"We might have to get lethal with this bastard," Grant said over his Commtact.

Kane's pause was enough to remind Grant of the potential nature of this beast. What was now a cyclopean horror might once have been an innocent person. Then again, nearly 20 feet and 3,000 pounds of rampaging muscle were hard to handle with kid gloves. "Whatever happens, we go home."

"Find you!" The titan's roar was such that Grant could feel the air shudder around him. Would any of their weapons hurt that thing? And given the kind of regenerative power he'd encountered among the Fomori in the Appalachians, would they cause it lethal harm? It was going to be a fine line that, despite the practicality he normally showed, Grant didn't want to cross without exhausting all other options.

There used to be a time when Grant would have killed a mutant monstrosity such as this outright, but years of battle, as well as learning more and more of Zen from Shizuka, had taken the quick edge off his aggression. It also didn't hurt that this thing was talking, giving it some semblance of humanity, and that he and Kane were able to keep skirting its attentions.

That wasn't going to last forever. But Grant wondered at something.

"Kane, we're gonna zap this thing with the Tasers. If that doesn't work, then we fill him with lead," Grant offered.

The breath of relief on Kane's end of the Commtact told Grant that the idea was greatly welcomed. If the current could go through the metal of a Spartan war bot, there was little doubt that it'd affect a flesh-and-blood humanoid with even better efficiency.

At least that was the hope.

The cyclops grunted, snorting as it was confused and frustrated by how easily it had lost its prey. Apparently its enhanced size came with similar benefits, such as hundreds of square feet of olfactory receptors through which it could smell its prey. Grant had to keep ducking through and past trees, at the same time avoiding rustling the undergrowth. Though large, he was lithe and capable of great agility and stealth.

The cyclops was keen of smell, but that singular eye of his at least helped out Grant. Depth perception and peripheral vision were both heavily curtailed by the lack of binocular vision, and thus, as a predator, it was left poorly off in close pursuit. Then again, a nine-foot reach forgave a lot in terms of grabbing at someone. If Grant was caught in those massive paws, not even his old Magistrate armor could prevent his being crushed like a grape.

It wouldn't even take a grab. Just a clumsy swat with a fist the size of a melon would be more than sufficient to shatter his ribs.

The cyclops's vision might not have been ideal for hunting, but as Grant inadvertently snapped the branch of a sapling as he scurried past it, the thing's head turned, attention locked on to that sound. The thud of a ton and a half of rampaging man-beast informed Grant of his deadly situation. He whirled with the shotgun, raising it and hoping the Taser launcher beneath would be enough.

The boom of Kane's shotgun was a sharp sound amid the ponderous steps of the giant and the cyclops stopped after two more steps.

"Damned...humans!" the creature growled. "Puny, worthless...humans!"

"Now," Kane whispered into the Commtact as the cyclops turned its back to Grant. Taking two swift strides, the big Magistrate bounded into firing range for the Taser and fired. The barbs struck the creature in its broad back, the barbed tines sticking into the thick hide.

"Hate you!" it bellowed. Grant didn't know how much louder the thing could get but he wasn't going to let it turn and try to rip him apart. He energized the Taser and, with a pull of the trigger, heard the snaps and cracks of intermittent voltage popping along the electrical wires. The cyclops groaned and grunted, gurgling, but it stood. Its arms moved stiffly, but even with its range of motion limited, it could still cause some harm, simply by toppling over. Luckily, it was so paralyzed and its legs of such great size and density compared to normal human limbs, that it stayed standing. In another moment Kane was out and firing. His Taser darts stuck into the cyclops and he cut loose with his own voltage.

Together the two Cerberus warriors hammered the giant with the output from both Taser batteries. At 50,000 volts, and with the Tasers operating at 3.1 milliamps—on the high end of less lethal, electric-shock technology— the cyclops received not just one zap of electricity, but each Taser was hitting him with 19 pulses per second, 38 times per second. For the space of thirty seconds, the giant's nervous system was overrun and abused by amperage. While the volts were a measure of the energy, amps were the measure of the force carried by each charge. Higher amounts of milliamps were lethal; 10 milliamps could cause a fatal series of convulsions in a 150-pound human. This was why the Tasers only put out a third of that, often only a fifth of lethal capacity.

Grant didn't know how that would work against an entity that was twenty times as heavy, but considering the paralysis the cyclops demonstrated, apparently it was enough.

Grant's Taser ran down, reaching the end of its thirty-second cycle. He swept the shotgun aside on its sling, letting his Sin Eater launch into the palm of his hand. The cyclops teetered, then fell to its knees, the ground shuddering beneath the soles of Grant's boots. A swallow cleared the lump in his throat at the thought of the massive opponent's collapse.

Sure, Kane and Grant felt fear in the face of enemies, despite the bravado and smart talk they fired off. But that was the whole point of being a hero. Doing what had to be done, no matter how scary it was.

Grant approached the stunned cyclops, seeing Kane enter the clearing at a right angle. His Sin Eater was out, as well. The beast had voiced its hatred of humans loud and long enough, so that if it did swing to kill, neither former Magistrate would have a single regret about putting it down with a wave of full-auto heavy slugs. But even so, they didn't want to cause undue harm.

One thing that had been part of their rebellion against the old barons and their villes was a rejection of cruelty and controlling the lives of others. They fought for freedom, and there was still a strong possibility that this poor beast was merely the victim of Charun or Vanth, mentally twisted by the same kind of hypnotic forces that had incapacitated Brigid.

The cyclops gave its head a shake, as if clearing the cobwebs out, and both Kane and Grant froze in their advance toward the mighty giant. When the thing lifted a seventy-two-inch-diameter arm, things were already apparent that the Tasers did work on it, but not as effectively as they would have liked. The giant's fist hammered the ground, striking with a force that made wrecking balls seem inadequate. Grant felt his knees buckle beneath him from the vibratory shock wave. Over the Commtact, he could hear Kane grunt as the surge of force transmitted through the ground gave him trouble.

Grant was so bowled over by the impact of the giant's fist on the ground, he couldn't see where his friend and partner had fallen, or stumbled. For all the big Magistrate knew, a tree could have fallen upon Kane, trapping him so that the monster could pounce upon him.

Grant let himself tumble into a roll, to give him a little more distance, and with a pivot, he was facing the titan. As big as it was, the cyclops had a hard time getting up from its kneeling position. Those legs were meant for keeping it standing, not for ease of bending so that it could stand from a fallen position. It crawled toward the tree line, where its long arms could be used to reach a tree trunk and help brace it to get back to standing.

"Kane!" Grant growled. "What's your status?"

"Staggered by that thing. It punches as hard as a mortar," Kane answered. "We can't let him back on his feet."

"No way in hell. Pop him in the head with the less-lethal. Distract him," Grant ordered.

Kane didn't ask questions, and the brawny Grant dropped his war bag. He found a coil of rope, the exact item he was looking for. The big man didn't know how well this would work, but it was better than nothing. The giant was still flesh and blood, and part of the dictates of a giant was the need to breathe and, hopefully, have a supply of blood to the brain.

It took a moment of guesswork, and Grant was glad he had inflexible rope; nylon that wouldn't stretch and give. He needed to choke the beast out. He also plucked out a steel collapsing baton that he could use as a handle.

As he was making preparations, he listened to the thunder and crash of Kane's shotgun, bouncing high-velocity neoprene rounds off the cyclops's head. The beast bellowed, cursed in its limited lexicon, thrashed and swung one arm toward Kane while keeping itself propped with the other. This was mere harassment, not a counterattack. Though the rubber slugs could break ribs, even snap necks at close distance, the knots of muscle and dense bone that made up this giant could continue suffering annoyance and prickling pain all the while.

There was little danger of causing it permanent harm.

Not like putting strands of strong rope around its throat and garroting it. Lack of blood to the brain would kill much faster than loss of breath.

Could kill. I just have to get to him first, Grant reminded himself.

With two quick strides Grant was at the thing's heels. The fat, flat, elephantine feet were nothing that would provide a handhold, but he threw himself at the top of the cyclops's heels, launching himself as high as he could, and was able to clear the four-foot ledge formed by the stumplike appendage. With two kicks, he was standing and racing along the calf of the giant. It was a platform that was wide and flat, easy to balance upon. The next level he had to hurdle was actually six feet in height, and was the cyclops's ass.

Grant drew his combat knife, knowing that he was going to need every ounce of leverage he could get. With a leap, he was clawing on at chest level on one of the giant's cheeks. He brought down the combat blade like a climbing ax, the sharp point digging into heavy hide and eliciting a grunt of annoyance from the cyclops. Still, that thick skin was strong enough that Grant could haul himself up higher on the butt of the beast. He dug his toes into the dimple of a lower back muscle when the thing pushed itself off of one arm, trying to get upright.

Grant planted one foot on the handle of his knife then swung the loops of rope upward with all of his strength. The coils snagged the creature, but he couldn't be sure where. Even so, he kicked off of the knife, planting the soles of his feet against the broad sheets of muscle that formed the cyclops's back.

Kane was back again. This time his Sin Eater blasted out single shots that elicited more annoyed snarls and gnashing of teeth, distracting the bestial giant. Grant finally was up on the titan's shoulder and pushing the ropes down under the cyclops's chin. It turned its head, swinging it as if to thrash Grant from its shoulders. The big Magistrate still held on to the coils looped around his foe's neck and swung on them, using his 240 pounds of muscle to wrench the rope tight around the thing's throat.

The collapsible baton snapped open with a flick of his wrist and Grant jammed the steel length into the slack of his noose. A hard twist and he soon had not only handlebars, but heard the croak and groan of the cyclops as it struggled for breath. Big, fat fingers reached up to snag the rope, but Grant cranked on his baton, twisting to take up any possible looseness in the lines. If the cyclops was able to catch a breath, there was a good chance...

The ground suddenly seemed to rush toward Grant in the corner of his vision and the burly Magistrate twisted his body with everything he had. The giant threw himself onto one shoulder and the force of that plunge produced a loud, sickening crack. It could be a dislocated shoulder, or the creature's collar bone, but either way, the sounds struggling past the giant's restricted larynx went up several octaves. It was definitely left in pain.

Grant felt good that the creature didn't roll onto its back. About the only thing that kept it from crashing its full weight onto Grant was its bent, massive leg. There would be little that could twist such a thickly muscled, heavily boned limb. Using the tension of the baton in the rope as leverage, he stood perpendicular to his giant foe's shoulders.

Grant's own legs pushed out, removing the absolute last of any slack around his opponent's throat. While he didn't have enough muscle to match the cyclops, he did have the leverage and more than sufficient power in his legs to constrict the big bastard's blood vessels and windpipe. Even with the thing's fat fingers clawing at its throat, trying to snag something to relieve all of the pressure, Grant flexed his leg muscles, digging into the beast's shoulder blades.

It started to feel as if he'd dislocate both shoulders from

the sheer amount of strain he was putting on the grip when Kane ran up to the baton.

Kane braced his back against the cyclops's wide shoulders, then hooked the steel bar in the step between his boot's sole and the raised heel. Kane pushed with all he had, and that tension held him up enough so that he could raise the other foot. The combined leg and torso strength of the two Magistrates was more than sufficient now, and Grant saw the giant's shoulders stop squirming.

"Enough," Grant ordered. "He's out."

Kane let his knees flex and dropped his feet to the ground. Grant dropped to the dirt, panting. His skin was soaking wet beneath the shadow suit, even as the high-tech uniform was hard at work, whisking his perspiration away to cool him. This level of exertion was something he hadn't maintained for a long time. His arms, legs and back ached. He watched the baton slowly twirl, the ropes slackening around the giant's throat. With the loosening, the deep, steady breathing of the cyclops reassured him that his plan was successful. They'd downed the mutant without having to slaughter it.

"We're going to need to be environmentally sealed so he can't track us by scent," Kane noted.

Grant nodded, watching his friend jog over to retrieve both war bags. Kane walked back, grunting as he extended Grant's war bag to him. He took it and tugged the loops of rope off of the monstrosity's neck, returning it to the bag. He hoped that the suffocation would keep for a while, but just putting his palm where the pulse would be on a normal man showed a strong, steady heartbeat.

"Sleep tight, One-eye," Grant muttered. "We don't want to see you again for a long time."

With that, the two merciful Cerberus adventurers pulled on their hoods and stalked off into the forest.

Chapter 10

Four people were all that moved on the old goat path through the hills. One man, who could be two smaller men by height and weight, and three women, each well-armed and clad in the seamless skintight shadow suits. They, of course, were Cerberus Away Team Beta.

Edwards walked at the back of the formation, cradling a massive shotgun identical to the ones carried by Kane and Grant. Should the CAT encounter any of the mindless, the enslaved, it would be his position to lay down less-lethal fire, stunning and staggering attackers in an effort to prevent harm from befalling the thralls of the Stygian couple—Charun and Vanth.

The next tallest of the group was Sela Sinclair, though her second place in height was a distant one. She also possessed a less-lethal, ammunition-loaded shotgun. It was Sinclair who had put together the crowd-safety weapons, and while Edwards would be smacking overly aggressive attackers with neoprene slugs, she took it upon herself to fire ferret rounds. The .12-gauge slugs would vomit forth payloads of tear gas, something that should make even the most powerfully mind-controlled victims pause. No amount of mental domination could stop the body's responses to powerful irritants such as the pepper extract within the tear gas shells. And when their enemy couldn't see, they couldn't attack.

The third member of the group was a young, olive-skinned beauty who seemed decades older than her true age thanks to her bone-white hair. This was Myrto Smaragda, the sole survivor of the Olympian expedition to this very countryside. Her presence was as much a healing process for herself as well as a hope for rescuing her lost platoon. Her choice of armament was a conventional assault rifle, just in case there were other forms of opponents under the control of the Etruscan godlings, or an appearance by one or the other themselves. Certainly, the other members of the group also had conventional firearms, as well. Even so, Sinclair had given Smaragda a gren launcher, loaded with larger tear gas shells, as well as smoke grens to hide and cover them against pursuit.

The last, as well as the smallest, of the group was their leader. Her size, however, did not mean that she was the least of this group. Though moving almost like an animal, scouting ahead of the team, she was the appointed leader of the group. Her experience, surviving in the Deathlands and later in the urban apocalypse known as the Tartarus Pits of Cobaltville, had sharpened her wits in ways that no mere scholarly education could hone a warrior's mind and skills. She didn't have any long weapons in hand, but her gun and her knife were sheathed at her hips, ready to flicker out in an instant. The rifle she had strapped to her back was something to fall back upon, just in case.

So far, nothing had showed up to keep them on their toes, but Domi, Edwards and Sinclair were professionals, as was Smaragda. Relaxation of their vigilance and dulling of their instincts was a quick road to doom. Then again, Smaragda was a living example of how even the most diligent of adventurers could end up on the losing side of a conflict. They were aware of the dangers that they approached, but even so, they were stepping onto the home turf of creatures capable of almost crushing an aircraft and stopping heavy machine-gun fire cold with energy fields.

Caution was the order for the present, as it always was.

Domi combined both her own feral instincts, sharpened in countless wastelands and danger zones, with the high-tech additions of the shadow suit hood. At first, she had been afraid of feeling more cut off from the world, but the electronic boosts were things that she could make use of. Now the hood was giving her access to spectrums of hearing and sight she'd only dreamed of, though she took care not to rely too heavily on the electronics, the same as Kane had with his point man's instinct.

Her ruby-red eyes were sharp at picking up faint light in the dark, but even they didn't have the preternatural ability to register ultraviolet and infrared wavelengths. The shadow suit optics did.

And so far things were quiet with the setting sun. There was also no contact over the Commtact. That meant in their hour of travel so far, Kane and Grant had persevered over the approaching monstrosity. No report on what they met up with, but also no distress call.

That was good news to Domi, because she knew that her comrades in arms would at least get a message out if they were in fatal distress. The two of them had stuck around to make contact, perhaps to be captured or to be invited into the arms of Vanth and her mate. With that as one option, CAT Beta was to sneak up on the home of the enemy, gathering information through stealth rather than infiltration.

Kane and Grant had been taken in by more than enough gloating enemies that it had proved to be a useful tactic to offer an olive branch, or simply be captured. Still, without Brigid Baptiste's presence, Lakesh would have said it unlikely for such a plan to work. Kane, Grant and Brigid's ploys and ruses worked thanks to what the ancient scientist called a "confluence of probability." Luck was on their side whenever they stood united.

Domi had little doubt that either Kane or Grant would be overwhelmed by an assailing monstrosity like a Gear Skeleton, but she also didn't suffer the delusion that they were invulnerable. If either was in danger, Kane would certainly give a loud and clear warning to Beta. Sure, some parts of her would rebel at the concept of her friends dying, but Brigid Baptiste had been adamant on teaching her practicality and logic.

Domi would mourn those two, but only after she was certain there was no other means of bringing them back. Kane hadn't given up on her, even when it had appeared she'd died in the detonation of an implode gren. Finding the Time Trawl on Thunder Isle had been Kane's means of rescuing her, plucking her temporally from before the detonation of the lethal bomb, saving her life. Even certain atomization by hi-ex hadn't stopped Kane from trying.

Domi could do no less for any of the rest of her Cerberus family.

She'd penetrated into the depths of the very base where she nearly died, looking for a cure for Lakesh as his mind began to fail. Her lover had been losing his mind, thanks to a bit of genetic vengeance cast upon him by Enlil, countermanding the same destructive nanobots that had rebuilt Lakesh from a two-and-a-half-century-old, half-artificial scientist to a man in his vibrant late forties. The slow robbery of Lakesh's intellect was ultimate vengeance against the man who assembled the Cerberus Redoubt to battle against Enlil and his kin, when he was first Baron Cobalt, then when he was Sam the Imperator, then finally his true Annunaki overlord self.

If Kane and Grant were in trouble, though, both men would have the foresight to send out a signal, one that was a tight-beam communication, nearly unjammable, up to satellites Lakesh and the Cerberus techs had hacked into. When that emergency dispatch was squirted out, Domi would have received the relayed message at the speed of light. Broadband jamming was one thing, but a full-power emergency pulse, focused like a laser, would *not* be blocked by whatever the enemy was using.

They were getting closer to a village now. Domi had been able to smell the village and its attendant flocks of livestock, but the road had been eerily quiet. Normally, at this range, when the smell was this strong, the bleats of goats and sheep would hang heavily in the air. This wasn't the case here. The same thing that Smaragda had observed before—the lack of life and spark in nature— was an oppressive weight on Domi's feral instincts. Every nerve in her was on edge, hating the ominous quiet smothering the countryside.

It was giving Smaragda hell, Domi could tell as she glanced back on the road, but the woman was a brave soldier, strong of will and willing to go into terror. The Domi of five years ago would have not even dreamed of stepping into such an unnatural void of life. Even the rotted shanties of the worst parts of the Tartarus Pits had rodents and flies and people all squirming and struggling for life; a wild energy that made the world feel right.

This was a nightmare of lifelessness, far more chaotic to her senses than a dark, dusky realm where any moment a knife could slide between your ribs. There were few cues for her as even the animals had seemingly gone mute. A fence loomed ahead and Domi waved for the others to stay still and silent. On silent, bare feet, she moved up to the closest post, keeping herself down in a crouch. The grasses along the fence had grown nearly three feet tall, both inside and out, something that already seemed out of place for the stench of sheep prevalent in this area.

Reaching the fence, she parted some grass and saw

that there were at least forty sheep penned into the area, but they simply stood in place. They'd eaten, but not with the same mindless industry that a usual flock would have. The animals were just taking in enough to sustain their lives, not grazing down to the nub and then moving on to another section. By the growth, Domi was able to put it at three or four months, putting the conquest of this small farm town right in the area of the first expansion of Charun and Vanth after their awakening. This was just as the CATs surmised upon their transit.

Approach on the road was too risky. The ovine brain wasn't one of the sharpest in the world, but certainly if the sheep were caught in a form of mental thrall, there was every likelihood they could serve as eyes and ears for the two Etruscan demigods. Domi slowly allowed the grass to bend itself back into position, in no hurry to let her presence be betrayed by the rustle of blades.

There was no wind, especially none at her back, so her scent wouldn't waft toward the sheep. With practiced stealth and grace, she returned to the rest of her team.

"Sheep. Just like the birds," Domi noted softly, keeping her voice low. "Numb."

"Why mind control sheep or birds?" Edwards murmured.

"The power needs to punch a hole to the other dimension," Sela Sinclair offered. "They want to open a door back to their home world, and doing that takes a lot of energy."

"So they're tapping free will? Souls?" Smaragda asked. "However that goes, it'd be a hell of a boon, technologically."

"If you don't mind robbing someone of their individuality," Sinclair countered.

"Maybe for prisoners," Edwards mentioned.

"Maybe we get out of here," Domi grumbled, her ruby

eyes narrowed to slits as she looked back toward the farm. "We skirt the town."

"And we shut the hell up," Smaragda added, gauging Domi's impatience.

The albino girl nodded. "Not so many words."

With that, Domi and her team backtracked, then gave the farm town a wide berth.

It would add an hour to their trek, but when it came to butting heads with alien menaces, there was little to be gained by rushing blindly into battle.

WITH NIGHT'S ARRIVAL, cloaking the world in darkness only illuminated by stars and a slim crescent of moon, CAT Beta had been able to move with a little more speed. In the inky shadows, they had the advantage of superior night vision, including Domi's ruby-red gaze, which made her sensitive to even the faintest of glows. She'd long since inured herself to daylight, but except on overcast days, she kept a pair of sunglasses ready to keep from being "snow blinded" by the burning sun.

It was after the arrival of dusk where she came most alive; a nocturnal predator entering her environment. The others were utilizing night-vision optics, and with the world cast in green via light amplification, the four of them were in far less need of keeping to foliage and such.

Sure, they meant to stay in the shadows, something that they could discern even in the night-vision optics. Domi eschewed that, as she was used to a lifetime of night hunting that she had honed to perfection. This was training and skill that she continued using, even with technology that couldn't honestly improve upon the senses she utilized. She could understand using IR and UV vision, as well as telescopic optics, but for night work, with plenty of natural starlight for her to see by, she didn't use the hood.

The four people kept their profile low, thanks to the camouflage aspects of the shadow suit's high-tech polymers. Though Domi didn't have her faceplate down on her hood, she did have it tucked up over her bone-white hair, so as to minimize the shocking contrast of it against the countryside. The same had gone during the day, as well. Her bare feet, though cast of the same alabaster as the rest of her albino skin, had been darkened and dirtied by years of trudging, so that she didn't have to worry about them sticking out like sore toes.

Domi heard the flutter of wings in the distance, then froze, the others coming to a halt behind her and crouching low.

"Bird?" Edwards murmured, speaking in a low tone.

"Lots," Domi returned. "Too dark to see us. Maybe."

Edwards and Sinclair immediately picked up on Domi's heightened agitation. Her language skills suffered in fight-or-flight situations, but that was all right with her two partners. When it came to fighting for survival, Domi's lack of elocution was balanced by downright eloquence when it came to the arts of violence. However, as they were closing in on the location of the missing parallax point, any bit of action would only draw down the attention of the godlings and who knew how many of their mindless slaves.

Though CAT Beta was made of formidable warriors, armed with powerful weapons, there still were limits to both firepower and skill in the face of superior numbers. Standing and fighting would be tantamount to suicide.

Their option was silence and a fighting retreat if necessary.

That retreat would get harder, though, the farther they penetrated into the realm of Charun and Vanth. There would be a larger perimeter to fight through, more lines of thralls at their backs to block their escape.

Together, though, the four of them knew that even if it came to blasting through the opposition, they were still limited by several things. They knew that their opposition was composed of innocents enthralled by the pair of winged demigods. And they had a limited supply of ammunition, even if they didn't care about causing lethal harm to the mental slaves.

As of now, Edwards and Sinclair were scanning the skies with their IR optics, picking up the heat signatures of several small birds in flight. They swept the air above them, staying as still as possible. There was a dull dread hanging in the night, if only for the fact that they knew their enemy had its own air force, the very birds of this area.

If there were raptors in the area, then there was also a likelihood that Vanth wouldn't even need to send actual troops to bring them down. A bird of prey hitting with its claws at over 50 miles an hour, up to 120 in some instances, was more than sufficient to slice through shadow suit and flesh easily.

"I'm watching for patterns among the birds." Sinclair spoke softly, only truly audible thanks to the Commtact's jawbone microphone pickups and inner ear stimulation. "They're not acting as observers. If one bird passes, it doesn't come back this way, not even making a wide berth."

"You're going by twentieth-century unmanned aerial vehicle surveillance tactics, right?" Edwards asked. "You had like…what? One or two up at a time?"

Sinclair nodded. Domi could hear her hiss of disgust as Sinclair realized that with all of the night flying, one bird wouldn't need to circle them to keep track. Not with waves of sets of eyes that could be in the air. Even so, the flights overhead didn't seem to be particularly concentrated. The whole thing reminded Domi of the sweep of that line on the circular radar screen, illuminating targets with each pass.

As long as they continued their slow crawl, as long as their shadow suits matched the ground beneath them, and as long as they only really moved quickly in the lulls between the mind-controlled eyes in the sky, they wouldn't be found.

As if that hopeful thought summoned down the wrath of Charun and Vanth, Domi spotted a flicker in the distance, the glow of multiple torches illuminating the movements of a patrolling group. Domi kept the team still. CAT Beta and Smaragda used the telescopic aspects of their shadow suit hoods to zoom in on those distant lights.

Three hundred yards away, they saw a group of ten people. They were locals, dressed in simple, handmade clothing, but each of them had either a brutal farm implement or a firearm. They were searching; a party of mixed men and women thralls.

Edwards spoke up first this time.

"They're actively searching for us," he subvocalized through the Commtact. "Their eyes are at least more animated now."

"Maybe Charun figured out that you were camouflaged near the Manta's landing site," Sinclair offered.

"It's weird. They're just below looking human," Smaragda mentioned, her voice also a low whisper. "Like…"

"Robots. Zombies," Domi muttered. She was put on edge by all of this, as well.

If there were people and birds out in the night searching, then there could have been other hunters. Domi swept the closer terrain. They were in waist-high grass, which meant there could be all sorts of smaller mammals present, but if there was one thing the feral girl was good at, it was spotting those little morsels that would keep her alive and surviving for another day, be it in a forest or a desert. Her instincts looked for mice, voles, rabbits and, with some relief, she came up with nothing. That didn't mean the tiniest of animals was ignored by the demigods, but it did tell the wild woman that those miniature mammals weren't being used as spies and seekers right here.

It was a small measure of relief.

"Do we wait for them to pass?" Edwards asked.

"No. But we stay slow and steady," Domi returned. "Birds, Sela?"

"None," Sinclair returned.

"Move," Domi ordered.

And she took the lead, her petite form crawling out, slender arms and legs carrying her along in a crawl that would approximate a fast walk as long as she wasn't among tall grasses that would sway with her passage. It was an achingly slow process, pausing every time Sinclair hissed and indicated something was in the air over them.

By the time that they reached the road where the search party patrolled, the thralls were out of sight, the glow of their torches having disappeared around the bend of trees. Even so, Domi flicked on her infrared vision and was able to capture the heat sources of those burning brands even through intervening foliage. She returned to her normal, natural vision, and waved the others onto the road with her. Their shadow suits shifted, blending into the dirt road, taking on tones of brown and rust to match the well-trampled earth that made up the path.

"There's a canopy of trees," Sinclair noted. "Sweeping for heat sources."

Domi nodded. They didn't dare move until they were certain that nothing was waiting on a tree limb or in a knot hole, serving as a living security camera for the Etruscan godlings.

Once that was cleared up, they continued moving, picking up their pace. Sinclair remained on infrared, counting on the heat given off by Domi's bare feet to mark a safe walking path, all the while keeping her head on a swivel. Tension, living and moving in the shadows or the breaths between moments without birds in the sky.

This was nothing new to Domi. This was where she was born, skulking in the shadows against authority and predation that would slam down upon her and end her existence. It was tense, it was tough, but there was one thing that would make this worth all the anxiety, all the stealth.

Freedom for those currently hounding them, freedom from Vanth and Charun's domination of their lives.

This deadly game of hide-and-seek had only one acceptable outcome for Domi and her friends, and that was the fall of the winged conquerors.

Chapter 11

Brigid Baptiste tested her weight on her foot once more. It had been an entire day since the others had left for Italy via interphaser. She'd been bedridden, eating aspirin and trying to relax her strained system thanks to a psychic battle against the song of Vanth. EKGs immediately after showed that her heart had irregular rhythms, rendering her in less than optimal condition to penetrate into enemy territory.

The aspirin pills were meant to bring her heartbeat back into normal parameters. They must have worked, since it was the morning after her friends had left and her EKGs over the past eight hours had proved normal. The acetaminophen had also worked wonders on her tender sprained ankle, as she was able to walk securely on it.

Of course, even if she wanted to take the interphaser, Kane and the rest of the Cerberus teams had thirty-six hours' worth of a head start on her. No, what she needed to do was to wait. Kane and Grant had done plenty of work making certain she was checked out on the Mantas, and she could fly them adequately enough. She wouldn't be an air combat ace, but she could land a Manta in a clearing, and keep control of it as it skimmed ten miles above the Earth at supersonic speed.

Her role was rapid response, so being "stuck" back here minding the store was a necessary evil. So far, the only thing reported from the field was Kane and Grant's encounter with the cyclops. The others had gone into radio silence, which made Brigid feel a little more edgy than normal. She was not a sit-back-and-wait kind of woman. She was an explorer, an adventurer. Her hunger for new knowledge, as well as her obligation to assist the helpless, demanded that she be up and around.

Diana had informed Brigid that she was free to keep herself in condition, mentally and physically, making use of the Olympian library as well as physical rehabilitation.

After ice baths and hot wraps, Brigid's ankle was feeling as strong as ever. She could put her full weight on it, and her ligaments had returned to full limberness. While there were medical facilities and a gymnasium back at the Cerberus Redoubt, New Olympus had far more cause and need to engage in physical rehabilitation. There were those who were catastrophically injured, to the point where amputations were needed to prevent suffering from gangrene. Then there were others with less dramatic wounds, so that Olympian doctors became a well-oiled machine when it came to pulled and sprained limbs, as well as broken bones.

Brigid continued flexing her ankle, pivoting on it to make sure she hadn't merely numbed it.

"You keep working that ankle at that rate, you'll ruin it again." Diana spoke up. "Then again, what would I know? I lost my feet years ago."

Brigid sat, laying a towel around her neck. She'd worked up a good sweat, hoping that her body's exertions would distract her. There was no such luck, and she was starting to grow sick of the walls around her. "Thanks for the use of the facilities."

"I'm surprised that you haven't been in the library," Diana noted, rolling closer.

Brigid smirked sheepishly. "There isn't much that I haven't already read there."

"Even in the original Greek?" Diana asked.

Brigid nodded. "I ended up learning Greek while doing background on the Annunaki's presence in ancient Greece. It's where I managed to pick up so much information about your country."

"And since you can read both languages…"

"Speed read," Brigid returned. "Whatever I hadn't read through in the past, I've been checking out since yesterday morning while sitting in the tub." Brigid casually gestured over toward the therapy tub and the two stacks of books next to it.

"You're that anxious about your friends," Diana said.

"I'm that obvious?"

The queen of New Olympus chuckled. "It kills me that I can't go out as a commander anymore in the field. The first few days stuck running this place, even with Ari's help, I was getting ready to chew my own leg off to escape this trap."

"Looks like you succeeded," Brigid noted.

Diana's laugh was loud and long. "Aristotle's about the only one who rides me and jokes about me anymore. I needed that."

"I figured. I've been watching and seeing how uncomfortable you are with all the adulation," Brigid said.

"And despite everything, I can't really order them to stop," Diana added. "They need someone to fight for. A standard to live up to. Which hurts, because I used to lead from the front."

"And you're looking for me to give you a means to feel like one of the boys again?" Brigid asked.

Diana shrugged. "Maybe."

Brigid nodded.

"It's hard to explain…I thought, maybe since we share a similar background…"

"You want to feel like you're doing actual work,"

Brigid said. "And you've been wired to feel like administration and being the leader isn't sufficient employment for you."

"Yes," Diana said. "I mean, I hardly get time to rest, but…"

"Do you have a cabinet, through which you can free up time?" Brigid asked.

Diana tilted her head. "A cabinet?"

"Maybe even make it more democratic, or representative. That might give you room so that you're not overstressed, but you're also not slacking in leadership. You and Aristotle are in charge. You want to engage in activity that may threaten the continuity of government. But, if you have someone to fill in, so there is no chaos should something happen…"

"I get back to being Diana, warrior queen," she replied.

"Technically, Hera," Brigid responded. "The inertia of recent history and the logic of Greek mythology do dictate that Zeus and Hera *must* sit atop the throne of New Olympus."

"Except Ari isn't much like Zeus. No sprinkling down into town as gold dust or mating with women as a swan," Diana added.

"You'd prefer that?" Brigid asked.

Diana shook her head. "No. But, hey, Zeus got to spend time away from the halls of the Pantheon. Why can't Hera be like that?"

"There is no reason you should allow yourself to be marginalized," Brigid returned.

The armrest on her chair beeped. "Hey, Di."

"Fast." Diana greeted her mechanic, Hephaestus. "Word on the Manta?"

"Yup. We managed to rig together a cowling," the top technician said over the radio. "Any time that Ms. Baptiste needs, she can hop in and get moving."

"That much is a relief," Brigid admitted. "Can I come down and see her?"

"Sure, if you have the time," Fast answered.

"Give me fifteen and I'll be right there," Brigid said. "Your Majesty…"

"Go. You've been idling around here long enough," Diana told her.

THE SUN HAD risen a half hour earlier and, judging by the distance Grant and Kane had "jumped" with the interphaser, it still would not be the break of dawn for Brigid and New Olympus for another several minutes. This wasn't much of a concern, at least for the two men, because they had managed to get snippets of rest.

Whereas they had sent Domi and the others along in a stealthy fashion, neither Grant nor Kane was actively trying to avoid patrols or detection. They continued their steady approach to the site of the "missing" parallax point, obviously armed and wearing their shadow suits.

The full capabilities of Vanth and Charun were unknown, but they hoped to provide CAT Beta with as much obfuscation as they could. They were the bait, the lamb in the trap to draw in a lion. So far, they'd pulled in enough attention in the form of a cyclops, but at this point, they were not certain of exactly how much they were facing.

They had managed to outpace the monstrosity left behind, so that gave them some feeling that they'd distracted the demigods so far. During the night, Grant informed Kane that birds were flying overhead, sweeping past their position as they'd encamped. Neither man needed nor wanted a fire in the dark, thanks to the environmental features of the high-tech shadow suits.

Even so, they built a small fire just to make themselves easier to find.

Now Kane could see, in the distance, a group of people walking along the road. They had torches, still lit in the morning gloom. Grant picked up on them, as well, and the big man flicked off the safety on his shotgun, just in case.

"I count eight," Grant stated.

Kane nodded in agreement. "And they're armed."

"Not quite a band of coldbloods, though," Grant added. "It's a mix of long arms and really sharp farm implements."

"Cover me. I'll try to talk to them," Kane said.

Grant glanced at his friend. "Well, we are hanging our asses out here for Charun and Vanth to grab."

Grant took cover behind the trunk of a thick tree. Part of what gave Kane hope was that the less-lethal shotgun slugs would fly far and true, unlike conventional shot, which would disperse and lose power over even thirty yards. From his standpoint, Grant could easily snipe any of the gunmen should things grow dangerous.

Kane slung his shotgun. If necessary, the Sin Eater on his forearm would flash into his palm, but as there was very little in terms of less-lethal ammunition for the Magistrate's signature side arm, he would only use it as a last resort. The day he couldn't protect himself from a group of farmers, especially ones under mind control, was the day he felt he'd have to hang up his shadow suit.

It was a mix of men and women, but there was no division among the sexes for the weapons they bore. There were only two torches among them, and already, having cleared the canopy of the forest, the bearers were dousing them in the dirt, grinding them out and smothering them. Later tonight, if they were still on patrol, then they'd be relit, but for now, they were annoyances.

The group locked eyes on him; sixteen orbs drained of color and vitality, with a milky appearance that glimmered in the sunrise, all aimed toward him like the sickly pustules. Kane swallowed, shaking off the unease at the slack, emotionless faces those blank orbs resided in.

Definitely under control, Kane thought. He wondered what kind of response he would get, burying the niggling fear of the "uncanny valley" before him. The people were absolutely normal in appearance, except they didn't act, didn't have emotion. This produced a kind of fear in most people, known as the uncanny valley. The closer to human an artificial entity appeared, the more disturbing it was. Every instinct in Kane informed him that these were *not* humans, more like something that wore people the way he wore clothing.

Though not a single gun was leveled at Kane, those eyes dug at him, relentless drills of eerie, silent inhumanity. He made certain the Commtact was set to Italian translation and spoke. He was glad for the fear, because fear produced adrenaline, and adrenaline not only boosted blood flow and reaction time, it also sharpened senses and made thought clearer. If they truly were a deadly threat, then he could explode into instantaneous action.

"I am Kane, of Cerberus Redoubt," he announced.

The faces were unchanged in response to his statement, but the person closest to him, a pallid woman with black curls spilling down to her shoulders, began speaking.

"Welcome to my land."

Kane's nose twitched as she spoke clear, perfect English without the necessity of the translation matrix. Her voice, however, was deep, resonant. The black-haired woman was far too wispy for such a tone of voice. Of course, the reverberation and tone were very close to the words of an Annunaki overlord, something that seemed projected across multiple wavelengths.

That made Kane all the more on edge, especially for the fact that the demigods were very much like the godlings he had been battling since the arrival of *Tiamat* and the evolution of the hybrid barons into their true forms.

"We come in peace," Kane offered, fighting off the thrash of thoughts suddenly racing through his mind. Thinking ahead, or solving mysteries, was one thing he could do, but not when he was within arm's length of a group of potential opponents.

The woman nodded. "And yet, you come knowing that something is wrong. Or do you merely come to retrieve your aircraft?"

"A little of both," Kane answered truthfully, frustrated that there was no emotional reaction to let him know what was going on behind those pale eggs that were supposed to be her eyes. "We came armed, because this is a dangerous world."

"As we are armed, as well," the woman told him.

No movement. No coughs. No shuffling of feet. Right now, the eight people were as motionless as statues, save for the lips of their spokeswoman. Any change only came when Kane shifted his own weight from foot to foot, because even without the black spots of pupils in their eyes, he could *feel* their eyes follow his motion. "You wouldn't happen to know anything about giants in the area, would you?"

Kane hoped to keep the situation defused, steering away the concept of the thralls being the danger he was armed against.

"The cyclops," the woman answered. "We thought it merely a myth, but it has come to my land. It is an annoyance."

Kane narrowed his eyes. "Annoyance?"

"The creation of those…not like me," the woman said.

"You are Vanth, then. That's who I'm speaking to, right?" Kane asked.

"Of course," she replied. "You know me by my husband. Charun. And presumably from your comrade, who managed to elude even my huntress senses."

"Yeah," Kane confirmed.

"I do not mind your pilot's evasion of me, nor of his attack against my beloved," the woman stated. "Charun is a formidable, fearsome warrior, more so in his war paint and battle gear."

"War paint," Kane repeated.

"You may inform your friend behind the tree that he no longer has to protect you. If you wish to accompany us back, you will come as guests." Vanth's voice echoed.

Grant's grunt of surprise over the open Commtact alerted Kane that the demigoddess had spoken into his ears, as well, despite a distance of fifty meters.

"Do you wish to disarm us?" Kane inquired.

The black-haired spokeswoman shook her head. "There would be no point. You are guests. Not prisoners."

Kane nodded. He glanced back quickly to make sure Grant was on his way.

"We are interested in you two, and the woman who usually accompanies you," Vanth said as Grant jogged forward.

"She's at home. Recovering," Kane answered.

"Baptiste was her name."

Kane's lips tightened. He had no real reason to be surprised, though. He had a suspicion about the source of Vanth's knowledge.

"Yes. I have heard of you, from the thoughts of others," Vanth stated.

"The missing New Olympian platoon and pilots?" Kane prompted.

Vanth allowed her thrall a smirk, the flex of lips. "Aye."

The search group turned as one, more indication of their alien nature, or the alien nature of the consciousness in control of them.

Grant stood shoulder to shoulder with Kane, watching the group as they proceeded, leading the way down the road.

"Either we're heading into the biggest trap in the world, or they think we're insects compared to them," Grant mused softly.

"Seems like a bit of both," Kane said. "After all, some of our biggest, Manta-mounted weapons couldn't hurt Charun, so why should guys on foot, with much smaller guns, be such a threat?"

"I apologize for the damage of your craft, Grant," a voice boomed from ahead. The two Cerberus warriors looked to see who was speaking, even looking up into the canopy of the trees, just in case Charun himself had flown to greet them.

It turned out to be one of the men, who slowed, dropping back to walk beside them.

The man was slender, but he spoke with the timber of a lion, each word bearing enormous weight as it was spoken. The man was equipped only with a sledgehammer, as if in echo of the original Charun himself. Kane wondered if the black-haired woman had a bow of some form, but then recalled that she had been one of the group snuffing out torches with the sun. Brigid's description of Vanth's torch flared freshly in his memory.

It all could have been a coincidence.

"You came toward us fast," Grant said.

A chuckle thumped from a chest too tiny to contain it. "Of course I did. My lover and I felt you breach the dimensions at the Oracle. We thought it enemies, returned to torment us."

"Who'd be your enemy?" Grant asked.

"The gods of the Isles…to the north and to the west," Charun said. "They sent their one-eyed minions to conquer us, and eventually, the hair-shirted humans who worshiped them came and tore down the empire of our children."

"The Tuatha de Danaan?" Grant asked. "Wait, one-eyed...like the Fomori."

Kane and Grant agreed to show very little foreknowledge of the Fomori.

"Yes. A bastard half-breed by the name of Bres...his minions roamed as far as my borders. I enjoyed crushing armies of them with my bride," Charun added. "Have you heard of him?"

"Only in respect to the Celtic gods," Kane answered. "The ones the Tuatha masqueraded as."

Charun nodded.

"It is a pleasure to meet the enemy of our enemies," Charun stated.

"Likewise," Kane answered.

Then Charun's puppet rejoined the rest of his group, leaving Kane alone with Grant.

There was very little wonder that they were being observed from tree branches by perched birds and other mammals. The moment the humans came into view, they had already been surrounded. The tiny, milk-white eyes of the mind-controlled animals followed them with the same penetrating dread.

Yeah, Grant is right, Kane thought. They think we're less than insects to them.

Kane ground his teeth.

And this time the bastard demigods might actually be right.

Chapter 12

Mohandas Lakesh Singh stirred from his too empty, lonely bed with the chirping of his Commtact, an alert that a signal had been received from Kane and Grant.

"I'm awake," Lakesh murmured, yawning and looking at the empty space where Domi should have been sleeping. He ran his fingers through his thick, gray hair, matting it back down even as the swift, tight-beam transmission was translated and transmitted via the computers.

"Contact made. Invited in. Everything mind controlled down to squirrels and sparrows."

It was Kane, subvocalizing and sending off the message with all the speed he could.

Charun and Vanth were so sure of themselves that they didn't even seem to care about the message transmitted by the two…prisoners? Guests? Visitors?

Lakesh was full of worry. While Kane and Grant were walking tall through the front doors of Charun and Vanth's kingdom, his love, Domi, was moving in stealthily, along with the rest of her team and one other. If there was someone who could travel undetected, it was the albino girl, a stalker of both wilderness and urban apocalypse. The same went for Edwards, a Magistrate who'd patrolled through the Tartarus Pits as a lawman in a dangerous fringe town.

CAT Beta was nearly as skilled and experienced as CAT Alpha, so he *shouldn't* have been so fearful for

Domi's safety. Logic dictated that, but Lakesh was someone who trusted as much in intangibles that lay outside the realms of hard numbers and mathematics. Things such as the confluence of luck, a manner of superstition that in the experiences of the Cerberus Redoubt "family" was more than just mystic mumbo jumbo. There was an entire quantum universe out there, one with multitudes of probabilities and realities, and somehow Kane, Brigid and Grant had proved to be the cornerstone of the movement, defying long odds and surviving.

True, the three of them were merely human, capable of being hurt. Brigid was getting over a sprained ankle. Grant still sported a bruise on his back and Kane himself had escape a serious concussion, or worse, by degrees. And yet their skills had been sufficient to send first the barons and then the overlords scrambling to the winds. They'd held off the invasion and near conquest of the Earth by one of Enlil's most dangerous sons, as well.

Through strength, courage and intellect, they had done the best to return humanity to ruling itself, shucking off the manacles of slavery to the alien Annunaki. Yet there were still so-called gods out there, struggling and conspiring to bring down humankind. Vanth and Charun stunk of such alien, monstrous heritage, of the same cruel dreams of conquest.

The video Brigid had transmitted back to Cerberus, Edwards's recordings of the missing New Olympian soldiers scanning the Manta's landing and Charun's fallen hammer, were proof positive that their powers of mind control were a deadly threat to any and all life forms on Earth.

Kane's assertion that even the beasts of the Etruscan countryside were enthralled only hammered home that point. It was one thing to have control of hundreds, even thousands, of human minds. Kane and the others knew how to deal with humans, even to the point of being able to take control of the situation without harming the hypnotized.

But how did you deal with swarms of rats or flocks of attacking birds? Domi had also transmitted the night before, having captured some footage of sheep on one farm that CAT Beta had neared. On enhanced resolution, Lakesh saw into milky, lifeless eyes as rams and ewes went about their life of chewing cud and yet existing as just more observers. Lakesh remembered in his youth, hundreds of years before, when he'd been at a petting zoo.

There were goats at the petting zoo, and while Lakesh was bored, having to hang around all the "kid stuff"— a pun he'd been pleased with himself over—he watched as one of the animal handlers began to have trouble with one of the rams. The sheep reared up and suddenly went on the offensive, slamming the keeper, a burly, barrel-chested man of six feet. The man collapsed, stunned by the sudden assault.

The goat continued its attack, biting at the keeper's cheek and ear, coming away with blood all over its snout, the human's face slick and red from such injuries.

That was one goat, only needing to use its horns once. The Italian countryside was full of such similar livestock, and the threat of all those jaws and teeth, formerly only meant for slicing tough grasses and twigs, suddenly became dark and deadly. Rats were equally as imposing, should they swarm and attack. There were tales of sewer workers who suffered countless lacerations and infections from stumbling into a nest full of the rodents.

Brigid had told Lakesh, as she'd told her compatriots in New Olympus, that Vanth promised to unleash those trapped beyond the dimensional doors to her home "world" like a plague of locusts.

Maybe the threat of invasion wasn't a physical one but

one of alien control. At this moment Charun and Vanth both appeared to be superhumanly strong examples of humanoids, but what if they were simply ideas? Concepts? What if they were spirits hurled across the gulf of the multiverse divides, finding their homes inside the flesh of two unfortunates?

What if the parallax point they were trying to breach only needed the merest of pinpricks in terms of an opening? The invasion wouldn't come in the form of living bodies, hurtling through a schism, a tear in time space, but a leak. Millions of alien minds flowing through a wormhole as if it were a vent in a dam? Thousands of ghosts or thought packets hurtling through per second, each seeking out the closest vacated central nervous system?

Brigid relayed that Vanth was seeking all of these minds for power, but what if the opening of that door was two ways? The emptied shells of the living, stripped of their intellect and free will, their emotions, their *souls*, would punch a hole through universes and then provide safe landing areas for those millions of invaders.

Lakesh shook his head at the concept.

"Boss, you got the message?" Bry asked.

Lakesh nodded, despite the fact that Bry was halfway across the redoubt. "Yes, yes, friend Bry. I have received the message. Have you relayed it on to Domi and the others?"

"Coded and direct-burst transmission made," Bry answered. "Hopefully, it cut through so fast our Italian bogeyman didn't hear a thing."

"There is that hope," Lakesh responded. "Though, as you may have heard, Kane isn't particularly convinced that Vanth or Charun is concerned about our interference or communication."

"You got that from six or seven words?" Bry asked.

Lakesh chuckled. "It's all in the tone. Plus, I believe he's been taking lessons from Domi in being succinct."

"That'd do it," Bry answered. "Are you coming to the command center?"

"I'll be there in a bit. We've got more information to go over, don't we?" Lakesh said.

"Yup. Vid of the first contact rode in on the same info dump," Bry responded.

Lakesh nodded. "I'll be there in a bit."

He swung his legs over the side of the bed. For someone who had lost over 150 years of aging and cryogenic suspension, and all accompanying ailments and aches, he still felt tired and achy being roused from his slumber. Lakesh knew, though, that his sleep was never as relaxing as when his beloved little Domi was curled against his side. She was at once a calming influence in her presence and a cause of worry with her absence.

He'd be much happier, much more secure, when everyone was back home.

The trouble was, if they had never gone out there in the first place, menaces to humanity would eventually seep their way back to Cerberus Redoubt.

There was duty putting them all out there in the line of danger.

It was a duty that not even Lakesh would feel right shirking.

By THE TIME they had traveled along the road toward where Charun and Vanth had set up their shop, Grant and Kane were tired. It'd been a brisk four-hour march, one that didn't show on the faces of their ensorcelled escorts, but was evident in the slowing of their step and limps that showed up on some.

Kane, younger than his partner, was not feeling as tender as Grant, but even so, he didn't think he had it in him to walk all the way back to their initial landing point. The reverse trip would take at least six hours at a saner pace, but the godlings wanted to meet the two human emissaries from Cerberus.

When the escort finally stopped walking, they were on a rocky, barren seeming countryside, with no sign of life, save for sprigs and individual blades of grass.

"This doesn't look like any ancient temple to me," Grant said, looking around. Since the parallax points were places where reality thinned sufficiently to allow them to receive communications, or even direct visits from the so-called ancient gods, humankind quickly grew into the habit of building shrines and temples at such places of power. This hill, while fairly flat and pyramid-like in shape, was nothing special. Then again, the fact that Grant immediately thought "pyramid" might have been a cue that the hill was not what it seemed.

"No, it doesn't," Kane agreed. "But you can feel the vibes, can't you?"

Grant glanced at his younger friend. "Not particularly, but the first thing I thought when I saw this was pyramid."

"A buried pyramid, like Xian in China? But this is nowhere near that scale."

"Let's keep heading toward the apex. That's usually where the actual center of power is on these things," Grant suggested.

Kane nodded and followed his partner. As they neared the peak, there was a faint rumble, the scraping of stone on stone as the point of this pyramid was pushed aside. The two men stopped, watching a long, powerful arm finish opening the top, then climb up and out of the hill. It was the same being he'd seen two days earlier, tall and long of limb, with muscles packed like tightened cables along his powerful frame. He did not have his batlike wings, but then, there was the possibility that those appendages were simply part of a flight harness.

This was Charun, his features much less twisted and distorted, the war paint having gone away. This was a god who was receiving visitors, not a captor.

Grant hoped that the situation would remain so.

"Greetings." Charun spoke, his voice sotto voce and rumbling through the air about them.

"Vanth was not kidding about war paint," Kane observed.

The giant's mouth opened into a smile. Charun still possessed tusks, but his face was not twisted in the semblance of rage. His skin was still coated in a fine patina of scales, meaning that his heritage was not much different from an Annunaki's, but his blue tint may have been a racial variation. Grant was used to being the tallest man in the room, but even he had to look up to Charun as he strode closer, towering at least two heads taller than him.

The Etruscan godling extended a big, beefy hand, and Grant accepted the offered handshake. The last time Grant remembered his hand being so small in someone else's was when he was a child, holding hands with his father. The giant was far too cordial, too smiling, to be at all concerned by the Cerberus pair's presence as Charun moved on to Kane.

"Welcome to our home," he said. He swept an arm toward the open top of the hill. "Mind you, be careful. The ladder was built for people of our size, not smaller. While it certainly will not collapse under your weight, you might not be able to grip it as firmly as one of us."

"Why...thank you," Kane said.

"Did you take the Manta down that shaft?" Grant asked.

"Oh, no...there is an alternate entrance," Charun said.

"However, we're going to keep that location secret from you."

"Understood. You don't need rats crawling in your back door," Grant agreed.

Inwardly, he felt bad for referring to CAT Beta as rats, but the alluded-to entrance was exactly what those four would need to penetrate into the depths of the Etruscan gods' pyramid.

Kane paused, looking down the ladder. "I didn't think that pyramids had been built in Europe. There've been plenty in Asia and South America…and naturally in North Africa…"

"There are more in what you humans used to call Bulgaria. A whole complex of them," Charun stated.

Kane was first down the ladder and Charun motioned for Grant to go next.

The huge demigod was correct about the sturdiness of the ladder, as well as the thickness of the rungs. However with their non-slip gloves and boots, there was little to fear from losing his grip and hurtling down the ladder. He took a glance up, and saw Charun following. Thankfully, the loin piece that the giant wore was a one piece that covered anything beneath, folded over a belt in the front and in the back.

"We're entering an ancient pyramid in Italy, and the only thing I can worry about is an alien up-skirt," Grant said into the Commtact for Kane to hear.

There was a snort, both above and below.

"You are welcome, Grant!" Charun exhorted.

"Busted," Kane added.

"Good ears," Grant said aloud.

"Having spent time inside the brains of you humans, I can pity the dullness of your senses," Charun called down. "And I can understand the disgust at some of the appearances of your own bodies."

"Yeah?" Grant asked. This conversation was going to make or break a lot of things. So far, Charun had demonstrated that there was very little that could escape his attention, part of the reason he even made the quiet aside to Kane. If Charun hadn't acknowledged it, then there was always the possibility of slipping up and speaking wrongly. Right now, Grant and Kane had to be on their best behavior. On the other hand, Charun's acknowledgment could have been because he wasn't some form of menace.

That bit of information didn't jibe well with what Brigid Baptiste had reported from her mental duel with the Vanth virus that had invaded her mind. Then again, Vanth presented herself as an angelic beauty—what was to say that she wasn't a mistress of deception, seduction and subterfuge? This wouldn't be the first schism between so-called partners, even among the gods. The fall of the Annunaki as a world-shaking power had been due to Overlord Lilitu's gambit to supplant Enlil as the highest authority. That scheme had fallen apart, as well as gutted the gigantic living star ship *Tiamat*.

Maybe Charun was a nice guy, but that still meant that Vanth was all the more of a trickster.

"We regret having to utilize the higher intellects of your people, and even your livestock, but Vanth and I are careful not to endanger the bodies of those we've borrowed," Charun added.

Kane hopped off the ladder upon reaching the bottom. Grant and the demigod joined him immediately.

"'Borrowed,'" Kane repeated.

"Yes. We've been looking for a sufficient source through which to open an aperture between this dimension and our home." Charun sighed. "You have a fine world here, especially with the stink of the Annunaki scoured from it…"

"Not quite scoured," Grant corrected.

"This area is free of their reek," Charun responded. "And thus, we no longer have to worry about them swooping down on us. You are to thank for much of that."

"We are?" Grant asked.

Sure, Grant was playing dumb for the moment, but he was still surprised at the kind of weight the New Olympian soldiers had put on the efforts of the Cerberus heroes. After all, they had fought with irrepressible courage and willingness to die for their countrymen. The final battle with the Enlil-empowered Hydrae hordes had resulted in casualties. Hundreds were wounded and scores had died, but the line was held if only for the stubbornness of the Greek warriors, either inside massive armored robots or merely on the ground, clad in leather and Kevlar.

That was a day of conflict that had been one unlike Grant had experienced before or since. And Grant had not been on the battlefield, fighting scale-hide-armored mutates and bloody-clawed giant sloths, but he'd also been with Kane aboard Marduk's scout ship, sabotaging it and wreaking havoc to keep the overlord and his Nephilim forces out of the conflict. Grant had thrown every dirty infighting trick in the book at Marduk, cheap shots and blindside attacks giving the big man those few extra ounces of edge against the seven-foot Annunaki demigod.

The hammering assault on the bridge of Marduk's scout ship bought Kane enough time to plant sabotage charges along the length of the scout ship, gutting it, slaughtering nearly half of its crew and forcing the overlord to abandon Greece.

Those memories should have been resigned to a side note in New Olympus history, but Charun seemed highly interested in this part of the pair.

Maybe he wasn't *threatened* by the humans, but

Charun seemed to be actively trying to engage their friendship and cooperation.

"You said you were only borrowing their minds. How… and how will they get them back?" Grant asked the demigod.

"Vanth explained that we're utilizing their higher brain functions as extra processors. We're dividing some extremely complex mathematical equations among a little over a million brain stems," Charun stated.

"You're using them as calculators," Kane said.

"Exactly. Essentially, we're doing what your ancient ancestors would call casting a spell. Except, we're doing it in the very code of which the multiverse is written upon," Charun explained. "Once we open up that door, we can go home."

Grant nodded. "That makes sense. But what are the number crunchers getting out of this?"

"They will be the ones who might just give you humans the means to spread out among the stars," another voice interjected into the conversation.

Kane and Grant both turned, watching the entrance of Vanth, tall, beautiful and half naked, striding as if she had not a care in the world.

"My beautiful, brilliant bride," Charun said.

Grant and Kane nodded; a subtle bow to the woman upon her entry.

"Gentle humans," Vanth said. "Welcome."

"Milady," Grant greeted. "The means of humans traveling to the stars?"

"The use of craft is all well and good, but the same roads that crisscross this ball of dirt are only a small factor of the equation that is the universe," Vanth stated. "There are similar roads, marked by magnetic fields, but they stretch from world to world, from star system to star system, and from galaxy to galaxy."

The brown-haired beauty stepped closer, a smirk brightening her features.

"With the equations your fellow Earthlings have been given, you can spill into the universe like unto a plague of locusts."

Chapter 13

The eyes of Vanth were like jewels set ablaze from within, anchoring Kane's gaze as her oddly harmonic voice buzzed both in his ears and his mind. This was the same kind of sensation that he'd felt, ever since Balam first "opened that door"—communicating with him through telepathy. It was a switch that never turned off, and Kane didn't like the tingles, the tickles of Vanth's power brushing across his brain, as if the folds on its surface were the hair of her lover. It was eerie, invasive, and at the flash of his anger of recognition, she withdrew, her smile fading.

"Lady Vanth," Kane greeted her, doing his best to stifle the tension in his vocal cords.

"Have you been giving these warriors the grand tour?" Vanth asked Charun.

The male demigod nodded. "The only thing that we're really missing is the third member of their trinity. The human woman, Brigid."

Vanth frowned, conveying an all too human disappointment. "What has kept her?"

"She suffered some minor injuries, so we did not feel that she would be up for the trek from the alternate parallax point we landed at," Kane answered truthfully. His will was a brick wall, and that was bolstered by Brigid's posthypnotic suggestions, sublimating his suspicions and worries deep, beyond the reach of a mere surface scan.

Using mostly intact truths would prevent her from sensing anything wrong.

It was not going to be a perfect solution, especially if Vanth's mental abilities were truly powerful. Kane's will had been tested by telepathic goddesses of late, and he didn't feel like pressing his luck. So far, however, he didn't feel as if she'd broken through anything.

Then again, it wasn't as if she'd leave a note pinned to the inside of his brain where he could find it. That was what truly sucked about this for Kane. He'd been made aware enough to know what was happening, but there was very little he could do by way of mental inventory that would give him an idea of how much his thoughts were rummaged and searched.

"Well, you surely have another aircraft like the one we requisitioned," Vanth stated.

"It was under repairs last we saw it," Grant answered. He nodded toward Charun. "This guy did quite a number on it."

"Ah, yes," Charun noted with a chuckle. "We have taken good care of your other craft. I hope you did not punish its pilot too much for fleeing from our arrival."

"We went easy on him. If he couldn't hurt you with the weapons mounted on it, there was no way he could deal with you carrying a mere side arm," Kane said.

Charun smiled, his shoulders straightening a little further, his chest jutting an inch or two more with pride over the power he had displayed and the intimidation he wielded as a warrior god. Kane couldn't tell if the demigod was buying into this through ego, or that he and Grant were simply good actors.

"So, you want me to pop over and bring Brigid?" Kane asked.

"Whoever wishes to fly the Manta, as you call it," Charun offered. "I would assume that you would go,

Kane, for your frame would allow more room for her as a passenger."

Grant looked at Kane. "He has a point."

"You are near the size of one of us, Grant," Charun stated. He rested a large hand on the big Magistrate's shoulder, making him feel as if he were a child once more. "There will be no harm to befall him under my protection."

"You're sure?" Kane asked.

"We shall have the ship readied for you," Vanth told them. "Then we shall have the three who are as one as our guests."

Kane was once more glad for the posthypnotic suggestions that drained any tension or relief from his features. This was feeling more and more like a trap.

Maybe the "virus" that had infected Brigid was either still alive or had managed to transmit a distress call back to its originator. Kane didn't have a clue as to how the goddess's song worked, but he wouldn't put it past Vanth to actually be able to fragment her intellect to the point where such a mind control effort could call back to her.

"How soon would that be?" Kane asked.

"We will take some time for you to rest your tired limbs and to fill your bellies," Charun stated. "While the appropriated Spartans carry the Manta outside, you'll have at least an hour of relaxation with us."

"Sounds good," Grant returned. Kane could feel the hint of sarcasm in his friend's voice.

Eat, drink and be merry, humans, Kane imagined the thoughts of the entities in front of them. For tonight, we steal your souls.

"You can't be serious," Brigid said over the Commtact.

"I'm as serious as I've ever been," Kane returned. "Vanth wants you to come visit us in the scenic, placid

Etruscan countryside. She promises wine and the mathematical secrets that will enable us to leave the Earth far behind."

"That is a tempting offer," Brigid replied.

Neither of them was speaking about it out loud, but the implications of all three of them being summoned before Vanth were dangerous. Brigid had done what she could to reinforce the minds of her comrades that had gone on ahead, and she had also self-hypnotized, compartmentalizing the memories she possessed of Vanth's viral knowledge entering her brain.

Such autohypnotic suggestion had carried her against the intrusion and violation of Ullikummis, so maybe it would work again. If not, it was unlikely she would ever know what happened. Her precautions could prove for naught against a superior hand at mind control, and the stresses of her battle against Vanth's projection still made her wary.

"And you won't even have to walk far on your game ankle," Kane added. "I can pick you up and fly you right here."

"Why can't I use the interphaser again?" Brigid asked.

"Because of the efforts of Vanth to open up a wormhole at the parallax point here," Kane explained. "So she and Charun could return home."

"All right," Brigid said. "When can you get going over here?"

"I'm outside with Grant. We're running down the checklist to make sure the thing is still in full flying condition," Kane told her.

"So far, looks all right," she heard Grant on the party line.

"You're not worried about staying there alone?" Brigid inquired.

"What could they do to me that they couldn't have a

dozen times over?" Grant answered. "I'll be fine. I can't wait to see you again."

Brigid admired her two partners in adventure. They maintained their calm, and sounded optimistic and trusting in the face of ultimate danger. Sure, she'd done a bit to keep their minds from betraying them, but even so, they were acting well. She could pick up inflections and tones in their voice that indicated they were speaking of their own free will, rather than repeating by rote or being intimidated into lying to her about the situation.

She knew that the two Stygian entities would be operating under a great deal of risk in sending Kane to her. Certainly, they had a hostage in the form of Grant, and there was a small tremor of doubt in Grant's voice, something she could pick up because of her familiarity with the man, but there didn't seem to be any duplicity, any subterfuge, going on at the present.

Together, Brigid and her friends had survived a great many traps, and this would be just another, and yet, the law of averages said that runs of luck would run out, no matter what. Certainly, they were prepared and skilled enough to handle unexpected troubles, just for when their luck *did* fail, and Kane and Grant proved to be brute tough enough to cope with problems that could only be solved with force of arms.

Blunt violence was something Brigid herself had become well versed in, as well. Early on, she'd turned up her nose at Kane and Grant packing all manner of hardware with them when they journeyed out on an expedition. Now, she carried the big, almost hammer-shaped TP-9 automatic pistol, which she slid into its holster. The TP-9 was a semiautomatic, civilian version of the old TMP-9 machine pistol, only slightly smaller than the Sin Eaters that Kane and Grant carried, and also carrying a 20-round magazine.

"Will she mind if I come armed?" Brigid asked.

"They haven't had us surrender our side arms, but let me ask," Kane responded.

Again, Kane was informing Brigid of the cockiness of his hosts.

"Vanth said she doesn't care what you bring. Just remember, we can't fit more than a grasshopper into the Manta with both of us packed into it," Kane offered.

And *there* was the tidbit of information Brigid had been waiting for. Vanth's confidence allowed her to repeat the term "locust" in speaking with Kane and Grant. When Kane mentioned "grasshopper," which locusts were a species of, Brigid had all the confirmation she needed about Vanth. It was a casual thing to say, though, and one that was actually true, as the Mantas were meant to be single-seat scram jets. Such a casual reference was easy to pass off.

Brigid, however, did not have any doubts that Vanth would get the hint. The demigoddess was a contemporary of the Annunaki overlords, and as such, had survived their schemes. Enlil and the rest were devils of subterfuge, and as guileless seeming Kane's comment was, it wouldn't have escaped her notice. And if there was such a possibility, Brigid had to err on the side of caution.

"I'll bring my pistol," Brigid returned. "And I'll make sure my ankle's taped up well enough."

Anything to make Vanth think she was at less than optimum capability would be a card in her favor. It would also give her options. She thought of what she could do with the taped ankle. Metal could be disguised as a kind of splint or brace.

"Sounds good to me," Kane replied.

Brigid said her goodbye and disconnected from Kane's transmission. Of course, Lakesh and the rest of the home crew back at Cerberus had been listening in on the conversation.

"Send me an interphaser," Brigid requested over the Commtact back to Cerberus.

That was code in itself. The interphaser was a piece of technology worth ten times its weight in gold, enabling anyone in possession of it the capacity to travel across worlds. As such, Lakesh was loathe to part with the device, especially since it was, in essence, an ever-developing prototype. When not overseeing the redoubt or applying his intelligence to the crises the CAT teams encountered, he was consistently tinkering with it. There were several proprietary bits of technology within the pyramid-shaped object, things that were hard to duplicate, but also there was the concern of others gaining control of it. Groups such as the Millennium Consortium, or the voodoo cult led by Papa Hurbon, could easily utilize the interphaser to conquer large areas.

Fortunately, since Brigid didn't need to use the interphaser to reach the parallax point, what *could* be delivered was something else. A fail-safe device that could tempt Vanth, all the while pretending that it was perhaps damaged in the flight.

And if the goddess was someone trustworthy...well, then, Brigid could continue on stating that they'd need to bring in another interphaser, while the small but deadly bomb in a rigged interphaser housing was left disarmed. If it was such an instance that Vanth was going to bring a deadly invasion into the world, the faux was designed to blow up with sufficient force to kill an overlord. Maybe, just maybe, it would prove enough to also slam the door on an interdimensional horde of attackers. Of course, detonating the bomb would be a final desperate act on Brigid's own part, likely killing her, her allies and dozens, maybe even hundreds of the thralls of Vanth.

The worlds of H. L. Mencken flashed through Brigid's mind at that thought. "To die for an idea; it is unquestionably *noble*. But how much *nobler* it would be if men died for ideas that were true!"

In all the struggles of the Cerberus explorers, she realized there was a truth—that men should be free from tyranny. The tyranny of first the hybrids, then their evolution into the overlords, was the first of many such unjust reigns that she was willing to die to stop. There were others that arrived. Cults, the predation of bandits and other such coldbloods, and especially the technocracy known as the Millennium Consortium, were all examples of the kind of man's own inhumanity to itself.

So if she had to be blown to oblivion to stop Vanth, then so be it.

"Nobler to die for an idea that is true," she mused.

WITH A FLASH across his windshield, Kane knew for certain that he'd reentered the atmosphere and was swinging the supersonic Manta into Greek airspace. He checked on his scanners, watching to see if perhaps he'd been shadowed by Charun or Vanth, but for now he was alone in the sky.

Brigid was at the temple of the Oracle, standing beside a small pyramidal device. He frowned, realizing that it was an interphaser. Bringing one of those into the presence of Vanth and Charun was not a good thing.

He recalled when the last of the pure Tuatha de Danaan on Earth, the mad god Maccan, came for the interphaser. Maccan's assault on Cerberus had left several dead and scores injured, including Domi, who had been tortured in Lakesh's presence to make him give up the interphaser.

The device was something he'd needed to return to his home dimension, thanks to a linkage in the great Martian pyramid. Grant, Kane and Brigid had rushed to Mars, dealing with little, mutated trans-adapts, pint-size humanoids designed for surviving in less atmosphere-rich environments, as well as being proportionately denser and stronger than a normal human.

With an army of such mutants in the Mars base, and Maccan himself setting up the interphaser to head home and then bring back an army of his followers, the trio had found themselves in a truly dangerous situation. Only by forcing Maccan's ancient glove weapon—the Silver Hand of Naudha—to unleash its power inside the pyramid had they managed to stop the scheme. The ancient building collapsed as the Silver Hand's power bolts tore through the roof, all while the Cerberus adventurers raced to the mat-trans to take them back home to Earth.

If one god was a threat with the interphaser, then letting Vanth and Charun have access to it would be even worse; at least that's what Kane assumed. Then again, Brigid was rarely a woman who did anything without purpose and plan. The tiny pyramid was an interphaser *housing*, but there was little guarantee that it had any of the proper components within. This could be a damaged prototype or something worse.

Kane swung the Manta over the center of the temple's remains, landing it among the Doric columns that were all that remained of the ancient structure. The ruins were large enough to land the compact scram jet, even with Brigid present.

He popped the cockpit for her. "So, you're bringing that along?"

"Yeah. Try not to fly too recklessly. The interphaser is used to just transporting itself and recalling immediately. Being jostled isn't in its best interests," Brigid admonished, climbing up and handing him the device.

Kane looked at the casing. It felt heavier than normal, but then Brigid caught his eye.

"Don't think of it," she told him.

And almost immediately Kane's thoughts became a

little fuzzier, clearing a moment later as the interphaser was cradled in his arms like a baby. "You sure this can take entering and exiting orbit?"

"If not, I can tinker with it," Brigid stated. "It's just a backup plan that might help our godling friends."

Kane nodded. He still knew enough to feel distrust of the Stygian aliens, those doubts forward in his mind... but something had slithered back into his subconscious.

Brigid squeezed herself in behind the pilot's couch, grumbling and complaining all the way. She was a tall, well-built woman, so slithering into such a tight spot was nothing fun for her. He turned and handed her the interphaser, wondering why his arms felt so achy and weak as he lifted it.

Kane dismissed it as tension and uncertainty. They were facing off with two alien humanoids that seemed to be capable of stealing a person's soul and breaching the barriers between universes. He wanted to talk to Brigid about this, but something in him whispered that she didn't want to know about his doubts and worries.

He ground his molars, feeling completely off balance, even as he went over the checklist for takeoff. It may have been overly redundant, as he'd just done it a few minutes ago before takeoff to the trip here, but he was a pilot. Not as good as Grant was, which was why he wanted to go over every variable, every condition, of the aircraft before risking his and Brigid's lives on takeoff.

The more he concentrated on the every day, the mundane, the better his mind and stomach felt. He wanted to ask Brigid if she had anything to do with this, but once again, a fog of obfuscation had him forgetting what he was going to ask a few moments later. It was a mental roller coaster, and one he wanted to get off of, but even wishing he could talk with someone else about it was making him feel worse.

"Kane?"

He turned and looked back to her. "Is Vanth attacking my brain?"

He managed to squeeze the words out, but it was as if his throat was a thin slit of cloth and as he pushed each syllable through, the canvas tore, threads popping, his larynx growing more and more raw with the effort.

"No. No," she said. She touched the side of his face, squirming to look him squarely in the eyes.

"What's wrong with me? My memory is going all crazy and I can't concentrate," Kane asked. "It feels like I'm not alone inside my head."

"Concentrate on me," Brigid told him. "I should have known that your will was too strong, that you were too aware of yourself to be able to ignore my posthypnotic suggestions."

With that statement he began to calm. "Posthypnotic suggestions. You've been helping me keep my thoughts aligned."

"But you are too smart. Too in touch with your own thought patterns that you were feeding into a loop of recognizing the dissonance, and then aggravating yourself more as your subconscious went to work burying it," Brigid said. "Your point man's instinct comes from your ability to see through the filter of your subconscious and pick up on actual details, not the usual tricks of consciousness that inform our daily perceptions."

Kane blinked, but kept his focus on her. Parts of him were upset with her, rooting around in his head, but then, he'd actually been one of the people for the act of altering his thoughts, protecting the Cerberus expedition from the intrusive powers of Vanth. It was merely his ego rebelling at the thought of his mind being manipulated by another.

"I've broken your conditioning by merely mentioning posthypnotic," Brigid offered. "Should we try this again?"

"I don't think so. If anything, it might make things worse for me, even if you managed to find a way to get me out of my loop of confusion," Kane said. "Who knows, she might not scan me casually…"

"Except you're returning with new stuff, new information," Brigid countered.

"Like the interphaser housing…being heavier," Kane agreed. He narrowed his eyes. "If we spend too much time here discussing this, she'll wonder where we disappeared to."

He finished his checklist and, satisfied that the Manta was ready to go, he glanced back. "All right, we're off. Make sure I don't bang the interphaser around too much, okay?"

Brigid took a relieved-sounding breath. "I've never been so happy to hear you play dumb."

Kane tilted his head. "What're you talking about, Baptiste?"

"Never mind," she concluded, sighing with exasperation.

Kane's lips pulled into a tight, self-satisfied smile.

Chapter 14

The four people in the CAT Beta squad had seen the departure of Kane's Manta from the mountainside and realized that something was up. From the direction that it flew in, Domi was certain Kane and Grant had ingratiated themselves into the house of the Etruscan godlings. That was always a good thing in Domi's mind; she didn't have to worry about putting on a false front to engage in the tiresome games of intrigue and false politeness with the alien entities. She was here, in the wilderness, where she was comfortable.

She was glad for the launch. Now she could start looking for a sign to track from where the robots had brought the captured Manta. With grim determination, she followed the back trail of the two Gear Skeletons as they trundled from the improvised launch pad on the side of the hill. Shadowing them was an exercise in the basics, as neither of the gigantic mechanisms was the quietest of devices, nor did their ponderous tread land lightly on the ground.

Even so, she didn't want to be lulled into a false sense of security, so she acted as if they were possessed of the sharpest hearing and the keenest of eyes. She stayed to the foliage and shadows, crawling along to pace them, but always keeping aware of where her next hand- or foothold should be, so as not to crunch a leaf or snap a branch.

The others were behind, keeping a distant watch, just

in case someone, somehow, picked up the feral huntress's trail. Edwards and Sinclair both had long-range rifles to provide her with overwatch, and they had night-vision and infrared capabilities that would pick up such a creature in pursuit of her.

So far, things were quiet. Of course, they were on radio silence, but Domi knew that if she did develop a tail, the others would fire. No matter what kind of silencer technology was developed, there was no way to make a rifle report quiet. She'd hear it.

Of course, if she heard it, then so would the gods within the mountain temple.

Domi focused on the mission at hand, living in the moment, as was her nature. All of that was how she managed to stay alive for her two decades of life so far, even in the face of inhuman opponents. Keep the basics, always move with absolute certainty and keep your eyes and ears peeled.

No technology, no tricks, were substitutes for the hard-won skills she'd developed.

The pair of giants reached a set of crags and an outcropping along the bottom of the hill. From a distance, it seemed like a natural formation and a casual glance would have mistaken it for a normally formed cave. As the robots continued on, Domi could tell that it was an entrance, with stones and slabs of solid rock positioned to conceal a metal-walled frame. The size of the "cave entrance" was also an indicator of the unnatural status of the opening, as the fifteen-foot-tall giants strolled through the doors as if it were nothing. Domi set her shadow suit to duplicate the rocky terrain, because it would be hard to hide herself among the barren hillside without a little bit of technological assistance.

With a few quick strides, she was out from the edge of the tall grasses and up beside the hand-built entrance to the mountain of Charun and Vanth. She peered around the edge and saw that the Spartans had gone down a hundred feet of corridor, thanks to their long strides, and were approaching a gate. She switched on the shadow suit hood's optics and gave a verbal order to search for cameras or electric eyes, things that even her finely tuned instincts couldn't discern in the shadows of the unlit hallway.

Domi didn't merely skim or glance; rather, she looked along as much of the wall detail as the telescopic zoom and light amplification would allow her to, which meant everything that wasn't obscured by the massive shoulders of the New Olympian war suits. There was no way she was going to endanger the other members of her team without a thorough examination of the artificial corridor. Fortunately, it seemed the only man-made objects were the ribs that upheld the rock walls, and the flat plates of steel that formed the roof and walls at the exposed entrance. No electrical wires were in evidence, and the metal looked as if it had been present for centuries, thanks to rust.

No wiring, no bulbs were in evidence, and there were no small mammals in the crags and holes along the walls of the deeper tunnel. She observed as the gate rose and heard the clank of chains and a pulley system lifting the iron bars. Domi remained still, so that if someone looked at her, she'd simply appear to be just another rock. Even her breathing was shallow, so that her shoulders and ribs didn't shift too much.

It was waiting, and those who knew Domi would have never thought she'd have this kind of patience, but this was not simply idling. She was observing, and staying low profile. She blended into her surroundings, eyes and ears peeled. She was not only watching for any holes in the Etruscan gods' security, but also if someone was coming up on her from behind.

So far, she was safe in her periphery, and hadn't missed

that the gate was large, heavy and dwarfed the pair of Spartans. There were also gaps between the bars, which the hood's optics immediately measured, displaying the dimensions of each gap. Getting through would be a task of phenomenal contortion even for the slim, tiny Domi, let alone any of the rest of her teammates and Smaragda. The only means of getting through would be to rely on technology that was left behind at Cerberus, or crudely spending time digging a channel beneath the gate, and hoping the surrounding dirt didn't cave in on the ditch.

The second option would also leave them vulnerable during the length of time it took to dig that hole, especially if it was to be large enough for Edwards to slither through. Domi's lips pulled tight as she realized their quarry had a good piece of security here.

She glanced back, scanning the mountainside with the telescopic optics for her friends.

Edwards and Sinclair appeared in stark contrast to the countryside as she picked up their passive IFF signature. She was out in the open and visible to them, but like her, their suits were configured to blend in with their surroundings.

Domi lifted her hand and waved for the rest of the team to come down. Sure, the idea of digging under the heavy iron gate was a bit foolish, but it was also so audacious that no one would consider someone try it. If there were any contraindications on the opposite side of the gate for making their entrance through there, then they could retreat.

Domi hoped it wouldn't come to that. She wanted to get inside before their friends ended up in deep trouble.

Something bothered Domi as she waited for the others.

There were only two Spartans lifting and maneuvering the Manta; the same suits she recognized from Edwards's vid footage. She wondered at the lack of the third of the suits. She recalled the heavy tread of a solo entity approaching their landing at the parallax point with Kane and Grant, but the two men had reported that it wasn't a Gear Skeleton that approached them. It had been some form of inhuman giant akin to the massive Balor they had battled in the Appalachian Mountains months ago.

That kind of a creature was an abomination crafted of human flesh, of a living, willing host, and often the dead and dying victims of the mutant. The Fomori, as they had called themselves, were on average about three to four hundred pounds, their bodies bulked up almost like cannibals, robbing the very parts of other people, stealing muscle, bone and skin to make them larger and stronger. This form of hideous transformation was part and parcel of a deadly being known as Bres, who was an inheritor of Enlil's, a half-breed who had molded himself into an object of perfection.

Stolen flesh, Domi continued to muse, looking down the tunnel. She began to wonder what a Gear Skeleton would resemble if it were given a coating of living humans, and the thoughts were uncomfortable. It only made sense…skeletons need muscle and meat.

And a hammer-wielding god such as Charun would need an opponent.

One whose bones could never break, being forged from an alloy version of orichalcum, and whose flesh could be healed and rebuilt, using the mindless and enslaved thralls Domi and her group had been avoiding for the past day and a half.

She wondered if the others would pick up on that. She had to remain in radio silence and avoid broadcasting the presence of CAT Beta to Vanth. She had to trust in the intelligence of her three friends that this threat could quite easily have been a replay of Helena Garthwaite's manufactured threat, that Vanth built something for Charun to slug it out with, finally having scored enough to make a true giant.

Of course, this could mean that some of Smaragda's own people could not be recovered, not if they were dissected and rebuilt to make new monsters.

Domi ground her teeth. She'd have to inform Smaragda of the fates she suspected, but hoped she wouldn't have to.

Domi prayed silently that she'd never have to tell the brave Olympian soldier that the comrades she had lost had been torn apart and reassembled as the muscle and skin of a robotic giant.

THE DULL RUMBLE of thunder in the sky alerted Grant that the Manta had returned. His instincts were buzzing, almost as if the tension he was feeling was emanating from him like electricity. Grant was glad to have Kane and Brigid both back at his side, but he couldn't help to think this was an elaborate trap, one that was intended to pull the three of them off balance.

Grant fought the urge to jump up and head to the ladder to see Kane bringing in the Manta from the peak of the hill. The hatch at the top was open, which was how he was able to hear the sonic boom of the Manta's deceleration as it reentered the atmosphere. Charun smiled at the sound.

"Your friends have returned," the eight-foot humanoid confirmed. His face was bright and happy at the sound; his eye lit with genuine pleasure at the prospect of meeting Brigid Baptiste. Grant felt bad for being so suspicious of Charun, but he'd encountered enough sociopaths, human and otherwise, who could put on a good mask of false emotion. If he turned out to be a noble and just being, then Grant would beg forgiveness of the Stygian.

He hoped he would be able to beg such forgiveness. The fact that the giant let him keep his side arms, even the bag of various weapons, was disarming enough an action, but it also could have been a sign of superiority. After all, Charun had faced the heaviest of small arms on the Manta and was unharmed. What mere man-portable equipment could injure such a being?

The truth was that Grant realized Charun's invulnerability had, in part, been due to the ancient hammer, an artifact of alien technology that was so powerful, it might as well have been magical. Sure, the others had *seen* the damage the hammer had wrought upon his Manta, but Grant was the only one to have been on the receiving end of the weapon in the hands of Charun. The aircraft had shaken violently. Even the inertial nature of the pilot's couch had conveyed the force of the hammer strike.

Charun was not an opponent to underestimate, and for all his cheer and amicability, showed signs of great intellect behind his attempts to seem simple and straightforward.

"I didn't want to seem too rude by hopping to my feet when I heard it," Grant told Charun as he rose from his seat.

"It is understandable, Grant," Charun said. "I have spent many a quiet hour in the company as an uncertain guest."

"In between your tasks as a chooser of the slain?" Grant questioned.

"My duties as a so-called psychopomp, as you mentioned before," Charun said. "The stories, as we've explained, have permutated over the many centuries."

"So, maybe it is a good thing that we have Brigid coming in to join us, so we can better understand what's going on," Grant returned.

"Vanth would explain much better," Charun admitted. "I was more engaged in protecting our borders from the minions of the overlords."

"Which makes you damn fine in my book," Grant

noted. "Enlil and his bunch never have been friends of mine."

"The enemy of my enemy is my friend," Charun responded. "Even in my time, it was an ancient saying."

Charun motioned to allow Grant to take the lead up the ladder. Without hesitation, Grant was up the rungs and out of the hatch on the peak. The wake of the Manta bisected a cloud, smearing the white fluff of it behind, creating a streak on the afternoon sky. He enjoyed watching one of these machines in action, even from thousands of feet away, its sheer velocity and nature. When not engaged in stealth mode, it was a vulgar, glorious display of the true scale of human creativity.

It was one thing to punch through dimensional walls, to squirt your atoms through a wormhole halfway around a continent, but really, Grant was a pilot. He'd been flying the Deathbird iteration of the AH-1 Apache gunship for decades, and nothing felt like the sensation of skimming over treetops at 150 miles an hour. With the discovery of the Mantas from the moon base, all dreams of velocity and agility were increased exponentially. There was no sense of movement in a mat-trans, no thrill with it.

Even the Deathbird was still a magnificent flying machine that moved and felt like an extension of his body, an *amplification* of himself.

Watching from the sidelines, he was still impressed with the sleek, transorbital plane.

Charun was up through the hatch and standing beside him. A glance at the giant told Grant that he was interested in the Mantas, too.

Charun followed it intently. He'd encountered the—to him—alien craft, and though he wore a harness that let him take to the skies with inhuman ease and wielded a hammer capable of splitting a Manta in two with a direct hit, the scram jet was wondrous to Charun. There was a sense of respect for the humans' tinkering.

The approach was clean from Grant's more clinical thinking, observing Kane's handling of the Manta. There was a difference between him and his younger partner. Whereas the Mantas were a joy, a drug to Grant, to Kane they were merely another means of transportation. There was no flourish, no excitement in his tearing between orbit and atmosphere.

Grant had to give Kane props for being precise and always in control, but that was no way to truly *fly*. Charun, with his wing harness, was someone who was more along the lines of what he experienced as a pilot.

Of course, all of this could have been projection, but Grant could see Charun nodding at the same points that he'd approved of in Kane's handling of the Manta. The scram jet switched to Vertical Takeoff and Landing mode, its engines swiveling so that it could hover and land on the clearing on the hillside.

Charun's head whipped around and Grant could feel the giant's tension increase.

"What's wrong?" Grant asked. He let his Sin Eater slide into his hand. Charun was suddenly on the defensive and he could see the demigod's hands flexing open and closed, sorely missing the hammer he should have had.

"We've got intruders," Charun stated. "They're coming in."

Grant was frozen in doubt for a moment but he kept his thoughts of CAT Beta deep within the back of his mind, buried under other mental processes. There was a threat, bringing Charun out of his curiosity, making the giant wish for a weapon. That wouldn't be Domi and the rest. The albino girl was a ghost when she wanted to be, just as stealthy as Kane himself.

No…someone was approaching, out in the open, and they were on a warpath.

"Should we have Kane take off?" Grant asked.

"No," Charun stated. "This should be nothing for me."

"But you're all itchy, ready to fight," Grant added.

Charun glanced at the machine pistol in Grant's fist. "As are you…"

"Your instincts kicked mine off," Grant replied.

"They come from that way," Charun stated, pointing down the hill. "I cannot quite tell the number of them…it is as if there is more than one mind or spirit per intruder."

Grant tilted his head.

Kane and Brigid were running forward, both of them with their weapons out, but leveled at the ground so as not to accidentally shoot someone as they rushed forward.

"What's going on?" Kane asked.

"Charun sensed intruders," Grant explained. "Coming from that direction."

Kane turned his head toward the forest that was pointed out. Brigid glanced down, too, but then returned her attention to the Etruscan giant. Her emerald eyes were wide as she looked at the titan from head to toe. Then she glanced at the hatch in the peak, blank-faced servants arriving carrying capsules the size of small melons in their hands.

Charun turned to the first servant, plucking the "ball" from his hand. He swung it up over one shoulder and Grant watched as straps suddenly stretched out from the capsule, winding around his chest. Then came the wings; crushed buds the size of Grant's forearms began unfurling into leathery wings, like those of a gigantic bat or reptilian pteranodons.

"The magic disappears when you look upon it up close, no?" Charun asked. He picked up another of the capsules and pressed it to his face, this one becoming the tusked, terrifying mask that, at this range, Grant could tell was the "war paint" Vanth had referred to. It was not much different from the shadow suit Grant himself wore. This one, however, put itself onto Charun, spreading down and increasing the unhealthy blue-corpse pallor of the titan. In a way, this was also close to what he saw when Enlil began armoring his Nephilim warriors with those little buds of smart metal.

"Nope, not a bit," Grant replied. "Pretty fantastic."

Charun flexed, feeling more himself as he "suited up" for war. There were still four more servants, all with their eyes empty, faces impassive as mind-controlled drones. Each held a different-colored capsule.

Charun picked up one that unfurled in his hand, forming a long metallic rod of great strength as it finished transforming. He plucked a second, stabbed it atop the shaft and it quickly formed a crosspiece, anchoring to the handle of the hammer. Charun took each of the last two, sticking one on either end of the crosspiece, each capsule forming into a deadly alloy wedge that was the last of the hammer's formation.

Brigid observed this, as well, and Grant intended to ask her, later, if he was right in the assumption of this technology resembling that of the Annunaki, especially the corrupted armor node that had turned Helena from a silver-skinned goddess into a rampaging engine of destruction.

"Let us gird our loins, Kane and Grant!" Charun bellowed. "The enemy is upon us!"

Grant saw Charun lift his hand, pointing toward an object hurtling up from the ground. It was a two-hundred-pound chunk of stone arcing into the sky, hurtling straight toward the Cerberus expedition and Charun.

Chapter 15

Kane saw the flying stone, and grabbed Brigid Baptiste by the wrist, pulling her down the hillside. Moments later Charun took a half step and swung his hammer, the head connecting with the two-hundred-pound missile loud enough to make Kane regret not pulling his hood up to protect his hearing. The impact was a direct slap in the face, pressure waves splashing against him and making him lose his footing on the rocky hillside.

"For the glory of Styx!" Charun bellowed, and Kane wasn't certain if his shout was even louder than that alien-tech hammer striking the granite slab that nearly crushed them.

With that pronouncement, Kane watched as Charun's "fake" wings glowed slightly and he launched into the sky, his tusked mouth a rictus of glee and ferocity, his insane hammer crackling with arcs of lightning across its head and shaft.

"You two okay?" Grant asked.

Kane blinked and shook his head. "My ears are ringing from that battle cry. Where did he knock the stone?"

Brigid pointed down the hill. "You mean the powdered gravel cloud he turned it into?"

Kane looked to see wisps of dust settling on the hillside. Well, we can eliminate our friends as being behind this attack, he mused. Even Edwards couldn't toss a two-pound rock like that, let alone two hundred pounds.

Charun flew forward toward the launch point of the slab of stone when his course jerked violently upward. A smaller, faster rock must have flashed at him faster than his reflexes could allow, and Charun somersaulted, tumbling through the air toward the ground.

"The antigravity elements of his flight harness will cushion his fall, but he may have suffered considerable trauma from the rock hit," Brigid noted. "We need to get to his side and protect him."

"You sure you know where he landed?" Kane asked her.

Brigid nodded. "I'll steer you from up here."

Kane looked down to her ankle. "Right. You're not rushing anywhere on that ankle."

"Hurry," Brigid admonished. "There's tree movement. Something quite large is smashing through the forest toward him."

Kane glanced at Grant and the two partners took off down the hillside, running and jumping.

"He mentioned more than one opponent," Grant said. "But apparently only one of them was big and strong enough to act as a living piece of antiaircraft artillery."

"Let's hope that's the case," Kane answered. He glanced back and saw that Brigid was hard on their heels, not quite as fast due to their longer strides, but she wasn't going to be left in the dust. "What're the odds we're going to run into our old cyclops pal?"

"I'd say they were even. One chance in one," Brigid said over the Commtact. "I doubt even Balor could cause such sway among healthy trees."

Kane grimaced, bounding down the slope. He was glad for the protection offered by the non-Newtonian nature of the shadow suit.

The main element of protection in the space-age polymers was that the fibers were fluid in nature until the moment an object struck them. The design was first discovered at the end of the twentieth century, enabling skiers to better handle high-speed impacts and crashes on the slopes. One moment the skintight uniform was flexible and supple, but when something like a collision occurred, the fibers became an almost steel-hard plate, blunting impact and preventing serious trauma. Taken to the extent of the moon base scientists, the shadow suits could even stave off light small-arms fire from anything short of a full-powered rifle.

More than once Kane had been saved from a deadly blow hurled by a foe of inhuman strength, the polymers blunting rib-splintering punches. His enjoyment of the shadow suit's protective properties, however, was extended toward the fact that he could slip and crash to a knee and not have the skin torn or split by bashing against a rock, nor would the sharp impact penetrate the cushioning effects of the polymers and cause a leg fracture. The soles of his boots also kept him from feeling it when he landed on a sharp stone that would have even given a conventional combat boot a puncture. The sides of the boots also would keep his leg rigid within normal range of movement, preventing a sprained ankle or a badly flexed knee.

The suits were made for all-out on terrain such as this, and Kane was going to need every bit of personal disregard to get to the fallen Charun in time.

The familiar bellow of "Hate you! Kill you!" reverberated off the trunks in the forest, making the cyclops seem even more deranged at this point.

Or maybe old One-eye was growing crazier, especially after being put down by Kane and Grant earlier. Failure and frustration were powerful motivators, but they also tended to make those who suffered such embarrassment crazier.

When you went up against eighteen feet of titan who was berserk and pissed off, chances were that you got to see just how good your fancy space suit could do against fists carrying tons of force. As Kane and Grant wove between the trees, Kane could make out a flowery fountain of light; infrared cameras picking up a flare of power that could only have been Charun's hammer.

"Just what the hell is all that light?" Grant asked. "Some kind of fire wall to keep the cyclops and his friends at bay?"

"Or maybe it's just pumping out another kind of energy and our suits can't quite identify it," Kane responded. "Just that there is a lot of it."

"Great," Grant murmured. "Well, I'm glad we sealed the suits. I don't need to be hit with hard radiation."

"Kane's right," Brigid called from above. "I'm trying to determine the output of the hammer. The readings are either pure gibberish or it's putting out the equivalent of a miniature sun down here. Light, radiation, magnetism…"

Kane looked through the fiery glow, seeing something massive swing down against the fountain of light. They were a hundred yards away, but the cyclops had reached Charun first and wielded another tree like a club. But when the huge log crashed down, it burst apart in the hands of the two-ton titan.

"Die!" the beast roared.

Kane unleashed his Sin Eater, slowed to a kneeling position and aimed at the figure in the distance. The cyclops was a big, easy target as they'd closed another twenty yards, well within the range of the Magistrate machine pistol. He pulled the trigger, ripping off a burst of 9 mm slugs toward the huge assailant.

The cyclops slapped at its chest, growling at the impact of the bullets. Kane frowned as he realized that as powerful as the Sin Eater was, capable of punching through the armor of a Deathbird or the windshield of a Sandcat, it had done nothing more than to annoy the giant.

The angry titan turned and its singular, bulging eye locked on Kane.

"I've got his attention," he said to Grant as nearly twenty feet of rampaging humanoid lunged straight at Kane. "Flank him!"

The gigantic creature's long strides accelerated it toward Kane, and once more, the Cerberus leader was astonished at the kind of velocity that a living freight train of muscle could achieve. He held his ground, firing single shots ineffectually into the titan's bulk until the last moment.

Within three of the massive strides of the cyclops, Kane hurled himself aside, diving out of the path of two tons of opponent. At that point, the creature had far too much momentum to stop and turn on a dime. The tree Kane had had at his back disintegrated as the titan plowed through it, branches and splinters flying from the devastated trunk.

Grant's Sin Eater roared as he pelted the cyclops with full-auto bursts.

Kane could see blood spattering under bullet impacts, but the creature seemed more annoyed than injured by them. Then again, the guns were designed to put humans down decisively, not organisms the size and mass of an elephant.

The cyclops spun and tried to slow, skidding on wide, log-size feet that dug up mounds of soil. Even that wasn't enough, so it reached out its long, massive arms and sank its fingers into the ground.

Finally reaching a halt, the cyclops glanced between Kane and Grant, who were both reloading their spent side arms.

"We had to run down here without anything bigger than our Sin Eaters," Grant snarled.

"You're welcome to run back and grab something," Kane offered. He took aim at the giant's singular eye and pulled the trigger.

The cyclops must have had incredible prescience and reflexes, because the large palm of the man-beast's hand rose, blocking the salvo that Kane launched. The skin on the thing's palm was torn up by the burst, but blood merely trickled from the ravaged flesh. There didn't seem to be too much in terms of muscle or guts that were usual in the hands of a humanoid. He'd slashed at enough hands with his combat knife over the years.

He fired again, hoping to penetrate further, or at least to keep the cyclops occupied. The ring of the high-velocity jacketed slugs on metal reached Kane over the rattle of the Sin Eater.

"Brigid, he's got a metal skeleton," Kane said over the Commtact.

As he told her, the cyclops reached out with his other arm to snatch a bough off of a tree.

"This is as I feared," Brigid pronounced. "Especially when you described the physiology of the beast to me."

"It's a Gear Skeleton?" Kane asked, whirling and throwing himself out of the path of the hurled branch. The wood striking the ground dug in to half its length, then split up its center.

That would explain a lot of things, especially considering Kane wasn't certain that an actual humanoid skeleton could support such strength and stresses as this twenty-foot cyclops would put on it.

Kane rolled to his back, aimed and fired, his burst striking the forehead of the giant, missing the thing's centered eye by mere inches, skin splitting under high-velocity impacts. It roared in discomfort, which meant that, somehow, there was living flesh wrapped around the orichalcum bones of that horror. And if there was living flesh wrapping the giant…

Grant appeared in Kane's peripheral vision, hurling a gren at the big creature. This time, the cyclops wasn't charging with the speed and force of a rhinoceros. Having overshot his target on more than one occasion, the giant had decided to take things slower, steadier, relying on a step that could take it twelve feet casually to outdistance its foes.

The gren caught the giant's attention and it whirled, clasping it in his fist.

"Stupid…"

Before the epithet that the cyclops intended could form on its lips, the gren detonated in a brilliant flash. Twenty feet of monstrosity rocked back on its heels then toppled, shaking the earth beneath Kane's feet, almost sending him back onto his ass.

"I thought you were griping about us only going after these things with only our side arms," Kane grumbled.

"That's why I decided to make a gren one of my side arms," Grant answered.

Kane picked up a wink and a grin from the normally grouchy Magistrate.

"Hurt Feem! Hurt Feem!"

Kane and Grant looked out into the forest. Their conflict with the cyclops had eaten up some time, time enough for the other intruders that Charun had detected to catch up with their gigantic leader. They saw the twisted, bulky, lurching things that had been called the Fomori when they'd encountered them in the Appalachian Mountains. They were big, but nowhere near the size of Charun, let alone the cyclops they called "Feem."

"Polyphemus," Brigid said on the Commtact, as she could hear everything Kane and Grant could hear. "That was the name of the cyclops Odysseus battled in his journey home from the Trojan war. They called him by his middle syllable..."

"Thanks for the legend lesson," Grant said. "Sorry I wasted my one gren."

"These suckers won't be wrapped around a Gear Skeleton," Kane replied. "But we have to know..."

Grant put his finger to his lips. Saying anything more would simply let Vanth know what they suspected about her. That the beautiful godling was a mistress of twisting and mutating flesh, and clad the skeleton-like giant robot in the meat of Smaragda's missing platoon, rather than being formed into the trio of terrors who'd just appeared.

That didn't make the prospect of fighting these entities any less distasteful. Kane wasn't going to roll over and die for anyone, but murdering people who'd been warped by Vanth was scarcely something Kane relished. His one hope was that the Fomori brutes had been people who had willingly surrendered their humanity for the promise of power and rank.

All these thoughts were pushed aside as the creatures closed to less than ten yards. Kane stiff-armed his Sin Eater and blasted six holes in the chest of one of the horror-sculpted abominations. The thing staggered under the impacts, grunting as heavy bullets punched through its hide and heavy sheets of muscle and bone. The Fomori, however, didn't fall from the abuse he suffered. Knowing the kind of permutations the other Fomori had gone through, it was likely that his vital organs were placed somewhere other than in the center of his chest.

Kane sidestepped as a second of the barrel-bodied, three-armed horrors leaped at him; three hundred pounds of muscle cutting through the air and missing only by inches. Kane opened fire, shooting the would-be tackler in the back, stitching him with a long burst where it appeared the thing's spinal column should have been.

The creature let out a wail and dropped to its knees. It caught itself with two of its spindly-seeming arms, but before Kane could put the thing out of its misery, the one he'd peppered in the chest lunged forward, two fists crashing against his chest. Once more, the protective qualities of the shadow suit proved its worth, as those twin hammer blows lifted Kane off his feet and hurled him four yards back. Only Kane's agility kept him from crashing into a tree and landing so that he could get back to his feet.

He rose to meet his twisted opponent as it lunged to follow up on its initial assault. Kane didn't shoot, knowing he only had a few rounds left in his magazine. Instead he charged, as well, snapping up his foot to kick the thing right where he'd blasted it in the chest. Blood gushed from the point of impact, the two bodies and their velocities adding together in the force of collision. Kane ran just that much faster to bring his momentum up to overwhelm his foe's. As such, he was able to ride the staggered Fomori to the ground.

As he did so, Kane aimed for the thing's skull and fired off the remnants of his Sin Eater's payload, the heavy slugs smashing apart bone and splashing brains all across the forest floor. It was a brutal, cruel bit of butcher's work, but at this point, Kane was in do-or-die mode. Distantly, part of his mind hoped that he was correct in the evaluation that the minds trapped in these twisted bodies had sold out their humanity for personal gain.

Kane dumped the spent magazine from his Sin Eater and reached for his last full one. He hadn't expected to run into a bulletproof titan and three of his equally durable partners. Magazine in place, round chambered, he looked up in time to see the second one he'd wounded making its charge at him.

Off to the side, he could see Grant in pitched hand-to-hand combat with the obscenity that targeted him. The two were locked in a test of strength, Grant's arms flexing with all the power in them and also giving lie to the "skinny" nature of the Fomori's limbs. The rest of its bulk, its doubled torso and neckless head, were so thick that they made even muscular arms seem anemic by proportion.

Kane sighted his second attacker's face and cut loose with two rapid shots—one bullet per pull of the trigger—to conserve his ammunition and maximize his accuracy and effect. The first shot seemingly had no effect, but the second one caused the creature to flinch, jerking as the bullet struck him. The hit only made the Fomori stumble for a step, but that was all the time Kane needed. His free hand drew his twelve-inch combat knife and slashed the thing across one of its reaching arms, the sharp blade carving through muscle and grating against bone. The flap of slashed meat flopped backward as the abomination wailed in agony. A second arm lashed up, clutching Kane by the wrist.

Kane twisted, using his entire body as leverage to keep the Fomori from getting a secure grip on him. As he did so, he brought his knee up into the torso of the misshapen humanoid. He was hoping to catch a kidney or something, but the solid impact he felt through the cushioning of his shadow suit told him he'd only struck muscle or bone. The one-eyed head whirled to face Kane, hatred glaring in the single, bloodshot orb.

Kane grasped his Sin Eater in his free hand, rushed up to contact range and fired, the muzzle spitting flame and metal into its mouth with the first shot. The creature jerked, its grasp loosening on Kane's wrist. Kane fired again and the bulging eye burst apart in a spray of milky goop, the top of its skull bursting open, petals of meat and skull fluttering in the wind at the slug's passage.

"Two down," Kane rasped.

"Three!" Grant grunted, twisting violently on the stocky, heavily muscled neck of his opponent. The crackling of bones breaking and tendons popping was grisly, but it was the surest sign the thing that Grant battled was long dead. Limp limbs dangled, as did its misshapen head as Grant lowered the corpse to the ground.

"I hope they don't have any more like that," Kane muttered.

"Kill friends!"

The unearthly roar caused Kane and Grant to look back to where the cyclops had toppled. The thing rose to its full eighteen feet in height. Its left arm had been flayed down to the brass skeleton, still dripping with blood from where Grant's gren had shredded its flesh. The thing's torso was also blackened.

"How much do you have left?" Grant asked.

"I'm on my last mag, maybe fifteen left in it," Kane answered. "No other grens?"

Grant shook his head. "You go left, I'll go right. Maybe we can get to the heart of the thing…"

"It'll still have Sandcat armor underneath all of that muscle protecting the pilot," Kane returned.

"Kill humans," the cyclops snarled.

"You're going to have to work for it, Ugly," Kane taunted. He clutched his knife and gun tighter, waiting for the titan to charge. The two men had fought plenty of powerful opponents across their lives, but this one looked just a little too large, was far too determined to give up. Without the kind of weaponry necessary to bring down

an armored vehicle, Kane didn't give himself much of a
chance against the cyclops.

"No…" came a rumbling growl from behind the cyclops.

Apparently, Charun was not completely out of this
fight, but could even the demigod stand before a meat-
covered war robot?

Chapter 16

Charun, the demigod, the mate of Vanth, rose to his full eight feet in height behind the gigantic cyclops that threatened to bludgeon Kane and Grant into pulps. Kane couldn't help but think that any impressive power he'd observed in the Etruscan godling in comparison to himself and Grant had somehow vanished in the face of the bloodied but still massive abomination standing between the three of them.

Certainly, equipped with his eight-foot-long war hammer, composed of four smart-metal subcomponents, he looked as if he was well armed to deal with any foe. But the foe in question was an ancient Annunaki Gear Skeleton, a piloted automaton composed of the alien alloy known as secondary orichalcum, one of the hardest materials the Cerberus explorers had encountered to date. That much was apparent from the bloody, glistening left arm, stripped of all meat thanks to the detonation of Grant's gren. Its skin was blackened, cracked in places, but the beast supported by the fifteen-foot war suit within seemed undiminished in intensity or strength.

Charun was also clad in his war paint—in actuality a form of smart metal armor akin to the skins the Annunaki had clad their Nephilim drone warriors in. Already impressive due to his physique and size, Charun was now a beast of terror, with oversize tusks and twisted features granting him a monstrous appearance.

Kane recalled the armored masks worn by the Tigers of Heaven in New Edo. The samurai warriors had carried on the ancient tradition of ornate helmets usually fronted by demonic masks to intimidate their foes. So be-tusked, so vile, the scowl scrawled across Charun's features, it would have broken the spirit of lesser fighting men, but in the face of the twisted, one-eyed giant, it was just a meeting of the ugly and inhuman.

About the only tool Charun might have that would even the odds was the antigravity flight harness strapped across his broad chest, attaching batlike leathery wings to his back. Charun, however, only had one wing out, flicking reflexively.

The huge rocks that the cyclops had thrown, or the out-of-control plummet from the sky, must have damaged the antigravity harness.

Eighteen feet of height might not have been much. Standing on each other's shoulders, Kane, Grant and Charun would have actually dwarfed the cyclops, but even together their combined weight wouldn't have matched the giant's—and that was part of where its brute power lay. Not only did the thing have an automaton as its skeleton, hydraulics adding to the mass of muscle tissue wound around the robot in a hideous mockery of the human form, but it had that once-living flesh as a part of it.

"Charun, just give the—" Kane began.

"You threaten the friends of Charun, abomination!" The demigod cut Kane off. "Fill thy hands, and challenge one who would be your match, coward!"

"Not scared," the cyclops snarled. "Came to kill you first!"

"Then do thy duty," Charun challenged.

The cyclops leaned to one side, wrapping its massive hand around a tree trunk. With two levering actions, it snapped the roots holding the tree to the ground, and lifted it like a club. Grant stepped closer to Kane, tossing him a spare magazine.

"At least we'll both be able to throw lead at that monstrosity while he's occupied with Charun," Grant muttered over the Commtact.

"Like that'd do anything more?" Kane asked. "Let's see what Charun can do..."

"And if he kills the poor bastard slurped into the Gear Skeleton?" Grant countered.

"I have a feeling the gooey innards were already torn out by the root by whoever made that abomination," Kane said. He didn't want to mention specifics, but both Kane and Grant were aware the possibility was strong that this creature was the spawn of Vanth. And if it were not the spawn of Vanth, then it was highly likely the creation of some other threat. Just because they were the enemies of the Etruscan demigods didn't mean that either side of this conflict was on the side of angels.

Vanth put on a pretty show as an angelic being herself; all beauty, unashamed nudity, and glowing, feathery wings. But Kane was fully aware that the deadliest threats hid under appealing, delicate skins as well as warty, reptilian hides.

The cyclops and Charun lunged to attack each other, each swinging their club at the same time.

Kane grimaced at the thought of "their ally" being outclassed in size and strength, but the demigod didn't hesitate to hurl himself into action. The tree came down like a thunderbolt, exploding as it struck the armored Charun, even as the cyclops was just out of the swinging range of his alien hammer. The destruction of the tree would have been deafening without the sound filters on their shadow hoods.

A cloud of splinters and sawdust filled the air, obscuring their view of Charun, but the Etruscan godling's hammer cartwheeled toward Kane and Grant. Before the thing reached them, it stopped, resting on its head, swaying slightly.

"Oh, not good," Grant murmured.

The cyclops waved, trying to push aside the cloud to see where Charun had gone. Suddenly a pair of hands reached up from the settling dust, fingers digging into either side of the cyclops's face, fingers spearing into cheeks. The abomination let out a roar, jerking upward and pulling Charun free from the ground.

The demigod, as he rode the cyclops upward, brought both feet up and hammered the hooflike boots of his smart-metal armor into the thing's clavicle. Flesh tore under the force of the kick, but the cyclops's secondary orichalcum bones didn't bend or break under the force of the double kick.

The naked hydraulic claw and the cyclops's still-flesh-wrapped hand grasped at Charun's waist, but the lithe godling used the monster's collarbone as a base to flip himself up and over the top of its head, out of the reach of those huge paws. In doing that somersault, Charun came away with handfuls of torn meat that used to be the giant's cheeks. The man-beast let out another hideous cry; a combination of pain and frustration as its smaller opponent stymied him.

Grant reached out for the hammer's staff, thinking to throw the weapon to Charun. Unfortunately the alien technology had its own agenda. A sizzling arc of voltage shot up the handle, popping loudly in the air. Grant winced, a nonlethal jolt of electricity causing his arm to contort reflexively. The effect was not very different from the Taser jolts Kane and Grant had used to floor the cyclops earlier, and both former Magistrates had Tasered each other to understand the effects. That didn't make the shock hurt any less, however.

"That's one way to keep your toys out of someone's hands," Kane growled.

Grant sneered. "I was trying to help him…"

"Well, the hammer isn't a mind reader," Kane said. "Or maybe it is…"

Grant glared at Kane, then looked back at the upended hammer. "Like it senses we're still distrustful of our hosts."

Excellent save, Kane thought. "Let me try."

"If it doesn't shock you, I'm calling bullshit," Grant murmured.

Kane reached out, his will sublimating any and all doubts about Charun. I'm helping your master, you damned hammer.

The next thing Kane knew was that he was hurled backward by a flash of lightning. His gloves smoked from the electrical discharge, and his head hurt, despite the protective effect of his shadow suit hood. His fingers throbbed inside the gloves, twitching uncontrollably with the aftereffects of the zap. About the only thing he could do to leaven the pain was to curse aloud. "Dammit!"

"All right, it doesn't like any human," Grant said.

Kane blinked, shaking his hands to get rid of the after-tingles from the electrical short. "Or maybe it's really clumsy…"

"The hammer is clumsy?" Grant asked.

Kane rose again and approached the hammer. He reached out quickly this time, no hesitation, no reluctance. The electrical jolt was there as he connected with the handle, but this time it was only painful, not electroconvulsive. He closed his fingers on the haft and pulled. At first the hammer didn't want to leave the ground. He put his other hand around it.

"Come on," he growled even as he felt the jolt and

crackle of energy surging up his other arm. "I handled the staff of Moses. I can lift you!"

Of course, the fact that the hammer itself was well more than a hundred pounds might have been what was slowing down his lifting of the device, he thought. The surge of electricity tickling his muscles increased again. The hammer grew lighter and soon he stood with it as if it weighed no more than his Sin Eater.

"The discharge," Kane said. "It was trying to make a connection to us. It's so used to cutting through Charun's smart-metal armor to link with him..."

"It didn't know that we needed a lot less energy to get through the shadow suits?" Grant asked.

"That's what I'm hoping, because right now I feel like a god myself," Kane told him.

With a few long strides Kane was up against the cyclops's massive leg. He swung the hammer around, his muscles flexing with more power than he could have imagined. Connecting with the secondary orichalcum leg structure beneath the flesh jarred him to a halt, vibrations rumbling back through the hammer and along Kane's arms. Still, the impact was loud and shattering, chunks of pulverized meat spraying from between the hammer and the anvil of the robot's leg. The huge hydraulic knee buckled under the force of the hit, pistons twisting and bursting.

The cyclops screamed and looked down at Kane. The feedback from the hit was such that Kane was unable to move, still stunned.

The abomination wound up to smash the human warrior, but Charun leaped down from the creature's shoulders, tackling Kane. The giant's massive fist slashed through the air, whipping up a wind that Kane could feel even through his suit's hood. The agile demigod curled Kane up against him like a child, running to dodge the cyclops's second hurtling fist. This time the log-thick limb crashed against the ground with a thundering boom.

"You wielded the hammer?" Charun asked with disbelief.

Kane nodded. "Yeah."

Charun set Kane down, and the man from Cerberus could see that he held the weapon in his off hand. "The hammer has near slain most men who touched it."

"Grant and I both got a shock, but we're still healthy," Kane responded. He doubted the truth of that statement right now. It felt as if he'd been running for the past seven hours, nonstop. His arms and legs were limp as spaghetti, and his stomach growled, begging to be filled as if he'd used up every nutrient in his body. "Still alive."

"The hammer is a fickle mistress," Charun said. "It gives and it takes. Let me handle this beas—"

Before Charun could finish the word, the cyclops plowed into the demigod. Even on its damaged knee, it still was barreling along at speeds of more than fifty miles an hour. Cyclops and Charun were one massive whole, and any tree trunk in their path was smashed open or snapped in two. Nothing short of a mountainside was going to stop those two as the pair of battling titans plowed through the forest.

Grant raced to Kane's side. "Talk to me…"

Kane took a deep breath. "That thing made me tap reserves of strength I barely knew I had. I feel like I pulled every muscle in my torso and arms."

"And now you're a limp noodle," Grant murmured.

Kane tilted his head. "To add insult to my injury, I didn't even slow down that one-eyed maniac."

"I wouldn't say that," Grant replied. "Before I clocked the big bastard at about seventy-five miles an hour. You took a third off his ground speed."

"Whoopee," Kane murmured.

The crashing of trees stopped in the distance, but now thunderclaps filled the air. Both men from Cerberus felt the ground shaking beneath their feet as blows were exchanged in the distance.

"We going to get closer to this fight?" Grant asked.

"You can go. I'll just sit here until my legs tell me they can work again," Kane answered.

"I can't take you anywhere." Grant sighed.

Another thunderclap shook the ground and several tons of meat and metal hurtled back along the tunnel the cyclops had torn in its initial attack on Charun. The winds coming off the flying abomination sent Kane sprawling and forced Grant to dig his feet in to prevent being blown over.

The cyclops struck the ground, producing another quake-like rumble, but after a couple more earthshaking bounces, it came to a halt. It struggled to its feet, most of its chest bared after being slammed by the alien hammer. Blood glistened on the brass and now Kane and Grant could see that the cockpit didn't have Sandcat armor plates.

"This…isn't one of the Spartans sent by New Olympus?" Grant asked.

"Also explains the three-foot height difference between this and the average Spartan," Kane added. "This was another automaton. Another kind…"

"So maybe we're off the hook when it comes to killing these things," Grant mused.

"We can hope, right?" Kane asked.

The cyclops swayed unsteadily on its legs. The huge eye in the center of its misshapen face was burst, deflated and dripping viscera in a milky flood.

Charun appeared beside them, leaning on the handle of his hammer. "This…was a formidable foe."

"No kidding," Grant mused.

"Still kill you." The cyclops spoke. Its voice was no longer an air-rattling bellow. It was a rasp and, with each word, blood spilled over its mangled lips. Through the metallic ribs, Kane and Grant could see lacerated lungs like huge bellows, struggling to take in and expel air.

Kane looked for the heart and found it. He drew his Sin Eater and took aim. Charun looked scarcely able to walk, and the cyclops took a menacing step toward them.

"No, you won't," Kane returned to the giant. He opened fire with his side arm, firing on full-auto. A couple of rounds struck the brassy alloy rib cage, bouncing away uselessly, but others slipped between the gaps in the robotic ribs, striking tough heart muscle. Those blows caused the cyclops to stagger, but it took another ponderous step toward the trio of warriors.

Grant looked at Charun, sagging against the hammer, and Kane's own sapped strength. The Sin Eaters could cause the cyclops pain, even stagger it with direct shots to the heart, but there was only one thing that could put the giant down for the count. Without a thought, he snatched the hammer from Charun and charged.

The alien artifact hummed through his bones, an adrenal high that called back to his musings on Kane's flying skills before. Grant's already formidable musculature swelled and throbbed with unearthly strength, power that was only going to cost him in the long run. But for now, the big, former Magistrate felt the might of a god swelling in his mighty thews.

He eyed the beating heart, the lacerated lungs, cradled inside the secondary orichalcum rib cage. The hammer seemed to sense its wielder's intent and rose, swinging directly toward the alien alloy breastbone. Having gotten used to a state of Zen in his practice of samurai archery under his beloved Shizuka, Grant didn't resist; he flowed with the path of the weapon, the hammer acting as an extension of him as much as he was a part of the hammer. The surging force was accompanied by a brilliant light, a charge of energy that bled off in streamers of plasma as the hammer head accelerated, lashing at the rib cage of the cyclops.

Grant could sense that the hammer had become blazing hot, the air slicing, sizzling with its passage. And then, contact.

The world turned a brilliant white, even the polarized face screen of his shadow suit hood unable to filter out the blazing glory of the hammer at the peak of its power. Tears flowed, trying to protect his eyes from a blaze that it wasn't truly feeling through the environmentally contained suit.

The air itself seemed to explode in a deafening wave the hood couldn't dampen even with its auditory electronics. Grant almost would have wished that someone had struck his ears with hammers than listen to that sound.

Blind and deaf, Grant staggered backward. There was no telling where the cyclops was because Grant was in a world of ringing eardrums and a burning afterglow hanging in his clenched-shut eyes. Right now he was helpless and anything could come upon him; he wouldn't even be able to tell if a Manta was landing right next to him.

Insensate, Grant whispered words, half in prayer, half in self-reproach, begging himself to recover from the hammer's landing.

Strong hands gripped his shoulders immediately, fingers grasping tightly, but not to hurt. They were also human-size, more or less, so they didn't belong to the cyclops.

"Grant, you got him." He could only "hear" it over the Commtact, the vibrations in his jawbone going directly to his eardrum.

"Can't see," Grant muttered. "Can't hear."

"It's all right, man," Kane said. His voice was coming through more clearly.

"Impressive." He heard Charun. "None but I have used the hammer like so."

Grant still felt the hammer's handle in his grip and realized the artifact was helping his eyes and ears to recover from the trauma they'd been subjected to.

Within another few moments he could see clearly again and the world sounded "right" again. He peeled himself out of the shadow suit hood and looked around. He handed off the hammer to Charun. Whatever the drain the device had inflicted upon Kane, it hadn't had that effect on him.

"Your arms and legs feel like rubber?" Kane asked.

Grant shook his head. "No. Were you fighting it?"

"It's a hammer. You manhandle those," Kane replied.

"Not this one," Grant told him. "It was alive. It worked *with* me."

"Both of you could lift it," Charun stated. "That is what impresses me. But you tapped its true force."

Grant nodded. "All that Zen learning from Shizuka. I allowed the weapon to guide me in its most efficient path."

"And that is what has bonded this weapon to me," Charun stated, hefting the warrior artifact. "We understand each other, and now you, Grant, have the same mental bond."

"Crazy," Kane muttered.

"But not outside of our understanding of the technology of the gods," Brigid interjected. "Such as when we saw how the overlords commanded their ships with mental power."

"The hammer lives," Grant said. "And you have to work with it. That way it won't beat you up and drain you."

Charun smiled, clapping Grant on the shoulder. "Well met."

Grant looked back at the remnants of the cyclops, the

"rib cage" of the robotic skeleton now sticking up like gnarled fingers, everything within charred to a crisp thanks to the plasma discharge. The abomination was dead. What was more, the beast *was not* the creation of Vanth, at least not using one of the captured Spartan warriors in their Gear Skeletons. There was an enemy out there, whether or not it was the goddess of the hunt, or some other entity. And it had access to horrors beyond the scope of anything they had encountered so far.

Chapter 17

Beneath the hill that Vanth and Charun called their home, Domi and the rest of CAT Beta moved silently, edging down the corridor first constructed from ancient iron framework, then hewed into stone itself, digging through the Earth. According to the readouts on Domi's faceplate, they had descended two hundred feet as they followed the corridor. This was off their current "altitude" and not in relation to the depth of the hill over their heads.

Their descent ended at the wrought-iron gate, and Domi was right after giving them a scan with the telescopic optics on her shadow suit. There was no way that anyone was going to slip through the bars, as the vertical crisscross left gaps about a foot wide, even more slender than Domi could squirm herself through. Edwards looked at the rock floor beneath the gate and frowned.

"So much for the dirt floor theory," he muttered.

Domi kept her ears open for the sound of anyone on the other side of the heavy gate.

"Think of something," she told him.

"I will," Edwards returned. He looked back at Sela and Smaragda. "We will."

Domi nodded, standing watch.

Within a few moments, however, there was the roar of an explosion outside that rumbled down the corridor to the surface, as if a massive bomb had gone off. The four infiltrators froze at the cacophony.

Almost immediately after the throb of the distant thunderbolt, Domi picked up the clank and thud of heavy robotic feet coming.

"Hug the depressions in the wall and go full stealth mode," Domi said. She quickly unpacked her boots and tugged them on. It was one thing to be barefoot out in the wild—the feral girl relied as much on the pads of her feet as her eyes and nose to detect potential traps or trip wires. However, to be invisible in the corridor against a furrow in the rock, she was going to need her complete suit. Luckily, the boots slipped on like socks, firming up as they sealed with the rest of her suit.

The boots would also nullify her infrared signature. Domi's feet, through a thermal camera, would have resembled a small mammal's, rather than point her out as a barefoot woman in a body-conforming environmental suit. However, in the close quarters of this wide and tall artificial cavern, a pair of naked feet would definitely attract attention. With great swiftness, she found a furrow along the wall and pressed into it. She tapped her forearm, bringing up the control menu, and set it for blend-mode. Miniature optic sensors picked up her surroundings and translated the terrain onto the skin of the suit.

Domi glanced around, reflexively holding her breath as the gate rose, clanking and rattling. A dozen of the Olympian soldiers came running through as soon as the gate cleared six feet in height, each of them carrying a rifle. In their body armor, they had their own helmets complete with electronic goggles and radio communications, but Domi frustratingly waited for them to pass. None of them seemed concerned with scanning the walls.

The Spartans, however, stood in front of the rising gate, floodlights blazing on their artificial heads. Domi was surprised when she counted all three of the missing Olympian war armors, which was at once a relief and yet only confused her even more. If the Gear Skeletons hadn't been the basis for the cyclops that Kane and Grant encountered, then what was?

She let those thoughts lay idle as the trio of robots rushed along in pursuit of the enthralled soldiers. As soon as the group was fifty feet away, Domi relaxed and waved to the others, pointing to the lowering gate.

Everyone, even Smaragda, made it through the gate before it closed, but once the wrought-iron barrier locked into place, the white-haired soldier looked through the bars.

"There should be more of them," she whispered softly, her fingers wrapping around the bar as she gazed on in deep concern.

Domi rested her hand on Smaragda's shoulder. "Some of them might have been held back, or put on some other duty."

"What about that explosion?" Sela Sinclair asked.

"Whatever it was, it gave us an opening to get in here. Let's not waste it by standing around so we're discovered," Edwards warned.

Domi nodded, and the group fell back into silence. She took the lead, following the route she'd heard the troops and the robots take. So far, except for an occasional torch here and there, the underground tunnel was unlit. The only thing they had going for them were their night-vision capability and infrared illuminators.

Domi kept using her illuminator intermittently, if only to prevent them from being seen by others further down these tunnels with their own night-vision optics. She kept them moving at a brisk walking pace, but her senses and instincts were on full alert. So far, no trip lines or electric eyes were in evidence, and there were no opponents lurking in the shadows.

So far, everyone had silent weapons out. Domi's knife,

its blade coated in phosphate black paint, wouldn't glimmer with a reflection. Edwards also had his knife, similarly dark coated, as was the custom of Magistrates, the foot-long deadly edge ready to sever an arm if necessary. Smaragda's falcata, like that of all Olympian combat blades, was dull in its finish, a dark gray steel. Even Sinclair's collapsible baton was coated in a nonslip rubberized coating, the thin layer providing a tacky feel that wouldn't skid, but did very little to cushion the anodized steel beneath the millimeter thickness. In the dark, the four of them had the means of delivering quick, silent death.

Domi didn't want it to come to that if they encountered any of the mind-controlled slaves of Vanth, but in a choice between her teammates and a potential threat, the feral girl would do what she had to, and mourn and regret it later.

The four of them eventually began to encounter more and more lit torches in the corridor, and slowed their pace. It was still quiet, but there was no telling if there was someone around a bend or in a side room standing guard. With their wills stolen, the sentries would prove to be silent and literally unblinking. Domi noticed there were doors to different chambers leading off of the corridor. The depth they reached now was over three hundred feet, and the hill itself extended another four hundred above "ground level." The air felt thicker and heavier down here, despite the lack of light.

Passing by each doorway was an exercise in caution and risk. So far, many of these rooms were empty of people, but there were supplies stored down here. This, however, was nothing like any redoubt Domi had ever encountered. The hill above seemed to be some manner of pyramid, buried under years of sediment and soil, perhaps even deliberately.

For all the exploration, all the hidden temples and underground vaults, even distant worlds that Domi and her friends had visited, she wasn't surprised someone had constructed, then buried a pyramid in Italy. She recalled the giant structure—Xian—in China, and how that had been dug out from hiding. She also recalled that somewhere in Eastern Europe was an alleged compound of buried pyramids, at least that's what Brigid Baptiste had said.

This was another undiscovered mystery, passed over and unknown from the days when humankind was allegedly at the top of its technological and scientific skills. And what horrors lay beneath were grisly indeed, if Vanth was the mastermind and soul stealer that the Cerberus teams suspected.

Domi pointed toward one of the rooms and then motioned for the others to enter there. The plan was simple. They would post up in an out-of-the-way position and allow Domi to sneak ahead. The small woman was much more likely to lose herself in the maze of tunnels should anyone be looking for her, and yet her tracking skills would allow her to trace back to where she'd left the rest of CAT Beta. As there weren't many things stored in the room she'd sent them into, there was little chance they'd be stumbled upon.

Granted, with Edwards in there, even being a "normal-size" room, it was crowded. The door closed easily and noiselessly. They'd checked to make sure there were no wires that could be connected to a security system, so opening and closing it wouldn't give them away.

Edwards leaned in close to Domi. "Thirty minutes. Then we come looking for you."

Domi nodded.

"Or if we hear something," Sinclair added.

"You won't," Domi said.

The door closed and the silent, feral girl stalked away,

keeping to the shadows as often as she could, no matter how empty the corridors were.

Eventually she made her way to a larger chamber. She paused before going in, but it had some form of bioluminescent lighting and she could see over a short balcony that there were huge rows of cages packed with humans and animals. Domi scanned first for sentries or other means of alarms, but none were positioned on the tier of walkway circling the cavernous room. Still, she crawled to the edge of the balcony, peering over and down.

She could see that there were dozens of cells, and started to count them, first by rows, then by columns, "horizontal and vertical" as she'd been taught by Lakesh when it came to figuring things such as area, but quickly, she realized there could have been millions down there. She unsealed her faceplate and took a breath, and smelled the stink of an entire city full of people and animals. She noticed there were people moving in the spaces between the cells and, resealing the faceplate, she saw that they were wheeling around carts of sludge, taking them off toward a side tunnel.

Of course being mind-controlled meant that you still required normal bodily functions. Those who were actually moving around were going about the task of keeping bodily wastes from making the air all but unbreathable. Domi scanned for other entrances and saw that there were different forms of carts being wheeled in from just beneath her. These were loaded with rice and beans.

Subsistence foods.

Domi smirked. "Explains the smell."

For whatever purpose these people were being kept, they were being kept alive and in good health. She didn't see any signs of abuse or more than token captivity. Those with the food opened the cells without needing to unlock them, and the thralls moved silently, orderly, receiving their platefuls of food and cups of water.

So much for keeping them all as slaves and prisoners, Domi mused. Vanth was actually providing for their well-being, so they wouldn't starve or dehydrate. Then again, keeping them alive and healthy might have been the only means of keeping her power sources. There was a mix of humans and animals down there that, together, could provide enough mental energy to do almost anything the demigoddess wanted.

Domi looked around and noticed a stairwell. She debated going down into the pit of prisoners, but also noticed that there was no room for one of the Gear Skeletons to climb the stairs. There must have been some other place of storage for the war machines.

The other reason she declined to go down there was that there was a good chance someone would be awake and alert enough to transmit her presence to Vanth. Better to observe from afar than to get in close. She took several digital photographs using the shadow suit hood, storing them for when they were once again out in the open. She slinked back along the corridor that lead here and heard the clanking of a gate in the distance. She froze in a niche in the wall, waiting for the arrival of the Spartans and the New Olympians that had appeared before, and had granted CAT Beta the means to enter this complex.

The movements of the mechanical giants seemed much slower now, and accordingly, the humans from Greece kept to the more leisurely pace of their robots.

Peering through the dark, she made out the figures as they carried something between them. It was Edwards's Manta. They hauled it along as if it were just a large chair between two movers. The mind-controlled soldiers stayed around them, guarding, but also using their flashlights to guide the giants and their burden. The group made it to an intersection then turned off.

Domi waited a few moments, then jogged off after them, keeping her profile low, her footsteps soft, though the heavy stomps of Olympian footwear and robotic claw treads made more than sufficient ambient noise to conceal a dancing dinosaur.

Domi stayed with her stealth training, never making a move or a noise that would betray her position, never committing to a movement that would leave her stuck out in the open to an observer. She shadowed the group, who didn't seem to care if they were followed or not. That didn't mean she wasn't remaining on her toes, though. One mistake and this whole mountain could come crashing down on her and her allies in CAT Beta.

She continued counting down the time to Edwards's deadline in her mind; she'd only been exploring for about six minutes. So far she'd managed to pick up a lot of information about the true scope and nature of Vanth. Continuing along, she paused as the Spartans took the Manta into an underground hangar, settling it down gently on its landing gear. With a quick scan of the hangar, Domi noticed that there was a third Spartan, matching the insignias of the suits taken by Vanth's song. It was standing in a stall next to the other two. These particular Gear Skeletons had similar but crudely painted insignias and decals that, by comparison, showed them for the frauds they were.

Domi also noticed one other thing. The "pilots" inside those armored giants were far from human. It looked as if someone had turned a person into dough and hurled them into a pilot's seat rather than an amputee or a dwarven pilot. She wrinkled her nose in disgust as the two suits strode over and parked themselves. Soldiers immediately began bringing food to the melted monstrosities inside the chests of the robots, unseemly heads turning and stretching on necks to gum at spoonfuls of rice and beans.

The insides of their mouths were without teeth and their tongues were bulbous, swollen and pink, flattening out to let the spoonfuls land on them, before slurping back between lips. It reminded Domi of a desert tortoise gnawing at a pulpy cactus, except the turtle was cute to the feral girl. This inspired her at every second to chop it into pieces with an ax then burn the remains.

Domi closed her eyes and took a cleansing breath, steeling her nerves against the disgusting sight. Her distaste at what was on display did not prevent her from snapping pictures on her hood's optics. The rest of Cerberus was going to get an eyeful, no holds barred. The things down here were atrocities, a familiar-seeming abomination, but these living spitballs, all tentacles and pseudopods, were something new that Brigid Baptiste would have to know about. The truth of the "servile" Spartans was a lie laid bare by the existence of these sluglike horrors.

The soldiers themselves took off their helmets and they, too, seemed to be far from the mindless drones that the Cerberus explorers had encountered so far. Their faces were coated in some form of dust or paint that made them seem pallid and lifeless. They were also not human, not if their glassy, milky eyes had anything to say about it. These things were naturally without any detail or structure to their eyes save for the pinpoint pupil at the center.

She kept "snapping" photos of these creatures. They were hairless, stretched and distorted in their appearance, the Olympian armor the only thing that made them appear normal. As they doffed their uniforms, Domi could see that their color was a natural grayish, and was immediately reminded of Quavell and the other hybrids. These weren't quite the same, though, as the similarities were vague enough to delay her observation of this fact. They might have been a part of Vanth and Char-un's true race, as the Quad V hybrids had been designed from the ground up to be one of the servant races of the barons.

Indeed, the barons themselves were hybrids, with ancient Annunaki DNA planted into the human race. When *Tiamat* returned and unleashed her signal to evolve, the barons literally shed their old skins, growing from five-foot spindly creatures to seven-foot, muscular and beautiful godlings. The Quad Vs had been removed from the equation, the hundreds or thousands of these creatures growing to six feet in height, their wills and minds sapped to become the Nephilim.

Domi narrowed her eyes.

The Nephilim were Quad V hybrids whose minds and individuality were stolen or sublimated and then mutated. Bres had also created his own warrior drones—the Fomori. All of this sounded a hell of a lot like the activity Vanth initiated with the Italians and the missing Olympian expedition; all those humans left milling around in their cells.

She tried listening in on the conversations of the unusual aliens, but they didn't speak. This added to their alien nature, if only for the knowledge that Vanth was suspected of possessing telepathic abilities, as well as other entities that they'd encountered. All of this made Domi keep herself hidden and camouflaged with even more paranoid urgency. Brigid had engaged CAT Beta in post-hypnotic suggestions that gave their surface thoughts good cover, should they be discovered. They were also utilizing their Commtacts to produce a form of white noise, rendering them invisible on radio frequencies the Cerberus scientists assumed telepathy operated on.

It was all experimental, and for all Domi knew, the creatures in front of her were simply humoring her, ignoring the nosy little ape as she crawled around their basement.

If that was the case, then Kane and the others were in great danger above.

Domi frowned beneath the faceplate of her armor. These things from Styx—"Stygians" as Brigid labeled them—were beyond the kind of threat they had been anticipating. All their less-lethal combat gear was intended to hold off innocent but mindless throngs of humans sent against them. There were humans and birds used as the eyes of Vanth, but it appeared that when it came to military action, these protean meat puppets were the ones to do that work.

Movement sounded in the corridor leading from the gate and Domi stilled and calmed herself, emptying her mind. There was one last Stygian, wearing the Olympian field armor, walking back. It carried a bloody lump of flesh in both hands. The lump looked like the squirmy, sluglike head of the things bonded with the Gear Skeletons. A severed head.

The soldier came closer and Domi continued to take pictures. The waxy eyes blinked, rippling, oozing flesh acting as lids, demonstrating that the severed part was still alive. Domi also got to see that the neck stump had fused with the Stygian holding it, the fleshy protuberance entering the opened belly of the armor and connecting to the thing beneath.

The soldier and its grisly charge passed her by, not noticing her, and continued into the robot hangar. Domi watched as the neck came unstuck from its bearer, and she fought the urge to shiver, her skin spawning goose bumps as the disembodied head was placed onto the flesh of one of the other "pilots."

The dully gumming creature barely acknowledged the new mind merging with its body, until the new head opened its wound of a mouth, moaning for spoonfuls of food. Then, the original head began licking the gore and blood off its new conjoined brother.

Domi steeled herself, ignoring the churning in her belly.

She didn't envy those who would see these pictures or this vid when she sent it back to Cerberus.

Chapter 18

It took a half an hour for CAT Beta to come close enough to the surface to transmit their findings home. Lakesh had been on the edge of his seat awaiting the news.

"Any problems?" Lakesh asked.

"Nope. As long as there was an open conduit to the surface, even with an iron gate in the way, the signal was clear," Bry said. "Of course, they had to transmit it to one of the satellites on their horizon, from their perspective."

"I'm glad you were able to maneuver one to be in line with the entrance to the underground pyramid." Lakesh sighed. "Otherwise, who knows how long we would have to wait for them to get out of…what is that?"

Bry glanced at the screen Lakesh was watching. Brewster Philboyd was on hand and turned away, spewing his coffee into a garbage can. Philboyd began dry heaving, his torment amplified by the echoes in the small metal bucket.

"That's—" Philboyd gagged "—nothing that should be."

Lakesh observed Domi's photographs of the contents of the Gear Skeletons inside Vanth's hangar. He'd already made notice of the three captured war suits, but the molten, distorted blobs of flesh and muscle sitting within the cockpits of the extant armors were at once disturbing and enthralling. Though he wasn't a biologist, he could see where the amorphous nature of the pilots was a boon to their ability to interface with the control systems, especially as he couldn't see where a command node could be inserted onto their forms.

He also was acutely aware of how similar a set of flesh sculpting had returned him from a 250-year-old cryogenically preserved man physically in his eighties to a man in his late forties. Flesh, bone and even his bionic parts had been broken down and rebuilt to the molecular scale by Enlil in his guise as Sam the Imperator.

That bit of transformation of old and dying cells to "new ones" was one of the few reasons why Lakesh could go out on missions, occasionally, and actually be a suitable lover to Domi. He realized that, quite easily, Sam could have made him into any manner of abomination. He looked through the pictures, eliciting grunts from Bry and Philboyd.

The armored soldiers, however, were an even greater revelation. Lakesh had been in on the Project of Unification; one of the great minds behind the barons and their means of crossing miles and keeping the great villes in touch with each other via mat-trans and the remarkable technologies stored within the redoubts. He realized that humanity's fate had been hijacked by tyrannical forces from the time that humankind was first crawling on all fours.

The Stygians were similar to the hybrids, but there was sufficient difference that Lakesh was wondering if they were some manner of prototype creatures, perhaps a halfway breed between the Quad V and Balam, the last Archon who had overseen and limited the growth of humanity's intellect and independence. Balam had wavered from his original mission as minion of the Annunaki and their baronial incarnations.

There was nothing to say that these creatures were not some intermediate form of servitor race. Over the past year Lakesh and the rest of Cerberus had been gaining new insights into the world when Annunaki overlords were the unsubtle rulers of Earth, before their hibernation, their descent into the background due to their accords with the Tuatha de Danaan.

The Igigi were what the Nephilim had once been, before Enlil's terrible act, lobotomizing the race into a seemingly endless army of warrior drones. Perhaps it wasn't a lobotomizing of an entire species, but a cloning and genetic manipulation. The Nephilim were not on display here, though. It was the Stygians, and Lakesh saw one of them enter, wielding the apparently severed head of one of its allies. Judging by the similarity of the appearance of the "skeleton pilots" and the fleshy linkage with the humanoid Stygian, this must have been another pilot.

Lakesh had received the report of the battle with the cyclops from Kane and Grant.

This had been the mind operating the giant warrior, the thing that CAT Alpha had fought, shoulder to shoulder with Charun, against. Grant may have showed that he was able to operate the deadly hammer of the Etruscan godling, but a small sliver of the creature survived, possibly for the sake that Kane and Grant had been spent after their war with the gigantic abomination and three of its smaller comrades. Tired, unwilling to stick around the abattoir, the two men and Charun returned to the buried pyramid, letting the "mindless thralls" do the cleanup work and to conveniently bring the surviving seed of the cyclops home.

Lakesh would have to ask DeFore about this. While she was nominally the chief medic at Cerberus, her strengths were in biology, so she would understand these things much better. If that thing could withstand a plasma discharge of the kind that Grant and Kane described, they'd need to know a lot more about these entities.

For now, Lakesh forestalled the ill feelings in his gut

and began composing a quick, cryptic note for Brigid Baptiste to receive during their next bit of contact.

Lakesh simply hoped he'd still be able to warn CAT Alpha of the true extent of their trap.

SMARAGDA WAS GLAD when Domi returned to their hideout in the storage cell. She'd been trying to process the memories of the passage of her fellow soldiers. Her alleged fellow soldiers.

Finally, when Domi returned and explained what she'd seen, the Olympian soldier let out a breath of relief.

"I thought my mind was playing tricks on me," she told CAT Beta. "None of them looked right as they passed by."

She looked over the pictures, shared via suit-to-suit electrical conductivity rather than by transmission, on her suit's forearm sleeve, configured as a monitor. "Then it's likely that my people are down in the pit?"

"I know you'd love to go down there," Domi said.

"Only if Charun and Vanth are kept busy," Smaragda stated. "Face it, we heard the sound of that hammer striking outside. We're all loaded up with some nice firearms, but that is some terrifying shit."

"Not looking forward to fighting him, either," Domi admitted.

"That much is obvious," Edwards murmured. "All right, so Myrto is not going to get stupid and jump the gun to rescue her partners. Great. We're all being smart about this."

"Smart is a relative thing. After all, we're stuck in here with aliens, including alien-piloted robots, and locked in by a several-ton, wrought-iron gate," Sinclair said.

"Always looking on the bright side," Domi answered.

"Well, you came back fairly quickly," Edwards said. "How much more did you explore?"

"We could look for another exit to the surface," Sela

agreed. "But the chances are, the way up and out would be right through the hangar where the aliens are."

"And going through them would raise enough of a racket to bring Vanth and Charun running. Or even if we snuck past them…" Edwards noted.

"We wait for them," Domi said. "Commtacts on passive pickup. Hear when they're talking."

"You think they'll bring them down here to see the prisoners?" Smaragda asked.

"Been dealing with enough of these types," Domi answered. "Love to show off. Show how smart they are. Their I-love-me wall."

"Even if that means it'll turn Kane and the others against them?" Smaragda continued.

Domi nodded. "Enlil never minded. Walked us all around his ship. Thought he was the shit."

Smaragda nodded. "Hera was the same way with you, too. The old Hera, that is. She let you in, even though you might have figured out her scam."

"She was balancing threats at the time. The Hydrae were now under the control of Marduk," Sinclair added. "And we were the only ones who could help her stop him. Well, Kane, Grant and Brigid."

"You helped, too," Domi returned.

Sinclair shook her head. "We all know who the stars of this show are."

"This world…more complex every passing day," Domi said. "We get involved as much as they do. We carry our weight."

"But every day, we get a little closer to being disposable," Sinclair murmured.

"No," Domi countered. "We're all needed to keep building. Protecting future."

"Yeah, Sela," Edwards added. "What'd that actor say? No small roles, only small actors?"

"Speak for yourself, Tiny," Sinclair countered. "All right. Just the way that Lakesh talks about their damn confluence of luck…"

"Hey, we're still here," Edwards said. "It's not like we're red shirts. Just keep going, one step after another. And don't be stupid. We weren't picked because we make mistakes."

"Just remember, we're human, not legends," Sinclair said.

"So're Kane and others," Domi added. "Smart enough to avoid mistakes. Tough enough to survive when we make 'em. Quick enough to learn from 'em, too. Why they picked you two. More 'n' one-dimensional."

"More than just hammers looking for nails," Sinclair agreed. "Okay. Even so, we're going to be waiting awhile."

"But now we know," Smaragda said. "We know they're not using our people as soldiers, and that one of our Spartan pilots didn't die to give Kane and Grant a good show as a cyclops."

"Things are looking rosy all over, but I wouldn't get too comfortable," Sinclair added.

Domi narrowed her ruby-red eyes. "Why you think sitting back at door?"

"All right. Just remember, someone has to take the role of the grumpy bastard," Sinclair told her. "I'm just looking on the bad side of things…"

"Expect worst. Enjoy disappointment," Domi concluded.

"You're getting too smart for your own good, girl," Sinclair chuckled.

Edwards smirked. "Let's hope we stay too smart for the good of Vanth."

Smaragda uncapped her canteen and took a sip. "I'll drink to that."

The four people passed the water can around, biding

their time, knowing that sooner or later the warriors of Cerberus were going to have to rise as one to do battle together against the Etruscan godlings and their Stygian minions. Thanks to Domi, they knew the odds, not limited to merely a dozen soldiers and three brutal robots, but also a million humans and animals kept in the deepest pit of the pyramid.

IT WAS A victory feast, with human thralls—women mostly—bringing food before the battered but victorious Charun and his honored guests. Brigid was included with them, for he claimed that it was under her observations and overwatch that Kane and Grant had been able to help the demigod prevail against the cyclops and his twisted brethren.

Brigid felt as if she were being paranoid as she sniffed and tentatively tasted each glass of wine and morsel of food. Indeed, they were dealing with aliens whose mental and physical capabilities were such that drugs or poison would be the furthest thing from their minds. Vanth herself demonstrated a song designed to infiltrate a human brain and leave the person it was attached to a drone without free will. Herbs or toxins were beneath such capabilities, and yet she couldn't help but feel the necessity to be careful.

Vanth smiled at her across the great feast table in the cavernous hall in which Charun conducted his revelry. Her golden eyes were at once warm and alienating, and Brigid partitioned her mind, burying her concerns and worries deep within, creating barriers of useless and nearly endless trivia.

"You are used to dining with those who may be devils, Miss Baptiste," Vanth observed, her voice smooth and sensuous, like silk reimagined as sonic waves.

Brigid wondered why she would even need her song

with seductive tones that threatened even to enthrall a straight woman as herself.

"Yes," she answered, sipping her wine. It was classic Italian wine, fortified concentrate, diluted with clean spring water. To drink the original fruit of this vine before its diminishment would be to risk one's health. She recalled that a goblet of fortified wine was how Caligula assassinated his brother, the sheer weight of its alcoholic content poisoning the young man, yet looking to the rest of Roman society as "an honest mistake."

"You say you have dealt with the likes of Enlil…so you know of our struggles."

"My ordeals have been with Marduk and his followers, co-opting our godhood. Before we were driven to our slumber, Charun and I saw him masquerade as Zeus. Charun and I were not guards, but those who cared for the souls and spirits of our people," Vanth stated. "Back then, the power of believers was something worth warring for. We gained our role as psychopomps in that we managed to rescue our worshipers from the overlord's dominion."

"Sometimes you brought them back whole and other times you were able to release their essences," Brigid surmised.

Vanth nodded. "I presume you are aware of quantum theory."

"Many aspects, though the math can be overwhelming," Brigid responded.

"Then you understand the concept that the reality that you and I currently sit in is something that is merely a shadow. A tesseract of an original," Vanth said.

Brigid nodded. "I've always been more of a fan of the beer-head descriptor. That we live in the quantum foam, while the totality of reality is actually the fluid we are floating on."

Vanth smiled. "Right. And each person, their existence,

their essence, while it might look like something different and unique, is all composed of the exact same cosmic energy. When an organic dies, the vitality that made them alive does not dissipate due to the laws of conservation of matter and energy."

"It returns from the quantum foam to the cosmic fluid," Brigid concluded.

Vanth took a deep breath, closing her eyes in almost orgasmic relief. Brigid bit her lower lip, steeling herself against the magnificence and sheer magnetism of the woman in front of her. "You do not realize how wonderful it is to talk to someone who can entertain these thoughts, let alone understand them."

Brigid glanced over at Charun, who was laughing as Grant and Kane joked with him. The eight-foot titan picked up his tankard of mead and took a deep draught.

"So, you are more in touch with this quantum whole," Brigid stated.

"We can trace the energies, the threads. Indeed, in returning to the foam-and-bubbles theory, our universe is from the next bubble over," Vanth said. "We've called our home Styx…but humanity has gone and made that out to be a river to the afterlife."

"Which, in the terms of quantum theory, a wormhole between our universes would be akin to such a river," Brigid said. "Not the river Styx, but the river *to* Styx."

"Which in your English would still be named the River Styx," Vanth said. "To give ourselves a common terminology. We can agree upon this, correct?"

Brigid nodded. She sipped some more. The food was delicious, but she couldn't help but wonder at where the rest of the population of this countryside had gone. There were far fewer humans working in the pyramid than she would have expected given the sparseness of the Etruscan lands.

According to the New Olympians, others had sent expeditions into this land, seeking out those who had formerly been traders and customers. Those expeditions faded into nothingness, never returning, and this was on the heels of the loss of three caravans traveling through. Even via satellite, the Italian peninsula was notably depopulated. One year ago, according to infrared scans, there were several hundred thousand humans, as well as attendant livestock, living in the surrounding terrain.

Now, except for the smaller animals, birds and a couple of small towns, there were barely two percent of the life forms visible.

While it was possible that Vanth may have exterminated them all, this pyramid was a significant source of heat. Measurements showed that somewhere in its halls and chambers, the heat signature of a million mammals was gathered.

"Right now, I have sequenced the people and livestock together in a telepathic algorithm," Vanth explained. "An organic search engine that is searching for the frequency through which we can open up our River Styx and allow for easy passage between the two."

"Even cattle and sheep can be used for figuring this out?" Brigid asked.

"Every brain cell can be used as a binary computer, even those of lower mammals and avians," Vanth stated. "The capacity of math as simple as one and none is there for even insects."

Brigid raised an eyebrow.

"No, I haven't hijacked the bugs," Vanth told her. "First off…I don't care much for the little creepy crawlies. And second, a million vertebrates is a perfect contiguous system for ascertaining the portal and opening it."

"You'll be able to open it without an Annunaki threshold or our interphaser?" Brigid asked.

Vanth nodded. "My torch is our technology for that purpose. We just need the combination to the lock, to use another analogy."

Brigid took a deep breath. "I hate to seem distrusting…"

"You have a proper purpose to be so," Vanth countered. "From the information I've gleaned about your history with other pan- and extraterrestrial entities, you cannot have gotten a good impression of our kind. I would love to inform you that not all of us are the same."

"No. We've encountered benevolence, as well," Brigid returned. "Enki is the greatest of these examples, as well as Balam and Quavell."

"But you see me, borrowing the minds of others of your species, without asking," Vanth admitted.

Brigid nodded. "That is a frightening and imposing concept. To be hijacked to become part of a massive calculator."

"They are all safe and well beneath the pyramid. They are shielded from even the mightiest of mankind's nuclear weaponry, cradled under one thousand feet of this arcology," Vanth told her. "You do sense the similarity between this and the megalithic ville you used to reside in—Cobaltville, correct?"

Brigid nodded. "Safe. What about their other needs?"

"They are being kept fed, bathed, and their accommodations are being hygienically maintained by humans we've programmed for that task," Vanth said. "And once we are done with them, then we will free them."

"Unharmed," Brigid returned.

Vanth nodded. "I swear upon my oath as defender of these lands. I have protected, not conquered. I have not taken that for which I have repaid. And the wonders I give unto humanity in repayment for opening the door back to our home shall be endless."

Brigid looked toward Charun and her fellow adventurers. Her instincts were tingling and her belief in the benevolence of Vanth was shaky for now. Was this demigoddess seducing her with soothing voice and lies by omission? Or was she sincere and genuinely pleading her innocence?

"Endless wonders," Brigid repeated. "Let's drink to that."

Vanth poured some more wine, for the both of them. To endless wonder...not endless horror.

Chapter 19

Kane could feel Charun's disappointment at being dragged away from the table, from feasting and carousing, and forced to accompany Vanth and Brigid on their tour through the mighty pyramid.

"This is not fair. We have won a mighty victory," Charun said.

"This is how Brigid celebrates," Grant offered. "Knowledge is joy to her."

Charun wrinkled his nose, sniffing in disdain. "Just as well. There is little fun to be had when carousing with insensate thralls. In their calculation mode, they agree to any and all suggestions."

"Not much sport in the already drugged," Kane agreed. "That immediately puts you ahead of most of the enemies we've battled."

Charun looked down at Kane, then roared with laughter, drawing stares from Brigid and Vanth up ahead of them.

"Use your inside laughter, my love," Vanth chided.

"This is my inside laugh," Charun countered. Kane saw the wink in the big man's eye in his response to her. It was a human enough action, disarmingly so. These entities had elements in common with him and Brigid, including the familiar chiding and joking together. If there had been a third member of their group, Kane would almost have thought these godlings had based themselves off...

"So how much did you learn about us from the Olympians?" Kane asked.

"Not as much as I would have liked, but enough to see that your reputation of courage and proficiency as warriors was not exaggerated by their memories," Charun stated.

Kane nodded. "Especially with Grant wielding your hammer."

"That was a surprise," Charun admitted. "But then, it has been a long time since you battled alongside the soldiers of New Olympus."

"All I did was not resist the weapon," Grant said. "It knew where it wanted to go and I helped it."

"You've said that before," Charun pointed out. As they were now, Vanth and Charun were both wearing their loincloths and nothing more. Weapons, armor and wing packs had been returned to their proper storage, for none would dare assail the home of the Etruscan gods, or so Kane imagined the thinking of these beings. He was busy projecting thoughts and likenesses onto them, but kept his true doubts and fears smothered deep down in his gut. He wasn't allowing his prejudices to rise to the surface, though, ever since he'd started adventuring alongside Brigid Baptiste, both he and Grant had leavened their old and cranky ways. There were still initial knee-jerk reactions, and tons of suspicions, but they didn't let them blind them to the real evidence of their eyes and ears.

They judged now on deeds, not words, but no one could be immune to negative first impressions, not when you'd spent a life in law enforcement and been trained to look for the worst, the signs of danger among those you meet. No, Kane was not the same man he was six years ago, but some things never changed.

Especially the tenet of "be polite, be courteous, but have a plan to kill everyone in the room."

Just because you weren't judging books by their covers didn't mean they still weren't full of lies and deceit, and often enough, those covers did match their contents. But now, Kane wanted to be absolutely certain, not to let prejudices color any evidence.

He returned to examining the pair. Vanth didn't seem to care that her feminine assets were all but bared for all to see, a string around her hips holding up the length of linen that hid her genitals in a token nod to modesty in mixed human company. Her full, luscious breasts were pert and, Kane had to admit, hypnotizing in their soft, rounded perfection. He noted that Grant tended to focus intently on her face or something else rather than get drawn into those tits.

Her comfort at near nudity almost seemed like a dare to either of the men. Her battle armor was nearly transparent, or it was designed with the same tapestry of her skin, so that when she went into battle, you saw her as if she were naked, but her flesh was protected against all elements and harm.

"Hell, if I had a body like that, I'd charge into battle naked, too," Brigid had admitted when they'd first arrived via Manta. That memory brought a smile to Kane's lips as the image of Vanth was replaced with Brigid herself, looking bare to all the world yet still wrapped in alien alloy cloth tough enough to turn small arms fire.

Baptiste, forgive me for that, he thought as they looked through halls decorated with ancient artifacts. The pyramid was clean, and it was a place that archaeologists would have killed to enter had they known of its existence in another age. Hell, there was enough gold and silver to bring in pirates from across the globe seeking wealth. Gemstones and artwork from the time when the gods let man assume he was the pinnacle of life on the planet were on display, as well.

The wealth of history here is incredible, Kane mused. In some rooms he saw the leather spines of books stuffed onto shelves, as well as wound scrolls and storage tubes for more of the same. Something Brigid had mentioned niggled at the back of his mind. "The library of Alexandria."

Charun looked down. "Ah, Alexandria. An almost impressive collection, much of it stolen from our lands."

Kane tilted his head questioningly.

"We were here first," Charun explained. "Without us, there never would have been a Greece, or a Rome. Alexandria was put together for *them*."

Kane understood the emphasis in Charun's statement was a curse toward the Annunaki.

Methinks you protest too much, Kane thought, tapping a line that Brigid had used on more than one occasion. He was starting to wonder if they weren't kith and kin to Enlil and his lot.

Once more, he found himself fighting against ancient prejudices, reminding himself that there were those of Annunaki blood who were not evil. Balam had a mixture of genes including that race, and he'd warned and aided Cerberus against the overlords. Fand's father was Enlil himself, and yet she was a trusted ally, calling upon Kane and the others in struggles against ancient evils. Then there was Enlil's brother, the benevolent Enki, and his spawn, the Nagah and the Watatsumi who'd splintered off from their Indian brethren across millennia and catastrophes. The mere presence of the DNA of the overlords was not a condemnation; it was just a sign that they were simply different from human. The Nagah and Watatsumi had demonstrated that they were just as human as anyone Kane had met.

Maybe Charun's disgust with Enlil was such that he

rejected his Annunaki heritage, or maybe it was all just a trick.

And yet, Kane had his Sin Eater on his forearm, his fighting knife in its boot sheath and was still clad in his protective shadow suit. The same went for Grant, and Brigid had her weapon, as well.

If they truly were tyrants, looking to usurp humanity, why would they have been allowed their minds yet? Why would they be left armed? Charun had even allowed Grant to replace his spent hand gren on his belt, the one weapon that could even the odds between a mere human and the godly hammer of Charun.

There was no way that Charun and Vanth would have been dumb or trusting enough not to consider the Cerberus explorers a threat. He wondered if his weapon would even operate. But even if there was some means of magnetically disabling the Sin Eater, that wouldn't render his knife or Grant's gren useless. Would it?

Or maybe they just don't care if they get shot or stabbed. Maybe they feel so physically superior that hand-to-hand with a knife would be suicide for any human, and mere bullets only sting, not slay.

You're projecting again, Kane.

"Charun, you look a little bored. Why not show us where the fun stuff is?" Kane asked.

"The weapons or the wenches?" the demigod asked.

"Or the liquor?" Grant added.

Charun chuckled and then gave Grant a tap on the shoulder. "Now I know why you and my hammer coalesced so well. You think much like me."

Grant shrugged and smirked. "The best things in life are simple."

"You are as wise as you are brave," Charun exclaimed. "Honey?"

"Yes, we heard. Even using his inside voice, Grant is not so quiet, either," Vanth replied.

The annoyance in her voice was not harsh, even gentle. As if she was having fun. Kane had been there many times before with Brigid in their conversations and interactions.

And there was that familiarity again, that mirror image between Charun and Vanth and Kane and Brigid. Over the course of his adventures, Kane had seen glimpses that his life was not confined to the body he currently inhabited, but rather he was a stream of energy, a thread of life entwining multiple people, from far back into prehistory and stretching to a distant future.

Kane wanted to ask Brigid if a psychopomp could pick up and pattern such things as souls.

And there was still the fact that Vanth's song had been in Brigid's head. Was it just her song or was it the demigod herself? Brigid had made very certain to hypnotize CAT Alpha and CAT Beta. Were their perceptions influenced by whatever remained inside Brigid's brain?

Kane had been stuck like this once before, with Neekra having allegedly torn him out of his own mind and stranding him in a comatose state. Time in the illusion passed quickly, so that he perceived the turning of centuries even though he was only out for the space of a day and some change. Maybe Brigid *thought* that she had been shielding the members of the teams against the psychic interference of Vanth and Charun, but in truth, she'd laid them bare and vulnerable.

Or almost all of them were rendered helpless.

Kane's posthypnotic suggestions were removed, his mind and willpower being too strong for such manipulation, rebelling at the command to forget and dispel his curiosity and thoughts. Had his own subconscious found a way to buck the system, to dispel whatever influence

Brigid had placed upon him? After all, the posthypnotic suggestions were conceived as a means of preventing their minds from betraying them by actually acknowledging their suspicions and prejudices.

The ways of the subconscious mind were such that Kane could have known exactly the kind of danger Brigid had been putting him into with her hypnosis, and then could have made enough of a fuss to get him to negate that conditioning. Of course, this now meant that Kane was alone, the rest of his allies against him.

Or would that actually be what Vanth and Charun *wanted* him to believe? The whole situation with these entities and their telepathic powers was one that could leave Kane doubting everything, even if he was seeing something right in front of his eyes. Traveling down one line of possibilities or another was something that could bring Kane to the edge of madness.

As he was trying to determine which end was up, he and Grant had entered the chamber where Charun said that the best of his "toys" were located. Kane wanted to call it a hangar, but there was no real exit to the outside skies. Here, he saw the Manta that Edwards had lost, as well as the three Olympian Spartan suits in stalls specifically designed for them. There were other stalls along the wall of the same nature, including two with robotic shapes hidden beneath tarps.

"You have your own Gear Skeletons?" Kane asked.

Charun nodded. "Yes. We kept them around and actually repainted ours to match those of New Olympus."

"To infiltrate?" Grant questioned.

"To keep our robots from being chopped to pieces. In fact, those were the suits that were transporting Edwards's Manta to and from the hillside," Charun said. "This is a courtesy as we did not want to create wear and tear upon the Olympian amputee pilots and their mecha."

Kane blinked in surprise. "No wear and tear on the pilots or the robots."

"The calculation process is not one that endangers those involved, so long as we have the staff to keep them fed, watered and cleaned," Charun explained.

Grant strolled along, looking over the Olympian suits, then lifted the tarp covering the two duplicates that had been utilized. Kane jogged up beside his friend, peeking behind the curtain. Charun strode over and pulled down the tarp.

"There are similarities in the basic construction, but we had to improvise some panels on ours to match the armored cockpits of your friends," Charun said. The front hatches to each of these armor units were open, and Kane could see the empty cockpits. He noticed that their torsos were larger.

"These weren't built for trans-adapts," Kane said. "Nor whatever midgets that piloted the original skeletons of the Olympians."

"No. These do not have the cybernetic interface nodule that can plug into a spine, either," Charun told them. "Rather, take a look at the headrest of the chair."

Kane squinted and noticed a small crown with stones, possessing the smoothness of river stones and the translucence of gems or quartz crystal. These were a familiar sight, his having noted similar artifacts in the Annunaki skimmers.

"The gems form a matrix around a sentient mind and respond to its commands," Charun explained. "Given your experience with our cousins…"

"The Annunaki. You admit to being related to them?" Kane asked.

Charun nodded. "Though we are not from the same world as they. In fact, you can say that the Annunaki are *our* twisted mirror images in *this* dimension. Thus our distaste."

"So you truly are from another universe," Grant mused. "We've experienced other casements, as well. Some of those realities echoed our own...some were vastly different."

"We haven't accessed those in a long time, though we're aware of other dimensions and pocket universes," Kane added. "One thing I want to know was that we brought our interphaser but you aren't interested in using it."

"If anything, your technology is not as ours," Charun told them. "Your device can be used to help open an aperture, but we *have* the means of opening that dimensional floodgate back to Styx. We just need the code to open it. And the interphaser won't do that for us. But you should thank Brigid for me. It was thoughtful of you."

"Thanks. I'll tell her," Kane returned. "Though, wouldn't Vanth be the one saying that, as they're both talking and touring side by side?"

"The truth be told, I'm not certain if Vanth's recall extends to matters of conversational courtesy," Charun said. "As you can tell, most men end up going stupid around her, and that tends to make women hate her. Fortunately you're among the rare of the apes that does not allow their hormones to distract them from the important things."

"Trust me," Grant interjected. "Kane tends to get plenty of distraction."

Kane rolled his eyes, pretending to maintain interest in the tour, the discussions going on between Grant and Charun.

All the while, he returned to his mind, trying to inventory itself, looking for signs of interference, of sabotage.

He recalled Brigid Baptiste's co-option, her hijacking by Ullikummis to become his godly prophet, his right hand as the villainous Brigid Haight. Though she had been under his control, there had still been a Brigid Baptiste inside Haight's head, locked into a mental version of a safe room to keep her true identity while allowing the son of Enlil to believe he was in command. When the time was right, Brigid restored herself to her original personality, successfully throwing off the fetters of Ullikummis and foiling his plans to wrest the Earth from his father and the humans he battled with.

Had Brigid given Kane an outside bit of suspicion, the doubt that Brigid was entirely herself when she worked to inure the rest of the Cerberus teams against Vanth's psychic song?

A shadow flickered in the corner of Kane's eye and it took everything in his will not to suddenly react to the new presence. There was a physical manifestation at his shoulder and he caught a glimpse of red-gold curls spilling across his peripheral vision.

"The word to break the conditioning of the others is *anam-chara*," Brigid's voice whispered in his ear. "I was erroneous in the belief that I'd dispelled the song of domination completely from my consciousness."

Kane nodded grimly to himself. Since this manifestation of Brigid was one solely perceptible to his consciousness, he didn't speak aloud. Was this why I started wondering if those two and their relationship was so close to ours? Because Charun calls Vanth his bride and you and I...?

"We are different. Something closer than they are, but I needed you to think of that term, I planted the crumb for you to break loose," Brigid said.

And just what am I supposed to do now? Kane looked around the arsenal. It was vaguely interesting, but the truth of the matter was, they were in an enemy fortress. This far down into the pyramid, his Commtact wouldn't pick up a signal. And am I supposed to break you out of your hypnosis?

"I can handle myself," the Brigid message told him. "But I told Domi and the others to hole up in a safe room. You should be able to pick them up as they have their Commtacts on passive."

Kane looked sideways at Charun and Grant. The two men were still conversing. He was free now, and his doubts were dispelled like smoke. Is Charun in this with Vanth, or is she conning him?

Brigid stepped in front of him, frowning. "Charun is the brains of this operation."

The demigod looked at Kane directly, his eyes aflame from within.

"Vanth is a willing accomplice, but it's Charun who is the wielder of the song and who has the telepathic capabilities," Brigid warned.

Kane frowned as Charun's tusks snagged his upper lip in a sneering, smug smile.

More movement sounded behind him, bare feet slapping the stone floor of the arsenal. Grant turned, dazed and confused at the arrival of the newcomers. Kane realized that trouble had arrived in the form of the Etruscan demigod's reinforcements. He clicked his Commtact to broadcast, all frequencies, knowing he'd need all the help he could get. Things were going to turn violent at any moment.

"Anam-chara," Kane uttered, but not before Charun snatched the jaw plate off his partner Grant.

"Oh, no… Kane has fallen under the control of Vanth, Grant," Charun stated, his voice stentorian, to the point where the Cerberus adventurer could feel the impact of each syllable. "You have to subdue him before he turns against us, Grant."

The big former Magistrate's eyes grew milky, watching as Charun staggered backward.

"Kane?" Grant asked. "Kane! Snap out of it! Don't shoot him! Kane!"

Suddenly, in the middle of the arsenal of Charun, Kane was confronted by the one weapon he could not destroy. His friend, his brother by blood, sweat and tears. And Grant lunged forward, the glaze of his eyes telling Kane that Grant felt he was completely out of control.

He wanted to speak another word, but a sudden grasp seized his throat. And Charun, sitting against the wall, grinned, his eyes twinkling as he denied Kane the means of breaking this spell.

Grant's fist hammered deep into Kane's stomach, and despite the non-Newtonian polymers stiffening to lessen the blow, all the breath was expelled from Kane's lungs.

Chapter 20

Domi and the others heard the voice of Kane over their Commtacts, meaning that he must have been close; otherwise the walls of intervening stone would have made reception impossible. His words were familiar, the affectionate term that he and Brigid Baptiste held for each other.

Anam-chara. It was a term from Celtic spiritual tradition, and was a belief that the human soul radiated all around the physical form in an aura. When two people came near each other, there were instances where that aura opened and channels of trust and understanding immediately opened between the two individuals. When that occurred, the Celtic tradition stated that one had found their soul friend, or in the ancient tongue of the Celts, the *anam-chara.* Though Domi doubted that kind of deep, almost symbiotic bond from the beginning, there was no doubt that each completed the other.

She'd also noticed part of that between Kane and Grant, as well, which was probably what Lakesh saw when he mentioned the confluence of personalities that always lead CAT Alpha to victory against imposing odds. However, between Kane and Brigid, this was what seemed strongest.

Domi, however, realized that she was inside a pyramid that Charun and Vanth *allowed* CAT Beta to infiltrate. The two demigods had drawn from Brigid the plans of both teams to deal with the Etruscan entities. However,

Charun and Vanth had not counted on the mental resilience of the flame-haired archivist. She'd hypnotized the group to the holes that they had funneled the Cerberus Away Teams toward, but there were other measures that Brigid had implanted in them. Rather than continuing to wander around the pyramid, allowing the minions of the demigods to entrap them, Brigid had arranged for them to seek out a truly defensible position.

This storage room was such a place. The door was sturdy enough to withstand attack, yet too small to allow one of the robotic warriors to reach very far into. The walls were simply too thick for even a skeleton of secondary orichalcum to sunder, and the chamber was deep enough to be out of range of a grasping claw. There were thick, durable crates that the four people had assembled into a barricade instinctively.

Fists pounded at the door and the CAT Beta members moved behind their assembled cover. Shelving units were stocked with weapons and ammunition, as well, providing Domi and her allies with the means to hold out against a prolonged siege.

Of course, all of those factors protecting the CAT meant that they couldn't rush to Kane's aid. Over their Commtacts, the four allies heard their friend grunting as he engaged in a melee.

The door shook as fists struck it.

"You are trapped, humans! Surrender!" came the shout from the other side. Domi recognized the alien resonance, as if the voice were echoing in upon itself, vibrating along different wavelengths. This was akin to the tones of the Annunaki, although these creatures hardly had the depth and power of the overlords. These must have been subordinates, mere minions, though their challenge was one of malice, so these weren't emotionless drones or thralls. "Throw out your weapons!"

"All right," Domi conceded, shouting loud. "Give 'em weapons."

Edwards smirked, his Sin Eater snapping into the palm of his hand. "Bullets first?"

"Duh," Domi responded.

Edwards winked at Smaragda. "That means we blow the crap out of these alien scum."

Smaragda chuckled. "I was hoping you meant that."

CAT Beta aimed their weapons at the door but only Domi and Edwards fired, the feral girl's .45 and the Magistrate's pistol having the punch to cut through the door between them and their opponent. The two gunshots were loud in the small room, even with their hoods on to filter their hearing, but the audio pickups rewarded the two shooters with the sound of strangled pain and a body dropping to the floor.

While it might have seemed more impressive for all four of them to cut loose, hosing streams of bullets through the door, they wanted to maintain their coverage as much as possible. Such a vulgar display of firepower would have been a waste of ammunition and weakened their first line of defense. Rather, the marksmanship of Domi and Edwards had eliminated one of their opponents without compromising the door.

That did not prevent their foes from opening fire, and from the racket, Domi could tell that the Stygians were using the captured rifles of the Olympians. The door's thickness absorbed most of the volley of return fire, only a few projectiles here and there managing to punch all the way through, their energy spent and turning them from lethal bullet into impotent rain clattering on the stone floor. Already, Domi was glad at their defensive position being an advantage that grew. As long as the humanoid minions of Vanth and Charun wasted their ammunition, they would be less likely and capable of bringing the fight to

CAT Beta, while the cooler, calmer heads of the four defenders waited for an opportunity to fight back effectively.

"Brains *and* brawn," Domi growled as she let the Stygians spend their energy and time in their futile initial assault.

BRIGID BAPTISTE HEARD Kane speak the words of her post-hypnotic suggestion, the key word that would break the conditioning that she'd unfortunately inflicted upon the others. She took a step away from Vanth as they entered one of the libraries she'd been boasting about.

The half-naked goddess casually followed Brigid's defensive movement, her efforts to create distance between them, and her lush, beautiful lips turned up into a smile.

"So, you've finally dropped your pretenses?" Vanth inquired.

Brigid narrowed her eyes. "You are the one who has been lying and subverting minds, my own included."

"Subverting my mind," Vanth mimicked, except as she spoke she turned Brigid's tone higher, whinier, showing disdain for the human woman. "Your minds? You were built from the ground up to be slaves, servants to alien gods."

"And yet we've sent them scattered to the four corners of the Earth, stripped of their power and superiority," Brigid challenged. She pulled the TP-9 from its holster, leveling it at Vanth. "I will not fire upon an unarmed, helpless opponent, but if you prove that you're not harmless…"

"You seek to instill fear into me?" Vanth asked. "As a child, I hunted the mightiest of beasts, naked, unarmed. The creature's tusk marks still line my belly, but I broke its neck."

Brigid glanced down to the stomach of the seven-foot woman, seeing the faint lines of a long-healed cut. She focused on the sights once more, matching Vanth's glare. "So, you believe you can take a spray of bullets without harm?"

"I am she who mothered the legends of Artemis and Atlanta," Vanth growled. "These limbs have shattered tree trunks as if they were twigs. Without a weapon, I am mighty. With them, I am invincible!"

Brigid circled back toward the doorway, relying on her impeccable photographic memory to navigate without looking where she stepped.

Vanth's lip curled in dismissal. "You threaten me with a rain of lead and fire, and yet you cannot pull the trigger?"

"And you just see me holding my firearm with one hand, not wondering what the other is doing," Brigid returned.

Vanth's eyes glanced to Brigid's other hand, which was empty. She looked back along the Cerberus archivist's path and saw a small disk lying on the ground.

A moment later a brilliant flare of light blazed in the room. Brigid Baptiste didn't delude herself that she'd carry enough firepower to wound a god, but if Vanth's vision and other senses were of the same superhuman nature as her physique, then the brilliance of one million candle-power blazing into her eyes would buy her moments, if not minutes.

Vanth screamed, agonized by the flash, and Brigid whirled, ducking into the hall. Though her own vision had blurred, Brigid relied on that photographic memory to map out her course of escape and evasion. Behind her, Vanth roared in fury, furniture shattering under hammer blows from those "bare hands" the demigoddess boasted of.

"Witch! I shall peel the flesh from your scalp, crush your skull and drink your brains!" Vanth bellowed.

Now I see the species resemblance to Charun, Brigid

mused as she hurtled down one corridor after another. By the time she'd run a hundred yards from Vanth, her emerald eyes could clearly take in her surroundings once more. Vanth's rantings and crashing fists were still distant behind, which meant Brigid had the opportunity to find the detour Charun had led Kane and Grant off upon.

That bit of navigation was simplicity for her, and she charged on, finding a stairwell that throbbed with the continuous explosions of distant gunfire.

"Domi and the others are awake, as well," Brigid mused as she descended the steps. "And Vanth lied about being the only two entities from her world to be on this side of the wormhole."

Taking the steps quickly, jumping when she could, Brigid was glad for the brace she'd wound around her formerly sprained ankle, as well as the day's worth of rehabilitation of the tender joint. Each landing was a spike of discomfort, but it was nothing more than a reminder of her mortality, not a crippling loss of footing.

Reaching the floor where the gunfire resounded most strongly, Brigid entered the corridor. She paused only long enough to pull more of her package of surprises from its hiding space inside her boot and the wrap at her ankle.

Vanth's screech at the top of the stairwell informed Brigid of the demigoddess's arrival. After seeing the way Charun had armored up, she knew that Vanth was also likely to be fully decked out with armor and her other gear.

Brigid put an adhesive patch on the back of her slim, flat automated munition, set it to motion-sensor mode and continued onward. The hi-ex device was designed for use in multiple manners, almost all of them antipersonnel and capable of damaging light armor upon detonation. In some instances, it could be used for demolition, could be buried and would go off with the vibration of a group of troops walking past, or stuck to a wall, utilizing infrared beams as trip wires.

It was amazing how clever mankind had been in the production of weapons of death and destruction, Brigid thought, but then she was thankful. There was an enraged goddess on her heels, so showing disgust at the aptitude of humanity toward warfare and armory was intellectually dishonest and incongruous. She glanced back to see Vanth hover down to the entrance to this level, glowing, feathery white wings unfurled behind her back.

"Now what toys do you hav—" Vanth began, floating forward. The munition on the wall detected her and the corridor shook as if a thunderbolt had struck it. Brigid kept going, knowing that Vanth's armor would provide more protection than the light mine could overcome.

Brigid entered an armory, seeing their lost Manta as well as a group of slender, pallid humanoids looking on toward some spectacle. She changed direction, letting the bulk of the transonic craft cover her movements, but as she neared the nose of the Manta she saw that Kane and Grant were engaged in a pitched battle with each other.

"Oh, that is unfortunate," Brigid murmured as Grant lifted Kane from the ground by his throat with both hands.

GRANT FELT THE flutter of fingers along his jawline, and then he was no longer in contact with the outside world via the cybernetic communicator he'd been wearing only a moment before. The plate, worn outside and attached via pintles to the bone beneath the skin, was another of the wonders of Manitius base technology that the explorers of Cerberus had added to their adventuring kit. They were meant to maintain a constant flow of communication between the CAT members and Cerberus Redoubt, ensuring that no one would be lost or out of touch for long.

The truth was that, as with any technology, there were

times when it wouldn't or couldn't work. Especially in the face of opposition that had its own communications networks and a modicum of electronic countermeasures and radio jamming. Still, the ease of the Commtact over bulky, regular radios was worth being stuck with a metal plate on your cheekbone that could be reduced to an expensive decoration rather than a phone to home.

Charun, beside him, had been jarred from his reverie in showing Grant around the Stygians' armory, turning and looking on in shock. "Oh no…Kane has fallen under the control of Vanth, Grant!"

The words had landed inside Grant's brain like an avalanche, the stones sharp and heavy as they battered against any thoughts he tried to entertain.

"…under the control of Vanth," Grant repeated. His vision blurred and his heart rate suddenly accelerated. Genuine shock and surprise bubbled up within him and suddenly Charun staggered, his chest splashed with blood. Grant easily recognized the chatter of a Sin Eater, which made his confusion all the stronger as he turned back and saw Kane, gun in hand, smoke wisping from the end of the barrel.

"Vanth betrayed me." It was a soft whisper in Grant's ear. He imagined it as a whisper, but in all probability Charun was speaking to him directly, mind to mind.

"Kane? What do you think you're doing?" Grant asked, stepping between the staggered, bloody Charun and his friend. He looked Kane over, but there were no words from his friend. If anything, Kane clawed at his throat, as if something was stuck there.

Anger flashed in Kane's cold blue eyes as he lifted the Sin Eater again, leveling it at the wounded demigod, his finger taking up the slack on the machine pistol's trigger.

"Kane?" Grant asked. "Kane! Snap out of it! Don't shoot him! Kane!"

With that shout, Grant hurled himself forward, heedless of the danger to himself. Kane raised his gun once more and Grant charged in, his fist a piston of steel slamming into his friend's stomach to keep him from pulling the trigger and gunning down the helpless, wounded demigod. The blow knocked the wind out of Kane, much to Grant's relief. The shadow suit's protective abilities prevented the possibility of an organ rupture, but also allowed enough force through to keep the gunman from firing at Charun.

Charun had just said that he'd been betrayed by his lover, Vanth, and that the selfsame goddess had seized command of his friend's thoughts. No matter what kind of control the alien witch could have wielded over Kane, there was little chance that he'd gun down Grant. Even so, he was glad the shadow suit provided some measure of small-arms protection.

With a leap, he was atop Kane, shoving his arm aside. The gun didn't fire, so that meant Kane did have some measure of self-control. Grant squeezed hard on his friend's wrist in the hope of making the smaller man drop the weapon. "You're not in your right mind. You can't kill Charun!"

Gunfire resounded in the distance, almost as if the floodgates of sanity had shattered, waves of madness flushing through the hallways.

Kane could only issue a croak from his lips and Grant took that as a sign of Vanth's command of his mind. In a flash, something hard slammed against Grant's jaw, snapping his head up and back. It wasn't Kane's closed fist, rather his forearm. Grant recognized the martial arts maneuver, one that was meant to apply the most force possible to inflict a burst of sensory input on nerves and blood vessels at the juncture of neck and jaw.

Properly placed, the blow could render an opponent insensate without causing bone damage. The impact was not delivered with a closed fist, as it would break knuckles and render fingers stiff and useless. Rather, a forearm or elbow—both thicker and more heavily protected than the lighter carpal bones—delivered the stunning attack.

Grant's instincts had kicked in swiftly enough that he'd avoided the bulk of the punch, but he was still dazed. Putting Kane down without killing him was going to be a challenge, as both men were equally well-trained, and where Grant possessed superior strength, Kane was faster and more agile.

Grant also possessed a longer reach, so he immediately pushed Kane away to his arm's length. The stiffened edge of Kane's hand sliced through the air, missing Grant's face. The karate chop was something a little more dangerous, but when focused on the side of the neck or that cluster of nerves and blood vessels, had the same effect as a forearm smash. The karate chop also had the potential of hitting *too hard*, possibly breaking an enemy's neck. Even with the non-Newtonian cushioning of his shadow suit, Grant realized that Vanth's mind control was pushing Kane to deadlier measures.

With a kick to the stomach, he vaulted Kane halfway across the floor.

"Don't make me hurt you, bro. Say something. Let me know that naked bitch hasn't got you as her puppet!" Grant demanded.

Kane gathered himself up, glaring silently back at him. He pointed to his throat, but still stood in a defensive martial arts posture.

Grant kept his distance, circling. He'd see white, slender figures in the corners of his eyes, but they faded the instant he tried to focus on them. They couldn't have been an active threat, not with Grant distracted like this.

The only reason they wouldn't be interfering…

They're not interfering because you're on their side.

Grant paused. Kane wasn't taking the offensive, and he wasn't looking for his firearm, either.

There were huge gaps in the logic of his battle with his friend, and that went double as he looked and noticed that the Sin Eater was still retracted, flat along Kane's forearm. He'd never unleashed it, and thus hadn't lost it when Grant tackled him.

Anger surged through the big man as he realized he'd just been duped, having fallen into an illusion cast by Charun.

Of course, he still felt the impulse to battle against Kane. This was something that had slithered under Grant's conscious defenses, which was doubly disturbing. Hadn't Brigid Baptiste implanted posthypnotic suggestions into the Cerberus expedition to protect them from this?

"Damned aliens," Grant snarled. He lunged forward and wrapped both hands around Kane's throat, lifting his friend up. It was an aggressive move, one that hadn't inspired an ounce of resistance from the voice at the back of his mind, shouting for him to put Kane down like the rabid dog he'd become.

Grant only hoped the collar of Kane's suit was absorbing the bulk of the force, as it had earlier with his initial punch.

"Kick that bastard in the head," Grant hissed to his friend.

Kane's eyes flared with recognition and agreement.

With a mighty surge, Grant whirled, hurling Kane toward the fallen Charun. Twisting in midair, Kane brought both feet up so that he could connect with the Etruscan giant. Soles stiffened to the hardness of steel plates and Charun found himself crashing against the wall with 200 pounds of fighting-mad Cerberus warrior kicking out. Kane's momentum was increased by the power of Grant's throw, and the two men had actually floored Charun.

The strange pressure inside Grant's skull disappeared in an instant.

"Anam-chara!" Kane rasped, finally able to speak.

Even more static dissipated from Grant's mind and he looked around to see the slender, pale creatures he'd barely been able to acknowledge under the ministrations of mind control. Of course, the moment they saw that he had been released from domination under Charun's spell, they immediately struck a retreat. They had showed up to enjoy the carnage that would have occurred when the two friends engaged in a bloody brawl, and foolishly did so without weapons at hand. Now, having underestimated Grant and Kane, they realized that discretion would keep them alive much longer than standing in front of two armed and trained warriors.

Brigid Baptiste swung around the nose of the Manta, her TP-9 in both hands and leveled toward the fleeing Stygians, making them run even more quickly away.

"We need to go now," she said. She must have realized the change in demeanor of the two former combatants. "Vanth is behind me..."

"This way," Kane croaked. "It sounds like Beta's in the middle of a firefight."

Grant let his Sin Eater launch into his grasp. "How rude. We invite them to all of our gun battles. Let's register some complaints!"

Kane grinned. "It's so much better having you on my side than against me."

As one, Brigid, Kane and Grant rushed down the corridor toward their besieged allies.

Chapter 21

So far, the Stygians outside the door to CAT Beta's hideout had wasted a lot of their ammunition, and had only succeeded in leaving ragged gaps in the door's panels. Domi turned and made certain that her allies were all in full hoods.

"Gas them," Domi said. She'd gotten a glance through the holes torn in the door and could tell that while they wore appropriated Olympian armor, they had forgone the helmets.

It was an uncertain strategy since there was no guarantee their body chemistry and biology were close enough to human to be adversely affected by clouds of pepper gas. However, if their sense of smell and touch, if they had similarly sensitive mucus membranes to humans, Domi could attest to the conclusion that tear gas would send them scurrying away.

Smaragda fired her under-barrel gren launcher on her rifle. The 40 mm shell punched through a weakened, bullet-eaten section of door, and when the round struck the far wall, it popped loudly. Hissing smoke gushed into the corridor and they were almost instantly rewarded with the sound of rasping coughs and gasps.

Sinclair and Edwards, who had switched to his shotgun on the command to gas them, fired their 12-gauge variants of tear gas shells, adding to the billowing, eye-burning mists that replaced the roar of autofire with the sounds of spitting, retching and wheezing.

"There's a reason why we wear helmets on the battle-field," Smaragda stated. She thumbed another shell into the breech of her launcher.

"What?" Domi asked bluntly, pointing to the round she loaded.

Smaragda looked down. "Flash-bang."

"Boom," Domi said with a grin. No longer needing their suits to be in camouflage mode, the team let the second skins return to their shadowy black, hoods turned translucent for the ease of recognition and communication. The black faceplates were good for stealth and intimidation, but a conversation lacking facial expressions was unnecessarily troublesome, especially for Domi, who tended to lose most of her vocabulary in times of stress and conflict.

Smaragda grinned in reply and fired the launcher.

The hoods protected the hearing of those inside the storage room, audio pickups filtering out the massive pressure wave, but for the Stygians trying to root them out, it was unadulterated pain. The stun gren shook loose splinters and remnants of door that had been hanging on by threads, and Domi could see one of the pallid aliens clutching the sides of his head. Though the creatures had no apparent external ears, that didn't mean they didn't have eardrums that could be ruptured.

The blast wave also did a number on their vision, as black, thick tears flowed from their almond eyes and slit nostrils. Domi recalled Brigid's explanation of the effect of dangerously loud flash-bang grens; that the sound was accompanied by levels of pressure that burst small blood vessels in vital areas such as the sinuses and eye lining in some cases. With their sinus membranes already under great stress due to the tear gas, the Stygians were undoubtedly going through hell as the already filled chambers of their skull were exacerbated and flushed with blood.

Gunfire rattled in the corridor, which caught Domi's attention. It didn't take more than an instant to recognize it was the gunfire from her friends' pistols, not the appropriated Olympian rifles. Slender, haggard figures lurched through the choking tear gas in an effort to flee the arrival of CAT Alpha.

A black-gloved hand reached in front of the door and gave a rap on a solid bit of remnant.

"Excuse me, is the man of the house around?" Brigid called out.

"And the ladies, too," Edwards shouted back. "What took you guys so long?"

"Would you believe acts of god?" Brigid asked.

Domi ran to the door, opening it for her friends. "We staying here or moving along?"

"I'd say we're moving," Kane returned. "Especially if Vanth isn't going to waste time on the scrambled Charun."

Domi snapped her fingers, waving the rest of her team into the corridor. Sela Sinclair led the way, motioning the direction from which CAT Beta had entered the bowels of the pyramid. Domi paused long enough to see Grant setting up a pair of flat demolitions charges along the walls.

"It slowed her down once before," Brigid said, starting to run and follow Kane and the others.

Domi nodded. "Good." She turned toward Grant, calling out, "Hurry up!"

"I'm coming!" Grant growled, punching the controls to activate the wall mines.

Domi caught the reaction of the big man as he looked away from the wall, then spun and raced toward them. Instants later the wall erupted under a thundering crash, a blast much larger than anything the trip-wire mine could have produced. Domi could have sworn, in the moment before the tunnel was shaken by the explosion, that she saw a black arrow slicing through the air.

Whatever the case, Grant skidded on the floor, then scrambled to his feet. "Vanth's here!"

Domi helped Grant get his footing again, and the pair exploded into motion, racing away from the spreading cloud of dust and debris.

Vanth had definitely showed up ready for all-out war, and she wasn't staying her hand, or the quiver of arrows she wore. Those arrows struck with the force of thunderbolts and, right now, the teams were equipped more for dealing nonlethally with mind-controlled minions than with deadly enemies whose archery was as destructive as anti-tank missiles.

"She's making room between us and them. She needs to get Charun back on his feet and into his armor," Grant explained. "Still, that's a hell of a bow and arrow set."

"Damn right," Domi agreed as they charged along.

Grant and Domi finally caught up with the others and saw Kane and Edwards hard at work cranking up the wrought-iron gate from the inside. Now that the Etruscan godlings knew of the presence of the CAT teams, there was little to be lost by using the official controls on the door. Working together, the two men used a lever and a set of chains and pulleys to lift the several-ton iron gate.

Brigid pulled the last of her paper-thin explosive charges and placed it along the chain.

"What's that going to do?" Grant asked.

"It'll slow down Vanth and Charun," Brigid said. "I'll detonate it by remote control."

"Did you see that arrow? Or did you forget about the hammer strike?" Grant countered.

"In close quarters, it'll put them at a disadvantage," Brigid told him. "Trust me, I'm thinking ahead on this one."

"Come on," Kane growled. "The longer we dither here…"

"And the prisoners?" Smaragda asked. "We're trapping my friends down there?"

Brigid gave Smaragda a shove past the gate. "We're not forgetting our promise to you and New Olympus. Trust us."

Domi and Grant ducked beneath the lowering gate, Brigid scurrying through immediately after. She tapped a control on her forearm and the sound of her munition detonating was instantly followed by the clattering of unraveling chains.

From there, it was a hard run back to the surface.

SMARAGDA SAT IN the forest, her arms crossed, elbows resting on her knees. She felt good to get out of the shadow suit hood, feeling the wind on her face and through her prematurely whitened hair. Though she was physically free from the constraints of the environmentally sealed suit, the world was dark and heavy around her.

The good news was that it wasn't her fellow Olympian troopers who were accompanying the robotic armor suits. They were not wandering around as mental slaves.

Instead they were corralled, like cattle, their minds hijacked for the purpose of punching a hole through to an alien universe. According to Brigid Baptiste, the flame-haired scientific genius of this expedition, their idle existences would be only a temporary condition, as once the dimensional warp was opened, there would be a need for bodies for the invaders.

"Charun and Vanth are likely Igigi," Brigid explained. "The nonelevated castes of Annunaki society. However, either by design or accident, their original identities were usurped and overwritten by transdimensional duplicates."

"If they can overwrite the Annunaki, then what chance do humans have?" Smaragda asked. "You're saying that my friends will cease to exist, and in their place, in their *skins*, fiends will appear and become a part of an army of conquest."

Brigid looked at her, lips sealed tight. Smaragda could see the thoughts churning behind the woman's eyes, and she immediately felt regret at claiming there was no hope. If there was a human being alive with the brilliance to rescue both her brother soldiers and hundreds of thousands of Italian peninsula dwellers, it was Brigid Baptiste.

"I'm sorry," Smaragda said quickly. "What would you need me to do?"

"Right now, we're going to let the enemy come to us," she said. "Vanth and Charun have been embarrassed, and they are angry. They will come looking for us."

"But we can tell that they haven't started with the search parties," Grant added. "According to Lakesh, who has three satellites looking down on their pyramid, there has been no movement from either of the entrances we've encountered. There are other openings, but no activity there, either."

"You found other openings," Edwards asked. "Air ducts?"

"Definitely," Grant confirmed. "Otherwise, things would become unbreathable down there."

"Given the human and livestock cells, it's not the healthiest atmosphere down in the pit," Domi said. Her nose crinkled at the memory of the smell. "But that was one thing Vanth didn't lie about. They've been taken care of."

"They want all the shells they can get," Kane muttered.

"Not to mention their squirmy little pale freaks," Sela Sinclair added. She glanced over to Domi. "Sorry, Domi."

Domi waved off the mention of the pallid nature of the alien humanoids. "How are we going to handle the two of them and their allies when they *do* come hunting for our heads?"

"It will depend on who they send after us," Brigid explained. "We're lucky to have Edwards as our pack mule... and you already have sufficient less-lethal firepower to deal with thralls sent in place of the standard troops."

"You think they'll take a shot at us with the locals and our missing Olympian platoon?" Smaragda asked.

"It'd be the one thing that would stay our hand," Brigid told her. "And, frankly, even if they send out a mob of human zombies, we're going to have to remain careful. Rubber slugs still can kill by breaking necks or snapping ribs and puncturing lungs. Also, while rare, tear gas can cause a respiratory arrest."

"So their best shot at us is throwing their captives down our throat," Kane agreed.

"If they wish to capture us," Brigid returned. "Don't forget their other weapons, if they deem it practical to simply exterminate us."

"We just have to figure out how much Annunaki asshole is part of their DNA," Kane offered. "If they are anything like Enlil, they'll snatch us up and drag us before them for hours of gloating and speechifying before putting us out of our misery."

"If that," Grant agreed. "Those bastards could talk Lakesh to death."

Domi pursed her lips. Edwards sat next to Smaragda and leaned close to her ear. "Grant just disrespected Domi's boyfriend."

"He *can* talk and talk," Domi admitted to Smaragda. Domi still glared at Grant. "Be nice."

"We're blowing off steam here," Kane said. "Right now, all we've got planned is waiting for the bad guys to attack us."

Smaragda looked around. "I wish that Vanth and Charun hadn't been so thorough in depleting the fauna of the area. If something were coming, we'd be better able to notice for the frightened animals."

Domi rose to her feet, even as Edwards rested a gentle hand on her shoulders.

"Don't worry. We've got the satellites watching the whole area, and we're already immunized against the illusion of the black fog by Brigid's hypnosis," Edwards told her. "There's no way we can—"

"Shut up, Edwards." Domi cut him off.

Kane stood, also looking in the direction where Domi scanned.

"You forgot about the black fog, Baptiste?" Kane asked.

"I did not. I merely discounted it as a form of psychic illusion, transmitted via communicator," Brigid returned. "But, apparently I was mistaken in the true nature of the Stygian flood. What are you sensing?"

"The birds, which shouldn't be reacting, are flying back toward the pyramid," Domi said.

Smaragda scrambled to her feet. "We've been wondering if they were being used as spies for those two. What if...?"

Smaragda focused on her memories.

...There were birds on the branches of the trees along the road, but they made no sound. They were still, no nervous tics that she'd seen other birds display as they, even in rest, continued turning their heads, making certain nothing was creeping up on them. The visible birds, however, was not what had truly disturbed her.

There were trees, heavy and dense with foliage, but the impunity of nests of hidden birds was not accompanied by the riot of tweets and chirps that warned any intruder of how outnumbered they would be if they dared enter the thicket. The countryside was silent.

Smaragda stepped off the road, closing on one of the

closest trees. Her men watched as she slung the rifle, then drew the falcata blade. With a twist, she rapped the spine against a low-hanging branch where a songbird perched.

The creature turned its attention toward her, blinked with eyes slow and gummy, but did not launch. Even the turn of its head was casual, unconcerned, not the flicker movement of a normal bird. Smaragda gave the branch another tap with the spine of her sword. The songbird took a clumsy sideways step further along the branch, then unfurled its wings.

Just before she could tap the branch a third time, the songbird took off, wings flapping powerfully, moving with the natural strength and speed of the creature, the limbs beating with the urgency necessary to keep the tiny thing aloft. It wasn't as if the songbird was in some sort of debilitating trance. It flew straight and true.

It just didn't seem to care. The normally skittish creature would have taken off on Smaragda's approach, let alone stay in place for two raps on its perch...

"Brigid, one bird flew away before the fog first appeared," Smaragda stated.

Brigid cast her eyes upward, a typical action of those seeking to remember exact details. This only took a moment as the swift-minded woman looked around. "Your notice of the animals and their odd behavior triggered the defense mechanism."

"Rustling all around us," Domi said. "All the small mammals I *haven't* noticed are back. With a vengeance."

"No wonder individual bullets didn't do anything to the cloud mass," Sinclair said. "Birds and hordes of rodents don't react to gunfire."

Smaragda grimaced. "Can these suits withstand the teeth and nails of rats?"

"Within reason," Brigid said.

The Greek warrior tugged her hood on; the others following suit.

"Run or fight?" Sinclair asked.

"Lay down tear gas and wait to see if they want to dare it," Kane returned. "Their instincts might make them turn away."

Grant and Edwards, both armed with the less-lethal loaded shotguns, opened up, firing into the forest surrounding them. Ferret rounds burst on impact with tree trunks, releasing the eye-burning gases. Kane and Sinclair rolled conventional tear gas grens, adding to the wall of choking, blinding smoke. Safe in their fully sealed environmental suits, they would be fine.

The only downside of their tear gas plan was that eventually the clouds would dissipate and the throngs of small creatures would make their way through.

Even now, Smaragda focused her suit's optics and saw the fluid, seething swarm. It was an easily identifiable black cloud behind the pepper-spray mist, blotting out the trees behind. It was also a solid entity.

"This is not good," Brigid said. "I was afraid of this. If Vanth and Charun could construct a cyclops or Fomoristyle entities, then they could alter the biomass available in the form of birds and small mammals into...that."

"Oops?" Sinclair asked.

Brigid nodded. "A terrible miscalculation and assumption on my part."

"We're also locked off from communication with Cerberus," Sinclair added. "Fortunately, if Vanth or Charun are releasing their songs, the filters are keeping it out of our Commtacts."

A tendril stretched through the tear gas cloud, lashing toward the Cerberus teams, and Smaragda opened fire with her rifle. The assault weapon chattered, flames belching from the muzzle. Edwards and Grant were also cutting loose, punching the ferret rounds into the lunging tentacle. The pseudopod of inky darkness twisted, losing its stretching momentum forward, and the shotgun shells shot out hot streams of gases from their tear-gas reservoirs. All of this sent the rubbery limb into retreat, back beyond the cloud.

By now, everyone was up, armed, ready to fight for their lives.

"Climbing," Domi announced, pointing toward a tree trunk that was now enveloped in the tarlike biomass of the Stygian horror. The blob surged upward as if it was under pressure, and Smaragda couldn't imagine how such a thing could exist without a skeletal structure. She then realized that it likely did have more than sufficient skeleton and muscle mass, considering it had the bone structures of millions of small creatures.

Kane fired on the branch, his Sin Eater chopping at the bough and snapping it off before the black abomination could loom above the group of adventurers.

"Retreat! Sela!" Kane shouted.

With that, Sela Sinclair whirled with her Taser in hand. There were lengths of the boneless mass behind the group, as they truly were facing an amorphous entity. Sinclair fired her Taser, and the tongs of the neuroelectrical weapon stuck in the inky skin of the creature. A pull of the trigger and a hundred thousand volts suddenly flowed into the bulk of the creature.

Black tendrils thrashed violently and the two arms of darkness suddenly retreated, making an opening for the Cerberus warriors to escape through. Smaragda paused long enough to turn and fire the gren launcher under her rifle's barrel into the body of the beast.

It was a flash-bang gren, and while there was no shrapnel put off by the 40 mm shell, what it did produce was a thunderous blast and a blazing bright light. The light wouldn't do anything to an organism that apparently had no visual organs, but if there was one thing Smaragda knew about sound, it was that it was amplified in fluid bodies.

The shock wave of the flash-bang gren was deeply muffled by the bulk of the creature, but the keening wail that unleashed from the entity made up for it. Smaragda whirled and followed the others as they charged through the forest. This was all too familiar to the horrors that had gone before, her wild charge to escape the monstrosity the first time she'd encountered it.

She couldn't help feeling like a failure now, but as she watched the Cerberus warriors pause and continue shooting at the bloblike abomination, she realized they were leading this thing to a position where they could counter it with strategy and intelligence.

Feeling a spasm of hope, Smaragda rushed forward, leaping over a flailing pseudopod and landing in Edwards's arms.

"Come on, whitey, we're going to show this snot ball how we treat monsters," he told her. His smile was just one more thing giving her a hope that they could rescue her brothers in arms.

Chapter 22

"Baptiste, what've you got formulating in your head?" Kane asked as he ran, keeping pace with Brigid.

That day of therapy for her ankle and the bindings had worked wonders, because she was easily at the lead of the pack. Her injured foot held up to this frantic gait, and there was little distracting her from the task at hand.

"So far, we have confirmed that heat and sound have negative stimulus on the creature," Brigid stated.

"Something hot and loud. Guns have both—"

"But the creature had been struck at near muzzle-contact range with the light machine guns mounted on a Spartan war skeleton," Brigid returned. "If the dark thing couldn't be warded off by the temperatures generated by an M-240 firing on full-auto, then we need something more."

"Dark thing?" Kane asked. "So why are they reacting so badly to the tear gas rounds? Those shouldn't be burning as hotly as muzzle-blasts."

"Then it has to be something in the tear gas itself," Brigid replied. She glanced back and saw the others following. She immediately began a mental breakdown of the ingredients for the gases used in those rounds.

Brigid immediately corrected herself on the presence of the pepper-based, oleo-resin in those CS canisters. Pepper spray and 2-chlorobenzomalononitrile had similar inflammatory effects on eyes and mucus tissues, but the cyano-carbon of tear gas was a different compound entirely. For one thing, OC spray was capsicum mixed with ethanol, which dried it out into a waxy resin. Subsequently, that material was carried in a solution called propelene glycol, which could cause severe allergic reactions but was not dangerous. CS gas, however, was dissolved in methyl isobutyl ketone, an organic compound that may or may not have been the active ingredient causing clastogenic mutation in mammalian cells.

Studies were not conclusive by 2001, which was when the world went to hell. But Brigid Baptiste found one focus point on the potential dangers and toxicity of CS gas. Clastogenic alteration was a chromosomal change, genetic damage.

The creature behind them was made up of avian and mammalian creatures, the sum total of thousands, perhaps millions, of mice and other rodents, as well as songbirds. If one portion of the aerosolized cyanocarbon could have a drastic adverse effect on the mammalian part of the alien entity, then there was little doubt that it was a direct injection of the tear gas via ferret shells that had caused the organism pain.

"We thought it was pained by breathing the tear gas," Brigid said, loud enough for all to hear as they made their way to an open field. "That is not the case."

"Direct injection?" Edwards asked. "Because nothing short of punching a ferret shell into the bastard seems to cause it to react...Myrto's flash-bang trick notwithstanding."

"Correct," Brigid responded. "We need to make this thing ingest the CS. It has a chromosomal effect on mammals, and this creature is at least thirty percent mammalian."

"And because the creature itself is a manipulated biomass, anything that hurts its DNA hurts the process making it a whole entity," Sinclair agreed.

"Simple. Shoot it," Domi concluded.

"Load up," Grant ordered. He plucked his hand gren from his belt and whipped it full-force toward the semi-fluid entity. "I'll give it something to chew on."

The small egg-shaped bomb spiraled through the air, bouncing off of the pudding-like skin of the blob. It rebounded into the air above the amorphous atrocity, and on its way back down, erupted full-force. Several ounces of hi-ex and a metallic core created pressure and heat, as well as a sheet of high-velocity splinters. Cut and slashed violently, the amalgamated mass shuddered and partially retreated to the tree line. There was a brief moment of respite as the battered blob seemed to observe its prey, trying to figure out an approach that would not cause it injury.

Kane handed off one of their remaining hand-thrown tear gas canisters to Brigid. He'd dumped the load of his shotgun onto the ground, leaving the neoprene baton slugs in the dirt while replenishing the magazine tube with more CS shells. The antibarricade ammunition might not have had the volume in it that the canister or a 40 mm gren held, but so far, those shotgun-launched rounds had managed to burn and deter the alien gestalt.

Brigid suddenly watched the thing collapse upon itself, disappearing as if its bodily cohesion burst apart.

"Watch your feet!" Brigid warned. "It's gone nearly two dimensional and is conforming to the ground!"

The grasses of the clearing began to move as if beset by phantom breezes. Though Brigid couldn't feel the moving air on her skin, her faceplate registered that there was no wind in the vicinity. Whatever caused the knee-length grass to rustle was movement caused from below.

"We need to make it pull into a more cohesive form," she said.

"Right. It's not big enough or thick enough to keep a shell inside it," Grant agreed. "Edwards?"

The burly CAT Beta warrior aimed his less-lethal shotgun at the ground, but rather than triggering the 12-gauge, he cut loose with the under-barrel Taser. The twin darts zipped out and into the moving grass blades. As soon as Edwards saw that the wires connected to the barbs were moving along, he triggered the battery.

Suddenly a tarlike mound bubbled up over the top of the grass, the amorphous creature unleashing its wail in a spine-scraping warble of a million different tiny voices. Tendrils whipped out toward Edwards, thick, cloying strands winding around his arms and shotgun.

There was a brief pulse of panic for Brigid as she saw those slack pseudopods tighten around his arms, but then Smaragda drew her sword and lashed at the snarling tentacles. Her falcata pierced the tarry blackness of the amorphous anomaly. At the same moment Sinclair gave Edwards a zap with her Taser, the shadow suit at once insulating her teammate against the voltage sent from her shock weapon and conducting the electrical energy into the remnant flesh that clung to him.

As the charge rolled through, tiny sparrows fluttered away on the wing, while rodents toppled to the dirt. Elements that had been halved by Smaragda's sword stroke fell in wet, bloody splatters.

Too bad there were no weapons that could direct electricity on a larger scale, Brigid thought, but she maintained her concentration. Where one "bubble" of the abomination faded, two more rose, and Grant pumped a tear gas shell into one of them. Domi's knife was out, and the feral girl slashed and flickered, intercepting pseudopods and tendrils, Kane mirroring her actions on the other side. Blades and tear gas cartridges were keeping this horror at bay, but they were battling a creature whose biomass was measured in tons, and the shocked elements being broken off measured in ounces per organism.

That meant a load of CS or ketone was going to have to be disgorged into the heart of the beast and that required an almost suicidal tactic. Then again, as Brigid recalled, the soldiers taken by this plasmoid terror were still alive.

"Kane. Gas canister," Brigid ordered. "Anyone else with a hand-thrown unit. To me!"

Kane lobbed his tear gas gren to her.

Brigid quickly drew a length of cord from a belt pouch, slipping it through the ring pins of the two grens. She was pleasantly surprised that Edwards had brought enough for the whole class. Seven of the shells lay on the ground in front of her as she quickly strung the cotter pins to be tugged out all at once.

At the same time, ferret rounds, bullets and blades slashed violently, batting away or burning into the writhing, surging Stygian force that threatened to overwhelm the Cerberus explorers.

Already, through her peripheral vision, Brigid could make out the slowing of her allies, their arms growing tired, not to mention that their supply of shotgun-based gas rounds was running out, and no one was interested in burning off the last of their more ineffectual rounds. Regular bullets were mere pinpricks to the rubbery flesh of this fiend.

"All right, let it grab me!" Brigid shouted.

"No," Smaragda called. "I owe this thing!"

Brigid looked toward the woman. She admitted to herself that she didn't relish the concept of being swallowed whole and smothered by the spawn of Charun and Vanth, but so far, she was of the opinion that she couldn't allow anyone else to go through this dangerous course of action.

It was her "harebrained scheme." She couldn't let anyone else risk absorption.

But Smaragda, behind the transparent faceplate of her shadow suit hood, was deadly serious as she extended her hand to catch the cluster of tear gas grens that she'd just made.

If there was one thing Brigid Baptiste was certain of, it was that the New Olympian soldier had more than sufficient motivation to deliver a load of chromosome-damaging chemicals into the heart of the creature that had frightened every lick of color from her hair, on top of kidnapping her closest friends and allies in the world.

Brigid lobbed the circlet of tear gas grens to the Greek woman, who put them into her breadbasket rather than clutch at the cord connecting them. Smaragda's wits were about her, and simply snatching one out of the air would have wasted that gren canister as she removed its safety pin.

Smaragda gave her *falcata* a whirl, handing it off to Edwards handle-first.

"Cover me," she said.

The biggest member of CAT Beta nodded grimly, his fist closing around the haft of the sword. "All the way to the gates of hell."

With that solemn pronouncement, the two people turned toward the bloblike horror. The five other Cerberus warriors stopped shooting and retreated, pulling back to let their friends become the bait for an abomination.

To Edwards, the logic was simple. The Cerberus teams might have been willing to sacrifice an ally to the formless alien monstrosity, at least as far as the callous Etruscan deities would have assumed. The Annunaki contemporaries were masters of cruel disregard. Edwards could even imagine Enlil assuming that CAT Beta themselves were nothing more than disposable cannon fodder to buy Kane and the others time to succeed, so Vanth and Charun couldn't be that much different.

And as soon as Edwards threw in with Smaragda, standing fast to shield her with three feet of hooked, battle-sharpened sword in his hand, the bloblike abomination realized that there was something up, something that could threaten it. Or maybe it was one of the demigods back at the pyramid who was doing the thinking for the tarry tons of biomass being wielded as a gigantic weapon. After all, no amount of the tiny brains of mice and birds could assemble into a single cohesive consciousness willing to endanger itself in battle with humans.

Edwards had yet to enter a field where birds were present and the flock didn't choose to turn and run, at least without the presence of eggs or chicks to defend. No, the abominable amalgam was being controlled by telepathic puppet strings. Powerful wings wrapped around Smaragda and Edwards, fingers reaching out to each other to intertwine and completely encircle the pair of warriors. Yes, this creature was doing things no normal mammal or avian would do. It was more amoeba than even the most coherent swarm.

"This had better work," Edwards said.

Smaragda remained impassive as she wound tape around the hulls of the tear gas grens. Now it was no longer seven loose canisters, but a solid whole. One tug of the safety pins and the spoons holding the nozzles shut would release. Tear gas grens didn't explode; they vomited out their payloads. And all Edwards had to do was to make a proper opening.

The creature swelled, and suddenly all of that pudding skin parted, showing off grisly pink inner tissues, raw nerve endings stretching out to web over the two humans.

Edwards realized that he wouldn't have to split open the outside of the creature to get the tear gas inside.

Tarry black lips of flesh elongated, blotting out the sky over the pair as Smaragda clutched her weapon as if it were a prize.

Edwards swung his sword, the keen edge severing threads of neurons and axons as if they were gossamer, continuing to put up the charade that he didn't want Smaragda and himself swallowed by their enemy.

Even inside the fully sealed shadow suit, Edwards realized there was very little that could be done to resist the horrible creature that was bringing down its rubbery bulk. He lashed out, the *falcata* cutting deep into a pink semblance of muscle, but more wormlike tendrils of pink, white and red flesh snapped out and seized his sword arm. Now, panic rushed through the CAT warrior. There was no need to act, as the strength of the Stygian entity was beyond anything he could hope to match. His boots left the ground and he kicked wildly. There was no leverage, so he was a plaything in the grasp of a giant that didn't respond to punches or bullets.

Suddenly an arm wound around his waist. This one had weight to it, but it was nothing like the grasping power slurping him up into the tissues of the alien shape-shifter. He couldn't see for the mass pressing against his faceplate, turning his universe into a window of tumors and throbbing polyps.

He didn't need to see Smaragda, however, to know that it was her. With Edwards in the midst of being swallowed, she'd leaped up and joined with him. There was suction tugging the skintight polymers from Edwards, trying to draw away the shadow suit to create a direct contact with his skin. He remembered Brigid and Smaragda's description of how the thing had swallowed an entire platoon of

New Olympian troops, and knew that the slightest touch to bare flesh would prove paralyzing.

That suction had to come from somewhere, though, and as soon as the turgid, inflamed flesh was around Smaragda, the whole throbbing mass suddenly began tossing Edwards as if he were trapped in one of the laundry machines back at the redoubt. Hurled and twisted around, he could now see that Smaragda was inside this cavity with him, as was the tear gas unit. Seven jets of white, eye-burning chemical blew outward, and the rippling pink flesh around them started breaking down, twisting apart as rabbits and squirrels started filling this chamber of mutated meat.

The *falcata* fell between the squirming voles and field mice, and Edwards reached for it. His first instinct was to begin chopping his way out, but to do that would be to give the tear gas a means of escape into the atmosphere rather than into its bulk. The birds provided enough of a skin and cohesion that it kept the spreading, choking clouds through its system. Whatever technology altered the cellular structures of the local fauna into this entity, at least for the mammals, was being counteracted by the chemicals that seemed to directly damage the chromosomes of a good portion of its total bulk. With coughing and wheezing tiny creatures twisting and clawing, gnawing for their means of escape, the tarry black form was being assailed from within in a second wave of torment.

Smaragda scrambled to Edwards's side, holding out her hand for him. He grasped hers and looked at the disintegrating walls around them. Chemicals and alien powers were waging war around them, as Edwards noticed some of these critters being slurped back into the biomass, but even with each mouse swallowed, a half-dozen squirrels were released from the bulky mass. Tear gas blinded and agonized animals chewed, and jets of blood erupted, smearing the whole mess.

"How much longer?" Smaragda asked, batting away at enraged or simply confused creatures bounding to escape the seething clouds.

Arcs of cracked blue rippled along the skin. Weakened and disoriented by the bad meal it had eaten, the tarry abomination was now victim to hundreds of thousands of volts of electricity from Tasers and stun guns Edwards had been hauling all of this time. As the shocks ripped through the creature, the sky appeared above them, sky that was filled with fleeing songbirds, crows and hawks, all bursting to freedom from the nightmare of oneness they had suffered under the forces of the Etruscan demigods.

Sinclair and Domi rushed to their allies as Kane, Grant and Brigid continued pumping Taser shocks into the remaining pieces. But this time, however, the blackened, rubbery entity was disintegrating without the inducement of electrical charges.

Vanth and Charun had released their tiniest of pawns, and now the Cerberus teams were together in a vacated field. The former segments of the biomass had separated, and except for a few scores of dead creatures, all of them were running or flying all out to escape the area.

"Did we kill the big bad beast?" Edwards asked, slowly getting to his feet as Sela and Domi had an easier time lifting the smaller Smaragda than they ever could hoisting him up.

"We dispersed its biomass sufficiently that Charun no longer maintained its structural integrity," Brigid said.

"Smaller words?" Edwards asked. The tug-of-war and rumblings in the belly of the abomination had left him with little patience for technical jargon.

"The mice and birdies are alive. The crap keeping it together is gone," Brigid clarified.

Edwards smiled. "That, I understood."

Kane and Grant gave the big man claps on his broad shoulders. "Feeling better?"

"Better how?"

"Not beating yourself up over falling once?" Kane added to his question.

"Are you going to hit me with that stale old shit about 'fall down once, stand up twice'?" Edwards countered.

Kane wrinkled his nose. "If you're going to put it that way…"

"I'm yanking you, man," Edwards said, disarming any tension with a chuckle.

"One threat down," Brigid pronounced. "But we've still got two demigods and their Stygian minions."

Edwards felt his shoulders slump. "I wish I hadn't understood that."

The thunderous footsteps in the distance warned the Cerberus adventurers of the gravity of their position.

This thing was far from finished.

Chapter 23

Charun sliced through the skies, headed for where they had lost contact with their protean emissary only moments ago. His wing harness propelled him along as if he were a bullet, any sense of wind resistance deleted by the very bubble of antigravity that pushed him along. The field deflected the air in front of him, part of the mechanism that allowed him to smash through Grant's Manta days before.

There was a touch of regret on the part of Charun as he sailed toward the battlefield, his hammer clutched in his mighty hands. Grant and the others, they had been so easily mentally disarmed, given to feel a sense of camaraderie with the two godlings, buying into a tale of need and mistaken identity or translation of thoughts. He could have had them as part of his world, if it all had not been for the damned woman, Brigid Baptiste.

Grant showed his worth, the way in which he was able to handle the mighty hammer, learning the true symbiotic nature of the intelligent metals that made up the weapon. Where Kane had struggled with the artifact, Grant knew that a Zen approach, a bonding with the hammer, was the means by which one took control of the deadly piece of alien weaponry and focused its power with deadly efficiency.

The body that Charun currently was burdened with was starting to lose its cohesion, while Grant's would give the demigod years more to survive in this world while the million brains at the bottom of the pyramid engaged in forcing open the aperture between universes, the route to home and to his beloved minions.

Back home was the true form that could contain the power of Charun's soul. The poor fool who had been present when his seed was planted. Not the beautiful, dark woman Nathalie, the one who actually sowed him, but rather the local guide, an Italian farmer well on in his years, who'd told her of the hidden pyramid.

Charun recalled having been tempted to make the woman his bride, to implant her with the genetic information to create a brand-new Vanth, but his hand was stopped by a subconscious command, a force from beyond him. The name Hurbon was associated with the hesitation, one that told Charun there were more important things for Nathalie to do than serve as a temporary shell.

Instead, simmering inside the skin of the now-erased farmer, Charun had returned to the man's home and found the local's wife. She had been as withered as Charun's "human suit," sixty years making her skin hang in wrinkled drapes on her skeleton. All it took was a kiss, a penetration of energy, and the seed that had been one became two.

The rest of the sons of Styx who inhabited the pyramid were composed of a chicken-coop full of birds. The genetic data, and the feast of the Stygians upon every other living creature in the barns of the farm, turned the small poultry into the reedy but powerfully built warriors who could be grown even larger and more powerful.

Once Charun had brought his family back together, there was only the task of amassing those necessary.

At first it was a town or two disappearing. Over the past several months the disappearances became epidemic; convoys vanishing, even expeditions from the coast arriving to wonder why the center of the peninsula became a black hole from where thousands were never seen again. Several hundred thousand human brains, and even all of the larger mammals that Charun hadn't crafted into the meat suit for their recently fallen cyclops, or the small creatures molded into the Abyssal blob, were now gathered in the city-size prison beneath the pyramid.

"This is disrupting us, love." Vanth spoke across the miles with her mind touching his. "We were so close to the final equation and now…"

"Continue your focus, my bride," Charun admonished. "The humans will surrender or they shall be crushed."

"Crushed," Vanth repeated.

Charun knew that tone of mind, her disdain stinging him like an open-handed slap. "Bride, mind thy words."

"They have cast down others of our ilk before," Vanth warned. "Just because you have girded your loins and brought yourself to them at the peak of your armor and weaponry does not mean that you will fare better."

"Already, you think that I have not learned my lesson," Charun growled as he hovered above the clearing where he and Vanth had last felt the presence of the Abyssal. He scanned around, his armor augmenting his already formidable senses, and yet found nothing on the ground. It was mere minutes after the savage battle and there was no sign of human life.

He alit, his draconian wings folding back against his shoulder blades. There were signs and elements of the battle, shell casings and the bisected corpses of sparrows and voles. He bent and lifted one halved creature.

He cursed the luck that they had come equipped to deal harmlessly with groups of mind-controlled people, and the very gases they intended to slow and dispel throngs of thralls had also proved to counteract the atomic matrices that turned millions of tiny creatures into an unstoppable whole. He crushed the half squirrel, its delicate bones snapping and its meat liquefying in his powerful grasp. He wiped his palm against the ground and stood tall, looking around.

During his flyover and hover, his augmented vision had swept for a mile in every direction, and though the men and women of Cerberus had been lauded for their physical prowess, there was no way they could have run as far and as fast as this.

That meant that they were present but had rendered themselves all but invisible and undetectable thanks to the optic camouflage technologies of their shadow suits. Without heat signatures and sealed airtight…they might as well have been phantoms.

Kane and his allies wanted to dictate the terms of their next encounter, which was something Charun could not allow.

The battle he'd forced Grant and Kane into had spilled back onto him and, without his armor, without his weapons, the frail flesh containing the power of his birthright was easily felled. With a body such as Grant's, he'd be unstoppable and closer to his original height and build.

Of course, Vanth had promised that with the incredible intellect of Brigid Baptiste, he wouldn't have to worry about shadows, mere substitute bodies. Their home world was almost open, and Charun's hordes would bring his slumbering form across, uniting him with the flesh that he was meant for.

"Humans! I grow tired of your games! Bring me the woman Baptiste, and we shall be gone from your lives evermore!"

Charun glanced around. "No taker?"

Charun drove the handle of his hammer into the soil and then stepped away from it. "What do you want?"

"You wish a fair battle?" he called as he peeled off the headpiece of his armor. "You, seven against one?"

He began pulling out of the near-fabric-like top of his smart-metal body armor. "You wish to prove yourself against a god?"

Nothing. No one moved. He was alone and apparently addressing a field full of mouse and bird corpses, stripping himself down. His head still hurt from catching the hundreds of pounds of force Kane had developed when he was hurled violently by Grant. That impact, and the back of his head crashing against a solid stone wall, had rendered Charun insensate and helpless. All he could do was watch as Kane, Grant and Brigid had fled the arsenal to rush to the rescue of their allies trapped in the storage chamber.

"We had all seven of you under our roof. We could have snuffed you out! But that is not our way. That was not our need!" Charun bellowed.

Within moments figures were at the tree line, but Charun knew that it was merely the automatons from his own arsenal. They stood there, scanning around, utilizing camera mounts of their own to sweep for signs of the humans.

Charun initiated a telepathic contact with his Stygian pilots. Have you made any contact?

Negative, sire. We saw none. We heard none. None struck at us.

"This is maddening!" Charun frowned.

"Where could you stupid little humans have gone?" Charun asked, hoping his mockery would inspire them into stupidity.

He spent fifteen minutes, walking around, finding only empty tear-gas gren hulls and other spent casings, but there were no footprints, no spoor and no infrared imagery. There wasn't even an active Commtact that he could use his own smart-metal armor to home in on as he pulled it back over his chest and arms.

Husband...return home. Leave the humans to wander around, confused and lost.

Vanth had a compelling point, and according to her, it would be only days, not months, until the resurgence of their portal. To crawl into Vanth's supple, loving arms and to taste even the withered shadow of her true flesh, would be the sweetest of release, a recharge for his next encounter with the men and women of Cerberus.

His leathery wings unfurled, stretched to almost translucent tautness. They appeared as living flesh, but they were more akin to the polymers that made up the suits of his human opponents, including the ability to either carry or insulate against the electric charges necessary to produce a gravity-defying ionic field.

Charun extended his hand and the war hammer rose from the ground, cartwheeling to his grasp.

With but a thought, he was airborne, spearing into the dimming sky.

His Stygian warriors, manning the Gear Skeletons, would continue their hunt through the night. Nothing could interrupt their telepathic contact with him, and with Brigid Baptiste's interphaser under their control in the pyramid, the Cerberus explorers were trapped and isolated.

Let the humans stew—let them fret and worry. Their ending would come, as had those of millions before who stood in the path of Charun.

KANE SCANNED HIS back trail, the growing shadows of evening being taken into account and adapted by his optic camouflage on his shadow suit. The arrival of Charun himself had been something of a surprise, especially as he hadn't expected the demigod to be hands-on in his hunt for the humans. The trio of Stygian "snot-pilots" in the Gear Skeletons seemed perfectly capable of crushing them on their own, especially since they didn't have the kind of fighting power that Charun had inadvertently bestowed upon Grant with his hammer. Moving with every bit of stealth and grace he had, he was a phantom.

He saw Domi motion, letting him know of her arrival at their rendezvous. They'd only traveled four hundred yards in the time it took for Charun and his bounding automatons to arrive, but it was still room enough for the seven members of the expedition to disappear into nooks and crannies of the ground, the foliage and the roots of the forest. Kane wasn't a big fan of hiding, but in the face of opposition that could crush a human skull with the same facility that a man could crush a grape, discretion was the better part of valor.

Right now he and the rest of the team were homing in on him, following the sound of clicks he made with his tongue. It was one thing to use something high-tech, like an infrared emitter that would show up on the optics of the robots, but the noises he made were in imitation of insect chirps. Unlike Domi, the others *were* visible to him, but only because he knew exactly what to look for in terms of signs of motion among his camouflaged friends.

Finally the small party was reassembled, and all hundreds of yards from the towering automatons skulking through the forest for their trails.

"I can't wait to pick up a rocket launcher and deal with those blobs," Grant grumbled.

"Me, either," Edwards agreed. "But how is that going to happen with the three of those things looking for us?"

"Brigid, just what was in that interphaser housing that you brought?" Kane asked.

The archivist smiled. "Oh, that little thing? I was considering different options when I had it brought in. The first thought was a fail-safe...a compact but powerful explosive device."

"That's what I thought when I handled it," Kane said. "But it was still too light to be even a suitcase-size nuclear warhead, and there's no way that anything else could have been packed in there with enough power to dissuade Charun and Vanth. If I didn't know any better, I'd have thought that you'd brought a regular interphaser in with the housing."

Brigid frowned. "And what would the purpose of that be?"

Kane smirked. "You brought in a working, full-powered interphaser so that the cavalry could be called in. At the same time, the extra mass has something to do with a jammer. A frequency jammer to do to Charun and Vanth what they've done to our Commtacts."

"I triggered the countdown for the broadcast of that frequency the moment I found you two," Brigid answered. "In five more minutes, the song of Vanth is going to disappear from the airwaves and a million people are going to awaken."

"That could get messy," Grant said.

"It could, if there weren't three Spartans ready to protect them from the Stygians, and Charun's armored minions were already occupied with us," Brigid said.

"That sounds like a great plan," Smaragda offered, but there was doubt dripping from that statement. "But the pilots of those armors are inside the cells hundreds of feet below the arsenal, if that's where they put your interphaser."

"That is exactly where they would have put the interphaser," Brigid corrected. "They think it to be a dangerous weapon, and the arsenal has been constructed so as to minimize potential damage to the rest of the pyramid in the instance of an explosion."

"But not in the instance of three Olympians being brought in through a parallax point," Smaragda concluded. "So..."

"Blowing up the very humans we're coming to rescue is highly counterproductive and against our ethics," Brigid added.

Kane nodded. "I was wondering what would even the odds. But how about us?"

"Activate your Commtacts now," Brigid said. "We should be in communication with our ride."

"Our ride?" Edwards asked. "The only ship we have access to is a Manta back in Greece..."

"Left with the incomparable mechanic Fast," Brigid added.

The crack of a sonic boom as the aforementioned ship entered the atmosphere punctuated Baptiste's statement.

"Mantas can carry one, two people at the most," Sela Sinclair noted.

"Inside its sealed cockpit? Yes, it's at best a crowded two-seater," Kane said. "But we're in full-body environmental suits. Suits that allow its wearers to walk on the surface of the moon with only an oxygen attachment."

Domi looked down, then smiled. "We can hang from the outside, on harnesses."

Edwards chuckled. "You are almost diabolical, Brigid."

"Almost?" Brigid asked, raising an eyebrow. "Which of you guys want to fly it? It's being brought in via remote control."

Kane and Edwards both pointed to Grant immediately.

"He's the best pilot we have," Kane added.

"Good," Grant said. "The weapons systems?"

"Hephaestus was told not to alter them," Brigid answered. She tapped her forearm. "You'll have the remote piloting controls on your shadow suit forearm display."

Grant looked down. "This looks awfully familiar..."

"Naturally. We needed you to be familiar with the operation of the Manta," Brigid explained.

Grant nodded. "Hang on...I'm going to give us a few more minutes before the armors harass us."

Brigid nodded. "That was anticipated."

As SOON AS Grant was plugged in to the Manta's remote-control network, suddenly he was surrounded in his hood by all the displays and control layouts necessary. As he moved his hands, he realized that he was inside of a virtual cockpit, and he immediately took control of the joystick and the throttle. Even the newly mounted weapon systems were part of the computer-generated command module on the Manta. Suddenly, the Cerberus pilot was where he'd been hours ago.

And the Manta switched to hover mode, guns deploying as he flicked controls.

At the edge of the clearing the three robots of Charun and Vanth stood, looking up at the newcomer and infiltrator. They each had some form of heavy machine gun in their hands, carried as if they were gigantic rifles. Before they could do anything, though, Grant activated the Browning machine guns on his Manta, spraying the lead ship with a wave of half-inch-wide, armor-piercing slugs. While the bullets didn't penetrate or damage the secondary orichalcum frame, the steel plates that protected the cockpit of Grant's first target suddenly became a sieve.

Hot lead burned into the pilot of the alien-controlled robot and its semifluid body structure did not make it immune to impacts capable of liquefying armor plate. The control couch beneath the amorphous pilot was also chewed awry, the internal systems of the Stygian armor bursting apart in a wave of destruction.

Gutted by heavy-caliber fire, the robot toppled backward. The others reacted to the sudden rain of fire and doom, scrambling to evade the hovering Manta.

Grant didn't intend to let his element of surprise get away from him for a moment, however. He hit the throttle and tore off, swooping low enough above the Gear Skeletons that they were bowled over by the Manta's thrusters.

Sent out of control by the sudden rush, Grant swung his ship upward, armed the unaimed artillery rocket pods on the ship, then looped back toward the ground. Missiles—77 mm—ripped from the pods, and struck either directly or in close proximity to Charun's robot minions. Hi-exes erupted with such violence, Grant could feel the tremors through the soles of his boots. He couldn't see what was happening to the twin robots he'd hammered with artillery rockets as he swooped the Manta up and away to keep the ship from crashing.

At least not right away. Within a moment he was able to get a rear camera view of the ground, and the dust-penetrating infrared lenses saw that while the nearly invulnerable frames of the robots were still extant, everything else that had been bolted on or was sitting in the cockpit had been forcibly removed by the pressures released on detonation.

Grant swung the Manta back toward the section of wood they were placed in. Along the way, he swept the skies in the direction of Charun's pyramid. The winged demigod was over there, but he was torn between the sudden mayhem under his roof and the violence occurring against his soldiers.

Grant brought the ship down and landed it in a clearing just large enough for the Manta. Security straps ran all along the top of the sleek ship, as well as new cowlings that could shield the riders outside from high winds.

different," Grant mused as he climbed up to the cockpit. "Space for six."

"And the pilot," Brigid said. "There are also replacements for the less-lethal ammunition in the compartment with you."

Grant reached in, pulling out two war bags. He took a peek in. "Real shotgun and 40 mm shells. Not the less-lethal."

"I said replacements, did I not?" Brigid asked.

Grant grinned. "What happened to getting tired about us talking about enough firepower?"

Brigid strapped herself onto the hull. "That goes out the window when you go in my brain and make me a puppet. You can hand me my Copperhead and gren launcher when we get to the pyramid."

Grant closed the cockpit, advancing through the pre-liftoff checklist with a broad smile.

This time, the gods were going to be the ones to feel a few thunderbolts.

Chapter 24

The wave of disorientation passed for Diana Pantopoulos and she was suddenly in a whole new area wherein old human weapons and artifacts were on display. Between her and two of her personal squadron mates was the interphaser that released them into the pyramid of Charun and Vanth. In the base of the device was a powerful transmitter that, by all accounts, should be drowning out the strange signal that had seized and controlled the hundreds of thousands of people on the Etruscan peninsula.

The three of them arrived without wheelchairs, but that was really a matter of convenience when they were around people who were taller than they were. Diana moved along on all fours, her strong arms and the stumps of her amputated legs giving her as much mobility as a young, swift monkey. Sure enough, Diana was glad to see the Spartan units up against the wall, their Sandcat armor plate chests open. So secure were the demigods that they hadn't left guards.

Why would they? They assumed that their seizure of this pyramid had cut it off from outside interference. Brigid Baptiste and the science team at Cerberus Redoubt had been doing a lot of number crunching, mind-bending dimensional physics that allowed them to pierce the bubble of power severing the parallax point from the rest of the planet.

"This is going to suck if they emptied the guns and the rest of the gear," one of Diana's squadron mates pointed out.

"We'll still have the Skeletons' limbs," Diana said. She snatched a handhold on the calf of one of the suits, and her well-muscled arms lifted her up. Climbing was easy, thanks to the fact that each of the amputee pilots present was a victim of lower-body trauma rather than upper-body stress. Every amputee was given hours and hours of re-habilitation training to render them able to move around, wheels or not.

Diana and her two partners, however, had been chosen for the fact that they had, pound-for-pound, the best upper-body strength and agility of any of the New Olympian pilots.

All that time in the gym with the weight machines made Diana feel a hell of a lot better, especially as now she was back on the front lines with her fellow warriors. She swung herself into the cockpit of the Spartan with grace and ease. The interface was still intact and she plugged it into her cyber nodule.

Once connected to the mobile armor suit, she was immediately back in business. The hands of the suit closed her cockpit for her as she checked all the displays. "Charged Energy Modules at full strength, guns are loaded."

"Same here," called her allies. Even through the closed shells of their control nodes, they heard the cries of alarm.

Artem15 took her first steps in a long time, crossing the arsenal and stooping to see a group of slender, pallid creatures racing down the hall. Each of them bore a rifle and opened fire on her as she appeared in the doorway. Bullets pinged impotently against the armored skin of her suit, and for a moment Artem15 thought that these poor, deluded beings could be spared. Then she realized that these aliens had taken more than twenty of her soldiers captive but also had thousands more under mind control, and they were rushing to the armory in an effort to prevent any rescue attempt.

The shoulder-mounted machine guns swiveled to life at her mental command, and she rested on the knuckles of her massive hands, allowing the weapons plenty of room to fire on the aliens. The twin light weapons followed the focus of her vision, at least in relation to the view screen in front of her face, and in the next moment both of them erupted, spitting thunder and fire.

The two Stygians at the front of the formation were still cutting loose with their rifles when slashing streams of 7.62 mm bullets ripped them in two. One of the M-240s had a rate of fire of 950 rounds per minute. With two guns cutting loose simultaneously, the wall of death hacking into the pallid aliens was an obscene display of force. It took only a few seconds to turn half a dozen armed troopers to six mangled, shredded corpses lying in pools of gore and burst tissue. The slain creatures were ignored for now as Artem15 and her allies headed out into the corridor.

The interphaser housing's jammer had made it so that Brigid and the rest of the CAT teams could inform Diana of the setup for the pyramid, one that now appeared on a data monitor just off her shoulder. If there was something that gave the New Olympian a sense of hope, it was that they were under the direction and guidance of one of the most thorough and intelligent women in the world. Having used the passive GPS information from CAT Beta's suits and their exploration of the lower levels of the pyramid, Artem15 and her Spartan guard were fully aware of the path to the captives of the Etruscan gods.

Artem15 led the way, her escorts pausing only to rip a door off of its hinges and jam it into the rock as a barrier against pursuit. The quarters for the fifteen-foot automatons were tight enough that they had to move down corridors in single file, but the last thing they needed was for Charun and Vanth to show up and easily make their way in pursuit of the mobile suits.

"Fiddy, set up a barricade here," Artem15 ordered. "Weapons free. Especially the explosive spears."

"Yeah. I remember the briefing about Vanth and her explosive arrows," Spartan 50, nicknamed Fiddy, answered. He accepted the sheaths for gren-tipped spears from Spartan 46 and her own.

"On me, Four-Six," Artem15 added. "We're going to look for a way out for the prisoners."

With that, the three robots became two. Artem15 hated leaving one of her own in the line of fire, but there were too many people in need of help and there had to be something that could hold the Etruscan deities at bay.

This being a Spartan expeditionary suit, and not the true Artem15, she didn't have her heat spear, a "hero suit" weapon. Instead the war spears were simply old RPG shells on sticks, thrown with more than sufficient robotic strength to burst the impact fuse on the warheads. Artem15's arsenal was both the standard explosive shells and a superheated spearhead on a conducting staff that could carve steel and stone let alone flesh.

That would have been nice to have, but she'd make mayhem with what she had. The shoulder guns alone and the powerful, wall-smashing fists of the Gear Skeleton would have to suffice.

And then, Artem15 and Spartan 46 were on the balcony overlooking the prison of the pit. The depth and breadth of the chamber was nothing short of epic, easily eclipsing every other structure she'd seen except for the Tartarus Crack in which Marduk had left his vast clone vats and the hundreds of ancient automatons that would become the backbone of the New Olympian military.

Looking through her cameras, Diana could see that the people down there seemed to be awakening from their hypnotic slumber. Not just humans, but also livestock in the form of cattle, sheep and horses were present. The yaps of dogs and yowls of cats also managed to reach her ears.

The pyramid shook.

"Fiddy?"

Another distant explosion resounded. "Winged bitch showed up and tried to impress me with her boom stick!"

"Fall back if you have to," Artem15 ordered.

"If," Spartan 50 added with defiance.

"As you were," Artem15 returned. "Come on. Let's look to see if there's a path out of here for the crowd. There had to be a way in for all of them, and not down the narrow ladders."

Spartan 46 grunted in agreement. "I can't recall the last time I saw sheep doing ladders, do you?"

Diana let out a chuckle. "Climbing time. We'll look for a major ramp."

The two robots dug their finger and toe claws into the wall and scaled their way down into the pit, aware of the precious cargo they had to protect from the demons above and their own footsteps.

THE MANTA ALIT on its gear and Kane hit the release on his harness. He carried his shotgun again, and this time instead of rubber slugs and tear-gas shells, he was armed for war. He paused only to grab a pack of spare shells for the weapon. Kane knew that using a gren launcher in close quarters would bring as much harm to him and his allies as it would to his opposition, given the general nature of the weapon, but these rounds were meant for punching deep through light armor and detonating inside their target without spraying indiscriminate shrapnel everywhere.

He hooked the ammo pack to his harness and thumbed the explosive 12-gauge shells into its tubular magazine. Charun had been pulled from the battlefield, even as his Stygian pilots had been torn to shreds under Grant's counterattack, and that meant there were allies in the depths of the pyramid who'd engaged Vanth and his other monstrous minions.

The last thing he wanted was to have even a fully armed and equipped Olympian Spartan stand alone against the two alien entities and their forces. Certainly, the pair had lost control of their amorphous giant, the creature who'd swallowed three such warrior robots and a platoon of soldiers, but that didn't mean they were completely disarmed.

Kane reached the peak of the mountain and saw that Charun had left the hatch open. He caught sight of a shadow moving at the bottom of the ladder, so the Cerberus leader pumped a single shot into the hole. The detonation of his shotgun gren was loud, and a bloodied Stygian guard limped into view, holding the broken pieces of his rifle in his hands.

Kane slung the shotgun and snagged the ladder. The friction of his grasp and the pressure of his boots on the sides of the ladder helped him slide down in a controlled drop that deposited him into the entrance foyer of the pyramid. The stunned and wounded Stygian let the broken pieces of his rifle fall away, one tri-fingered hand plucking a knife from his belt even as Kane let go of the ladder and dropped the rest of the way to the ground.

With the reflexes of a panther, Kane ducked beneath the wounded alien's slash, realizing the creature he was up against might not have been operating at peak capacity but still possessed prowess equal to the finest of the Magistrate corps. The Stygian reversed the point of its knife and stabbed, the point snagging the shoulder of Kane's suit. Polymers split, slicing open, but still managed to protect the human skin beneath.

Kane spun, as if to whirl away from the deadly attack of his alien foe, but dropped down to one knee and swept his leg across the ankles of the humanoid. The Stygian's spindly legs snarled against each other under the swift, savage lash, and it comically windmilled its arms in an effort to stay upright. In the next moment he'd crashed on the hard stone floor, and Kane pounced, coming down with his weight focused onto the peak of his elbow against the breastbone of the alien minion.

Ribs snapped under the elbow drop, Kane's joint protected by the non-Newtonian polymers hardening like steel. That very protective quality also made the force of the blow increase as the elbow was now as if it were encased in armor plate, rendering the protective cage of bone around the humanoid's vital organs a mass of splinters stabbing and slashing through lungs and blood vessels.

Inky-green blood spurted from the abomination's lips and its colorless eyes blinked in shock and horror.

Kane rolled away from the fallen foe's torso, spinning on his backside so that he could bring his booted feet around to bear on the opposing entity's head and neck. A swift scissor kick pulverized jawbone and ground vertebrae to chunks, ending the thing's suffering within moments.

Kane scrambled to his feet and looked up the ladder, Grant taking the lead down the ladder, Brigid above him.

"Beta, I'm picking up comms from the Olympians. They're looking for the exit. The main exit," Kane said.

"Uplink with Cerberus and look for that door leading underground and go that way!"

"Sure you won't need us?" Edwards asked.

"Over a half million humans need you more than we do. Now go!" Kane ordered.

"On it," Domi returned.

"Close the door, Baptiste," Kane said. "And leave a surprise in case we chase them back up this way."

Brigid braced herself at the top of the ladder and Grant handed up a larger version of the flat mine she'd hidden in her ankle brace earlier.

"This should shear even an armored Annunaki in two," Brigid said, securing it.

"Then don't arm it too soon," Grant offered.

"As if I'd forget that, or any step," Brigid replied.

In moments they were down with Kane, guns out and ready.

THE SOUND OF Lakesh over her Commtact made Domi feel whole again, his Indian accent and deep voice soothing her nerves like salve on a burn. It didn't matter that she was in full run down the side of a mountain, loaded with grens and a Copperhead rifle. It didn't matter that, a few hundred feet beneath her, two alien entities claiming godhood were still trying to get to over half a million human captives and assorted livestock.

It just mattered that her love's voice was in her ear.

"We're looking for the main entrance to the Etruscan pyramid, and using ground-penetrating radar as well as uploads of the layout transmitted by both you and Brigid. We've found a strong possibility," Lakesh said. "Adjust your heading forty degrees west, beloved."

"Thank you, Moe," Domi said. "How big is the opening we're looking for?"

"It's actively concealed," Lakesh responded. "Some

form of camouflage netting is over the cave, and there was no thermal reading on the crack."

Domi skidded, adjusting her heading. Behind her, Sinclair, Edwards and Smaragda took to the new course, as well, Edwards laden down with one of the two war bags that had arrived on the Manta. Domi led the way with her Copperhead, which should be sufficient for even a Stygian soldier wearing New Olympian armor, thanks to its high-velocity armor-piercing bullets. But if that wasn't the case, she had a bolt-action, magazine-fed shotgun attached in front of the trigger guard, in the place of the old foregrip handle. The XM-26 was a 5-shot 12-gauge that stripped off shotgun shells from its box, and could be rapidly reloaded.

Of course, Cerberus Redoubt had loaded the war bag with light antiarmor shells intended for vehicles akin to Sandcats and Deathbird helicopters, and hopefully that kind of firepower would be sufficient to hurt Charun and Vanth. Domi didn't envy that Kane would get a shot at them first, especially since she was dead certain there were likely other threats guarding the cave entrance.

They reached the camouflage netting and Domi slung her rifle. Grabbing her knife from its sheath, she started slashing, creating a hole in the cave entrance. She could see that the ramp was easily fifty yards wide and tall enough for even the New Olympian Spartan mobile suits to walk without stooping. Her eyes adjusted to the darkness and she snagged a handful of netting to use as a climbing rope to descend. The entrance continued beneath her, a slanted field that would disgorge onto ground dozens of yards farther. It was just simpler and quicker to drop down from the upper lip of the cave entrance.

As she got down, her ruby-red eyes scanned the darkness. There was something wrong, something dangerous that spurred her instincts to full life. She brought down the Copperhead-shotgun combo.

"Slow and easy," Domi called upward. "Company down here."

Dust rained from where her comrades stopped at the roof of the cave entrance, reassuring her.

"I'll scout," she informed them.

"Dammit," Edwards cursed.

Domi ignored his frustration and treaded into the cave. She alternated between infrared illumination and her already light-sensitive eyes. The setting sun had turned the cave inky-black, but something was present that her already canny senses could *feel* but were not showing up on her shadow suit's optics or audio pickups.

Then she heard the faintest of rustles, saw small clouds of dust and sand falling from rising shapes.

Of course. They hid under tarps, hiding them as we hide in our shadow suits, she thought. Her instincts hadn't let her down, realizing that there would be guards present, and they would seek the same means of concealment as had been used across millennia of human warfare. Domi whirled toward one of the rising figures, letting the Copperhead snarl out a salvo of high-speed death.

The tarp shook and vibrated under the rain of bullets, but the form beneath continued surging forward, a deep, vibrant growl resonating inside a deep, powerful chest.

It was a Fomori-style creature and probably something that was also protected by bullet-resistant fabrics or fabric-like metals. It was too close for her to risk the shotgun gren or to do anything else but throw herself into a somersault as the tented titan lunged forward. Domi hit a tuck-and-roll, getting out of the path of the monstrosity, its camouflaging tarpaulin fluttering to the ground and revealing its massive, deformed bulk. Domi was on her feet in an instant, tracking and shooting at the creature's exposed back.

While 4.85 mm rounds might have been effective on human-size foes, even behind ballistic body armor, to the Stygian giant her salvo of automatic fire was nothing more than the scratching of an irritating itch. At more than seven feet in height, and looking to weigh in at five hundred pounds, the creature boasted four thick arms and one and a half faces, a trio of glistening eyes locking onto her. The one and a half mouths were ugly scars that twisted into a gleeful pair of smiles, and four large hands opened, a dozen fingers clawing the air for her.

"Food!" her Commtact translated for her.

Domi triggered the M-26 and the antiarmor shell boomed loud enough to rattle her teeth in the confines of the cave. The Fomori whirled, one of its quartet of arms hanging by threads of skin and stretched sinew from a ravaged torso.

Despite that horrific damage, it still continued its single-minded approach, two more of the things throwing off their disguises, gibbering laughter echoing in the cave.

Domi worked the bolt on her under-barrel shotgun when the snarl of Edwards's Sin Eater heralded the eradication of the alien abomination's skull.

Sela Sinclair and Smaragda cut loose with their shotguns, chopping a second of the horrors apart with a salvo of armor-piercing, explosive slugs, thunderclaps striking quickly and certainly.

The third of the Fomori was caught flat-footed, left indecisive as to whether to attack the small black-clad girl, charge toward the newcomers or flee to fight another day. That moment of indecision meant that Domi and Edwards were able to both take good aim at its misshapen skull and rain damnation onto it. A flurry of 9 mm bullets and an explosive slug sent a rain of blood and tissue misting across the interior of the cavern.

"Told you wait," Domi said. She took out her magazine and loaded two replacement shells into it.

"And we heard there was a party going on," Sinclair returned. "Ain't no party like a CAT Beta party."

Domi smiled. "Thanks."

"Anytime, boss," Edwards said. "Now let's get to the pit."

The four warriors continued down into the darkness.

Chapter 25

Vanth tore her tattered wing harness from her shoulders, hurling it to the ground in disgust. She watched as her lover approached, hammer in hand, trepidation slowing his gait.

"My bride?" Charun asked.

"You had to bring the interphaser into our armory?" Vanth asked. Her smart-metal armor sleeve was healing its tear, quickly, but the wing harness, having received much more damage, was shorn apart.

"That was how they got in? But how did they get—?" Charun began.

"How did they activate the three battle robots that you left with quivers full of exploding spears?" Vanth asked. She drew her torch, then extended the flame like the blade of a sword. "How did they render me as an Earthbound fool by throwing said bombs at me with the force of a giant?"

"My love…" Charun started to speak but Vanth slashed at the air between them, letting out a screech of frustration.

Vanth glared at him. "Let us invite them under our roof. They will suspect nothing. Our song has already subjugated their greatest mind."

"Still your tongue!" Charun bellowed. He scanned around the corridor and saw that Vanth's arrows and quiver were not present. "Where is your bow?"

Vanth's rage flashed to morbid guilt, her beautiful, lush mouth turning downward at the mention of her archery.

"You lost it to a human?" Charun asked.

"My arrows detonated," Vanth admitted, stepping back. "My arrows detonated because you—"

Charun snatched the female by her wrist, dragging her off balance, disregarding the flaming sword in her grasp. "Because I what?"

"Because you invited those…mewling little apes under our roof!" Vanth shouted.

Charun let his hammer hang in the air, backhanding his bride with every ounce of strength he could muster. Her cheek and jaw were left livid, lips dripping blood beneath the split mask she wore. Even behind the shielding for her eyes, Charun could see them welling up with tears of despair and rage. "Because you were foolish in your invulnerability."

Charun slapped her again, her metal mask peeling even further away, her lips burst like overgorged worms. He tightened his grasp at her wrist, pulling her in closer until her cheek was punctured on one of his tusks.

"You blame me for your failures?" Charun whispered. "You tell me that it was my fault that *our* scheme didn't work?"

"The humans…" Vanth began.

Charun threw her to the ground and took the torch from her hand. "The humans. The humans are too mighty, too willful. Brigid Baptiste somehow managed to stave off your suggestions because she was brilliant. Do you not recall the origin of this species? The simplicity and complacency inserted into their DNA? They were born to kneel and serve!"

Vanth looked up, her blood dripping on the stone floor beneath her.

Charun observed the intersection and he saw scattered segments of the black bow that Vanth wielded, a holy device made of the same materials as his own hammer. They had been driven apart, and scorched, charred by the detonations of powerful energy crystals. That explained the shredded wing harness of Vanth's. She had survived the chain-fire explosion of her deadly arrows only by using her own wings as a shield; after all, that was part of the purpose of the appendages. Certainly, they allowed for easier steering and maneuvering in flight, but the wings' main purpose was to protect their backs, and their ability to fold around their front was a feature that had carried the battle for Charun on many occasions.

Absently, Charun gave the torch blade a twirl, admiring its balance. It was nothing compared to his hammer, and yet, with it, Vanth had showed the ability to carve mountains...such as this one. The detonations of her arrows showed the sturdiness of the granite halls she'd carved through the interior of this mountain. Even after thousands of years of hibernation, this homestead stood mighty against the elements. Certainly, it had been buried under soil and rock, and entrances had to have been reconstructed by the mightiest of their Fomorian forces, but the Stygian pyramid was indeed still powerful.

How could he have been blamed for thinking that the interphaser was some form of bomb, especially since he'd been reading that in Brigid Baptiste's thoughts all the while he thought he had them all under his influence? Had the bomb in the housing gone off, all they would have lost would have been anything not constructed of secondary orichalcum, a mighty alloy that few powers on this planet could dent.

And yet there was that failure to completely infiltrate and connive inside the mind of the human woman. She had managed to delude Charun and Vanth all the while making it seem as if she were their perfect puppet, even leading *both* of the Cerberus teams into ambush situations, trapping them firmly. The plan had been to leave them seemingly unaware of how easily they had gotten through the front door, only to be ensnared in a web spun by one of their own.

But she'd known.

She'd put the blocks in place to make it only seem as if they'd walked into the trap. Once there was a proper command given, the meek lambs to slaughter showed just what kind of lions they were, flattening Charun and stunning Vanth. They had lost a dozen Stygian humanoids then.

He felt the sudden input, the shock and ache of three of his Fomori shock troops at the ramp entrance to the pyramid. All of them had died. That meant the Cerberus warriors were invading from below, making their way directly toward the throngs of mammals assembled for the purpose of housing an army of a million Stygian demons. The apes and their livestock would be transformed into the shock troops of a conquering interdimensional army, but all of that was under assault now. The kind of energy necessary to make that wormhole opening was gone.

Their brains were freed. The whispers and murmurs of all of those minds threatened to wash Charun's own thoughts away. Too many of them were present. The breakdown of the tethers on the sentients and even the droning thoughts of food were becoming a rising tide that menaced his individuality.

"Vanth, my bride, I apologize for the mistake I've made," Charun said.

She was quiet now, her hands folded to her face. Maybe he had gone too far this time with his rebuke. After all, the two of them thought they had everything under control. Any failure on her part was weighted against him, as well.

He knelt beside her, resting his hand on her shoulder. "My bride…"

"The humans," Vanth whispered. "Angry. Confused. Do you not feel them? Hear them?"

"Take your torch," Charun ordered. Her eyes were bloodshot and full of tears. This was far more than Charun's slaps, the pain, swelling and bleeding he'd inflicted upon her. This was psychic trauma. "My bride, your torch will shield your mind."

Vanth lashed out, her nails raking his war mask, the smart metal parting under sharpened claws of the slightly greater, far less flexible hardness. Through the rip, Charun felt the thoughts of their captives, no longer enthralled, no longer dominated by the task forced into their minds by the song of Vanth. He pressed his own war mask shut and the smart metal stitched itself closed, sealing against the external pressure of hundreds of thousands of consciousnesses.

"Diabolical humans," Charun growled. He pulled Vanth to her feet, pressing her mask closed. "Ignore them, shield yourself!"

"So many...so angry," Vanth repeated again and again. "Too much..."

"Shield yourself!" Charun roared, pressing the edges of her ripped headpiece together in a vain effort to isolate her from the collective humanity in the pit beneath.

"They..." Vanth began.

She turned away from Charun, looking back from where he'd entered.

There was Kane, standing between him and the war hammer, shotgun in hand. Grant and Brigid were behind him. Though they were clad head to toe in their shadow suits, their faces were visible through the faceplates on their hoods, and each of them regarded the pair of demigods with grim resolve.

Charun pushed Vanth aside, wielding her torch. "There is no hope for you, mortals."

"If that's so, why are you so eager to fight?" Kane asked.

Grant touched the hammer's handle, closing his fist around it. He gave the mighty weapon a tug and Charun watched as it wobbled.

Brigid Baptiste's smile was blasphemous against the Etruscan deity. "Having trouble concentrating?"

"'Concentrating'?" Vanth repeated.

"What are you doing?" Charun asked, holding the flaming spire of the torch between him and the humans. He tugged on Vanth's shoulder, trying to get her behind him.

"Scrambling your particular brand of telepathy," Brigid answered.

"'...of telepathy,'" Vanth repeated. Charun felt her nails stab through his leggings, pricking into his thighs.

"Or you could say your frequency," Brigid corrected herself. "The same one you've been using on your prisoners."

"'...your prisoners.'" Vanth mouthed the words as her claws sliced into the skin and muscle of Charun's left leg. He backhanded her hard. She barely budged.

"No way to treat a lady, Char," Grant said. He upended the hammer, giving it a twirl. He twisted the handle and suddenly the four-piece unit broke apart, a smaller hammer going to Kane's hand.

"We could do this with our shotguns," Kane mocked. The smart metal of the hammer seemed to mold to the image of what a warrior like Kane would wield: a plain Celtic-style battle-ax, complete with swooping beard, adding cutting length and depth to the blade. For Grant, his weapon retained its hammer styling, except there was a blunt, flattened end and a spiked point at the back. "But you were so keen on Grant handling the hammer that..."

Charun concentrated with all of his might and suddenly the two humans were spun toward each other, their weapons also spinning toward each other. This was *his weapon* and no mere ape would—

Charun staggered, his concentration broken by the detonation of a 12-gauge gren against his war mask. Only the power of his armor kept him from harm, but as he staggered backward he could see Brigid Baptiste riding out the recoil on her shotgun.

"Yeah, getting poetic with your own weapons was stupid," Grant growled. He opened fire and Charun's ribs received a hammering blow that sent the titan reeling once more. With a flourish, he swung the torch and a wave of heat and light smashed against the trio of Cerberus warriors, bowling them over.

Vanth's torch hadn't quite put out the kind of power he wanted. Charun was too distracted, too stunned, by the onslaught to focus all of his energy into commanding the weapon. As well, it was attuned to Vanth, and her face was slack and beset upon by waking nightmares.

"To me," Charun growled, and the four sections of his hammer flew from where they had been dropped, reaching his hand.

More hammering explosions peppered Charun's broad chest, even as he wrestled his chosen artifact into its original form. "Run, Vanth!"

"…anth…anth…Vanth," the female demigod murmured, crawling forward on her hands and knees.

Charun sneered as he finally assembled the hammer.

The roar of machine guns filled the air, but Charun felt none of that. At first he attributed the lack of sensation to the puny nature of human weaponry, but a spray of blood splashed on the floor at his feet. He looked down and saw his bride, riddled with bullets, her blank eyes glazing over.

"Vanth?" Charun asked.

Spartan 50 lurched into Charun's view and the angry Etruscan deity brought the war hammer up. The detonation of an explosive spearhead shook the entire corridor, but Charun had shielded himself and his mate. Her armor was still split, torn open, and the human form she wore was riddled with bullets beneath. The frail old woman, despite being pumped with the strength of a god, had been unable to deal with the onslaught of blazing bullets punching into her.

Charun looked up from the lifeless form at his feet, regarding Spartan 50 as his hammer's shield burst bullets in midair against its shimmering plasma screen.

"She died at your hands?" Charun asked.

"It's about time she went down," Spartan 50 challenged. "You next."

Charun let the hammer lay and leaped at the Gear Skeleton. His fingers tore into the Sandcat armor around the robot's cockpit. He roared at the top of his lungs, the same kind of nail enhancements that had drawn his blood making short work of the steel plating meant to protect the amputee pilot of the Olympian battle suit. Metal peeled and parted under his onslaught, even as the hammer's plasma field melted the barrels of the shoulder-mounted machine guns.

Tearing his foe's shielding free, he looked at the amputee within. Strong arms, nubs of legs cut off at mid-thigh, a beard. He wore a simple coverall and there was little about this baby-like humanoid, this mewling ape, that distinguished him as the kind of warrior to slay a goddess.

Even then, Spartan 50 pulled a handgun from a holster on his chest, aiming it at Charun's face.

"You expect me to beg?" the pilot asked.

Bullets rang off of the facial armor of the demigod as he sank his fingers into the Olympian's chest, shattering ribs and lacerating heart and lungs. With a mighty wrench, Charun tore the organs from his bride's murderer, letting gore splash all over him.

"You maniac!" came a shout from behind.

It was Kane, and the man opened up with his Sin Eater. The hammer swatted bullets from the air, but the warrior from Cerberus emptied his whole magazine in an effort to draw blood from Charun.

"Maniac? *Maniac?*"

Charun wrenched the corpse of the pilot from its couch and hurled it as a missile at Kane, bowling the man over. "My wife is dead at the hands of your misbegotten species, and you dare insult me?"

"Don't use the shotguns," Charun heard Brigid say. "His hammer is detonating any projectiles sent toward him."

Charun looked down at the waist of the mobile battle suit and found one of the warheads in its quiver. "Yes. If you will not blow yourself up, then I shall do the job for you!"

Grant plucked something from his belt and rolled it low, rebounding it off the wall so it went past the demigod in his resplendent armor.

"What are—?"

The corridor became a ball of light and thunder.

THE EXPLOSION OF several spear grens, cooked off by Grant's own hand-rolled gren, bought Brigid and him enough time to drag Kane from beneath the corpse of the murdered Olympian. Standing at ground zero of so much devastation would have totally obliterated any other creature, but the thing stood there, blinded and deafened by the multiple blasts.

Kane grimaced as he kicked to his feet while being dragged along by his friends, and then he clapped both of them to let him know he was about to move on his own.

"So, we're back to shooting this bastard?" Grant asked.

The ground shook beneath their feet. Charun had gotten his hammer back in hand and he'd tapped the floor. At several feet thick, the stone slabs that made up the structure between the levels of the pyramid were great at transmitting the kind of vibrations that rattled the three of them.

"Well, he dealt with that amount of explosives without concern," Brigid said. "I don't think even the armor-piercing shells we have can do anything against him."

"He's pissed," Kane added. "We're dealing with only one of them now, but he's gone full berserk."

Grant paused as they got to the foyer. "Brigid..."

"I disarmed it via radio," she said.

Grant surged up the ladder, snatching the explosive mine from where she'd placed it. He opened the hatch and got out onto the top of the pyramid. There, a few yards down from the peak, the Manta was parked.

"Can the two of you buy me a few moments?" Grant asked.

Brigid nodded as Kane joined them.

"Distract him?"

"Slow him down," Grant said. "I'll be in the Manta."

Kane gave a one percent salute to show that he was willing to follow his friend's lead. He took Grant's war bag.

"Any idea what he's up to?" Kane asked.

Brigid nodded. "I'd rather not say anything, though. He might be listening."

"Through several feet of solid stone?" Kane asked.

"I could hear you on the far side of the moon, you sniveling monkeys!"

Charun's rage and volume were unmistakable. Kane reached into the war bag, looking down into the hatch. The demigod strode into the open, wielding his hammer, glaring up the ladder.

"You wish to slow me?" Charun asked. He spread his arms. "Do your worst!"

Kane decided to oblige the ancient alien, dropping a couple of live grens down the hole. Brigid was on the lid, slamming it shut to contain the explosion.

Kane's teeth shook at the rumble, which seemed unusually strong for a couple of gren blasts.

"Shouldn't the countersignal be interfering with whatever doomie powers Charun has?" Kane asked.

The top of the pyramid shook once more, seething and cracking under a powerful force bursting from within. Kane and Brigid lost their footing, but he recovered, bracing her from falling into a crumbling rift in the peak.

"Let's get off the top of this," Brigid replied.

Kane didn't argue; he simply grabbed her by the waist and the two of them bounded across the growing chasm in the hilltop. As they reached the other side, another thunderous boom resounded. This wasn't the explosives anymore. Someone was literally tearing the top off of the pyramid, and a slide of dirt and pebbles washed the two Cerberus explorers another several yards down the hillside.

With a last, powerful surge, one section of the peak disappeared and Charun and his hammer erupted through the broken stone. His wing harness lifted him through the hole, and Kane was surprised to see that the wall he'd punched through was easily three feet thick. The hammer sparked with arcs of blue plasma.

"Humans," Charun snarled.

"Maniac," Kane returned. He brought up his shotgun as the bat-winged horror hovered.

"Prepare to pay for your trespasses," Charun warned.

A moment later something bigger, darker, loomed behind the flying warrior.

Charun looked back over his shoulder.

Grant's Manta hovered, ten yards from the Etruscan titan. He powered up the spotlights for the craft, casting

Charun in silhouette for Kane and Brigid. Over the loud-
speaker, Grant's challenge was unmistakable.

"Pick on someone your own size, asshole."

Chapter 26

Charun hovered in front of Grant. With his armor and war mask, he was easily eight feet in height. His betusked features twisted; a face that was born of ugly hatred echoed in his actions and words over the past several minutes. The beaklike nose of the blue, pallid man-beast was set between eyes that were red and livid with a mixture of suffering and anger. Batlike wings that spread to a span of twenty feet waved and undulated. They didn't beat, but they didn't have to as they were more for steering, maneuvering and shielding, the actual impetus of Charun's flight originating with a field of ionic energy that severed gravity's grasp upon him.

In the meantime, Grant was in a stub-winged, sleek, bronze craft that bore more than a passing resemblance to the sea creature from which it took its name. The Manta. The ship had been built for the purposes of Manitius Moon Base, but had quickly grown in utility for the explorers and warriors of Cerberus Redoubt. Not usually equipped with guns and missiles, this time it had been so armed, as well as recently bedecked with streamlined nacelles in which it could carry passengers outside. Of course, that transport could only be done safely within the confines of a Manitius-designed shadow suit complete with its environmental seal, even under the protective windshield shells.

Grant tilted the Manta further away from Kane and

Brigid, hover jets lifting the ship from the broken peak of the pyramid.

Charun rose, as well, but he didn't seek to stay the same distance from the scram jet.

"You wish to pit your flying skills against mine? In the same thing I broke when first we laid eyes upon each other?" Charun asked. His voice was loud and clear over Grant's Commtact. Brigid's ploy of breaking the radio jamming of Charun's hammer, as well as the mind-clouding song of the deceased Vanth, had cleared the airwaves for such communication.

Grant nodded, then grimaced, forgetting that his opponent could not see through the cockpit glass. "We battle in the sky. You and me."

Charun rolled his head back and laughed, but there was no mirth or warmth in the cacophony leaving his twisted lips. "You expect me to care enough to allow you a fair fight?"

"I didn't think you were that much of a coward, Tusks," Grant taunted.

"Maniac. Coward. Just for that, after exterminating you and your pathetic friends, I will create a death camp and slaughter millions just in response to your insults," Charun said. With that, he burst skyward, accelerating far faster than Grant could have imagined, going from zero to supersonic in the space of instants.

Grant let his pilot couch tilt back and he took off in pursuit of his enemy. Man and machine versus alien and nearly magical technology, and already, Grant was aware that he was behind the curve. G-forces, the results of high-velocity maneuvers and the crush of acceleration, were something Charun apparently could ignore without care. The shadow suit and the pilot's couch in the Manta provided some compensation for such stresses, but the

Etruscan demigod was taunting in the ease with which he defied physics.

Grant hit the throttle and followed Charun's course. All the while the weight of inertia squeezed him. He knew that fighter pilots could handle g-forces, the equivalent of one level of gravity on a human body, up to nine Gs while engaging in dogfighting over the space of a few minutes. However, in the instance of using an ejector seat, people could survive up to forty-five Gs for an ejector-seat launch. It was an iffy set of circumstances, though. The Manta's maneuverability, only in the direst of maneuvers, could easily top that as he flew the ship in the form of a dogfight. With most of his artillery rockets having been used, all he had left were the .50-caliber heavy machine guns mounted on the ship.

Machine guns that Charun's hammer had "de-fanged" in an earlier dogfight against Edwards.

In moments Grant was supersonic, at a much slower rate than Charun had gone, and already he was looking at the radar screens for signs of his opponent.

Charun was approaching from the rear of the Manta at Mach 3, and Grant hit the thrusters on his ship, jetting higher into the sky. He didn't think that altitude would have an adverse effect on the demigod, but if there was one thing Grant could hope for, it was to negate any of his foe's advantages. That meant reaching escape velocity. He kept the ship climbing higher and higher.

Fireballs of blue plasma slashed through the night, showing up on his radar screens as solid objects themselves. Grant found himself both relieved that Charun wasn't hurling rocks, but the plasma bolts were moving with speed that could eat the distance between the two of them. They were at twelve miles in height and he spiraled the Manta into evasion of the discharges from Charun's mighty hammer.

"I thought you said you wanted to battle! Not run around like a frightened chicken," Charun called out. "You were the one mocking my strength of will and resolve!"

"You act like your shit impresses me, Char," Grant returned. Fifteen miles, twenty miles. He used the rearview camera to see how Charun was maneuvering; his wings had gone from undulating to flat and still.

And for every maneuver Grant made, Charun adjusted, as well. He just wasn't doing so as fast. The air was thin enough that those artificial wings couldn't grab and carve against wind resistance. However, Grant could also see that those wings were glowing with electrical energy.

The sensors on the Manta indicated they were highly ionized and were producing pure thrust to make those maneuvers.

"Come get some," Grant said finally. He hit the brakes, twenty miles up, allowing Charun to close the gap between them.

Charun cut loose with his hammer, but the plasma blasts were wide of Grant and his ship.

"You looking for me to flinch, Char?" Grant asked.

"I'm looking for you to die, ape!" the alien snarled. "My bride—"

"Is rotting where she belongs. In a tomb!" Grant shouted, cutting him off.

Get him mad. Get him to forget everything.

The hammer in Charun's hand released a blaze of rage and, for a moment, Grant feared the fireball was a huge wall of energy coming straight for him. No, that wasn't the case. It was multiple streams of plasma that formed the walls of a tunnel between the two airborne foes.

"Come to me!" Charun bellowed.

Grant hit the afterburners on the Manta and accelerated toward the winged entity.

As soon as they were within two miles of each other, the range closing swiftly, Grant triggered the Browning machine guns. Their recoil and the forceful slugs they spit were too much for the moorings that connected them to his craft. The .50-caliber blasters were torn from their pods, spiraling off into the night, the nuts and bolts sealing them shorn by the sheer physics of the situation.

The sight of the machine guns falling away elicited a chuckle from the demigod. He let go of his hammer, letting it hover in the air.

Yeah, I figured you could do that, Grant thought. After all, it had flown back to Charun's side before, and he had nearly forced him and Kane to bludgeon each other to death with the damned thing. Hovering was a minor stunt for the ancient technology.

Charun stopped and started flying backward after a few moments, allowing the Manta to touch him. His clawed toes scratched at the cockpit of the ship.

Charun perched on the nose of the Manta, his smart-metal gloves and boots allowing him to stick to the aircraft, even as they hurtled through the thin atmosphere at twenty miles up, the speed of sound long passed.

Grant opened the cockpit and the demigod laughed.

"You want to make this a fist…"

Grant's Sin Eater drowned out whatever the Etruscan creature wanted to say, his bullets slashing at the armored war mask. Charun and his wings formed a stopgap windshield, but even with that, even with his shadow suit providing environmental protection, icy cold slashed at Grant. This didn't matter, though, as he took the deadly mine he'd taken from the pyramid hatch.

The Sin Eater clacked on an empty chamber and Charun's bloodied features were visible through his shredded armor.

"You thought that could do something to me?" Charun asked.

Grant hurled the mine, and its electro-adhesive base stuck solidly to the alien's head. Grant's toss also carried enough force and momentum to rock the demigod on his heels, rock him far back enough for him to hit the controls to close the cockpit.

Grant hit the thrusters, taking the Manta to orbital velocity. Even in the minimal atmosphere at this altitude, Charun's wings served as enough of a parachute to pry him off the hull of the scram jet, all the while he battled with the mine that clung to his naked face as well as his smart-metal armor.

The jolting alterations of momentum, and Charun's sudden deceleration, weakened the wing harness drastically.

A radio signal detonated the mine.

All of that ionized energy being put off by the flight systems on Charun's armor died out. If the mine hadn't taken off the demigod's head, it had deprived him of his wings, of the thrust that could sever him from the grasp of gravity.

Whichever the false god's fate, Grant knew one thing. Falling from twenty-two miles above the Earth, "godly armor or not," was not survivable. Even if he landed in the Mediterranean, he'd strike with such velocity the water would be as solid as basalt.

Grant adjusted course, slowing so he didn't tear the Manta apart as it made its way back to the pyramid.

Every mile of the trip, Grant kept his eye on the radar, but all he saw was a large, inert form sailing back under the greedy grasp of gravity.

"THE HAMMER DISAPPEARED from radar, but only because it was heading beyond Earth's orbit," Lakesh explained as the heroes of Cerberus and of New Olympus were gathered. "Vanth's torch also took flight, joining the hammer as it flew into space."

"Didn't Charun and Vanth say they were from another universe?" Diana asked at the head of the feast table.

"They did," Brigid explained. "But they operated on Earth with the Annunaki. They originally inhabited the bodies of lesser Annunaki, and had stolen their technology."

"So, the hammer and the torch went back to Nibiru?" Kane asked.

Lakesh nodded. "The path of the artifacts would have put them on a course somewhere beyond Jupiter, which was where we assume is the Annunaki home world."

"Any regrets about not being able to use their secrets to reach their home dimension?" Aristotle asked Brigid.

Brigid shook her head. "The Stygian realm and their inhabitants, at least through the doorway we can access on this world, is not a place we should seek to make contact with anytime soon. I can vouch for over half a million Italians that keeping that door closed is in the best interests of all involved."

"Here, here," Aristotle agreed. "Though, it is a shame that Charun's tantrum closed off so many sections of the pyramid."

"When we have the time, we'll start excavations," Lakesh promised. "We still have much of your base to break from isolation."

Aristotle nodded. He looked over at Diana, who for the first time wore her hair pulled back in a ponytail. She wasn't hiding her features. The infiltration of the Etruscan pyramid had helped her shed her own feeling of isolation and alienation. "Speaking of alone, where did Grant go?"

"He is around," Grant heard Brigid say. "He has his own thoughts to go over…"

Spartan 50—Ignacio "Fiddy" Phoebus—was being honored for his ultimate sacrifice. His grave was added to the honored dead of the nation of New Olympus. He'd perished in battle against false gods, having brought the end of Vanth by his initiative.

No one compared to the accomplishment of Grant in eliminating Charun. Both men had overcome their foes through the use of technology and wits.

And yet Grant stood aloof from the mourners. He hadn't had a chance to know the young Ignacio as anything more than just another face in the crowd, remarkable only for that he sat in a wheelchair, signifying that some earlier battle had left him diminished enough to fit into a cockpit meant for a smaller species of humanoid.

Spartan 50 was dead, but his memory would live on. No one else would take that name, as was the case for all deceased battle suit pilots and their call signs.

This much was made clear as there were Spartan call signs that reached into the low 200s, many having died in the Hydrae wars.

Grant noticed that Edwards had wandered off, hand in hand with Myrto Smaragda, the two of them sharing quiet whispers and tender looks. The shade of gloom that had hovered over Edwards's features since his domination by Ullikummis had faded, at least in the presence of the young warrior woman.

Smaragda's shock of white hair hadn't showed signs of darkening, but the loneliness and isolation she'd displayed had lessened, her platoon returned. When Ignacio Phoebus was lowered into the ground, however, the tears had come to her cheeks unashamedly. Tears had come unashamedly to all the warriors present, men and women.

They had become brothers and sisters for the simple fact that they risked their lives in the protection of those who could not fight, either for lack of strength, lack of skill, lack of arms to engage in that battle. Humanity, in crawling from the wreckage wrought upon it by Annunaki interference, was showing signs that it had learned from the petty tribalism of the ancient days. Be they the soldiers of New Olympus, the samurai of New Edo, the troops of Aten, or the CAT teams of Cerberus, they had all allied for a single cause.

Defense of the weak.

No, Grant wasn't feeling a lick of satisfaction for having killed a god. His anger was assuaged, but the sense of loss he felt with the murder of Spartan 50 still hung on his shoulders.

Kane and Brigid appeared, Kane having brought a bottle of ouzo from the celebration of Ignacio's life and the mourning of his passing.

"Deep thoughts?" Brigid asked.

"You have to ask me that?" Grant inquired back.

"Not really," Brigid responded.

Grant accepted the bottle of ouzo and took a long drag on it. He liked the hint of licorice that leavened and sweetened the spirit. He swallowed, the burn tingling in his chest.

"Thanks," Grant told Kane.

"I was afraid you were going to do something stupid back there," Kane told him.

"Like what? Open my cockpit at the edge of space with an angry giant looking to tear me apart?" Grant asked.

"Nah," Kane said. "You punch gods in the kidney every Tuesday."

Grant chuckled.

"I think he's referring to feeling like you didn't accomplish anything," Brigid said.

"I stopped Charun. A lot of people are safe because of that," Grant told them.

Kane nodded. "We've bought some more time for mankind to crawl up from the wreckage."

Grant smiled. "Isn't that what we've been doing since we first blew out of Cobaltville all those years ago?"

"That goes without debate," Brigid said as she took the bottle and downed a swig. "Now come on back to the feast."

She handed the bottle off to Kane.

"What's the rush?" Grant asked the archivist.

"Because sooner or later, your God-punch Tuesday is going to roll around again. And given our recent string of opponents...I have a feeling it'll come much sooner."

"Let's celebrate some life before that," Kane added.

Grant nodded.

The three soul friends returned to the great hall.

Eat. Drink. Be merry. Someday they would all pass from this Earth, but until then, freedom would be protected and fought for, and life would be lived.

* * * * *

COMING SOON FROM

GOLD EAGLE

Available September 1, 2015

GOLD EAGLE EXECUTIONER®
SYRIAN RESCUE – *Don Pendleton*
Tasked with rescuing UN diplomats lost in the
Syrian desert, Mack Bolan is in a deadly race
against time—and against fighters willing to
make the ultimate sacrifice.

GOLD EAGLE SUPERBOLAN®
LETHAL RISK – *Don Pendleton*
A search-and-rescue mission to recover a high-
ranking defector in China leads Mack Bolan to a
government-sanctioned organ-harvesting facility.

GOLD EAGLE DEATHLANDS®
CHILD OF SLAUGHTER – *James Axler*
When Doc is kidnapped by a band of marauders
in what was once Nebraska, Ryan and the
companions join forces with a beautiful but
deadly woman with an agenda of her own…

GOLD EAGLE ROGUE ANGEL™
THE MORTALITY PRINCIPLE – *Alex Archer*
In Prague researching the legend of the Golem,
archaeologist Annja Creed uncovers a string of
murders that seems linked to the creature. And
Annja is the next target…

COMING SOON FROM

GOLD EAGLE®

Available October 6, 2015

GOLD EAGLE EXECUTIONER®
UNCUT TERROR – *Don Pendleton*

Mack Bolan sets out to even the score when a legendary Kremlin assassin slaughters an American defector before he can be repatriated. His first target leads him to discover a Russian scheme to crash the Western economy and kill hundreds of innocent people. Only one man can stop it—the Executioner.

GOLD EAGLE STONYMAN®
DEATH MINUS ZERO – *Don Pendleton*

Washington goes on full alert when Chinese operatives kidnap the creator of a vital US defense system. While Phoenix Force tracks the missing scientist, Able Team uncovers a plot to take over the system's mission control. Now both teams must stop America's enemies from holding the country hostage.

Joan of Arc's long-lost sword. A heroine reborn. The quest to protect humanity's sacred secrets from falling into the wrong hands.

Rogue Angel is sophisticated escapism and high adventure rooted in the excitement of history's most fabled eras. Each book provides a unique combination of arcane history, mystery, action, adventure and limited supernatural elements (mainly the sword). The series details a young woman's transition from an independent archaeologist who hosts an American cable television show to an action heroine with a surprising connection to Joan of Arc and a role in French mythology.

Available wherever Gold Eagle® books and ebooks are sold.

GOLD EAGLE®

GERA2015A